THE CITY OF SEVEN HELLS

GEBOFAL

N. CHADWICK PRAGGASTIS

<u>**Note from the Author:**</u>

In these end times, Satan has grown bolder because he knows his time is short. He no longer obscures himself. He is no longer in the shadows. As believers, we cannot be complacent, but we must fight against the powers of darkness with the light of Jesus - the One and Only Begotten Son of the Father. We should never fear the demonic realm. Although it is a realm with real world implications, it is also a defeated world.

But unlike Hollywood which portrays light and dark as a yin-and-yang of evil and good caught in an eternal struggle, we know there is no parity. Satan is *not* God's equal. We testify to the authority of the triune God and His supremacy over all creation. Jesus has already won. As Christians, we must remember that we fight *from* victory, not *for* it!

TABLE OF CONTENTS

CHAPTER 1 - Boston, Massachusetts

"But understand this, that in the last days there will come times of difficulty. For people will be lovers of self, lovers of money, proud, arrogant, abusive, disobedient to their parents, ungrateful, unholy, heartless, unappeasable, slanderous, without self-control, brutal, not loving good, treacherous, reckless, swollen with conceit, lovers of pleasure rather than lovers of God, having the appearance of godliness, but denying its power. Avoid such people." - 2 Timothy 3:1-5

rank Rogha and his wife Asiya met while he was writing his dissertation in Anthropology at Boston University. Fleeing religious persecution, Asiya had come to 'Beantown' to study Egyptology. They shared a few classes. He was a senior; she was a freshman.

Frank was raised in a traditional blue-collar Irish Catholic family. He had put his familial reservations aside for the sake of his love for her. He knew that his parents would not accept a woman from Egypt into the family, but he had fallen headlong in love with Asiya. Their marriage and the arrival of their son came shortly thereafter.

Despite his upbringing, Frank was agnostic. Asiya had been raised a Coptic Christian and subsequently converted to Catholicism after a friend from work invited her to the local parish. To Frank, religion was a self-imposed crutch for the unintellectual—a means to cope with a world of pain and nihilism. To Asiya, religion and her nearby parish were a source of support and comfort.

Frank and Asiya had not been to church together since the baptism of their only son, Ishmael. Yet on this day, he was compelled by his devout wife to attend church. They ran late. Traffic had been impossible to avoid. It was Easter Sunday.

The sky spoke in deep rumbles. The dark clouds hung low, and lightning flashes lit up the spires of the cathedral. South Boston was known for many parishes, but Holy Cross was the most beautiful, the most ostentatious.

Ishmael's five-year-old legs had difficulty navigating the wet steps to the entrance of the church. His mother tugged at his tiny hand. The foyer was abuzz with activity. The Rogha family stood at the ingress, befuddled. Families with little children, older ladies wrapped in shawls, and middle-aged men adorning the vestments of the clergy paraded into the sanctuary. The church was alive with chatter. The pews were packed.

Asiya led her husband and Ishmael to a seat at the periphery. Ishmael sat in amazement at the grandeur of the sanctuary. The wooden ceiling accented the cream-colored spires that flanked the nave, and the two-toned white marble floors shone from a fresh polish.

"...and on this day, we celebrate the resurrection of our Lord..." Father Dunnigan leaned forward toward the microphone; his raspy baritone voice reverberated throughout the cavernous hall.

Ishmael's hazel eyes peered at his mother. He had the eyes and almond skin of his beautiful mother. His hair, however, stood in direct contrast to hers. His reddish hair bristled and fought against the heavy application of hair gel.

Ishmael squirmed nervously in the wooden pews, which felt cold against his wool slacks. He stared at his mother. Asiya looked back at him and smiled. The tiniest of crow's feet appeared in the corners of her gentle eyes. His father looked uncomfortable and gazed into the distance.

With arms extended, Father Dunnigan presented a round wafer to the congregation.

"In Matthew 26:26, it states,

'...as they were eating, Jesus took bread, blessed and broke it, and gave it to the disciples and said, Take, eat; this is My body. Do this in remembrance of me.'" He held up an ornate gold chalice with intricate engravings. *"This is the cup of my Blood, the Blood of the new and eternal covenant which was poured out for the forgiveness of sins."*

Pausing at each pew, the ushers corralled the parishioners into singular lines. Asiya looked at Frank; he appeared indifferent. Asiya took her son by the hand and led him up the stairs to the altar.

As she waited in line to partake of the Eucharist, she looked back at the crowd behind her. Elevated on the steps, she beheld the massive expanse of the sanctuary. She loved how elegantly the columns rose to the ceiling, arching slowly... How beautiful, she thought. How majestic.

Suddenly, Asiya felt the weight of the queue fall back on her. Two ladies in front had borne the weight of a man collapsing to the ground. All three stumbled backwards, hitting other bystanders as they fell.

Mr. Browning had fallen; his head struck the marble floor. Gasps and one singular scream echoed in the sanctuary. Blood alluviated into a growing pool. His body began to twitch grotesquely. A crowd encircled him.

Asiya rushed Ishmael back to his seat and began praying for Mr. Browning.

"What happened, Mommy?"

Asiya worried for her son. The blood expanded into a large pool on the floor. She put her hand over his eyes.

"Come on, Frank, let's take him out of here."

She grabbed Ishmael's hand and led him to the foyer. Father Dunnigan and the clergy tended to Mr. Browning.

Minutes later, flashing lights could be seen refracting off the wet streets. The ambulance crew stormed the sanctuary. The crew attempted to resuscitate the old man, but to no avail. His body convulsed, and his eyes danced. The team of paramedics bowed their heads. They pulled a white sheet over his body as the crowd began to dissipate. Many of the parishioners had left; others were still on their feet.

A congregation of patrons gathered in the foyer to opine about what had gone wrong. Asiya and Frank joined them. Ishmael's mother looked down. She had been lost in conversation.

"Frank, where is Ish?"

"I thought you had him with you..." he blubbered.

"Where's Ishmael?" she asked frantically, searching the room.

The paramedics had failed to see a five-year-old kneeling at the corpse of Mr. Browning. He had slipped into the sanctuary. With one hand, he had lifted the veil, and with the other, he was cupping Mr. Browning's face.

"Ishmael, NO!" his mother yelled.

Head bowed, Ishmael was lost in prayer; his mouth moved, but his mother could not make out his words. She ran to him. The remaining parishioners all turned their heads. She tugged at his arm, but he resisted.

"Wait, Mommy..." He muttered one last word, "Amen."

Asiya squatted down to scold her only child when her attention was drawn to the deceased man. Coughing and gasping could be heard from beneath the plastic veil.

Mr. Browning sat up. His eyes were bloodshot, and he coughed violently. The sheet fell from his face, and all eyes fell on him. The remaining parishioners gasped. A shout could be heard from the distant corner of the sanctuary.

"It's a miracle!"

The paramedics stood incredulously; the clergy were amazed, and Father Dunnigan stared pensively at Father Azikiwe. The crowd grew animated.

"Did you see that?" said one.

"How did he do that?" said another.

The crowd gathered around Ishmael. The clergy ushered the Roghas into a hidden room behind the sanctuary.

Father Dunnigan paced in front of a large oak desk; his cream-colored chasuble swayed back and forth. He and the other priests exchanged looks. Father Azikiwe stared at Dunnigan. The Nigerian positioned himself with his hands clasped behind his back. Asiya stood next to him, her tiny stature dwarfed by his six-foot-five-inch frame.

Asiya chimed in, "What happened, Father?" Her gaze was fixed on Father Dunnigan.

"I am not sure. It is premature..." He paused. "But from my observation, it seems as though your boy... uh... healed him." Father Dunnigan's baritone voice echoed in the small room.

"Healed him?" She gestured with her hands. "He wasn't dead, Father. I'm sure it was just a coincidence. The man was probably still alive," said Asiya.

"No. No, I don't think so. He lay there for several minutes. The medics called his death ten minutes earlier," Father Dunnigan insisted.

"So, what are you saying? That my son healed him? Brought him back from the dead? Come on, Father."

He stared into Asiya's brown eyes. "Has he ever done anything like this before?"

"Healed someone? No," she stated emphatically. Asiya deferred to her husband.

"Never seen anything like that... never," Frank stated stoically.

The Father bowed his head and stroked his closely cropped beard. An awkward pause ensued.

"But he does have dreams," Asiya added.

Frank turned to look at his wife with concern in his eyes.

"I would like to talk to your son as soon as possible," the Father said, staring at the couple.

CHAPTER 2 - Boston, Massachusetts

"Come now, let's kill him and throw him into one of these cisterns and say that a ferocious animal devoured him. Then we'll see what comes of his dreams." - Genesis 37:20

t never changed. The dreams were always the same. Ishmael woke up. It was early. His disheveled, curly red hair stuck out at odd angles. He had hardly slept.

His mother's visage appeared in the doorframe. "Time to get up, darling!" Her dark hair fell sloppily onto her shoulders. She wore a dark blue robe tied tightly around the waist. "Your father has breakfast ready for you downstairs."

Ishmael staggered downstairs, half awake. Frank was attentive as he poured the batter onto the flat griddle. Irish folk music blared from the speakers. "Here you go, son." He shoved a plate in front of his son as he took a seat at the table. Ishmael's tiny stature fell deeply into the Windsor dining chair.

"You want butter?" His father's large frame swiveled. "How about some peanut butter... and some syrup?" He cut the pancakes into bite-sized pieces.

The pancakes were nearly at eye level, and the sweet aroma filled his young nostrils. Ishmael boosted himself to his knees and leaned against the rectangular old table. The toddler stabbed awkwardly at the bits with his fork cupped in his left hand.

"Honey?" Ariya came downstairs with her hair in a bun. "Did you hear that? The doorbell..." She made her way to the front of the house. "Frank, can you turn that down?" She opened the front door.

Father Dunnigan and Father Azikiwe stood back with their hands crossed behind their backs in a non-threatening stance. "Father, Father." She nodded and yielded the hallway.

Asiya ushered them through the Victorian house. They came in politely, adjourning to the living room. They waited for permission to sit. Asiya waved her hand and spoke, "Please."

They both wore similar clothes—black blazers, clerical-collared shirts, black wool overcoats, black pants, and black leather shoes. The rain had beaded into stellar patterns on Father Dunnigan's matching fedora.

In the salon sat Ishmael, playing with his yellow Tonka truck. The boy made engine noises as he slid it along the tiled floor.

Asiya poured the clergymen some Earl Grey, then took her seat. She sat demurely with a delicate porcelain teacup clasped tightly in her cold hands. She sipped the hot tea. Wisps of steam wafted to the ceiling.

"So, what is this about?" Frank began.

Father Dunnigan put his tea on the side table, then leaned forward in the chair. "Do you mind if I smoke?"

Frank consented with a defiant nod.

Father Dunnigan took a Cuban from the inside pocket of his blazer and a matchbox from his other pocket. His wrinkled, forty-two-year-old eyes squinted as he lit his cigar. He took a deep drag as the cherry tip crackled and popped. He exhaled. The white smoke hovered ominously above them. He looked up.

"I am sure you know why I am here." He shook the match, and it threw black smoke circles into the poorly lit room.

"You want to talk to our son," Frank stated matter-of-factly. He made eye contact with the Nigerian. "If you want to talk to Ishmael... you do it in front of me," he stated unequivocally.

Dunnigan paused. "Can I know about his dreams?" The priest glanced at his smoldering cigar.

Asiya interrupted. "He talks a lot about his dreams." She paused.

"And what does he say?" Father Dunnigan broke the silence.

"He talks about things he has seen—images mostly. He describes people's faces, colors, places..." Asiya was reticent about revealing the details. Although Father Dunnigan had been her priest for six years, she was not willing to reveal anything that might compromise the safety of her beloved son. "Why do you ask?"

"No reason..." He took a puff on his cigar. The smoke rose above his balding hairline. "It's just that... what we witnessed has provoked some thoughts that I'd like to share with you." Father Azikiwe nodded in agreement.

The priest leaned closer. "Mrs. Rogha, we believe your boy to be... to be... well... special. He may have..." He took a deep drag on his cigar and blew the smoke toward the ceiling. "...abilities. Has he ever done anything like this before?"

Frank stared at the priest. "He has always done things we couldn't explain."

"For example?" the priests inquired.

Frank interrupted. "When he was younger, he predicted things."

The priest inquired, "What things?"

"Well... One time, he must have been about three. He ran over to me and grabbed my arm, preventing me from taking a bite of salad..." Frank paused. "...a salad with walnuts in it."

"And what does that mean?" Father Azikiwe inquired.

Frank sat back in his chair. "He'd had a dream that I was choking on a bean. He called it 'a bad bean.' So, you see... well, I am deathly allergic to walnuts, you see? And the salad, well, had walnuts in it. I might have died. Now I don't know how he knew because I had never told him. He just knew..." He looked over at the caramel-skinned boy. "That day I might have died." Frank beamed with pride, peering over lenses that fell to the end of his nose.

Both men of the cloth looked at each other.

"Are there any other times he might have 'known' things?"

"Several times, as a matter of fact. One time at the stoplight—you remember that one, honey?" Asiya deferred to her husband.

Frank's guard fell slightly as he recounted the events of his gifted child. "Yeah, the light was green. I was about ready to go through when I heard Ishmael say from his car seat in the back, 'Wait, Daddy.' And he said it so authoritatively. So, I waited... and you know what? Damned if a truck didn't just skid out right in front of me! And dumped an entire load of tomatoes right in the intersection, right in front of me!"

"Are you saying that Ishmael was able to see it before it happened?" asked Father Dunnigan.

Frank looked at the priest. "Look, I don't know. I don't know how to explain it. All I am saying is that we would have been broadsided by that truck... no doubt." Frank paused and stared at the priest. "Father, is my boy clairvoyant?"

"Mr. Rogha," Dunnigan glanced at Father Azikiwe, then leaned in to address the couple. "Tell me about his dreams."

Frank stared at his wife briefly, then Asiya felt compelled to take the narrative.

"Sometimes, he wakes up yelling. When we ask him about the dreams, he just repeats..."

"He repeats what?" Father Dunnigan chimed in.

"Gregowee!" A juvenile voice came from the corner.

All four adults simultaneously turned their attention to the redheaded boy who sat without looking up. The redhead continued playing with his truck. His mouth struggled to make motor noises as he swung the yellow truck through the air.

Father Dunnigan rose slowly and proceeded toward the boy.

Frank sat up. His wife put her hand softly on his forearm. She stood up. Asiya looked at the clergyman with concern.

The Father stopped mid-room, bowed at the waist, and grabbed his knees, leaning toward the boy. His black fedora was held crumpled against his knees.

"Ish?" He spoke using Asiya's term of endearment. He stared at the boy ominously.

His mother stood up and then interrupted. "He said, 'Gregory.'" She paused and looked at the clergy. "He also speaks of numbers."

"Numbers?" Dunnigan stared intently.

"Random numbers. The other day, he kept repeating the number two hundred. Not sure what that meant, but... look, I think that's enough for today." Asiya stepped between the priest and her son.

"Mrs. Rogha, does your son bear any distinguishing features? Marks of any kind?"

"No. Why?" Asiya spoke inquisitively.

Father Dunnigan looked at Azikiwe and then straightened his blazer as he rose. "Okay, Mr. and Mrs. Rogha. Thank you for your time. We'll get back to you."

Father Azikiwe's massive stature rose from the sofa. Frank stood up too.

"Father Dunnigan, tell us what you know." Frank grew impatient.

"Let me talk it over with the archdiocese, and we will get back to you."

"No. You need to tell me what's going on!" Frank's tone boomed.

"Try to understand—it is premature, and I do not want to speculate." Father Dunnigan promptly stood up. "Let us do some research. We will talk with our archbishop and get back to you. In the meantime, we would like to offer you some protection."

"Protection from what?" Asiya jumped in.

"Let us just be safe." Dunnigan gestured to Father Azikiwe.

"Get out of here, priest! If you can't tell us what is going on... if my son is in danger, then we have nothing else to talk about!" Frank yelled. "All you are doing is inciting fear... Get the fuck out!" Frank stood assertively.

"Please, Frank, you are not helping!" Asiya approached him and put her hands softly across his chest.

"Hon, you can't be okay with this. They're talking about our son." Frank stared at his wife.

"Hon, I trust Father Dunnigan. He is trying to protect us."

"Protect us from what? What the fuck do we need to be protected from?" He turned his gaze back to the priest. "It sounds like you have an idea." He stared defiantly at Dunnigan. "I have a right to know if my boy is in danger... Tell me!"

The priest adjusted his black fedora. "Please, Frank, I want to tell you, but for me to tell you my opinion—it would only be speculation at this point." He turned to address the other priest. "Father Azikiwe, you ready?" The Nigerian nodded his head in agreement. The priests moved toward the ingress.

"That is just an excuse for control," Frank rebutted. "Religion has always been about control! He doesn't care about us. He cares about his coffers, isn't that right, Reverend?" He glared at the priest with condescension.

"Frank, please... don't," Asiya said in a soft voice. She had an unearthly calm about her. She turned around to face the priest. "Father Dunnigan, we will wait to hear from you. Thank you for your time."

Frank looked at his wife, shook his head, then turned and walked into the kitchen.

Asiya showed the priests out.

CHAPTER 3 - Rome, Italy

"Come, I will show you the punishment of the great prostitute, who sits by many waters. With her the kings of the earth committed adultery, and the inhabitants of the earth were intoxicated with the wine of her adulteries." - Revelation 17:1

t was a cold, dark February night in the Eternal City. A delicate rain fell onto the cobblestones of Via Del Circo Massimo. The lights formed a kaleidoscope of refracted rays. The pavement glistened, and the cars violently crossed the intersection.

The two men arose from the belly of the Metro, and, as if choreographed, both men donned their black umbrellas. The clerical collar of the older gentleman was barely visible beneath his Armani trench coat. The other man was considerably younger and considerably shorter—foreboding and well-built. Their black umbrellas cast shadows from the streetlights, further darkening their faces.

The elder priest bit a Gitanes cigarette from a pack and lit it with a silver Zippo lighter. He inhaled.

"There is a rumor about a boy." He exhaled, then looked pensively over the enormity of the grassy knoll where once charioteers battled to the death. "E' rosso, a redhead." The smoke collided with the cold and formed a cloud. He spat the tiny particles of tobacco from his mouth. Claxons sounded in the distance.

"Ah sì? And what do you think?" The muscular Calabrese struggled with the English.

"But he does not bear the mark. Yet, this case holds the most potential that we have seen in years. He is not like the others." The Jesuit drew hard on his filterless cigarette.

"In what way?"

"He has exhibited supernatural powers." He took another drag on his cigarette.

"Soprannaturali?"

"Apparently, he has healed... and not just mere healings. We have in good faith that he brought someone back from the dead..." He paused. "...a resurrection." The priest sucked on his cigarette. "And he has dreams as well."

"Eh sì? So, what kind of dreams?"

"Some say he is prescient."

"Perhaps, it is time? Che ne pensi?"

"We will act when we hear from the order—not a second sooner. We will have to protect him from falling into the wrong hands."

CHAPTER 4 - Boston, Massachusetts

"The thief comes only to steal and kill and destroy; I have come that they may have life, and have it to the full." - John 10:10

rank awoke to an uneasy feeling. He had heard strange noises coming from the backyard. Frank opened the back door several times and peered into the darkness. His mind was playing tricks on him. He felt childish for feeling afraid. Frank turned off the kitchen light and headed upstairs to rejoin his wife in bed. Ishmael had fallen asleep several hours prior.

Suddenly, an intruder grabbed his neck from behind. Frank struggled. He couldn't breathe. He gasped and choked. Frank pushed his weight into the assailant. The intruder pushed back. Frank's six-foot-one frame collided with the banister. Frank let out a grunt. He squinted his eyes in the dimly lit room. His attacker had donned a ski mask. Immediately, the grotesque figure pivoted and threw a left cross, which knocked him to the floor.

Frank fell headlong into the shadows in the corner of the room. He landed on the metal hilt of his umbrella and rose swiftly, swinging it wildly. With one circular movement, Frank hit the intruder on the side of the head, which sent him reeling backward. With a dull thud, he knocked the assailant backward into the sideboard. The wooden credenza shook, and the man fell forward onto the floor. A cry of pain escaped his lips.

Asiya's eyes flew open. She flipped on the light at her bedside table and noticed the indentation where Frank had been. Asiya crept into the hallway and froze. She heard sounds of struggle coming from downstairs.

"FRANK?!" Asiya yelled.

"Get Ish and lock the door!" Frank's response was riddled with fear.

Asiya ran to Ishmael's bedroom. She scooped him up from his bed and bolted back to her room, then locked the door. Asiya gently placed him on her bed. Ishmael was groggy and confused.

"What's wrong, Mommy?" He was barely awake.

"I need you to stay in Mommy's room, okay sweetheart?"

Asiya quickly dialed the police and frantically responded to the operator, "I think someone has broken into our house!!" She gave her address and stayed on the line, waiting for the police to arrive. Asiya was trying to stay calm for Ishmael, but her heart pounded in her chest. Was Frank okay? Would the intruder break in...

Her thoughts were interrupted. She heard the beams creak from the floorboard in the hallway. He was coming in! The door handle...? Rising incrementally faster toward the handle, she heard the footsteps quicken in the hallway. She leapt forward and let out an involuntary scream. The assailant grabbed the other side of the handle, and a tussle ensued.

Asiya was yelling, "In the name of Jesus, in the name of Jesus..." Her back to the door, Asiya fell to the floor and wedged her heels deep into the shag carpet. She pushed defiantly with her legs. The handle contorted and twisted, and then came several thumps as the man kicked near the lock to free the frame from the door. He grunted and hissed from beyond the portal.

"NOOOO!" She gave out a shriek.

At that moment, a siren could be heard in the distance. The intruder paused and quickly retreated. His footsteps could be heard scuffling down the stairs and along the stone path outside. Flashing red and blue lights reflected off the ceiling. Still on the floor, she took a deep sigh.

A deafening silence ensued as Asiya held her breath. A voice blasted from the front door, "Ma'am, are you in there? Boston P.D. Open up!" They kicked at the door, and it gave way from the impact. Frank's corpse and his umbrella lay in a pool of blood on the foyer floor. His throat had been cut from ear to ear.

Asiya heard heavy footsteps moving steadily up the stairs. The officer peeped into the bedroom.

"Ma'am, are you all right?"

Asiya sat on the bed clutching her son tightly. She nodded with the slightest movement of her head.

The officer directed, "I'm going to need you and your son to step outside while we check your residence."

They proceeded by Frank's corpse, which had been hastily covered with a sheet.

While sitting on the curb in the front yard, an ambulance driver offered Asiya and Ishmael a blanket. She gently bundled her son in fleece and sat him on her lap. The stout officer finally emerged from the entrance and walked toward Asiya and Ishmael. She stood abruptly and placed Ishmael down.

"Can we speak privately?" said the officer.

"Yes, of course."

Officer Tate led her away from the earshot of the young one.

"What happened?" Her voice trailed off.

"Your husband was attacked. Unfortunately..."

Asiya could hear the officer talking, but his words seemed foreign to her. Dead? Frank was dead? She had denied the obvious. No, there must be a mistake.

"Ma'am, I think it's best if you stay somewhere else tonight."

Asiya tucked her hair behind her ear and stared across the lawn at Ishmael. Ishmael was watching as the paramedics loaded his father's body into the ambulance. Her home had become a crime scene.

CHAPTER 5 - Boston, Massachusetts

"And he will send his angels with a loud trumpet call, and they will gather his elect from the four winds, from one end of the heavens to the other." - Matthew 24:31

he police station bustled with activity. Asiya sat discontented in the lobby. Irritated patrons complained loudly to the clerks about matters Asiya could not ascertain. Daydreaming, Ishmael looked out the window at the patrol cars covered in dew.

A man approached the carefully groomed Egyptian woman. "Good morning, Mrs. Rogha, I'm Inspector Malech," he said, extending his hand. "I know this is a very difficult time for you, but I have to ask you a few questions." He turned to the toddler. "Is this your boy?"

Asiya nodded. "Yes, this is Ishmael."

She playfully tousled Ishmael's copper curls. The inspector leaned over to address him.

"Hi, buddy. Nice to meet you."

Ishmael was indifferent.

"Perhaps it is better to leave your son out here. What we have to discuss may be..." He paused. "Disturbing." He gestured toward the redhead.

"Ishmael stays with me," she stated matter-of-factly.

"Please follow me, then."

Malech led the Roghas to his office and offered them a seat. The walls were devoid of any pictures. The young detective sat deeply into his reclining black leather chair. His desk bore the metallic frame of the stock desks provided by Boston P.D.

Malech's elegant appearance stood in contrast to his sterile office. He was in his late thirties. He sported a black pinstripe suit with a white cashmere turtleneck sweater. The cuffs of his slacks slid loosely over black tassel loafers. His stark black hair was tightly cropped around his ears yet left longer in the front. Several rebellious locks of hair fell in front of his lightly wrinkled brow.

"Mrs. Rogha, do you have any idea why an intruder would break into your home?"

"No," Asiya said flatly.

"Does your family have any enemies?"

"No, no one."

"So, you have no enemies? Is that correct?" he repeated.

"You've already asked me that," Asiya replied astutely. "Can you tell me what is going on now? Please, I have answered all your questions."

"Well, we are inclined to believe that Frank was not the target but rather..." He nodded his head at her, "or perhaps," then to Ishmael, who was busy looking at the ceiling. "The assailant dropped a few items, including some zip ties."

Asiya was shocked. "What? Why would someone want to kidnap us?"

"That's what we need to find out, Mrs. Rogha. In the interim, we would like to place you in protective custody."

Protective custody.

Asiya's mind raced back to the conversation with Father Dunnigan and Father Azikiwe. *"In the meantime, we would like to offer you some protection."*

Is this what they wanted to protect Ishmael from? she pondered.

"Yes, thank you. I'll think about it. Right now, we are staying with friends," Asiya replied.

"I strongly encourage you to take us up on our offer. We want to keep you and your son safe," urged the inspector.

"Thank you, Inspector."

Asiya stood abruptly and took Ishmael by the hand before exiting the station.

CHAPTER 6 - Boston, Massachusetts

"For the Lord your God moves about in your camp to protect you and to deliver your enemies to you. Your camp must be holy, so that he will not see among you anything indecent and turn away from you." - Deuteronomy 23:14

he moved swiftly to the church office, pulling Ishmael behind.

"Mommy, too fast!" the boy complained.

"I'm sorry, Ish. We're in a hurry!"

Asiya was welcomed by a mousy receptionist wearing black-rimmed glasses.

"Hello. How may I help you?"

"I need to speak to Father Dunnigan," Asiya insisted.

"I'm sorry, but the Father is not available," Mrs. Klein stated apathetically.

"I'll speak to Father Azikiwe then. It's an emergency!"

Mrs. Klein stared blankly. "Hold on." She walked into the back of the office.

Father Azikiwe entered the room. "Good afternoon, Mrs. Ro—"

"I need to know what you know!" Asiya demanded. "My husband is dead, and Ishmael was almost abducted!"

Azikiwe paused and then answered, "I'm so sorry for your loss. Please tell me what happened."

Father Azikiwe guided her and Ishmael into an empty conference room. Through her tears, she told the priest the horrible details of Frank's death and how the police believed the intruder intended to kidnap them. Father Dunnigan entered the room after listening through the door.

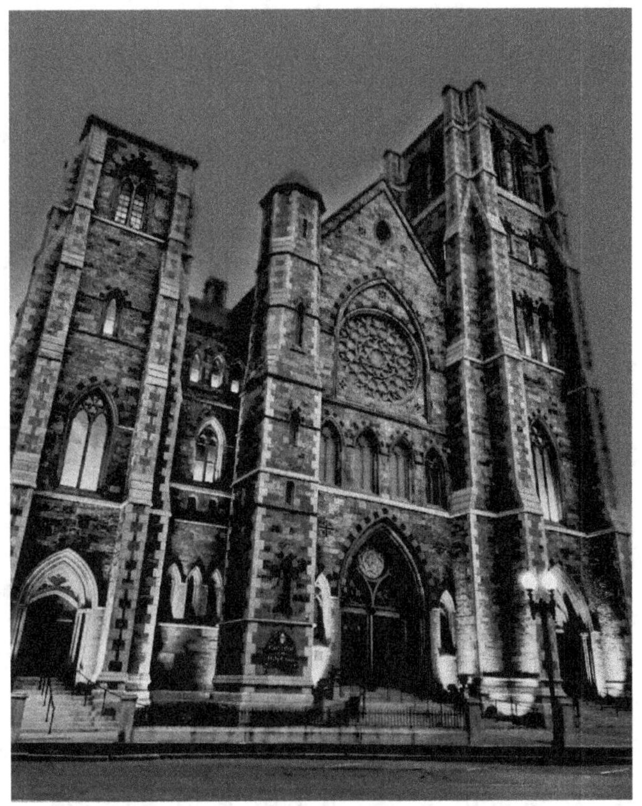

Asiya collected herself. "I need to know what's going on. Please help us," she pleaded with the priests.

"Your son is in danger." Dunnigan paused. "He is being hunted." He took out a cigar from his pocket and took a long drag. He looked at the disheveled woman. "What do you know of the occult?"

"Wait... what? Cult? Like... like Jim Jones? What do you mean?" Asiya was stunned. *Why would they want Ish?* she thought.

"Sort of." He paused to choose his diction. "The word means, hidden."

"Hiding what?"

"Knowledge."

"What knowledge?"

"Knowledge to manipulate reality, Mrs. Rogha."

"Give me a break, Father! What is really going on?" Asiya was livid.

"Mrs. Rogha. Look, to state it bluntly, the occult represents a very real and present danger; and we believe..." He glanced at the Nigerian, "...that they want your boy." Then the man of the cloth took a hard puff on his cigar. Awaiting Asiya's reaction, he exhaled and watched the smoke rise.

"Let me say it this way." He looked directly into the eyes of Asiya. "We believe that there is a satanic coven active in South Boston and... they may have a vested interest in your boy."

"What?! Why?" Asiya's voice grew more distraught.

The priest took a long drag, then looked intently at Asiya. "They want him because of his abilities. They want his ability to heal, and particularly for his prescience."

"But he can't control it... He is just a child." She looked at little Ishmael with dread in her eyes. Asiya paused. Her body deflated. The gravity of the moment began to sink in.

"What do I need to do to protect him?" she stated resolutely.

"These people are true believers, fanatics, willing to murder and torture for their dark lord." Dunnigan scraped the ash from his Cuban cigar. "Of course, the police are unaware of this. They do not know what they are up against and therefore may not be prepared to handle this situation. It is better if you let the church help you."

Satanists? Evil forces? she asked herself.

"You must go into protective custody—our custody. And the authorities must not be informed."

"Why?" she mustered.

"Mrs. Rogha, these are very powerful people, and it would not surprise us if there were moles at Boston P.D. They have foot soldiers everywhere. You must trust no one. And you must decide now!" the priest stated in a tone that almost seemed like a scold.

"What do you mean? Now?"

"I mean you must not go home for any reason. You must enter a witness protection program effective immediately. You will leave this building in a car of our choosing. A driver will take you to a safe house, from which we will establish contact. Shortly thereafter, a more permanent solution will be found. But under no circumstances should you leave this building without our protection. Do you understand, Mrs. Rogha?"

"Wait. What? What about Ishmael? What about my car? What about my things? What about my house? What about our family and friends? We haven't even had Frank's funeral." Asiya embraced her child.

"Listen to me, Mrs. Rogha!" He grabbed her arms and squeezed. "These are not petty thieves, strung-out teenagers, or mixed-up addicts. These people are murderers, and they will not think twice about killing you and your son. These are people who have made a conscious Faustian choice to serve Mephistopheles. They will kill anyone in their path. They are evil—pure evil."

"I can't believe it. I can't believe this," she stuttered.

"Your boy is clearly not safe in Boston, Mrs. Rogha. And we simply cannot afford the boy falling into the wrong hands. We must act—and we must act NOW!"

Asiya felt compelled to do what her priest told her. *Give up everything? Go on the lam?* What would happen to them? She missed Frank's soothing presence. Through the fog of emotion, Asiya consented.

"Okay, Father Dunnigan. Just tell us what to do."

"Very well then." Dunnigan went to the door, peeked through it, and gestured to two men waiting in the hallway. Two hulking men stood in the door frame.

"You will go with these men. Do exactly what they tell you to do." The priest put his hand on the nape of her back and led her softly toward the exit.

The two men wore jeans; one wore a bomber jacket, the other a dark blue hoodie with a black baseball cap. Asiya imagined that both were capable of extreme violence. Yet neither bore any distinctive features—nothing that would set them apart from the crowd. Both approached with awkward smiles on their faces, but one seemed more ominous than the other. They bowed their heads consensually.

Ishmael and his mother were led to the rear of the sanctuary and down into the stomach of the parish, into the basement where the pipes protruded from the wet walls and the odor of mold permeated the air. They kept on.

They walked into a dark corner of the basement. The larger of the two men removed an artificial façade that led to a tunnel, a tunnel that traversed the adjacent road and then led to a nondescript building on the south side of the street.

Asiya helped her terrified son brave the long, poorly lit corridor. The two men cautiously led them into a garage harboring a dark blue Ford Buick Riviera. The two men bid them into the back seat while they got in the front.

"Stay down," said the driver.

The Roghas laid sideways on the seats. The cold brown leather sucked the heat from their torsos.

"Mommy, I'm scared," the boy murmured.

"I know, baby. We're gonna pray to Jesus now. Come on, pray with me. Okay?" She cupped his cold hands in hers and began to pray.

Asiya's senses were heightened. She became acutely aware of every aperture in the road, every bend, every sound.

The driver stopped briefly at a light when, suddenly—Crunch! The back end of the car folded.

An International Metro delivery truck rammed it from behind. The Riviera lurched forward, throwing Ishmael to the floor. Asiya braced herself, wedging her knees into the back of the seat. Raised voices and shots could be heard from behind the buckled trunk door. In a flash, the passenger-side door swung open; one of her priestly protectors stepped out wielding a pistol. With a wild expression and an even wilder aim, he fired four shots. He went down immediately as buckshot riddled his body.

Ishmael buried his head and cupped his ears. The sounds were piercing. Shots ensued. Glass shattered, throwing shards into the air. A bullet pierced the car's frame and entered Asiya's left shoulder, sending a cry of pain to her lips.

An ominous figure stepped from the driver's seat of the delivery truck. He cradled a Mossberg assault shotgun, his face obscured by a black ski mask. He walked methodically toward the driver's side of the Buick, pumping round after round into the driver as his figure was thrown violently into the street.

Asiya shielded Ishmael from the attack. Her body quivered as the man swung open the car door. The tall man in the mask plucked the  toddler from the car floor as he screamed and squirmed. Asiya flailed for Ishmael.

"Nooooooo!!" Grasping in vain for his ankle, she screamed, and the blood rushed to her head. She could hear her son's screams halt suddenly. Asiya looked up to see the man impaling a syringe into her arm. Her vision tunneled, then she lost consciousness.

"Ishmaaaael!!"

—--

Ishmael awoke to the sound of a train's whistle. His room was barren. He shook off the drug in his veins.

"Mommy?"

The boy sat up in the squeaky bed. His hair danced out at all angles. Inspector Malech sat in a chair facing the bed.

"Where's my mommy?" the boy lamented.

"I am afraid your mother didn't make it, little one." The inspector said it so callously that one would have thought Ishmael were a grown man.

Ishmael stared at the inspector. "Where's my mommy?" he complained.

"I am sorry, my boy, but we did what we could." The inspector's gaze was fixed on the teary eyes of the little boy.

Ishmael was inconsolable and cried incessantly for days.

CHAPTER 7 - Mortlake, England - 16th century

"And if I have prophetic powers, and understand all mysteries and all knowledge, and if I have all faith, so as to remove mountains, but have not love, I am nothing." - 1 Corinthians 13:4-5

ncient crypto-codices lay before the distinguished men—manuscripts that only a few scholars could decipher. At the center of an old Tuscan table stood a singular silver candelabra, casting fleeting shadows of two huddled silhouettes in deep study. The two aristocrats puffed nervously on pipes that filled the enormity of the library in a shroud of smoke.

"So, tell me again about this dream." The alchemist shifted his gaze to the doctor.

Edward Kelley carried with him a pungent smell of cooked tobacco, as he had smoked his pipe since dawn. Known in certain circles as Edward Talbot, he carried a sordid past—an expert in foreign languages and ancient religions, yet also known as a charlatan. Indeed, rumor had it that he had been kicked out of Oxford for forgery and necromancy. Yet to Doctor Dee, Mister Kelley had provided useful insights into the occult. And through their initial correspondence and the passing of time, they had developed a camaraderie vested in their common interests.

"Not a dream, really..." Doctor Dee lit his pipe with flint and steel. "...nor may I say a prayer. Let us say deep meditation. But kneeling in my quarters, there came upon me a great light; it overshadowed me. A most elegant and majestic being emerged—his radiance lit every precipice of the room, and his grandeur dwarfed my presence. I must tell you, it was quite emotional, yet he bade me, 'Fear not,' and he identified himself as the angel Uriel.

The angel told me that he had been dispatched from the heavenlies to task me with a divine ordination. He told me that I would finish the work of *Loagaeth*, and we would commence *Gebofal*. Then he gave me this amulet."

The doctor moved his ruff collar to the side and exposed an opaque, rotund pearl crystal hanging from a gold chain.

"Uriel told me that it was a conduit to the angelic world. He stated that I would be able to scry with the deities."

"Lovely story, my Lord, but dare I say without offending—it is quite incredible," remarked Edward.

"If you are saying that it is a futile pursuit, I am beginning to agree with you, for I have had no success in cracking the code." He gestured to the necklace. "This blasted 'shew stone' has no power to do anything but arouse my anger," replied the doctor in exasperation.

"And I presume that is why I am here," Kelley responded.

"Let us say I am aware of your interest in antiquity, as well as your knowledge of Greek and Latin—not to mention your affinity for ancient relics, and of course, nar' I say, your exploits in alchemy as well." The doctor raised one eyebrow suspiciously.

"One should not give credence to the *quidnuncs*, my Lord."

The doctor stood up and paced. "To be forthright, I was hoping that you could elaborate on some writings and perhaps help me to communicate with the deities. Yet, I must make it known that what we do here must remain clandestine. I do not want to suffer the ire of the aristocracy nor dishonor the Queen. Nor do I want to conjure a malicious spirit or invoke some curse down upon my family. We must hold fast to scripture and pray daily. Do you concur?" the man inquired.

"But of course, my Lord. But dare I say, the clergy may see our endeavors as..." He paused and gazed into the shadows of the library as if he saw something odd, then spoke generically, "...sacrilege."

The physician strolled closer to his younger colleague. "I am aware, Edward. And it is precisely for this reason that I must stress that we hold prudence and the utmost secrecy about our theurgical endeavors."

"How may I be of service, my Lord?" Edward said sycophantically.

"Verily, to commence, assist me with this." He dropped the amulet awkwardly onto the table. "Help me to understand its mysteries."

Edward stood up and removed his cape. He meticulously laid it over the back of the chair. "If I may..." Edward plucked the jewel from the table. Approaching the candelabra, he lifted the translucent white crystal to his face.

"Quite interesting. The crystal must be..." He paused to select his words carefully. "...in the mood to reveal her secrets."

The doctor looked at him incredulously. "You speak as if it is sentient?"

"No. The crystal is not, but the spirits on the other side... well, let us say, they can be a bit temperamental. My Lord, if you don't mind, I would like to adjourn until tomorrow after I have had a chance to prepare some things."

Edward put the shew stone back on the table.

"Very well." The doctor led the alchemist to the door and bade him farewell.

Rays of orange and purple shone through the stained-glass window, illuminating three rectangular tables on the ground floor of the library. The stained-glass window contained a sun rising from the sea; the sun held within it the symbol of the philosopher's stone—a talismanic square encapsulated by a circle, enveloped by a triangle.

The library was impressive, boasting more than four thousand ancient tomes and half again as many original geographic, political, astrological, and topographical maps. The rafters hung high above, hosting a singular rectangular black iron chandelier. And if needed, the room could be further lit by matching iron sconces impaled to the six columns that supported the second tier of shelves.

Although the library was expensive and expansive, it was not public. It belonged to astrologer, astronomer, navigator, inventor, linguist, mathematician, esotericist, and consort to Queen Elizabeth I—Doctor John Dee.

Edward sat wearing a long brown garment that fell to his buckled leather shoes. His collar stood upright, revealing a fluffy champagne-colored undergarment that concealed his neck. His head was adorned by a black hat that covered his ears. He held the shew stone so close that, at times, its chain hid in his pointed beard.

With one hand he held the stone; with the other, he wrote frantically. As if possessed, he labored throughout the day, transcribing symbols. He continued into the evening, pausing only for the occasional libation or to pack his pipe.

"May I?" the doctor inquired. He leaned over the scribe and reached for some of the parchments cast about the table. "What do they mean?"

Without lifting his gaze, "I don't know, my Lord. I have yet to decipher them."

"You mean to say that you don't know what you are writing?" Dr. Dee probed.

"Not yet, my Lord."

The doctor looked closely at the script. This was no random scrawl. Each parchment contained a mathematical grid of twenty-one characters. Each cell was filled with a grapheme resembling ancient Aramaic, Hebrew, or perhaps Syriac. It was an alphabet.

And Mr. Kelley had meticulously partitioned the glyphs into consonants and vocalic consonants, disambiguated by the insertion of elaborately illustrated diacritics.

Most impressive! he thought to himself.

"I think we are onto something! I think we have the alphabet of Enochian. Bravo."

"I have transcribed a few texts as well, but without a working knowledge of the glyphs, it will take some time to decipher them." Kelley's gaze lay fixed on the stone.

The texts were arranged into forty-nine tablets by forty-nine tablets.

"And what are they then?"

"I think they are the Tables of Loagaeth, my Lord."

"No! They cannot..."

"Yes, my Lord, it is as you have foreseen," Kelley affirmed.

"What is this ink you use? It has a peculiar smell."

"Yes, my Lord, it is blood." He dipped his quill in the inkwell and returned to his writing.

"What?" the physician retorted.

"Yes, I am afraid so. Lamb's blood. It was a prerequisite. They... um..." He looked up from his task. "They required it."

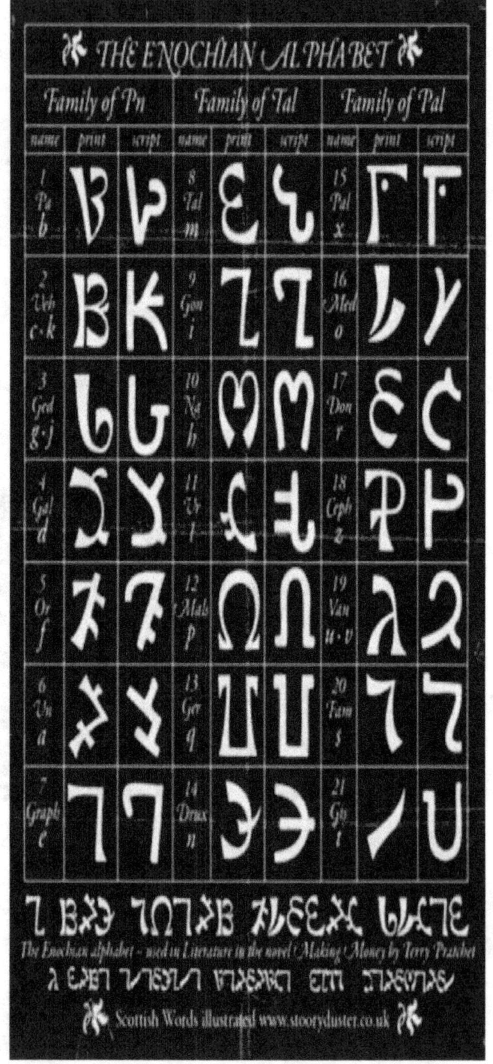

"They?" The doctor stared back.

"Yes, Uriel and Raphael."

"Are you sure? How do you know who you are talking to? How did you come to this knowledge? How do you know they are not demons? You know they thrive on deceit."

"I do," the scholar rebutted. He put down the shew stone. "Shall I stop?"

The physician stroked his beard and thought for a moment.

"No, though please tread carefully."

Chapter 8 - Chicago, Illinois

"Now the Spirit of the Lord had departed from Saul, and an evil spirit from the Lord tormented him." - 1 Samuel 16:14

hen morning came, mourning came. They stalked in the early hours around three or four o'clock. They brought with them confusion, angst, and a deep foreboding that permeated his body. He didn't know why they tormented him. Yet he knew their disquieting presence, their suppression, their familiar caress. Thoughts of violence, thoughts of perversion, thoughts of blood, thoughts of long ago, thoughts of future events plagued his mind. To numb his senses from the incessant echoes, he would masturbate violently, partake of recreational drugs, or walk in circles talking to himself. In the past, he played his guitar, eliciting the complaints of his foster parents. Yet there was no respite ever—just an incessant, insatiable hunger.

Ishmael's long auburn hair flew wildly as he lifted his head from the pillow. He fell to the wooden floor face down. He put his feet on the side of the bed and planked his body. He took a deep breath and pushed. He coordinated his breathing and managed sixty push-ups. He stood up, touched his toes, and twisted at the waist. His morning ritual required another four sets. After finishing his morning workout, Ishmael's twenty-one-year-old, six-foot-two-inch, one-hundred-and-eighty-two-pound frame stood erect. He was awake.

He crossed the loft and entered the five-by-five-foot corner designated as the bathroom. Ishmael reached behind the shower curtain and ran the water. Steam rose to the rafters of the tiny loft. He peered into a small circular mirror nailed to the wall. A rosary hung from its frame. His caramel freckled skin appeared green in the fluorescent light. Stubble covered his angular jaw.

He finished his hygiene routine and threw four eggs into a pan on the small burner, which sat on a makeshift kitchen counter—a flat particle board attached to the wall. The frigid air from Lake Michigan whistled through a tiny crack in Ishmael's singular window. He finished his breakfast, threw on some clothes, and descended the creaky stairs to the gym below.

The Title Boxing Gym was abustle with activity. It had been a landmark of the Windy City since its founding in 1923. Ishmael pushed through the swinging saloon doors and was confronted by Alfonso.

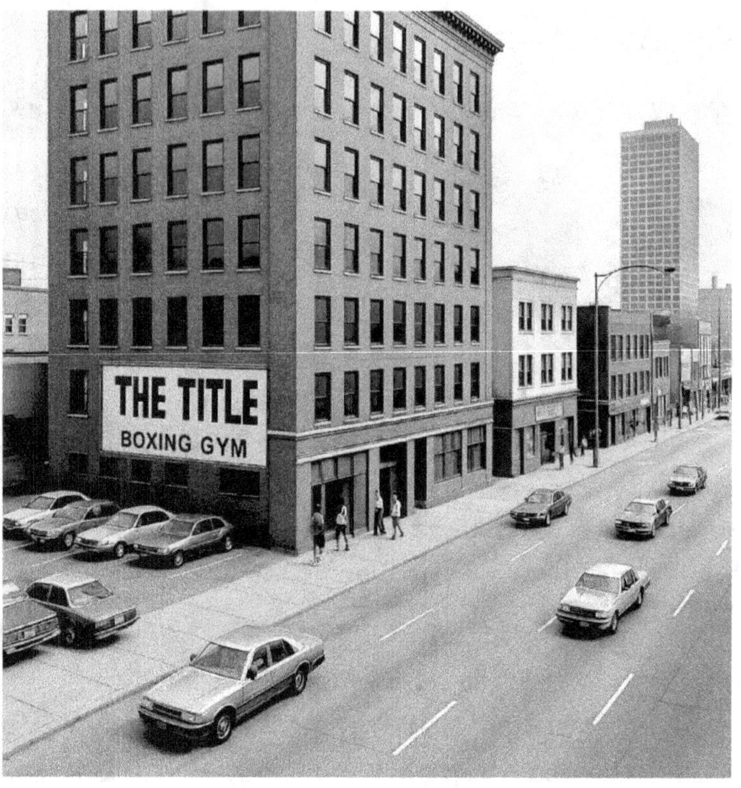

"Good morning, Red. How you doin'?"

"Awright. How are you doin', Alfonso?"

Alfonso DiGiorgio was one of the three personal trainers on staff. Although never claiming any major titles, he had been a fierce fighter in his day.

Ishmael made his way to the custodial closet, grabbed a broom, and started his rounds. The ceiling of the gym was twenty-four feet to the rafters. The length was twenty times its height. Its long rectangular expanse was partitioned by several hanging punching bags, a few stationary bikes, and open spaces flanked by mirrors where boxers could work on their technique.

Some fighters jumped rope, others shadowboxed, still others sparred in the ring. The walls were adorned with corkboards, fliers, and paper posters of famous pugilists. The impact of gloves hitting leather bags and simultaneous grunts echoed throughout the gym. Trainers yelled. Above the ring hung a banner: *Welcome to the Richmond's Citizen Boxing Club*, and above it sat a cartoon tiger with boxing gloves. The ring obscured a narrow hallway at the back that led to a weight room where Ishmael would train after closing.

The founder, Monty "Snow" Griffith, was a fixture in East Chicago. He had trained with Muhammad Ali and managed several contenders who had competed for the World Championship. Flanked by the other trainers, "Snow" sat ringside in his usual spot on raised wooden bleachers. The three were immersed in their daily discussions—boxing strategies and comparisons between the fighters du jour and how they might have fared against those of yesteryear.

Snow had allowed Ishmael to stay in the loft provided he kept the gym clean. Ishmael lived rent-free and was privy to the gym at all hours. Griffith trusted Ishmael; he had even given him a set of keys. But this trust had not been earned overnight. Ishmael had begun training at The Title seven years earlier.

After escaping from foster care at the age of fourteen, Ishmael had been living on the streets of East Chicago. Aside from the boys at the group home and Carrie, his girlfriend, he knew few people. The gym provided food for the local homeless, and Ishmael had come for a hot bowl of chicken noodle. He walked in the door and subsequently challenged a veteran pugilist. Snow told his boys to lace him up. Ishmael had thrown hands in foster care many times, but he was not prepared for a seasoned fighter. He took an uppercut to the chin that laid him out, unconscious.

The owner took an immediate liking to the boy; he admired his moxie. Over time, Snow took the boy under his wing, let him hang out at the gym, and even paid him for menial tasks. Soon, Ishmael was training daily, living in the loft upstairs, and working for his keep. The boys at the gym called him "Red."

Ishmael had just finished mopping when Cylas Wilson kicked over his pail, spilling soapy suds all over the tongue-and-groove wooden floor.

"Oops. Maybe watch your step, huh, Red?"

Ishmael looked up at Cy, then over at Snow.

"You gonna keep voidin' me?" Cy eyeballed the redhead.

"Aright, Cy, let's go."

Ishmael let the mop handle fall hard to the floor, wiped the red locks from his face, then gazed intently at his mentor. Snow gave him a nod, curious as to Red's impending reaction.

"So, you got it today, bitch, or what?" Ishmael felt his body adrenalized.

"Oh, you know it. It ain't like last time," Cy retorted calmly.

"Took a while for that shiner to go away, huh?" Ishmael smirked. He walked and disrobed at the same time, throwing his garments to the floor.

"Alright. We about to see..."

Cy stood two inches taller than Ishmael and outweighed him by fifty pounds. The two walked calmly to their respective corners. One trainer approached one corner, the other approached the opposite corner; each trainer held a pair of red gloves dangling from worn strings. After lacing up their gloves and headgear, the trainers put in their mouthpieces.

Snow jumped into the ring, squatted, and leaned in toward Ishmael's face.

"Remember what we've been workin' on. He is taller than you, so when you attack, come in low—but watch for that uppercut. If he overcommits, fake to the other side, then come back quick. He won't see that comin'. When you deliver, watch your footwork and imagine punching through to the back of his head. Don't get caught up in his facial expressions, and if he starts to wobble... attack! Remember your left cross and don't stop until he is on the ground."

Snow slapped him hard with an open hand to the chest.

"You got this!"

They came together at the center of the ring. Ishmael ignored the stares from his opponent. He gazed straight ahead.

Alfonso said, "Keep it respectful. Keep it safe. And move on my cue or I'll shut this shit down, understand?" He looked intently into the eyes of both fighters. Ishmael didn't blink.

"Let's do it."

The fighters bumped their gloves and returned to their corners.

RING!

The fighters met in the middle of the ring. Cy came out swinging haymakers—left and right—he swung wildly. Ishmael pivoted left and threw a left jab to Cy's left eye. Cy blocked his second jab and caught Ishmael in the ribs. Ishmael's air left his lungs.

"Get down, Red!" Snow screamed from the corner.

Ishmael winced in pain, then stepped backward. His opponent recklessly threw another predictable haymaker. Ishmael countered with a straight cross. Cy misjudged his direction. Ishmael's counteracting force caught him directly on the chin, knocking his jawbone into his neck. He let out a shriek, staggered, and fell backward into the ropes.

Ishmael pursued. Gaining counterforce, bouncing off the ropes, Cy's body ricocheted, propelling him headlong. He swung awkwardly with tremendous force. He harnessed all his strength, throwing it into a wild right hook. Ishmael saw it coming, channeling all his momentum into a left-handed uppercut. It penetrated Cy's defenses and landed squarely on his chin.

Cy's legs gave out and his body folded. He went directly to the floor, bouncing his head on the mat. He was unconscious momentarily, then began to gather himself. Ishmael stood over his victim.

"That's it. Call it, Alfonso. That's enough," the boss bellowed from the sidelines.

Alfonso rushed in and held Ishmael back from the fallen Goliath.

"Nice anticipation, my son. Go get cleaned up."

The fighters hit the showers.

———

The air nipped. The rain fell heavily on the streets. And the swell of three—Cylas, Daniel, and Carrie—waited outside the iconic Marge's Still in Northern Chicago. Ishmael arrived last. He noticed the bandage over Cy's left eye. Ishmael approached his petite blonde girlfriend and gave her a kiss before addressing Cy.

"You alright?" Ishmael inquired of the giant.

"Yeah man, I think that's the fifth shiner you've given me. We just had to make sure you were ready."

"We?" Ishmael asked.

"Yeah, the crew."

"Ready for what?" Ishmael realized what he meant. "Oh, shit! No?"

Cy smiled. "Come on in. It's supposed to be a surprise. Don't tell Snow I told you." He walked into the pub.

"Are you shittin' me?" Ishmael's mood had lifted.

Carrie followed him as he rushed into the long tavern, tore off his fleece-lined jeans jacket and his cream-colored beanie, threw them hastily on the stack of cloaks piled in the booth by the entrance, dodged half-drunk patrons, then proceeded to the table at the back where Snow sat with two of his trainers, Mannie and Sal.

Ishmael stood over the table. Alfonso threw darts.

"Tell me. Just tell me. Did I get it?" Ishmael could not contain his enthusiasm.

Snow and Alfonso started laughing. "It's only an expedition fight."

"FUCK YEAH!!! Oh, fuck yeah!" With a goofy expression, Ishmael did his goofy happy dance and then waved his hands in the air. Cy and Carrie jumped in, synchronizing their happy dance.

"Woooo, woooo, woooo..." they chanted in unison.

Ishmael pushed his way into the booth and sat opposite his African-American mentor. The waitress came to the table carrying five foamy Guinnesses. She laid out all the beers in front of the patrons.

"I'll be back shortly with the rest," she announced and walked away from their table.

"But hey, listen, it's in one month at the Windy City Boxing Club. And your opponent ain't no chump, neither. Leon Murphy. You know him?"

Ishmael nodded. He had seen him fight when he was fifteen.

"And you better bring your shit, because he's a local champion. He represented Chicago at the Intercity Golden Gloves a year ago. I was there. He knocked out his first two opponents in the first round."

Ishmael sat back and thought hard—it would be a challenge.

"Listen, son, if you don't make weight, you forfeit. To do that, we need to shave ten pounds off you. So after tonight, it's protein. Understand? So, you go ahead and enjoy that..." Snow gestured to the beer in his hand. "Because for the next four weeks, it's rice, meat, eggs, fish, and vegetables. Come tomorrow, early, we are hittin' the gym."

Ishmael was flooded with emotion. He knew the next month would be grueling.

Ishmael rode his black Triumph Bonneville T140 past the old Greyhound bus station, then turned into a small arcade where his girlfriend worked. He got off the bike, took off his helmet, and scanned the restaurant for his girlfriend. He had been dating Carrie since she was eighteen. She was a waitress at Tortorice's Pizza in downtown Chicago.

"Ishmael!" Carrie called from across the room. Her face lit up when she saw him.

"Hey baby!" Carrie chirped with delight. "So, how was your training today?" she asked.

"Intense. Snow is pushing me crazy."

"That's no surprise. Can I get you somethin'? Do you want a beer?"

"No, I can't drink until after the fight. I have to make weight. I'm going up against Leon Murphy. He's the real shit."

"I know you're going to kick his ass! I'm really busy, babe. Can we hang out later? My place? I get off work at 10:00..."

Carrie grabbed a tray to serve some customers, then turned back to Ishmael. "Take me on your motorcycle later?" she mumbled as he left.

To Carrie, "hanging out" meant drinking cheap booze and having sex. And despite Snow's restrictions, Ishmael was up for it. He needed to let off some steam. The fight put a great deal of pressure on him, and his unsettling thoughts were becoming more frequent.

Ishmael would find himself humming tunes in the shower, repeating phrases he had never heard, singing songs he had never learned, and scribbling symbols he had never seen. Although they weren't songs, but more like... chants... and they weren't languages per se, but rather unintelligible, visceral, semantic grunts and moans. In his visions, he saw himself in the third person—understanding, communicating, navigating through space and time with purpose and conviction—as if he were transcendent, as if he had a secret that no one knew... not even himself.

CHAPTER 9 - Chicago, Illinois

"And you, my son Solomon, acknowledge the God of your father, and serve him with wholehearted devotion and with a willing mind, for the Lord searches every heart and understands every desire and every thought. If you seek him, he will be found by you; but if you forsake him, he will reject you forever." - 1 Chronicles 28:9

The day came earlier than most. Ishmael had trained for four weeks. He had neglected nothing. He had made weight, and he was in good shape, but despite his dedication, his dreams flooded his head, compromising his focus.

"You alright, son? You look a little teary-eyed. Are you okay?" Snow consoled his protégé.

Ishmael gave a half-hearted shrug and fell back into his thoughts. He never knew his parents, or at least he couldn't remember them. He was told that he had repressed his memories, probably due to their traumatic nature. Sometimes in the early morning, he woke with images of extreme violence in his head. And recently, his dreams had become more intense—more graphic. He heard gunfire and screaming. He saw fleeting images of glass shattering, of his mother pulling him out of bed, and of a man in a ski mask.

He remembered bouncing from group home to group home, fighting, struggling. He especially remembered Mr. Russell, who had sodomized him at the age of six. He remembered the Delfinis for beating him with a broomstick. And the Smiths for depriving him of food. Ishmael had run from every group home. Social services had classified him as emotionally disturbed. And that label followed him until he showed up at The Title. In fact, Cylas Wilson was the only good thing to come out of it. And if it had not been for Carrie and Snow adopting him, Ishmael would have lost it a long time ago.

His trainer slapped his face. "Hey! You in there?" His thoughts were not in the fight.

The crowd noise could be heard ebbing and flowing from the auditorium. One trainer tightened his laces, another rubbed his shoulders, and Snow filled his ear with advice. The crew threw the young fighter into the congested corridor where people slapped him on the back. Carrie and Cy followed. The shouts grew progressively louder as he approached the arena. The crowd propelled him forward. He put his hands on his trainers' shoulders, looked at the floor, and thought about the fight.

They led him to the ring. He looked at the sidelines to catch a glimpse of Carrie's worried expression. Ishmael stepped through the ropes and peered at his opponent. Leon Murphy was cut and refined. He seemed intense. Ishmael knew that he was in for a duel. He turned around and bounced on his toes. He cracked his neck and focused on Snow. He inhaled heavily and then sat on the tripod chair. Snow meticulously stepped through the ropes and squatted in front of Red.

"So, you remember your training, remember what we worked on... He is going to come with it, right from the beginning."

Snow's strategy was to weather the first rounds and look for a knockout in the latter. Despite Murphy's muscular appearance, he felt Ishmael could outlast the champ. Ishmael's amateur record of 13–2 was wrought with wins in the latter rounds. He was known for his second wind. He was best when he was down, when he was threatened.

"Stay away from the ropes. Jab and move, jab and move. Keep him at bay. He wants you in close, to set up that left-left-right combo. If you can weather the storm, we can take him into the later rounds and we come out on top. Okay? Let's go!"

He slapped him open-handed on the chest.

Ishmael nodded. He thought about his mother, and then shook it off. He put in his mouthpiece, inhaled through his nose, sucked in the menthol from his upper lip, and then stared at his opponent.

RING.

Just as Snow predicted, Murphy came out aggressively. Crossing the ring in four paces, he swung hard for Ishmael's head. Ishmael did not expect the sweeping left hook, and it partially landed against his forehead, sending him reeling to the ropes. Ishmael covered his head and abdomen as best he could from the assault on his person. Murphy delivered a barrage of body shots.

"Get out! GET OUT!" He could hear Snow screaming ringside.

Ishmael leaned against him and pushed both his shoulders backward toward the center ring. Murphy took a step back, gathered his momentum, stepped forward with his right foot, then leaned left, setting up his patented triple combo. Ishmael saw it coming but faked like he didn't. Avoiding Murphy's cross, he pivoted to the right, deflecting his blow and countered with a right-hand cross over the champ's shoulder. He struck pay dirt, hitting him on the side of the face. The champion recoiled and backed up. Murphy's strategy for a quick knockout was dissipating.

Murphy tried repeatedly for the quick knockout, but Snow's training had prepared him for a long bout.

The bell rang. Ishmael stared defiantly at the champ. Their gloves fell and they went to their corners. Snow was in his face, but his words fell away as if the volume had been turned down.

RING. Round two.

Ishmael and the champ squared off in the middle. Ishmael threw two crosses, missing horribly. The champ countered, hitting Ishmael in the gut. Ishmael let out a grunt as his wind left him. Murphy hit Red again in the stomach. Sensing weakness, the champ swung upward as Ishmael doubled over, catching him on the chin. His jaw was jarred, and his mouthguard flew to the asphalt floor outside the ring. His legs failed, and his face hit the cold canvas. He lost consciousness.

Images flowed... Locked in chains... more violence... 200... blood flowed... familiar... someone hurt... someone betrayed... a girl... a beautiful girl in pain... foreign faces, foreign lands... a massive crowd of people... so cold... terrifying... desecration.

The audio came back. He could hear the crowd yelling. He heard Snow's booming voice.

"Get up!"

He jumped up. He was disoriented but checked in. How much time had passed? He didn't know. He shook off the fog and forced his eyes to focus on the referee, whose fingers shook in his face.

"...seven, eight... Look at me. Look at me, Red. You with me? Can you go on?"

Ishmael nodded. The referee stepped back and motioned for the two fighters to resume.

Murphy came in aggressively, looking to finish it. He pranced forward too confidently, leaving himself open for a nanosecond. Seizing the moment, Ishmael baited him. Murphy wound up, but before the champ could deliver the impact, Ishmael countered with a distracting jab and three successive crosses. Ishmael moved left as he threw his lightning-quick punches.

The first hit the champ's glove. The second deflected off his glove, forcing him to lower it. And the last two connected with his nose and jaw. The champ stammered backward as if walking the wrong way on a treadmill. He overcompensated, trying to regain his equilibrium, then stumbled to the floor.

Shouts erupted. The referee held Ishmael at bay. Then his fingers came out again.

"One... two..." He shoved them in Murphy's face. "You alright? Look at me. Look at me... three... four..."

The champ stood up immediately and nodded in agreement. The referee stepped back, and the fight resumed.

The two pugilists bludgeoned each other for twenty more minutes. Ishmael didn't win, but he had gone seven rounds with the champ and forced a split decision. Snow was very proud.

CHAPTER 10 - Boston, Massachusetts

"Woe to those who call evil good and good evil, who put darkness for light and light for darkness, who put bitter for sweet and sweet for bitter." - Isaiah 5:20

ather Samuel "Sammy" Morado grew up in the *barangay* in Cebu, Philippines. He was transferred to the Holy Cross at the age of twenty-six and ordained seven years later. Dunnigan had taken him under his wing.

The young priest stopped by the church office and saw a copy of the *Boston Herald* sitting on a table in the reception area. He picked up the paper and moved to his small office. As was his habit, he sifted through the newspaper for the sports section, pulled it out, and discarded the rest on his desk. On the cover page, the headline read: *Celtics Fall to the Pistons*. Samuel checked the scores, put the paper on his desk, and returned to his duties. One last glance revealed a picture and a familiar name: *Unknown Fighter Goes the Distance with Local Champion*. He read the article, thought about the name, then picked up the phone.

"Yes, Mrs. Klein, can you let the Father know I would like to speak with him?"

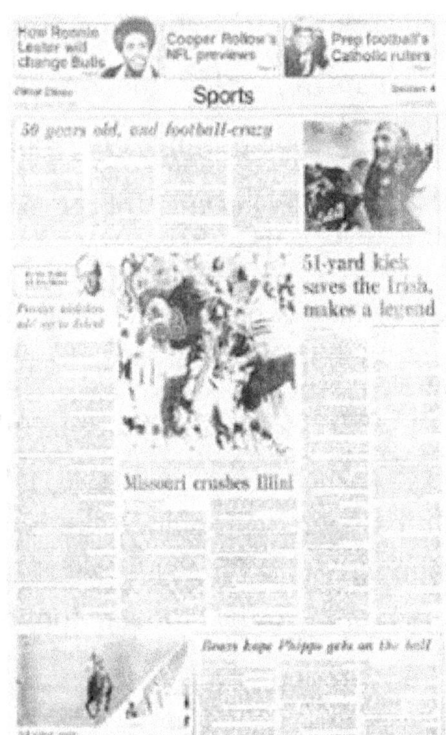

Although privy to many of the parish's operations, Father Morado knew little of the miracle-worker. But he had heard the name Ishmael, and he knew about the red hair. He had heard the ubiquitous murmurs surrounding the healing of Mr. Browning and the boy's subsequent disappearance. He calculated his age and stared at the boy's photo. The young Filipino picked up the phone on his desk.

"Father Dunnigan, sorry to disturb you, but I just read something very interesting. I thought you might like to know."

"Yes, Father?" Dunnigan's baritone voice came through the line.

"Have you read today's paper?" the Filipino asked.

"Not yet. Why do you ask?"

"In the sports section... So, do you remember that boy, Ishmael?"

There was silence on the other end of the line. "Go on."

"How old would he be if he were alive?" the young father inquired.

"I don't know. Why do you ask?"

"I think he is in the paper." Father Morado listened for a response. There was an awkward silence.

"Why don't you come by after work, and we can talk about it?"

"Okay, Father. See you tonight. I look forward to it."

Father Dunnigan opened the front door to his brownstone on Gloucester Street to find Samuel on his porch in street clothes.

"Please come in, Sammy."

The young Filipino scaled the stairs to the entrance. Father Dunnigan closed the door behind his guest, still donned in his clerical garments.

"Would you care for some refreshment?" Dunnigan walked him into the kitchen and gestured toward a crystal carafe of whiskey.

"No, thank you," Samuel responded.

"So, what's your information?" Dunnigan demanded.

"I thought you'd want to see this story."

"So, what do you know about Ishmael?" he asked nonchalantly.

Samuel responded, "I've heard rumors about him healing a dead man at the Holy Cross long ago. I guess he and his parents disappeared shortly afterward." He pulled a torn page from his pocket and unfolded the excerpt from the newspaper. "But this is him, right?" He extended it to Dunnigan.

"Let me see." Dunnigan put on his readers and squinted at the black-and-white photo. *Ishmael Taylor.* He was much older and had a different last name, but it was undoubtedly the boy.

Father Dunnigan placed the article on the counter, closed his eyes, and breathed deeply. Then, Dunnigan unzipped his pants and began to stroke his penis. He turned around to expose his erection. Samuel stood in front of Dunnigan's protruding phallus.

"Turn around!" he growled.

The submissive Filipino dropped his pants. Father Dunnigan bent the young priest over and began to thrust violently into Samuel, who braced himself against the counter. Beads of sweat formed on his forehead, and his eyes grew black. Dunnigan pulled a cincture from his pocket and wrapped it firmly around the priest's neck. The young priest became more aroused, moaning loudly. Dunnigan pulled the cord tighter with each thrust.

Father Dunnigan began to climax and chanted, his voice growing in volume and intensity as his chanting was interspersed with groans of ecstasy. Samuel began to lose consciousness. The

Filipino's movements, once slow and lust-ridden, became contorted and violent as he realized his predicament. Dunnigan tightened his grasp as the priest struggled to breathe.

The crystal carafe shattered on the floor as his arms flailed desperately against the attack. His hands grabbed futilely at his throat. Abbreviated attempts at speech could be heard through the gurgling saliva. His body contorted violently as he took his last desperate breath, then collapsed forward onto the counter.

The young priest's legs twitched. Dunnigan pushed hard into him, penetrating the dying man. Then, with a blood-curdling cry of exhaustion and ecstasy, his body twitched as he shot his last drop of semen into the dead man.

Dunnigan let go. Morado's body collapsed hard to the floor. Dunnigan's eyes grew black. He zipped up his pants, ran his fingers through his sweaty, blondish, balding hair, and straightened his clothes. He took a knife from the drawer, bent over, and cut the cord loose from Morado's limp neck.

He removed a cigar and a box of matches from his pocket, lit a Cuban, and inhaled deeply into the flame. Dunnigan picked up the black push-button phone from an end table and dialed.

"Hello? Yes, it's me. I have a carpet stain. I need it removed."

Chapter 11 - Mortlake, England - the 16th Century

"The Lord will send on you curses, confusion and rebuke in everything you put your hand to, until you are destroyed and come to sudden ruin because of the evil you have done in forsaking him." - Deuteronomy 28:20

he driver snapped his leash heavily against the horse's back. The conductor knocked on the wooden frame of the carriage below. And the man sitting opposite Doctor John Dee was not Edward Kelley, his companion of nine years, but rather a personal escort of Emperor Rudolfo II, the "mad king" of Prague, the Emperor of Bohemia. The king, heir to the Habsburgs, had commissioned the physician and Mister Kelley to conduct theurgical practices in the service of his court. The pair had become famous in Eastern Europe. The two had led royal families to nightly séances, tarot readings, divination, necromancy, and astral projection. The two had become fonts for the royal classes to the obscure and metaphysically perverse. They were the latest entertainment.

Dee did not know that a short time later, his fellow "scryer" would die, diving from a tower window where he had been imprisoned by Emperor Rudolfo II. He would survive the initial fall but die later of his injuries.

Dee's escort held up one finger to signify one mile to his house at Mortlake. He was exhausted from the journey; it had taken three weeks. His underside was saddle-sore despite having been transported in a lush carriage replete with cushioned bench seats, oak wood interior, golden inlay, and burgundy drapes. He had made haste from Prague. Without protection from his Queen Elizabeth, he worried about his home, his collections, and his library. The coronation of James I had ushered in the Jacobean era—an epoch riddled with the persecution of the occult and esoteric practices.

Dee leaned his head out of the window to listen to a gathering crowd of angst-ridden city folk outside the grounds of his house. Some held clubs, others gardening implements. The weight of the crowd caused the iron gates to bow. He told the driver to speed up. The crowd turned to the growing sound of galloping hooves, then enveloped the caravan. Doctor Dee yelled, "Stand aside!" and waved his hand. Several people were knocked to the ground as the muscular horses trampled them. But the crowd would not be dissuaded—they wanted blood.

The gates opened prematurely as two hired hands swung the metal frames wide. The carriage came to the inner sanctum of the entry to the disembarkation platform. The crowd grew frenzied and pushed the gate open. One hundred and sixty townsfolk descended on the doctor's residence. The royal escort and the driver unsheathed their swords and yelled at Dee to enter the house. He ran inside and beckoned for the two guards. They entered, slammed the doors, then slid the enormous iron bolt into the lock. They stepped back and listened to the crowd as they banged on the large wooden doors.

From his vantage point, Dee could see rioters throwing projectiles. A large rock smashed through the stained-glass window. Dee had had three weeks to anticipate what he would grab in this exact scenario. It had played out in his head several weeks prior. The reality was starkly different. He was scared.

He entered the darkened library. He heard people banging on the door and the yelling of his staff. He only had a few moments. He thought he could run, but they would chase him down. He could fight, but that would only arouse their anger further. He decided to protect his most treasured possession—the manuscripts that he and his fellow alchemist, Edward Kelley, had meticulously transcribed, the key to transcendental spiritualism, the Enochian writings, the *Liber Loagaeth.* Perhaps his work could outlive him. Perhaps he could pass on his knowledge. Perhaps someone, someday, would ascend the *Gebofal.*

Hurriedly, he took out a key that hung from a chain attached to his belt. He shoved aside some books to reveal a hidden door. He opened it with the key and sifted through the parchments. He identified the writings of Enoch and removed them from the rest. He crossed the room to another cabinet that held a wooden jewelry box with a red felt interior—a box intended for Queen Elizabeth before her premature death. He unlocked it and removed a false bottom from the box. He slid the parchments into the hidden compartment. He locked it, then slid the jewelry box back into the hidden cavern.

No sooner had he replaced the books and exited the library than a mob of angry protestors seized him in the corridor and beat him to the ground wildly. He did not know at whose hand he would perish, but he knew that he would finally be able to communicate with the angels. He bled into the hallway of his beloved library. Unlike Edward Kelley, Doctor John Dee would survive his wounds—but his beloved library would not. That is, nothing but the *Loagaeth.*

CHAPTER 12 - Chicago, Illinois

Though they plot evil against you and devise wicked schemes, they cannot succeed. You will make them turn their backs when you aim at them with a drawn bow. Be exalted in your strength, LORD; we will sing and praise your might. - Psalm 21:11-13

now pushed the youngster back from the Everlast vertical bag. "Watch. Red!" He scrunched over and held his fists up over his face. "Make sure your fighting stance is here. Then here, and then switch feet to give that uppercut power..." He illustrated the technique, then hit the bag. "Now, you try."

Ishmael stepped back into his stance, leveraged his weight, and struck the bag. The bag swayed.

"Okay, now practice that one hundred times, both sides—fifty each—then hit the shower."

The boy repeated the strike over and over. His three-hour workout was done.

"Alright, Snow, I'm going to shower up now," Ishmael mumbled.

"Alright, my boy..." Snow nodded, then returned his gaze to the other fighters sparring in the ring.

"KEEP 'EM UP!" he scolded.

Ishmael climbed the stairs to the loft. He threw his clothes in a bin and ran the hot water for his shower. The hot water felt great. His muscles were sore—but in a good way. He let the hot water run heavily on the back of his neck. His thoughts raced as they always had.

The visions returned. Lustful thoughts of violence and depravity... veiled faces, with recognizable voices... spoken languages that he understood but could not explain... nor recite... a beautiful woman... smells of sulfur... agony, indescribable agony... strange names and images of ancient peoples in ancient times... so confusing... large men shrouded in mist and hoods... and frail tiny women... someone dying... always the same, yet never quite the same... never-ending...

He was awoken from his vision by a car door slam. He put a towel around his torso and walked to the window. A yellow checkered Marathon taxi had pulled up to the gym entrance on West Monroe. An ominous figure had stepped from the taxi wearing a black weaver's hat, a white butterfly collar, a black leather jacket with wide lapels, and black slacks that flared out over leather shoes. The elderly man lit a cigar from a box of matches and walked to the entrance of the gym.

As he approached the building, Ishmael got a glimpse of his face. He had deep eyes and blondish-grey hair that shot out from underneath the beanie. Ishmael was enthralled with his gait, his presence... There was something so familiar about this man.

The redhead sat obscured in his loft, hiding behind the pane, peering out his fogged window. After a few moments, the gentleman entered the gym. A short time later, he promptly emerged, returned to the waiting taxi, and left. Ishmael put on some clothes and went downstairs.

"Hey, Snow." Griffith sat in his usual place, bellowing across the gym. "Move! MOVE! Yeah, my boy, what you got?"

"Did a man just come in here?" Ishmael inquired.

"Matter of fact, yeah. He spoke to Alfonso. He dropped this off." Without lowering his gaze, he dug in his pocket and pulled out a card. "Here."

Ishmael took the business card and looked at it:

RODNEY D. ARMSTRONG – PROMOTER

In the bottom left-hand corner lay three unusual, yet oddly familiar symbols. They were gold, celeste, and black in color. *They seem like Egyptian hieroglyphs—or maybe something older,* he thought.

He had received a lot of notoriety from the Murphy fight. People had stopped into the gym without warning, pretending to know him—lost acquaintances from years past, people with alternative motives that he could not decipher. Some wanted money, some wanted favors.

"Said he wanted to promote you... sounds like you movin' up, my boy." His mentor supported the backside of a vertical bag as one of the local fighters pounded it. Snow smiled, then noticed Red's lack of enthusiasm. He dismissed the other fighter so they could talk.

"What is it?"

"Nothing." Ishmael was perplexed.

"You know that guy?" Snow inquired.

"Not sure."

____

The evening was predictable. The crew got there about nine o'clock. The Still was crowded on Friday nights, and that evening was no exception. People bled into the streets. Congregations of Chicagoans stood outside the pub arguing over the latest sports teams. Music blared from the speakers in the pub.

The boys went in and ordered Guinnesses. Alfonso played darts with Carrie, the boys stalked the pub for girls, and the trainers argued about who was the greatest fighter.

Cy sat alone with the redhead in the booth.

"Hey, you believe in God?" Ishmael inquired. He had had seven pints and felt drunk.

Cy rolled his eyes, then reached over and took his beer. "Okay. That's it, you're cut off."

"I am serious." He grabbed his beer and took another sip. "You know, I have a few faint memories of my mother." He looked at Cy. "And I remember that she had an immense passion for Jesus. I remember that she would come pray with me at night to scare the dreams away."

"What do you mean, 'scare the dreams away'?" Cy said.

"Yeah, my dreams... She used to come and pray with me to make them stop..." He paused. "They... they sort of have a mind of their own... like... personalities... It's hard to explain."

"Awright, brother. If you say so. I think I'll wait till morning to hear that one."

"I am not drunk..." He said as his eyes attempted to focus and his head swayed. "All I'm saying is that I have seen shit happen."

"So?"

"So, it came true." Ishmael was not lucid, but he was adamant.

"It came true?" Cy rolled his eyes.

"Yes."

"Like exactly as you dreamt it? Or maybe you just imagined that you saw it? Or maybe you just thought it came true? Or maybe..."

"No." Ishmael interrupted. "I mean, I saw it before it happened, and then it happened. I mean... it happened exactly the way I dreamt it." He paused in doubt. "...Or at least, symbolically anyway."

"Symbolically? Oh okay, Mister Prophet," Cy said sarcastically.

Undaunted, Ishmael continued. "Sometimes I see it seconds before the event, other times, I see it from far away—a long way off... And the further it is... the more symbols. It only comes into focus when it wants... I have no control over it."

"I don't get it."

"There are images. They look like symbols, sometimes numbers too." He pulled out Armstrong's business card. "Like this." Ishmael held out the card.

Cy looked down at it and noticed in the upper left corner, three unusual symbols, separated by a triangle, indented into the card stock and written in three distinctly different colors—light blue, gold, and black. They all lay against a white background.

"And this means something to you?"

"Those specific symbols? No, I mean… I don't think so… but I have seen many like it."

"Where did you see them?"

"In my head. Or perhaps somewhere else…" Cy rolled his eyes.

"That is what I am trying to tell you. These signs, symbols, or whatever the fuck… they pop up everywhere—in my dreams, when I am eating, when I am out—wherever. They follow me. I even see them in my bouts."

"In the ring?" Cy asked.

Ishmael nodded in concurrence.

Sally swooped in and dropped two new brews onto the table in front of them. Ishmael waited until she was out of earshot to reply.

"Yeah, man. They consume me. But whatever time they take, they give back."

He looked at Cy, who looked confused.

"So… it's like this… my head might be clouded for a moment, then all of a sudden, I get a bucket of images… they just come… they communicate with me… and I can't tell where they come from…" He took another sip of his dark beer. "And in an instant—literally in nanoseconds…" He snapped his fingers. "It all makes sense. Everything is clear. And I know exactly what to do…"

He paused to look at his friend. He took a sip of his beer, then stared over his mug at his brown-haired friend. Cy looked incredulous.

"And here's the thing…" He sipped his Guinness, then wiped the froth from his upper lip. "They're back. Every day, I am getting these symbols thrown at me. They are more and more frequent and much more vivid than before… I haven't had it this bad since I was a child. Something is going to happen. Something big—I can feel it."

"Okay, Nostradamus. Well, if you get any vibes—oh, sorry, 'symbols'…" He put two phantom quotes in the air. "…on the horse races, let me know. Or maybe we should go to Atlantic City, play some blackjack?"

Cylas paused to notice Ishmael's withered body language, then paused introspectively.

"Look, man, I love you. In my experience, I ain't never seen anything like that... but if you say that shit happens, then that shit happens." He took a sip of beer. "I know that your dreams bother you..."

"Yeah... dreams." He paused to look out the window at the cars passing in the rain. "But they seem more like memories." He swallowed the remnant of beer in his glass. "...even the ones that haven't happened yet."

He looked around for Sally, bid the boys a good night, and grabbed Carrie's hand before they stepped outside into the rain and hailed a cab.

The cab took them south on Sedgwick toward the loft. He leaned his face against the cold glass, the weather combined with his drunken condition creating luminary streamers in the frosty night. His mind gave way to visions of men in cages... the speaking of tongues... screaming voices... and the constant smell of sulfur...

Carrie interrupted his thoughts when he felt her teeth gently nibble his ear.

"Hmmm," she whispered. "I can't wait to get you upstairs."

The cab stopped at The Title, dropping them at the entrance. He stumbled out of the cab, then ransacked his pockets for the large L-shaped key. He fumbled with the key, all the while trying to keep his mind focused on the stranger's face in his mind. Carrie kissed his neck and giggled.

He turned the lock and pushed the heavy twelve-foot wooden door. He hit the light switch. The electricity traveled through the cables, creating a humming noise that preceded the activation of the lights.

The couple started kissing passionately. They wobbled up the stairs, undressing each other as they went. When they reached the top of the circular staircase, Carrie took a few steps and fell headfirst onto the pillow on his bed. She turned around slowly, and Ishmael began to kiss her breasts, then climbed on top of her. Carrie pulled Ishmael's head down and pushed her hips up toward his mouth. He buried his face between her legs and moved his tongue in circles until Carrie began to moan. Ishmael lunged forward to plunge inside her.

They both grunted together, louder and louder as they neared climax. Carrie loved to talk when they were having sex.

"Oh yeah. That feels so good!"

Ishmael soon began to ejaculate, thrusting deeply inside her with each release before rolling onto the mattress. He stared up at the rafters in the ceiling.

"That was amazing, baby," said Carrie with satisfaction.

"Yeah, it was," he replied in agreement.

Ishmael put his boxers back on while Carrie found her panties and pulled on one of his T-shirts before getting under the covers. He laid back and turned off the lights before falling into a deep sleep.

Ishmael had failed to notice the black Cadillac Seville sitting deep in the shadows of the alley. The soft glow of a cigar pulsed from the driver's seat. The driver watched as the couple entered the gym. His mind schemed, and he chanted under his breath.

He was five years old again... The smell of his mother's perfume permeated his nostrils... The ceiling was so high above... celestial... symbols, recurring symbols... stained glass windows... Who was Gregory? ... Two hundred what? ... The pews were packed with people... so many people... His mother looked so beautiful, and his dad sat belligerently with his arms crossed... Someone was about to die... But was this the past? The future? Something so familiar... Gebofal... A baritone voice echoed in the grand cathedral... Carrie was in pain...

Suddenly, in his mind's eye, he was floating, navigating the rafters of the grand cathedral, peering down at the priestly podium... There stood a priest holding a chalice...

ARMSTRONG! The priest! That's it! Armstrong was the priest! But why would he show up now? What was that smell?

A sweet ether-like scent filled his nostrils. A large black figure bore down on him. The masked man struggled to cover Ishmael's mouth with a chloroform-soaked cloth. Ishmael tried to kick at the dark figure but realized his feet were being restrained by another man. Ishmael let out a cry, but it was muffled by the wet cloth.

His left hand was free, so he threw a hard strike at the man's solar plexus. The assailant groaned in pain, releasing the cloth from his face, allowing Ishmael to breathe the cold air. He threw his forehead wildly forward, colliding with the man's nose. The figure dropped the cloth to the floor. He murmured something in a language that Red had never heard before.

The man's weight shifted from Ishmael's chest, allowing him to arch backward. This time, Ishmael brought the full strength of his abdomen. He threw his forehead violently forward, headbutting the man's mouth. Ishmael could feel the man's flesh tear beneath the ski mask. The intruder recoiled and cursed loudly in Italian.

"Mortacci tua!"

Both of Ishmael's hands came free. He grabbed the second man from behind his cranium and pulled his head into his bent knee. Both men staggered backward, both with broken noses. Ishmael would concentrate his successive strikes on those wounds—Snow had taught him well!

Ishmael noticed yet another man wrestling with Carrie as she fought for her life... She fell unconscious to the chloroform cloth. The masked figure dropped Carrie's limp body to the bed and looked up to see Ishmael flying headlong into the air. He was a human projectile. His speed and body weight culminated on the jaw of the masked invader. The dark figure's large frame slammed heavily against the refrigerator.

The assailant let out a loud shriek. The lamp suspended from the ceiling shook violently, and some empty beer bottles shattered on the floor.

The other two culprits regained their footing and grabbed Ishmael from behind. Ishmael leaned backward and twisted at the torso, striking one assailant with an elbow to the broken nose. Screaming loudly, the man fell backward to the cold wooden floor.

Ishmael turned to throw another blow when...

"EY! Guarda qua! Hey Romeo, LOOK AT ME!"

He held Carrie's unconscious body aloft by her hair, and with the other hand, he held a medieval dagger to her throat.

Ishmael gasped. "OKAY, okay, okay, stop, stop... just don't hurt her!" Ishmael stood up, wearing only his red boxer shorts. "I'll do whatever you want." He held his hands open in submission.

The other two men stood up as well. They tied rope around Ishmael's wrists, fastening his arms behind his back. The larger of the two took out a black hoodie and started to fold it over Ishmael's face.

"Ey ragazzo, guarda qua... Look at this!" His heavy accent echoed through his mask. Ishmael turned his head to the voice just as the invader plunged the dagger into Carrie's throat; he stared directly into Ishmael's eyes as he slowly sliced the girl's neck from ear to ear. Blood squirted across the loft and onto Ishmael's bare chest. The dark figure then dropped Carrie's lifeless body awkwardly to the floor.

"MOTHERFUCKER! I AM GOING TO KILL Yooooouuuuuu!" With his hands still bound, Ishmael hopped up on one leg. He shook off the hoodie and then delivered a swift kick to the side of the knee of his captor, who buckled over in pain. He then brought up his knee into his face, knocking him to the floor.

The other captor struggled to restrain the redhead. He broke free momentarily, leaned forward, and charged Carrie's murderer. Using his momentum, he plunged his shoulder deep into his chest. The speed of the collision hurled the pair through the third-story window into the cold, cloudy night. Along with shards of glass, splintered wood, and bent metal, the two crashed heavily to the cement below. Ishmael's entire weight fell on the chest of his foe, crushing his ribcage and vital organs. Bloody gurgles filled his last attempts at speech. He was dead.

 Ishmael had only a few moments. He spied the dagger glistening near the entrance of the gym. He ran awkwardly and sat backward. Grabbing the blade with his fingers, he cut the ropes that bound his hands.

Ishmael could hear the two behemoths coming down the stairs. He pulled his keys from under the fender of his Triumph. He jumped on the bike and turned the ignition. His enemies sprang from the gym, slamming open the large wooden doors on their hinges. The bike started, and Ishmael pulled the throttle back hard.

One of the goons ran up and hugged the boy from behind. Ishmael accelerated, causing the man to drag his feet through the parking lot. Ishmael tucked his head and pushed the man's arm free of his body. The man collapsed awkwardly; his masked face bounced on the wet asphalt.

Speeding from the parking lot, Ishmael pushed the Triumph to capacity. He took a hard left toward Lake Superior. His bike hydroplaned on the wet surface, nearly tipping it to the ground. Suddenly from behind, a black Cadillac Seville fishtailed onto Cermak Road.

Still wearing only his boxer shorts, he throttled the bike and leaned into the frigid air. Ishmael squinted to see three figures in the pursuing car. The car closed the distance as his bike screamed along the avenue. His senses were heightened; his focus was unequivocal. His body was frozen, yet on fire at the same time.

It began to rain. The droplets felt like pellets against his skin, and the lights glistened from the road. He weaved his bike between the cars, missing them by centimeters. The driver of the Cadillac sped up but then strategically waited until Ishmael approached a grassy knoll. The car gently kissed the backside of the bike. Ishmael's bike slid sideways, throwing his body headlong one hundred feet into the air. His body contorted and slid along the grass and then flew into the hedges. His bike tumbled down the road, finally crashing into a telephone pole. Ishmael felt an immense blow to his head and plummeted to the ground.

 The Cadillac screeched to a halt. Two figures emerged—one stalked forward holding zip ties, and the other, a dagger. Twenty yards behind them, a black 1967 Ford Mustang Fastback skidded to a stop. A red cherry sat atop the canopy, spinning defiantly. The red glow of lights formed candescent rings in the fog.

A silhouette jumped from the driver's seat and immediately began shooting, splitting the frozen air with slugs. The driver of the Cadillac quickly sped away, abandoning his comrades to their fate. One man fell from a blast to the back, collapsing onto Ishmael. He weighed heavily on Ishmael's chest, preventing him from moving. Blood spilled all over Ishmael's chest.

He gazed through blood-stained eyes as the second figure suffered two blows—one to the chest and one to the neck—that nearly decapitated him. His body fell lifelessly to the grass.

Ishmael attempted to push off the fallen corpse, but his strength had left him. Ishmael's head injury was too severe; he fought against it but reluctantly collapsed into unconsciousness.

Ishmael heard a high-pitched humming sound. He opened his eyes and listened, trying to determine the source of the noise. It was coming from outside. He sat up in bed to glimpse flashes of light across the sky.

Leaning against the pane, Ishmael peered through the window at a clear starry night. There was no sign of a storm. He was compelled to investigate.

Ishmael opened the front door and crept outside. In the distance, he could see a massive cloud moving toward him that emitted metallic flashes of light. Ishmael was frozen in awe and fear. The cloud descended on him.

A creature emerged from the cloud with giant wings that extended upward and the beautiful face of a human, whose body was engulfed in flames.

"Son of man, do not be afraid. You are called by the Lord to bear witness to His glory."

Ishmael felt a radiant light enter his body; he was drawn upward... The luminescence gave him comfort for the first time in many years. The angel presented a scroll that contained strange glyphs.

"Soon it will be revealed unto you the significance of these revelations."

Ishmael reached out toward the angel and felt a searing pain on his left wrist. With a flash of light, the angel disappeared, and the radiant warmth abandoned him—leaving only cold darkness again.

The Sisters of Saint Anne in Chicago took Ishmael into their care after the incident. Malech would not risk taking Ishmael to a hospital for fear of his exposure to the coven. Ishmael slept for several days, only waking up to take sips of water or broth. Sister Mary Catherine stayed at his side by day, and Sister Ruth by night.

The sisters were afraid of encephalitis, but he was alert when finally roused from sleep. "Hello, Ishmael. It is so good to see you awake!" said Sister Ruth, touching his shoulder.

Ishmael recoiled from her intimate gesture. "Who are you? Why am I here?"

"You are at the convent at Saint Anne's. Sister Mary Catherine and I watched over you after the accident," explained Sister Ruth. "We were very worried about you."

"Thanks," he replied weakly.

Ishmael lay in his bed for several more days and refused any offer of "fresh air" from the sisters. His memories came rushing back to him—the attack at The Title, Carrie's death, and the chase through the city. He couldn't endanger his friends by going back to the gym. Ishmael felt he had nothing left to live for. He buried his face in his hands.

When he looked up, he noticed a red branded wound on the inside of his left wrist. His vision flashed through his mind. He saw the angel holding a cryptic scroll and felt the burn against his skin. He touched the evidence of this encounter but wasn't ready to grasp its magnitude.

Malech visited him in his room a week later. "How are you feeling, son?"

"Never better," Ishmael responded dryly.

"Have you ever been to Italy?" asked Malech enthusiastically.

"What are you talking about?" he snapped.

Malech looked deep into Ishmael's eyes. "I have a friend in the Catholic Church who will arrange for an apprenticeship for you at a monastery in Umbria. It would be a great opportunity for a fresh start—to lay low… in a safe place."

"There are no safe places," said Ishmael with dread.

"No one would know you there. You could assume a different last name… Ishmael, you have nothing left to lose. Please consider it," urged Malech.

CHAPTER 13 - Rome, Italy

"So, she let them down by a rope through the window, for the house she lived in was part of the city wall. [16]She said to them, "Go to the hills so the pursuers will not find you. Hide yourselves there three days until they return, and then go on your way. - Joshua 2:15

ary/Chicago International Airport was less conspicuous than O'Hare. Ishmael had changed his appearance by cutting and darkening his hair. He also wore new clothes that were atypical for him. Ishmael sat comfortably with Azikiwe and Malech in a leather-backed circular booth. Voices echoed in the hangar:

"Mister Peterson, please report to gate thirty-three, your flight is ready to depart. Paging Mister Peterson…"

Malech's upright posture accentuated his pristine black-and-white pinstripe suit, and Azikiwe's massive priestly frame filled the booth beside him. Ishmael sat, nursing a coffee in his hand.

"Honestly, after the head injury, I needed some down time… It took a while before I remembered you… In fact, it wasn't until recently that I remembered what happened to my parents. I must have blocked it out. I'm still trying to get my head around this whole thing," Ishmael confided.

"We have watched you from afar for some time. With some supernatural providence, we were able to come to your aid. And I would say just in the nick of time, huh?" Malech's black hair was neatly coiffed.

"Why does this always happen to me?"

Azikiwe leaned forward to gulp down his scrambled eggs. "You experienced a lot of trauma, my boy. No one should experience what you have experienced…" He waited to chew his food before continuing. "I am sorry, my boy, but for reasons we cannot understand, the Almighty has allowed this to happen. And we may never understand His will, this side of the grave. We must fall back on what we do know. God is just. His will is supreme. He promises never to forsake us. He will never forsake His chosen."

"Chosen? Ha! That's rich! And is that supposed to be me?" Ishmael laughed sarcastically. "Am I 'chosen'? Chosen for what? To suffer? Yeah, no thanks." Ishmael raised his hands, making air quotes in a mocking fashion. "Not much 'free' will if it is already written!"

Azikiwe took a sip of his coffee. "Prescience is not causation, my boy…"

"Where was your God when my father died? Where was your god when my mother died? Or Carrie? Huh? Why was I able to heal a no-name geriatric in the church when I was a child but not my own father and mother? Or my girlfriend!? HUH? ANSWER ME! HOW IS THAT FAIR?!" Ishmael stood to his feet, his voice escalating in volume. Malech motioned for him to sit down.

Azikiwe answered calmly, "Fairness requires balancing the free will of all beings. We cannot judge God's decisions because to do so would require tangential knowledge of every possible variable, every possible outcome—to be, in essence, omniscient. God balances the free will of four billion people, my son, and that does not include the metaphysical realm." The massive Nigerian finished his toast and then gestured to the waitress for another serving.

"But why me? Why is this always happening to me?"

"Have you ever considered that your path has been harder because your calling is higher? Simply put, you are different. You have gifts that a certain group of people are trying to exploit." Azikiwe leaned over to speak to Malech. "Hey Inspector, do you have his passport?"

Malech slid the blue passport across the table. Ishmael caught it before it fell to the floor. Inside, there was an envelope of cash. He opened it and read the name: *Ishmael Di Scala.* Di Scala? Weird. But it didn't matter—he never knew who he was anyway. What's in a name? He was used to getting new names.

"So, if your God is so good, why does everyone I love have to die?" Ishmael said, rage burning in his eyes.

"Look, I'm not the right person to ask on these matters. I am sorry, my boy. I wish I could give you a satisfactory explanation, but the answers you seek require more insight and explanation than we have time for." He finished his last bite of breakfast. The mammoth Nigerian wiped his mustache with his napkin. "You will find the answer to your questions in Umbria. There, you will find your purpose."

CHAPTER 14 - Rome, Italy

"Woe to those who plan iniquity, to those who plot evil on their beds! At morning's light they carry it out because it is in their power to do it." - Micah 2:1

t one end of la Piazza della Rotonda lies the Pantheon, one of the few historical buildings to be spared the ransacking of Rome. At the center of the square, surrounded by an elaborate fountain, lies the Obelisco Macuteo, an Egyptian obelisk. It is one of thirteen in the city of seven hills. It was excavated in 1373 and originally placed in the Piazza di San Macuto, adjacent to the statue of Sant' Ignazio—the founder of the Order of Jesus Christ, otherwise known as the Jesuits.

Dressed entirely in black, the collared cleric sat at a circular metal table in the square, sipping his cappuccino. He lit a Gauloises and then took a deep drag. He admired the architecture of the Pantheon—the Corinthian columns, the pediment, the frieze, and the dome. He imagined what it must have been like before the exaltation of Christendom, in the pagan days where Zeus, Athena, and Hermes were venerated, before it became a Catholic church. He smiled to himself and spoke quietly to his associate.

"We know where he is."

"Ah sì? After so many years?" The Calabrese spoke with a strong southern accent.

"Yes, and we cannot lose him again. We must act now," the Jesuit emphasized.

"How did we lose him?" The Calabrese wore a brown tweed flat cap, a collared white button-up shirt, black wool slacks, and black leather shoes. His brown leather jacket concealed his pistol (a Beretta, .380 caliber), which was held in a holster under his arm. He also carried a compatible suppressor that he had made himself.

 "He slipped our surveillance... when he left foster care." The Jesuit's expression diminished. "He let himself out a window in the early hours. After that, we had no information as to his whereabouts. We heard nothing from the other side either. And we know what would have happened if they had found him. He must have left town because we would have spotted him. He was probably living with a friend or... or on the lam..." He stared intently at the dark-skinned southern Italian. "But we have found him. After his little sabbatical, we have finally found him." He repeated, "We believe that he is in a suburb of Chicago. We sent in a squadra. But we must assume that the enemy knows what we know. Ergo, we must act now. And we must prepare for every possible contingency. We will have to prepare for damage control. It may get messy with local law enforcement." The priest took another sip of his beverage. "But we already have a few assets in play."

"Ah sì? And what if the others get to him first?" The Italian took a sip of his espresso.

"We must make sure this does not happen. We need him. They will stop at nothing to obtain the boy. He is the key to the Gebofal." The priest noticed a change in his friend's countenance.

The Calabrese watched as an elegant lone man, sporting priestly shoes, turned down the via and stepped into a kiosk. His stomach told him there was something off about the man— the way he glanced, the way he moved, his body language. Something he could not explain. Something irregular. He had only a visceral sentiment, but over the course of twenty years, he had learned to trust his instincts, however irrational.

"Father, I think you had better head back to the Vaticano," he warned the Jesuit priest.

Despite not perceiving the threat, the priest had learned to trust the instincts of his associate. He stood abruptly, then proceeded down Via Della Minerva and took a hard left into a small vicolo.

The Calabrese stood abruptly, then walked briskly toward the kiosk. As the man in the indigo blue cardigan exited the kiosk, he saw the muscular figure approaching him. They made eye contact. The mysterious man proceeded to escape into a small alley. The Calabrese's pace quickened. In full view of the public, he pulled his pistol from his pocket and screwed on his silencer.

He turned the corner of the alley with his pistol extended. The target had scaled a black Ducati Desmo. He revved the engine, then released the clutch, spinning the tires. The bike fishtailed, then fled in the opposite direction. The Calabrese took aim and fired two shots in quick succession. One hit the façade of a brick building; the other hit home, forcing the rider to swerve directly into traffic. He was struck violently by an approaching car. His body flew up in the air, knocking him to the *pavimento.*

The rider quickly got up. His shoes scuffled wildly on the cobblestones. He ran, glancing back frequently to see the black-haired Calabrese meticulously approaching. The Calabrese took aim once more and fired thrice. The bullets took their mark in the back of the upper thighs of the escapee, forcing the man to the ground in agony.

The man put up his hands in a futile defensive gesture, then pointed accusatively. "You have no authority here... you will lose. The end is written."

Still ten meters away, the Calabrese took the kill shot, obliterating his right eye.

Pedestrians gathered, talking amongst themselves. The Calabrese turned and yelled in defiance to the crowd.

"Ma chi ti fici a guarda'? Dìgghili chissu ca vidisti... Eh?"

He raised his pistol, and the pedestrians scattered.

He turned to his victim's pockets. Nothing.

Police sirens echoed in the canyons of the city. He sprang up, holstered his pistol, walked hastily around the corner, peeled off his hat and jacket, threw them in the dumpster, put on some sunglasses, turned the corner onto Via Dei Pastini, then descended the stairs to the Metro.

Chapter 15 - London, England

"...And do not let your people practice fortune-telling, or use sorcery, or interpret omens, or engage in witchcraft, or cast spells, or function as mediums or psychics, or call forth the spirits of the dead. Anyone who does these things is detestable to the Lord." - Deuteronomy 18:10-12

The esoteric writings of Edward Kelley and Doctor John Dee had filtered down through history; only a few manuscripts remained. They had been smuggled out of the library in a hidden compartment of a jewelry box and then sold at auction to a local confectioner, who gave the box to his fiancée as a wedding gift. She was widowed shortly thereafter. And as chance would have it, her chambermaid unwittingly opened the box, throwing parchment to the floor and into the fire. The Lady of the House pounced on the manuscripts before the vestiges of papyri were consumed in the fire.

Knowing the jewelry box had been bought from the estate of the infamous Doctor Dee, and having been told of his reputation as an alchemist, the Lady realized immediately their potential value. She salvaged as many as she could and then sought the advice of some clandestine people in the London underground. She was offered two hundred quid for the writings, which she happily accepted. She and her chambermaid were murdered shortly thereafter.

The documents were examined religiously. Although they contained the secrets to angelic "Enochian," the manuscripts were indecipherable. It was collectively decided by the occult hierarchy—i.e. the lawyers, the doctors, the bankers, the political aristocracy, and the royalty—to hide them away. And for the subsequent two hundred years, the secret papyri lay in obscurity. Competing groups such as the Freemasons, Rosicrucians, and the Jesuits voraciously sought them, but to no avail. They had been lost. That is, until the turn of the century...

Mister Aleister Crowley, known ubiquitously as the most evil man to ever live, was led by his esoteric research to a gypsy caravan deep in the seedy underbelly of London.

A thirty-third-degree Mason, heroin addict, and official warlock of the local chapter of the *Ordo Hermeticus Aurorae Aureae*, Crowley was a true believer. The Hermetic Order of the Golden Dawn—an organization founded by William Robert Woodman, William Wynn Westcott, and Samuel Liddell Mathers—was the center of Crowley's devotion. The Order was founded on Eastern mysticism, namely the theurgical, geomantic, and more specifically, thaumaturgical arts. To the layperson, that meant communicating with spirits to obtain secret knowledge, manipulating nature, and gaining demonic favor.

All media were used toward this goal: fortune-telling, spells, incantations, divination, necromancy, drugs, sex, cannibalism, pedophilia, and of course, occultic languages... The clergy used anything that could bridge the barrier between the physical and metaphysical worlds. No act was forbidden, no act too immoral— in fact, the more profane, the more the spirits moved. Self-indulgence was key. Crowley summed it up thusly: "Do what thou wilt shall be the whole of the Law," expressed in his *magnum opus*, a text he maintained had been dictated to him by a non-corporeal entity named Aiwazel.

In fact, it was this demon who had told him where to find the lost Enochian manuscripts, also known as the *Liber of Loagaeth*. Crowley could read the manuscripts—or at least partially—and he could write, or at least reproduce the script. But his articulation of the glyphs was a complete fabrication. He was forced to rely on his knowledge of ancient Aramaic and Hebrew, and on modern-day pronunciations of the languages in the Semitic branches. No one could say for certain how the first language ever created was spoken.

Crowley had studied the parchments exhaustively, yet to his dismay, the sacred forty-nine tables were missing—possibly lost in the fire. To achieve Gebofal, the tables must be read with perfect pronunciation and perfect interpretation, followed by perfect obedience.

On this Sabbath evening, there were seven new initiates to the Dawn, a motley crew of intellectuals from the university and one thirteen-year-old pregnant mother. In the Romanian community of London, she was known as Miss Euphemia Anastasius. Yet on this day, she would be re-anointed, reborn, and consecrated into the first tier as a neophyte to the Outer Order of the Golden Dawn. She would be known as Regina Amaruel Tiranicus. She held within her womb a child conceived in sin— conceived in the ceremonial orgies held by the Golden Dawn. Who the father was she did not know, for she had had intercourse with six hundred and sixty-six men, including Mister Crowley. The event had spanned three days—a Black Sabbath weekend of blood and carnal debauchery. On the eve of the following morning, Regina had sworn her life and posterity to the demon prince, Lucifer.

Crowley, the self-proclaimed reincarnation of Edward Kelley, recited from the unholy scriptures in the Enochian tongue. He pushed himself from the lectern and circled the sanctuary where the initiates stood in a queue, awaiting their baptism. Each candidate wore tau robes with hoods that hid their faces. The sanctuary was lit by six hundred and sixty-six sage-scented candles. An inverted red pentagram had been inlaid into the black marble floor around the lectern. The walls were adorned with all sorts of occult symbols and blasphemous imagery.

Crowley waded into the basin filled with the blood of lambs and menstruating young congregants. He gestured to the first person in the queue and bade her into the pool. He dipped his fingers into the blood and wiped it across his bald head, drawing an inverted cross on his forehead. The silence of the congregation was broken by softly spoken tongues.

Crowley welcomed the first convert into the warm pool. He held his hand around the person's waist, then lifted his other hand to address the congregation.

"We come together to act as unholy witnesses—an unholy testament to the consecration of this soul to the pursuit of forbidden knowledge and to eternal damnation, to the glory of our father, Satan."

He continued to chant as he lowered the witness into the blood. The congregants chanted as well. A cacophony of competing voices erupted. His arms tensed, extending her further into the quagmire of plasma. Crowley held the initiate under until her arms flailed and splashed—drops of blood splattered all over his face and garments. An expression of pure sadism fell over his face. He forced the person deeper into the blood. His nostrils flared. His eyes went black, and his face grew red with excitement. The voices in the hall grew to a fever pitch.

Finally, at the last moment, he relented, letting the young woman rise. Regina Amaruel came up gasping and wheezing, a terrified look upon her face. Her face was no longer obscured by the hood of the robe but by a mask of crimson. Her hair coagulated into clumps. She looked back at him in terror and awe. Crowley moved to the side so she could exit the pool.

"Welcome, my sister," he said flatly.

Regina was told to stand at the flank until the other initiates had been baptized. Blood dripped profusely from her soaked hair and garment all over the sanctuary floor. The congregation's chants subsided. Crowley held out his hand for the next initiate.

CHAPTER 16 — Assisi, Italy

"Then I will give you shepherds after my own heart, who will lead you with knowledge and understanding." - Jeremiah 3:15

shmael looked out of the car window. The sunflower fields scrolled by in a bucolic brownish yellow; the pastel colors of late autumn painted the idyllic Umbrian countryside. He peered into the distance. The Papal Basilica of San Francesco di Assisi was perched upon a picturesque hill surrounded by olive and cypress trees.

The Umbrian settlement of Assisi was founded circa 1,000 BC. It became a Roman *municipium* after the Battle of Sentinum in the 3rd century BC. It gained popularity twenty-two hundred years later with the birth of its patron saint, San Francesco, an aristocrat born to affluence. The young Francis received a vision from an icon of the crucified Christ in a chapel just outside the hilltop town at San Damiano: "Francis, Francis, go and repair My church which, as you can see, is falling into ruins." After receiving the vision, the young Francis devoted his life to the spreading of the gospel and to a life of asceticism.

Rain began to pour down onto the roofs of the brick houses and cobblestone streets. The red 1979 Alfa Romeo Alfetta Sport pulled up to the *piazza*, which was blocked off by heavy iron chains. Ishmael stepped from his taxi with his suitcase and pondered the *cattedrale* named for the famous ascetic. He made his way up the slow incline to the entrance of the monastery.

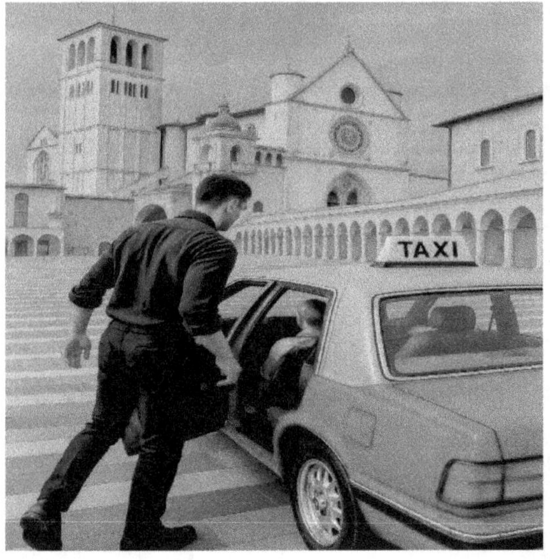

Reaching the ingress, he grabbed the large round knocker of the massive medieval wooden door, then beat it against its base. Scuffled footsteps could be heard from the other side. A balding elderly monk with kind brown eyes opened the door.

"Buona sera. Come posso aiutarti, figlio mio?"

"I'm here to see Father Rodrigo," replied Ishmael, brushing the raindrops from his hoodie.

"Ah. *Sì! Sì!* Come in, come in. I am Padre Giovanni Scaramucci." He stepped back and laboriously opened the door of *La Porta del Collegio*, then led Ishmael Di Scala methodically across an internal courtyard.

The meticulous masonry of millions of bricks was partially covered in ivy—ivy that sprang from purposely positioned pots. The verge hugged the immense walls and seemingly stretched into the *celeste*. A thirty-three-year-old man with a thinly groomed black beard waited patiently with his hands behind his back. He stood stoically by a marble effigy of San Francesco.

Scaramucci turned slowly and motioned for Father Rodrigo.

"*Buenos días!* Welcome to the Papal Basilica of St. Francis, Ishmael. It's so nice to finally meet you." Rodrigo extended his hand jovially.

Father Rodrigo Ruiz-Fuentes was charged with the overseeing of the young lad. On this day, Rodrigo had opted to wear a cassock. He gazed at the lad, assessing his presence.

"Let me show you to your quarters." Rodrigo stepped aside and gestured toward another set of enormous wooden doors.

"*Después de ti... Dopo di te.*"

Rodrigo noticed the quizzical look on Ishmael's face.

"So, you cannot speak Spanish or Italian? Hmm, I thought it would just be intuitive to you," Rodrigo said to himself.

Ishmael feigned comprehension with an exaggerated nod. Rodrigo led the black-haired boy through a grand hall, and finally to the entrance of the *Sacro Convento*, a narrow corridor flanked by many rooms. Ishmael stopped and took in the ambiance. He gazed in awe at the frescoed walls offset by magnificent stained-glass windows and overhanging wooden beams. The rain had ceased, and the sun illuminated various saints who were immortalized in colorful tableaus.

Rodrigo stopped in front of a door and pushed it open.

"This is where you will stay, *amigo.*"

The room was replete with a bed, a Spanish terracotta-tiled floor, a hand-sized crucifix affixed to the wall, cream stucco walls, and one singular window. He dropped his baggage on the bed and walked over to the window to witness an amazing view of the Umbrian countryside.

Rodrigo continued, "The bathroom is down the hallway. Meals are served in the dining hall. As part of your apprenticeship, you will assist our grooms with the horses in our stables each day, except on Sunday when you will attend Mass. In the morning, you will meet with Father Scaramucci, who will manage your studies."

"Studies? What? Like college?"

"We will instruct you in the way of the cloth, if that is God's plan for you."

"And what if it is not?"

"Then you may leave. You are not a prisoner here. Do you have any questions, Ishmael?" Rodrigo turned away and started down the hall.

"Yeah, is there anything fun to do around here?" Ishmael followed.

Rodrigo turned around.

"You're looking at it, *amigo*!" Rodrigo said with a laugh and held up his hands. "You may want to explore the town after your work in the stables. Just remember, we expect you to return by your curfew at 22:00, *entiendes*?"

"Yeah, I got it."

The work of tending to the horses was more strenuous than Ishmael had expected. His responsibilities included turning out the horses into pasture while he mucked out the stalls and tossed the hay. The other grooms stoically worked in silence even when Ishmael tried to make conversation. The head groom, Monsieur Bernart, scoffed at his attempts to care for the horses.

"No, no! You must start at the heel and work toward the toe when cleaning hooves, Monsieur Di Scala!"

Ishmael suppressed a seething urge to punch him in the face. He needed this apprenticeship. It was the only thing he had to hold onto to steady himself from the storm that was his life.

When Ishmael finally lay down in bed, his body ached. He was too exhausted to dream—at least for a while.

It was dusk. Shaded from the fallen sun, the two silhouettes paced beneath the porticoes in the courtyard of the basilica. The twilight left the belltower's western facade awash in red and purple. Whispers could be heard but not understood. Leather-soled shoes clapped against the wet cobblestone.

"So, how are you finding yourself?" Father Rodrigo turned to Ishmael.

"It is different."

"And you are finding your duties overwhelming? How is the apprenticeship program working out for you?"

"I mean... aside from Bernart busting my balls, I don't know. I just keep to myself." The young man hesitated. "I appreciate all that you have done for me, and I respect your beliefs, but I don't know if I am on board with this whole church thing. I don't know if I could be a friar, a priest, or whatever. I mean, I am not even sure God exists, to be honest."

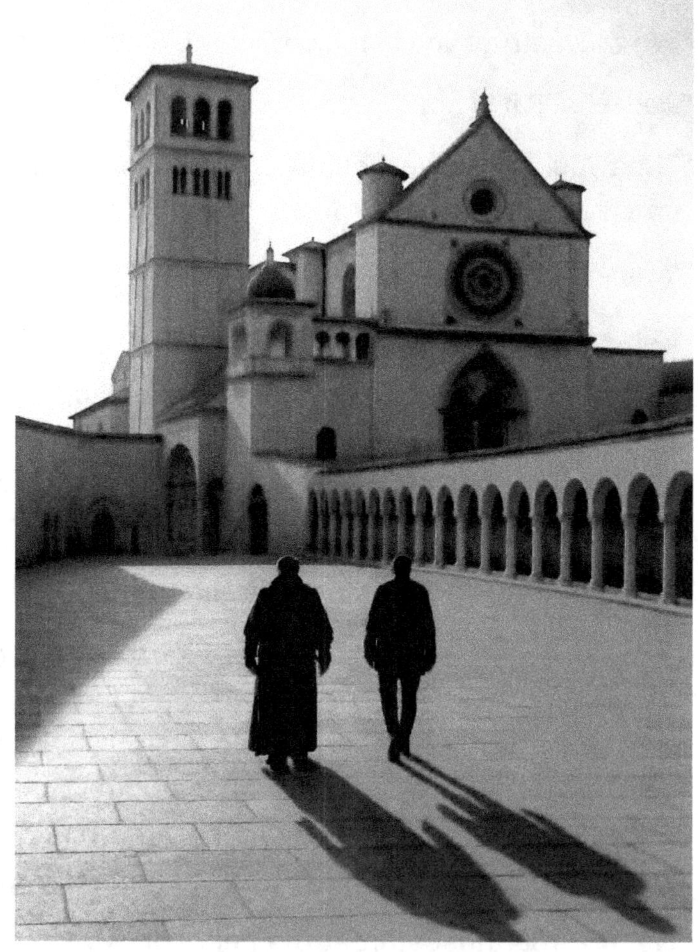

Rodrigo paused politely and contemplated his words. He then spoke in monotone. "Yet I would imagine that you, of all people, would be aware of the supernatural world," the priest pried for information. "...For you have seen it, have you not?"

Normally guarded, Ishmael reluctantly responded. "I have seen some things I cannot explain. I do not know if I would chalk that up to a god."

"I don't imagine, however, it should be a grande leap to believe in a supernatural intelligence? No?" Rodrigo turned inquisitively.

Ishmael decided to trust the young priest. "I don't know why I see things. If you want to say a 'god' gave me these abilities, fine. But I wish he would take them back and just leave me alone because everyone close to me dies." From beneath his darkened hair, Ishmael's auburn roots were starting to show. "Look, I am here because I have nowhere else to be."

Rodrigo turned. "Many people called by God initially refuse. Look at Jonah—he sailed in the opposite direction."

Ishmael scoffed. "Jonah? Am I called by your god? And then what? Am I going to be swallowed by a whale? Is that what you are telling me?"

Rodrigo waited patiently before speaking. Then he stopped and looked pensively at the horizon. With a small smile, he hesitated, then spoke. "It is the carnal man who shakes his fist at God and says, 'Show me and I will believe!' But I imagine God would say to us, 'Believe and I will show you.'" The Spaniard continued his slow pace through the courtyard. "You see, we must approach God on His terms, not ours. We must accept His reality. We must stop kicking against the goads."

"You ask a lot, priest." Ishmael looked toward the horizon.

"Please understand, mi hijo. I am here for your protection."

"That just means you'll be the next to die." Ishmael's cynicism was evident.

"If I die for the calling of Jesus, so be it!" the Spaniard stated defiantly.

Ishmael looked at him in awe. "And what of all those who don't choose 'The Only Begotten Son'?"

The young Spaniard collected his thoughts. "The layperson has no concept of the world in which they live..." He adjusted his frock. "The atheist, the agnostic, the indifferent, the 'lukewarm'—do not perceive the metaphysical realm, mi hijo. They are blinded by the enemy. They suppress the truth in unrighteousness. He has convinced them that they are on a mindless, godless trajectory where life has no meaning and this world is all there is... They are caught in an evolutionary matrix of hedonistic temporal decay. They do not see that even the most menial of decisions..." Rodrigo put his hand to his face and made a gesture with his fingers. "...are contested, manipulated by the enemy. The evil one has blinded them to the spiritual realm; it is inaccessible to the carnal mind."

Ishmael was uncomfortable with the conversation and the new attire. He preferred jeans and a T-shirt, but the monks had insisted that he wear a frock.

"Many who follow him are not aware that they are allied to Satan," Rodrigo continued. "But rather, they believe that they are exercising their own free will. They are the worst of slaves because they believe that they are free!" The air grew colder, and a light mist began to cover the courtyard. "Much like the heroin addict who acts on his 'freedom' to stick a needle in his arm, the non-believer makes decisions for his own temporal pleasure, his own finite gain, according to his own will, which leads him into eventual bondage."

"Bondage?" Ishmael quipped.

"Satan grants them what they want temporarily in exchange for torment eternally. He entices them through the fulfillment of their desires, which always entails an insatiable appetite for money, sex, and power." He stopped momentarily to look at the tower. "It is always the same."

"Like Faust," Ishmael exclaimed.

"Aww, tú sabes... sí... sí... exacto, señor. And their souls lie in the balance... all power granted comes with a cost." He paused again and turned to the cascading sunlight as it hit the catedral. He stared at Ishmael directly. "And that choice is the eternity of life itself!"

At the other end of the courtyard, the heavy cast iron doors of the commissary creaked and slammed open. A monk with his cappuccio drawn over his face latched the massive heavy frame to the adjacent wall.

"Ah, comida. It looks like they are about to serve some food... Are you hungry?" he said in his Spanish accent.

The two turned toward the commissary with their hands folded in their sleeves; light from the commissary cast their silhouettes into the courtyard. Rodrigo took a deep breath and exhaled.

"In the end times, the Bible says that there will be a great falling away and a global pursuit for singularity."

"Singularity? What does that mean?" Ishmael looked at Rodrigo intently.

"Lucifer's time is short, mi amigo, and he knows it. He wants the whole world and a global government to control it. His followers are growing, and he is gathering power to crown his anointed. He has enticed many to join him. His desire for domination is absolute, and it is at hand!"

"Anointed?" Ishmael inquired.

"The Antichrist, Ishmael." The Spaniard stared intensely into Ishmael's eyes. He then adjusted his frock. "For millennia there have been whispers in the satanic realm—murmurs of a boy, 'bitten by fire,' 'a moonchild,' a child from the descendants of Esau, an Edomite. This has traditionally been interpreted as..."

"Red hair," Ishmael interrupted.

"Sí." Rodrigo stared at the redhead.

"So, they think I am their 'holy one'?"

"Well, let us say that they believe this 'rojo' will usher in the son of perdition. In fact, I don't think anyone knows exactly how it will play out. We do not understand what his role is. But we know that there are prerequisites... It is said he will possess superpowers."

"Superpowers?"

"Supernatural powers." He stopped mid-step and peered at the potential initiate.

Ishmael ignored the question. "And do you believe that I am the one?" Then he looked toward the sky. The horizon swallowed the sun in rays of deep purple and dark blue.

"Perhaps." The rain had increased in intensity, and a cold wind whistled its way through the porticoes.

"If what they say about you is true... then perhaps." They approached the center of the courtyard. Then Rodrigo donned his cappuccio and said flatly, "But there is a problem."

"Yeah? What is that?" Ishmael inquired.

"You lack the mark."

Ishmael stared into the eyes of the young priest, subtly pulling his sleeve down over his left wrist. He remained silent.

CHAPTER 17 — Assisi, Italy

"Fools don't want to learn from others. They only want to tell their own ideas." - Proverbs 18:2

eeks had passed.

Lightning strikes crashed in the distance; a storm was approaching the tiny Italian hilltop town. Violence erupted in his mind—vivid, captivating imagery of dismemberment, death, blurred faces, blurred images, and blurred plans echoed in the deep chasms of his consciousness.

...Gebofal...shrines of sacrifice...one hundred ninety-seven souls...a beautiful face...a girl with dark hair...suffering...betrayal...someone was in agony, screams of pain rang out in the streets...a bald priest from the past...a legacy...Gregory...crowds chanting his name...symbols and more symbols...

Ishmael awoke and rubbed his eyes. What did it all mean?

He immediately planked his body with his feet elevated on his bed. He pushed out fifty push-ups, then rose and walked to his window. He watched as the black thunderclouds rolled over the farms. A crack in the window let in a cold, premature winter air. The lights from the homes could be seen against the backdrop of darkness.

He put on his cloak and headed up to the other side of the grounds to the eastern tower.

Scaramucci's office was well lit; his eight-by-fifty-foot stained-glass window faced the eastern hills. His office was a converted insulation shaft combined with a supply closet. The room was extremely narrow but deep and covered by a lofted ceiling thirty meters from the fourteenth-century wooden floor.

One wall was covered from top to bottom by bookshelves. The books at the top were accessible only by way of a steep rolling ladder. The counter wall was adorned with an assortment of taxidermy heads, cartographical selections, Da Vinci-like sketches, samples of fungi and flora, and etymological samples that had been sloppily pinned to the wall.

The room was completely cluttered with boxes—cardboard *scatole* that overflowed with mechanical *apparati*, microscopes, and disorderly parchments.

Father Scaramucci, a balding, stout older man, sat at his desk with a screwdriver in hand, plucking at the backside of an old typewriter.

"Hello?" Ishmael called into the narrow space. No answer.

Frantically typing on his typewriter, the Father was undaunted. His remaining white hair shot out at all angles.

"Permesso?" the redhead reiterated, one of the few words he had picked up since his sojourn in Umbria.

He waited again, then pounded on the door. The door swung open. The disheveled older man turned around and peered through his books like a mad scientist peering over his beakers.

"Yes?" He noticed the young lad peering in his doorframe.

"I was..."

"Si. Si. Come in, *figlio mio*. Careful. *Non rompere le scatole...*" The father laughed to himself, amused at his own joke.

Ishmael weaved through the labyrinth of boxes and then sat down in the chair opposite the scholar. Ishmael's eyes were preoccupied with the makeshift kitchen and the regalia on the wall. Ishmael nodded and smiled strangely.

There was a long, awkward pause. They both sat and stared at each other.

The father turned back around and continued tapping on the typewriter again. There was another pause.

"Why am I here?" Ishmael finally blurted.

"I don't know. You came to me." His comment came amidst a barrage of clicking.

"I was told to come and..." He paused. "...study something."

"To study something or to learn something?" The priest typed voraciously on his document.

"To learn... I guess. What am I supposed to learn?"

"I don't know. What do you want to learn?" The father kept typing.

"What if I don't want to learn?" Ishmael replied.

Scaramucci stopped, then turned his body half-heartedly. "In that case, *arrivederci*." Undaunted, the padre returned to his typing.

Ishmael slammed the door and left.

CHAPTER 18 — Assisi, Italy

But as the days of Noah were, so shall also the coming of the Son of man be. - Matthew 24:37

shmael had elected to forgo his studies and focus on his chores and his boxing. He had also managed to finagle a temporary side gig at a local motorcycle shop, repairing Vespas.

The stables had been meticulously cleaned—fifteen stalls—and he was still pumped; he had too much nervous energy. He knocked out some exercises on the floor of the stables, then grabbed some boxing gloves he had hidden under a bench seat. He stacked some hay bales. He stretched a bit, then began punching and practicing his technique on the bales. He recalled the advice of Snow: stay low, counter... counter... then attack. His mentor's voice echoed in his head. His blows came faster, with more precision and ferocity. His torso twisted, and his footwork was impeccable. His breathing increased, and sweat flowed from every pore. Right, left, right, left... His exertion, stress, and exhaustion gave way to a hallucinogenic state.

Memories of his mother came to the surface... his mother was in pain... symbols... he was in the streets of downtown Assisi... but it was cold, spiritually cold. A shiver fell on him... darkness was around him and a low fog hugged the streets... the smell of death was in the air... someone was going to die... a crash! Something was coming.

Monsieur Bernart wore a vintage hunting hat, a white collared shirt, and tan riding shorts tucked into shin-high black leather boots. He had a pitchfork in his left hand. "There are still fifteen stalls to clean. What are you doing?" he said condescendingly.

Ishmael kept boxing.

"Salut, idiot!? Can you finish cleaning? The cardinal is coming this evening."

"Yeah, sure. I'm just taking a break."

Monsieur Bernart was not part of the clergy and lacked priestly decorum.

"Mon dieu, you make me look so bad... do it now!"

Ishmael ignored him.

Bernart walked up to Ishmael and pulled him by the arm.

"Do it now, stable boy! The cardi—"

His words were interrupted by a fist to his mouth. The groomer was knocked back. He fell to the ground, bleeding profusely from his torn lip. His expression aghast, he dabbed his wound, then looked down at the blood in his gloved hand.

"MERDE! Putain!" Bernart said something that Ishmael couldn't understand.

"I AM GOING TO KILL YOU!"

He jumped up and charged Ishmael with the pitchfork still in his hand. Ishmael anticipated his movements. Bernart extended the weapon, thrusting the teeth at Ishmael's abdomen. Ishmael leaned back, then spun to his right, advancing; his spinning punch hit home on the side of the jaw. His attacker dropped. Knocked out.

By this time, the other occupants and hands had gathered around. A hushed murmur turned into shouting voices. Ishmael couldn't understand what they were saying, but judging by the gesticulation and raised voices, it was not good. One of the bystanders whispered in his ear, "You should go..."

Ishmael walked calmly to his 1970 Piaggio Vespa that he had borrowed from the garage. Several hands shouted obscenities at him. He headed back up the hill to the monastery.

He pushed his Vespa full throttle. It shook violently as it hit the potholes. The cypress trees lined the road and fleetingly blocked the view of the pastures below. His bike grunted, spewing smoke from the exhaust. The buzzing Vespa rounded the corner and in the distant courtyard he could see three opaque figures.

He led his *motorino* to the ingress of the porticoes and chained it to the metal railing. He braved the long march to the top of the courtyard, where Father Rodrigo, Father Scaramucci, and an unknown figure dressed lavishly in red awaited him. The enormity of the cathedral dwarfed the men who stood tightly huddled together.

Ishmael approached. Dispensing with pleasantries, Rodrigo spoke first.

"Were you hurt?"

"So, I guess someone told you?" Ishmael retorted.

"Did you check to see if Bernart was okay?"

"Why would I do that? He tried to kill me. I had no choice," Ishmael said flatly.

"That will be addressed, but what about your part? There is always a choice, my boy."

Changing the subject, Rodrigo continued, "You have met Father Scaramucci, and this is Cardinal Müller."

The cardinal extended his hand.

"Guten tag," he said in a deep Austrian accent.

Ishmael shook his hand customarily.

"Ishmael, we believe it is critical that you continue to develop here in our community. We strongly recommend that you talk to Scaramucci... let us say..." He paused and grabbed his chin. "...three times a week? What do you say, Father Scaramucci?"

The Father nodded.

"No, thanks," Ishmael grunted.

"In that case, you are free to go…"

The Cardinal's tone was unequivocal.

"Go? Where do I go?" Ishmael felt vulnerable.

"However," the Cardinal continued, "if you decide to stay, we would insist that you attend classes with Father Scaramucci—academic and otherwise," he turned toward the balding priest, then back, "beginning tomorrow morning."

"You mean counseling?"

"In no uncertain terms," he said matter-of-factly. "Yes."

He skipped his morning routine; he didn't even eat breakfast. He was too tired. He got dressed and then walked the long hike to the eastern tower where Scaramucci had his office, although truth be told, it was more like a laboratory, kitchen, loft, library, classroom, and custodial space all in one.

He scaled the circular stairs and then knocked on the door.

"Anyone here? Permesso?"

"Si. Si. Si. Vieni… come in, please." Scaramucci methodically stepped from the vaulted ladder.

Ishmael entered and sat in the chair opposite Scaramucci. The scent of cooked onions and garlic permeated the air. The Father held up a bowl of risotto and gestured to the redhead. "Want some risotto? I just made a fresh pot. This one is especially good—my mother's recipe: manzo, spinach, and mushroom, mmmmm…?" He raised a thumb to his cheek in true Italian fashion.

Before Ishmael could respond, a bowl of hot risotto was placed in his lap. "You want some parmigiano?"

He held up a giant wedge of cheese encased in waxed paper.

"Sure."

The Father stood over him and grated the classic Italian cheese over his bowl. He sat back down, took a big spoonful of risotto. His cheeks puffed out like a squirrel.

"So?"

Ishmael took a bite and realized that he had never had risotto before—at least nothing like this. The cream of mushroom melted in his mouth and the *parmigiano*...

"Oh my god! This is amazing."

"Si? Bravo. Now you understand my culture, my boy. Welcome to my country—the Veneto," the priest said proudly.

Ishmael took another bite. "You are from Venice? Lots of canals, right?"

He took another bite of the Venetian dish.

"Asiago, actually," the priest corrected.

"So, what are we here for? You gonna psychoanalyze me? Ask me about my childhood?"

"In time, figlio mio, but right now, I have only one question."

The priest stuffed his mouth with another mammoth bite of risotto; some fell in his lap.

"The same question I posed the last time we met..."

Ishmael had a hard time understanding him with his accent and mouth full of food.

"What do you want to learn?"

What do I want to learn? Ishmael thought hard this time.

"Angels."

"Angels, huh? Or maybe demons, I think."

Scaramucci stopped chewing and stared at the young man with his mouth full of risotto.

"Interesting choice. And what kind of angels?"

"There are different kinds?"

"Ohhh. Sí. Sí. Seraphim. Cherubim. Thrones. Dominions. And what Paul called 'principalities.' They are spiritual beings just like you and me—just as unique, just as individual."

"Wow. So, were they created? I would like to know about that! About their history. In fact, I would like to know history in general," Ishmael chirped.

"Ahh, another great choice. Whose history? Egyptian history? Sumerian history? Secular history? Biblical history? Assyrian? Persian? Greek? Roman? Modern? What?"

"All of it! But let us begin with something basic... Let's start at the beginning."

The priest laughed heartily, choking on his risotto. His belly shook as he wiped his mouth with a giant red cloth. "The beginning is anything but basic; it is the most complicated part!" He stared into Ishmael's eyes. "Are you familiar with the Apocrypha?"

CHAPTER 19 - Assisi, Italy

For Ezra had given his mind to learning the law of the Lord and doing it, and to teaching his rules and decisions in Israel.
- Ezra 7:10

e got up late. Ishmael had been up until three o'clock. Exhausted, he ran up the stairs of the eastern conical tower. He was eager to pepper his teacher with questions.

Scaramucci's "laboratory" was cleaner than the last time. The Father had freed up some walking space by stacking the boxes higher against the wall. Garlic and onion scents, the aroma of hundreds of bowls of risotto, had permanently seeped into the pages of his books.

The balding cleric stood thirty feet in the air, suspended on a rolling ladder. His head was buried in his collection of papyri.

"Ciao, figlio mio. Dammi un momento, per favore." Wearing a brown frock, he shimmied down the ladder.

"Non c'è problema." Rodrigo had taught him some phrases.

"Do you want some risotto?" the priest offered.

"You eat risotto in the morning?"

"Certo. When isn't it a good time to eat risotto?"

"No, thank you..." He paused until Scaramucci had time to get a bowl and collect himself at his desk, which had been cut in half to accommodate the confines of his extremely narrow office.

"Did you read Genesis like I asked?" The redhead nodded. "So can I ask you some questions?" the priest said through a mouthful of rice.

"Sure," Ishmael said flatly.

"Okay. So why did God send the flood?"

"Because humanity was sinful."

"Genesis 6:5 says, 'GOD saw that the wickedness of man was great in the earth, and that every imagination of the thoughts of his heart was only evil continually.' They were wicked. And not just sinful—and not just humanity—but the angels and the Nephilim too."

"Nephilim?"

"The Nephilim were a hybrid race of giants that existed before the flood, what we call the antediluvian period." He leaned over to the bookshelves to his left and pulled the pseudepigraphical Book of Enoch from its perch. "Eh, andiamo…" He looked around for his glasses. He pulled them out from underneath some papers and began to read:

When the sons of men had multiplied, in those days, beautiful and comely daughters were born to 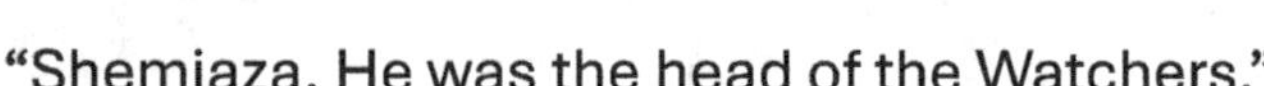 *them. And the Watchers, the sons of heaven, saw them and desired them. And they said to one another, 'Come, let us choose for ourselves wives from the daughters of men, and let us beget children for ourselves.' And Shemjaza, their chief, said to them, 'I fear that you will not want to do this deed, and I alone shall be guilty of a great sin.' And they all answered him and said, 'Let us all swear an oath, and let us all bind one another with a curse, that none of us turn back from this counsel until we fulfill it and do this deed.' Then they all swore together and bound one another with a curse.*

The priest looked up after reading.

"Shema… who?" Ishmael asked quizzically.

"Shemjaza. He was the head of the Watchers."

"The Watchers?"

"Sì, a host of angels charged with safeguarding humanity, known in the Book of Daniel as the Grigori."

"Gregory!" Ishmael whispered to himself. "So that's what it means?" He spoke to himself. "So, they were like the police?"

"No, figlio. There were twenty of them. Twenty angels in charge of ten angels each—two hundred in total. They were told to 'watch' but not to intervene, to protect humanity. They broke this sacred trust; they rebelled. They were tempted by the beauty of human women. Shemjaza, their leader, decided to entice the other angels into committing a sin—a violation of God's laws: the taking of human brides."

"So, angels had sex with humans? And had human babies? I didn't think an angel could do that," Ishmael said incredulously. "How could an angel impregnate a human? How could a human give birth to a giant? I mean, wouldn't she... uhh... you know, burst?"

"Good questions. Many have conjectured what could have happened. But they might have been born regular size, never ceasing to grow—much like the dinosaurs. As for the ability to combine spirit and flesh, well, this is, in fact, quite common in ancient biblical literature. Our Lord and Savior is one example. It seems the fallen angels were given some power to bend natural law, seed thought, manipulate human emotions, and navigate the metaphysical and physical worlds." He took a deep breath and a swig of wine, then stared blankly at the redhead as if choosing his words carefully. "Here, let us read God's reaction as He speaks with Enoch..." He flipped forward in the book and adjusted his glasses. "Here, chapter fifteen, listen carefully..."

Why have you left the high, holy, and eternal heaven, lain with women, and defiled yourselves with the daughters of men, taken wives, and begotten giants as your sons? Though you were holy spiritual beings living eternal life, you've defiled yourselves with the blood of women and begotten with the blood of flesh. As children of men, you have lusted after flesh and blood like those who die and perish. Therefore, I have given them wives to impregnate and beget children by, so that nothing might be lacking for them on earth... Now the giants who are produced from the spirits and flesh shall be called evil spirits on the earth, and on the earth shall be their dwelling. Evil spirits have proceeded from their bodies because they are born from men and from the Watchers; they shall be evil spirits on earth. The spirits of the giants afflict, oppress, destroy, attack, do battle, and work destruction on the earth, causing trouble.

"Wow." Ishmael was amazed.

"Yet I must tell you, to speak of the powers of the demons is a field better addressed by a colleague of mine, Father Pasquale—our resident exorcist..." He collected his dish and walked to the back of the loft near the base of the stained-glass window, where he had made himself a makeshift kitchen. He put the dish in the sink and then downed the last drop of his Chianti. He then resumed his lecture. "The Nephilim were the giants of old, enormous beings with incredible strength and appetite. They towered above mortal men—some may have reached two hundred feet in height. They were said to have enslaved mankind and devoured all the resources. Famine was extreme."

"Giants? Really? Come on." Ishmael's doubt was obvious.

"Yes, giants born of angels." Scaramucci stopped his cleaning of plates and returned to the desk. He leaned down and looked at Ishmael from behind his glasses. "Son, the fossil record is definitive. There were giants on the earth! There are too many skeletal remains, too much evidence for the existence of giants to be discarded. Giants existed. The question is when."

"Hmmm. And so then, what happened to them?"

"Sì. They consumed all the produce, all the food. And when the resources had been consumed, they became cannibals—eating men and women. When mankind escaped to the mountains and caves, the giants turned on each other. Evil fed on itself, becoming more and more perverse."

"More perverse than cannibalism?"

"Si. Infatti. The earth became a cesspool of debauchery and gave rise to transhumanism. These fallen spirits fornicated with animals, creating the monsters of old—hybrids of the most hideous kind, beasts described in the pantheon of gods, offspring that were half beast and half spirit, the horned, scaled, and winged creatures of myth."

"Like what? Centaurs?"

Scaramucci continued undaunted. "From the line of Cain arose all the polytheistic traditions we know today—from Rome to the Vikings, to Egypt and the Sumerians. Even modern-day comic books have been inspired by this lore." He sat back in his chair and then continued.

"Four angels approached God's throne—Raphael, Uriel, Michael, and Gabriel—who had remained true to the Creator. They pleaded with Jehovah for justice. God gave the four angels authority over the fallen, with a holy mandate to imprison Shemjaza and his two hundred followers, or *grigori* in the original tongue. After a lengthy battle, Michael and his soldiers prevailed. The Watchers were thrown into a subterranean cell known as Tartarus, locked away until the Day of Judgment."

Ishmael's attention piqued. "Gregory," he said to himself. He stared longingly at the stained-glass window. His thoughts meandered, and then his vision blurred...

Ishmael saw them in their dungeon... symbols... He saw them in Tartarus... in pain... he saw them with more clarity than before... angelic hosts screaming... the smell of sulfur... two hundred... he had had this dream before... and now he understood.

Scaramucci noticed Ishmael's glossed-over glare. "What is it? You saw something, didn't you? What did you see? Tell me!" The priest's enthusiasm resembled that of a child.

"I always see them—all two hundred—locked away. I can hear their screams echoing in my head. I can smell the sulfur. I can even feel their pain. I have had this dream since I was a child. I can't get it out of my head… I can never get it out of my head." He looked down and shook his head. "They are calling me. They never stop calling me!"

"Wow. So, you can see them?"

"I can even understand them." Ishmael looked at the priest.

"Whatever you do, do NOT engage them!" The priest's decorum had changed drastically.

"Engage them? What do you mean? I don't know what I see. Could just be some bad risotto," Ishmael rebutted.

The priest did not relent, pressing the redhead further. "Do not speak to them! Under no circumstances should you speak with them. *Capisci?*"

"Why?" Ishmael said innocently.

"My son, never engage the spirit world other than to approach the throne of God through Jesus. Do you understand me? We must speak with Pasquale about this." The priest was adamant.

Ishmael nodded his head. "So why create them then? I mean, God is supposed to be all-knowing and all-loving, right? Why did He create them if He knew they would choose to disobey?" Ishmael ventured.

"Si, si, the age-old question that has been debated for millennia. If God is all-loving, why does He allow suffering? If God is all-knowing, how can He condemn people to the Lake of Fire?" Father Scaramucci leaned back and sighed. Then he leaned forward and spoke methodically.

"Well, let me say that in thirty-three years of study, I can tell you definitively that I do not know, my son. I cannot reconcile the two. I don't believe anyone can." He poured himself another glass of Chianti. "But I can tell you this: if God says that we have free will, then we have free will. We may never know this side of the grave the answer to that one… but we do not…" He paused and took a sip from his wine glass. "How do you say this in English? 'Throw the baby in the dirty water?'"

"Yes, throw out the baby with the bathwater…" Ishmael corrected him.

"Si. We must not throw out the baby with the dirty water…"

Ishmael smiled.

"Yet it is ironic, is it not?" the cleric continued.

"What is?"

"…that the person who shakes his fist at God claiming he has no free will, has freely chosen to shake it, has he not? Is it not a self-defeating argument? For he exercises his free will in claiming that he has none."

"I never thought about it like that." He paused to let the words sink in. "But what about disease, famine, war?"

"'Why is the world cursed? Why do babies get cancer?' you ask." Scaramucci leaned forward and spoke in a soft tone. "Saint Maximus the Confessor once said, 'Man is a microcosm of a macrocosm,' meaning we are but a smaller piece of a larger sinful whole. In 2 Chronicles 7:14, God tells us, 'If my people, who are called by my name, will humble themselves and pray and seek my face and turn from their wicked ways, then I will hear from heaven, and I will forgive their sin and will heal their land.' If we sin less, if we repent, our land will be healed...

So, to answer your question, it is symbiotic. Just as the sin in nature affects us, so also our sin directly affects nature. Nature directly reflects our depravity."

"Hard to accept that." Ishmael looked at the mounted impala head on the wall.

"But there is also hope, for this means that we can change... We can choose. God gave us free will to show us His love, *figlio*. One cannot love someone forcibly. To express His love, He created people with the choice to refuse it."

"So, if I refuse, I am sent to the Lake of Fire. Not much choice," Ishmael posited.

"God is loving, but He is also just. God did not make hell for humans. Saint Matthew tells us that He created it for the devil and his angels. You do not have to go..."

"Couldn't He have created a place without fire and torture?"

"Hell is where God is not. Therefore, the *Logos*, or the manifestation of all systemic order, is absent. Result? Chaos. God's hope and love are absent. Result? Hate and despair. Comfort? No. Understanding? No. Relief? No. You understand? If you tell God that you do not want Him, He is loving enough to respect your decision... He must punish evil!"

"But why does it have to be forever?"

"Because, my son, we were created flesh and spirit. You have an immortal soul. And God is immortal... Death is a perversion. It is not the intent of God that you should suffer eternally."

"Why the cat-and-mouse then? Why not just poke His head out of the clouds and say, 'Hey people! I am God.' No more mysteries, no more guessing?"

"When I was a child growing up in Asiago, in the Veneto, I used to steal the *caramelle* from the local market. I never stole any when I was with my father. Did I have the same 'amount' of free will as when I was alone? Of course. But I would not have done it because I was afraid of my father's reaction. The same is true of God. He does not want us to obey because we are afraid... He wants us to obey because we want to. That is true free will."

"I don't have a choice. The cardinal gave me an ultimatum. I have nowhere to go."

The priest countered. "The martyrs killed in the Coliseum were given the choice of renouncing Jesus or death. Many chose death. There is always a choice, my son! Staying here or leaving is a choice. It may not be a choice you like, but it is still a choice!"

CHAPTER 20 - Assisi, Italy

"Start children off on the way they should go, and even when they are old, they will not turn from it." - Proverbs 22:6

t was midnight. Ishmael couldn't sleep again. He dipped to the floor and knocked out fifty push-ups. His thoughts raced. The discussion in Scaramucci's loft had unsettled him. He sat on his bed and closed his eyes. ...screams in the dark... symbols, so many symbols... blood... he saw himself above the street, floating, an out-of-body experience... he was high above and someone was dying on the street below... someone was going to die!

Ishmael rose and put on some street clothes. He opened his door slowly, then stuck his head into the corridor. The black iron sconces held dimly lit candles with flames that struggled to survive. Luminary configurations danced on the walls. He pulled his hoodie over his face and then slid down the hallway. The redhead could hear chatter echoing from the sanctuary.

He slipped past unnoticed. He came to the large courtyard and crouched at its perimeter. He searched the courtyard for movement. Nothing. He ran light-footed to the exit/entrance. With two hands, he lifted the heavy bolt of the medieval gates. He pushed his way through and then quietly closed it behind him. He walked quickly to

distance himself from the monastery. The young prodigy resumed a normal pace when he reached the edge of town.

The early spring had descended on the medieval town of Assisi, but the cold winter temperatures still held sway over the northern breeze. Ishmael walked down Largo Gregorio toward the Church of Santa Chiara. He put his hands in his pockets and kept his head down. Fleeting chatter, alcoholic laughter, and the occasional tire screech broke the night air. Observing the local eateries, he looked for some *pizza al taglio*—nothing too commercial, a mom-and-pop shop, something rustic, and preferably Neapolitan.

L'Osteria Dei Consoli provided an outdoor eating area and a window accessible to the main street. The passerby could approach the establishment and select from the fresh pies on display or choose an outdoor table. On this evening, the outdoor tables were still teeming with vociferous patrons, twirling their forks with fettuccine and drinking Spumante and Lancers. A dapperly dressed couple sat at a table as the congregants clanked their forks against wine glasses, then collectively shouted, "Bacio! Bacio..." It was a wedding reception.

Ishmael stepped to the open window that accessed the street and purchased two slices of the margherita. The vendor wrapped up the pizza in some wax paper. Grease dripped from the bottom of his cone-shaped slices. He took a huge bite. The mozzarella was amazing. *Wow. Unbelievable,* he thought. He turned downtown to enjoy his *camminata.* In fact, for the first time in a long time, he almost felt free.

Ishmael noticed a shadow out of the corner of his eye. He was being followed. The fighter in him was tired of reacting, running. He made a beeline for the obscure figure. Realizing that he was about to be confronted, the obscure figure turned on his hinges and slipped into a nearby *vicolo.* Ishmael rounded the corner and saw the man in full gait, so he gave chase.

"HEY!" Ishmael yelled.

The man, dressed entirely in black, began to run. Then he came to a dead end. Confrontation was now unavoidable. Ishmael came to the aperture in the street and stopped. The man was no longer alone but flanked by two other masked men of similar dress and stature. They all held medieval-looking daggers—daggers Ishmael had seen before.

The trio advanced on Ishmael. Ishmael's rage was heightened, his senses attuned. The first came at him wielding the blade, thrashing with wide strokes. Ishmael dodged his blade, pushed his arm past him, and delivered a strike to the abdomen. The man doubled over. The next man came at him, stabbing for his stomach. Ishmael took a step back, then came down hard on his wrist, knocking the blade to the ground. He then delivered a roundhouse to his jaw. The man fell backward, grunting in pain. Ishmael picked up the dagger, wielding it at the third assailant. The third was more reserved. He danced with him, then took two deliberate strikes for his neck.

"Attenzione, lo abbiamo bisogno vivo."

The voice came from one of the three, but Ishmael could not tell from whom. Sirens rang out in a nearby street. The assailants were taken aback; they looked at each other, then escaped immediately, each heading off in separate directions.

Ishmael could hear the approaching *polizia.* He tucked the blade into his pants and then hopped a fence into a private garden. He lay flat under some hedges, observing the police's approach. Between the slats, he could see the policemen exit their car and search the surrounding area. He waited for his moment, then scuttled along a stone wall and slipped away.

Ishmael came in through the southside porticoes hoping to remain undiscovered, but Rodrigo was waiting for him at the entrance of the courtyard.

"You broke curfew," he stated flatly.

"Yeah, sorry about that, I uhhh…" He didn't know what to say.

"We cannot protect you if you continue to play the *vagabondo.*" His demeanor reflected both concern and anger.

Rodrigo pushed in the large, black, grease-soaked iron bolt, then closed the mammoth medieval gates. They walked side by side.

"You must be careful. If you are who many think you are, then the fate of humanity could be hanging in the balance."

Ishmael rolled his eyes. "I am nobody. They just think I am somebody and…" He looked directly at the Spaniard, "…they know I am here."

Rodrigo stopped and turned. "They? Oh, you mean… How do you know?"

"I was attacked in town. Three men in masks. I got the best of them. The cops came."

The priest paused, then retorted. "Could be local hoodlums."

"No way. They were armed with these." He withdrew the blade from his trousers and held it in his open palm.

"Wow." The priest examined the blade. "This is old, maybe… the fourteenth cent…" Rodrigo paused mid-sentence. Then grabbed the redhead by the wrist. "How long have you had this?" He pulled Ishmael's wrist closer to his eyes.

The dim light had betrayed Ishmael. He was exposed. He had unwittingly shown the priest the celestial symbol. He paused pensively. Rodrigo answered his own question.

"Not long ago, I think… Looks like it is still healing!"

He then let go of Ishmael's wrist and put his hand on the redhead's shoulder.

"Come, let us go inside. We have much to discuss!"

CHAPTER 21 - Perugia, Italy

"So, David left Gath and escaped to the cave of Adullam. Soon his brothers and all his other relatives joined him there. ² Then others began coming—men who were in trouble or in debt or who were just discontented—until David was the captain of about 400 men." - 1 Samuel 22-28

*a Grotta* restaurant was in the peripheral town of Monticelli, located just north of *Perugia*. Perugia was the largest city in Umbria and only a few kilometers down the road from Assisi. La Grotta was a restaurant of historical significance. It had been dug out of a mountainside in an ancient, exhausted quarry of taconite. The local municipalities had partitioned the mine and sold it for commercial use.

Patrons who frequented the establishment entered at the surface level, then stepped down into a cavernous enclave that harbored hundreds of tables. The vaulted ceilings were softly lit by crystal chandeliers that were appended to metal sconces embedded in the rock.

Following the head waiter, Ishmael and Rodrigo descended the staircase into the belly of the earth. Father Scaramucci, Cardinal Müller, and another gentleman sat impatiently in the shadows at a table in the back. All three wore street clothes. In fact, the lighting was so sparse that Ishmael could barely decipher the facial features of his company.

Rodrigo approached the table. "Buona sera, come stanno?" Normally, the three men would have stood and exchanged the cheek-to-cheek greetings so prevalent in Italian society, but on this occasion, they remained seated. In fact, they just nodded.

Rodrigo remained standing and waved his hand in a papal gesture. "Ishmael, you know Father Scaramucci and Cardinal Müller, but I don't think you've met Father Pasquale."

Father Pasquale leaned over the table and shook Ishmael's hand. "Piacere." He spoke with an English inclination, as if he had been schooled abroad.

Despite the lighting, Ishmael was able to make out a few of his features. There was nothing exceptional about his appearance. He had dark skin that was accented by a white beard and a full head of white hair. He wore a dark cotton V-necked sweater with a collared shirt and oval glasses with fine metal frames that wrapped around his ears. Despite his uptight appearance, his countenance was relaxed— even commanding.

Scaramucci spoke. "Father Pasquale is our resident exorcist." He sipped his white wine then continued, "But I should qualify that, because he spends most of his time either traveling abroad or in his office in Rome. He has taken some time out of his hectic schedule to bless us with his presence."

"You flatter me, padre. But I did not come for *you*." He smiled and looked at Scaramucci. "I am more interested in our new companion here."

Turning back to the redhead, he stated, "So I have heard a great deal about you, Ishmael."

"So, you've heard of the 'holy moonchild'?" he said facetiously.

"Well, no. I do not assume anything. I reserve my judgments. In my line of work, I cannot afford to make assumptions." He paused. "May I ask you a question?"

"Shoot," the redhead offered.

"May I see the mark on your wrist?"

Ishmael extended his hand and pulled up his sleeve. Pasquale leaned into the light and examined the scar.

"Hmmm. How long have you had this?"

"A few months."

"And yet it has still not healed?"

"Yeah, I was going to get some medicine but…"

"And how did you get it, if you do not mind me asking?"

"I was working on a bike. Leaned against the exhaust pipe."

"Hmmm. Interesting." The priest held his tongue.

Ishmael rolled his sleeve back up. "So, you are an exorcist? I guess you're going to tell me that demons are real?"

"I am not here to convince you of anything. I am just here to get to know you a little, with your permission, of course." The priest was diplomatic.

"Not much to tell, priest. And I'm sure the others have already filled you in."

Cardinal Müller rarely spoke, and when he did it was germane. "Look, Ishmael, we are convinced that you are the 'boy bitten by fire,' foretold for centuries. You are the bridge, the key. And our enemy is relentless. We cannot guarantee your protection all the time. We know that you can handle yourself with your fists. All we are asking is that you take that focus and do the same in the spiritual realm. Understand?"

The cardinal leaned back in his chair. "Think of it as training."

"Training? Training for what?"

The cardinal continued. "We do not usually welcome anyone into the world of exorcism. We screen our initiates extensively. They must be believers. They must have certain characteristics… and they must engage in intense study, learn the Bible, learn church tradition, learn technique, learn strategies—and not just our strategies but those of the enemy as well."

"What if I don't want to?"

Scaramucci chimed in. "You have never been our prisoner. You know that, Ishmael."

Father Pasquale continued in his perfect English. "Whether or not you stay at the convent or come with me will determine your future. But to do nothing will leave you defenseless on the most savage and bloody battlefield you can possibly imagine. You would be completely vulnerable—a sitting duck. And in good conscience, we cannot allow that to happen."

"So you are forcing me?" he asked.

"No, I am asking you as an equal to come with me. If you want to leave, so be it," Pasquale stated matter-of-factly.

Despite his words, with the magnitude of what was at stake, he knew that they would never let him leave. They could not afford to.

"All right," Ishmael reluctantly agreed.

CHAPTER 22 - Vienna, Austria

"They went across the lake to the region of the Gerasene. When Jesus got out of the boat, a man with an impure spirit came from the tombs to meet him. This man lived in the tombs, and no one could bind him anymore, not even with a chain. For he had often been chained hand and foot, but he tore the chains apart and broke the irons on his feet. No one was strong enough to subdue him. Night and day among the tombs and in the hills, he would cry out and cut himself with stones." - Mark 5:1-8

he four-hour flight from Ciampino, Rome, to Vienna International Airport was devoid of serious conversation. Airport terminals and long flights were not conducive to discussions about the paranormal. A black Mercedes 280 SE collected them at the airport; two Austrian priests in clerical garb, including scapulars, sat at the helm. Pasquale and Ishmael climbed into the back.

"Thank you, my friends, for your hospitality," Father Pasquale spoke first.

The priest in the passenger seat responded. "Natürlich. Always a pleasure, Levi." He spoke with a thick Austrian accent. "So nice to see you again, my friend."

Ishmael looked out the window at the ubiquitous green verge and rolling hills, then turned to Pasquale. "So why are we here?"

"An interesting case study."

"Case study?"

"Yes. There is a man here in this city who needs our help." He paused, then looked out the window.

"And how do you know these people are not just mentally ill?"

"We don't—at least not initially. But there have been many cases that, after investigation, we have deferred to a psychiatrist. We have many doctors on staff... but there are signs that are definitively satanic."

"Like what?"

"...superhuman strength, otherworldly knowledge, the violation of natural law..."

"Violations of natural law?" Ishmael was obstinately curious.

"Yes. Abilities to bend light, access occult (or hidden) knowledge, alter atomic structures, defy gravity, increase wealth, manifest other demons, project astrally... to name a few."

"Astral projecting?"

"Astral projection is the ability to project oneself through the metaphysical ether—to effectively transfer one's spirit into the body of another, rendering the recipient a marionette. However, it is a skill reserved for extremely powerful Satanists and requires the conjuring of very powerful demons. The recipient must be completely under the jurisdiction of the acting principality."

Ishmael looked quizzical. "Sounds like a comic book."

The priest continued, "The devil has achieved great success in cloaking his activities in myth, folklore, materialism, and even mental illness. The average person is completely oblivious to the preternatural world. But listen to me carefully, Ishmael..."

Ishmael stopped looking out the window and gazed at the white-haired priest.

"The spiritual world is the real world. Our reality is a lesser facsimile. We are in an inferior simulation."

The grey sixteenth-century architectural facades stood in stark contrast to the red trams that clogged traffic. The low-hanging clouds hid the Gothic finials on Stephansdom, providing a lead ceiling that seemed to contain, even oppress, the city. The driver looped quickly through the Ringstrasse, zipping past the crowded coffee shops and high-end clothing storefronts.

"Demons can only act within the 'legal' jurisdiction given to them by the free election of the person possessed. Those who are possessed have made choices—or choices have been made by their ancestors, either intentionally or unintentionally—to invite the demons into their lives. The devil must have a window, an entry point—legal access."

"Legal access? I don't recall making any decisions to 'invite' him into my life."

"Oftentimes, it is the ancestry of the demon-possessed that has provided the access. There are different levels of demonic involvement. There is a difference between obsession and possession. You have been harassed, my son, because you are a threat!"

"Not sure about that... How do they get in?" Ishmael asked introspectively.

"It could be palm reading, Ouija boards, yoga, idols, fornication, habitual sin—or, as in your case, childhood trauma. This is very common, especially through physical and sexual trauma."

"So, they got in because of my trauma?" Ishmael inquired. "But that is not free will! I didn't choose my childhood. I didn't choose my descendants. I don't have control over what my ancestors did. Why should I suffer the curse of Adam?"

"God respects the free will of your predecessors as well. And we live in a world of ramifications—consequences that reverberate through the ages. The rock cast into the water disappears, but its waves continue. You must understand that God balances the free wills of five billion people, all with the ability to navigate the physical and metaphysical ethers. It is much more complex than the temporal and superficial. The demonic intellects that we fight against are far beyond ours, and they are allowed, within certain parameters, to exercise their free will as well."

The engine revved and sputtered, turning east toward the Danube, then the car lurched forward as it hit a pothole. The streets were in disrepair. The horizon was obscured by the monolithic, monochromatic buildings that enveloped the priestly posse.

"You must understand that demons are unique spirits—unique individuals. They have specific personalities just like you and me. They have habits, proclivities toward certain behaviors, opinions, even fetishes. They have free will. They can even rise against the satanic hierarchy—and often do. But unlike God's divine order, which runs on free election, the dark kingdom is run by coercion and violence. And if/when they disobey, they are swiftly punished by their evil overlords. Fear keeps them in check. As exorcists, we are commissioned with breaking these bonds, and to do so requires closing those entry points."

"How long does it take to… umm, 'close those doors'?"

"Closing the doors is simple. Keeping them closed is another matter. But the length of the exorcism is entirely subjective. Some exorcisms take a few minutes, and others require multiple visits over months, even years. We proceed according to the dictates of the Church that have been passed down through the millennia—the *Rituale Romanum*."

CHAPTER 23 — London, England

"You shall not allow a sorceress to live."- Exodus 22:18

 fter her purification by blood, Regina Amurael Tiranicus had been accepted as a member of the Order. Since Regina was an "undesirable," the coven did not seek the care of a doctor. If the baby or mother had died, their bodies and blood would have been offered as a sacrifice. Not that they needed a supply of babies for their rituals—social services were replete with orphaned and runaway children to sacrifice. However, if she and her baby had survived, Regina would have become a powerful priestess in the coven.

When Regina was finally ready to give birth, she did so in an abandoned one-room house in the slums of Southwark, London. The previous inhabitants had died of consumption, so the house was temporarily unoccupied. Regina, or Euphemia as she was known, had been a prostitute before joining the Order; she was familiar with the area. The inside of the house was damp and drafty as it was near the River Thames. Sisters Chastity and Prudence accompanied Regina during the birth. Sister Chastity was the coven midwife and had assisted in many Satanic births.

To prepare, the sisters drew a pentagram in chalk on the wooden floorboards and placed black candles on each point of the figure. Powerful demons were summoned to inhabit the baby upon birth. The smell of incense permeated the room, and its smoke danced around the candlelight when the legions were evoked.

Regina was laid on an old rusty cot near the pentagram. It was a long and painful labor that ravaged her undeveloped body. She cried out in agony as the baby's head began to tear her apart as it moved through the birth canal. After pushing for hours, the baby girl's cries were finally heard.

"It's a girl," said Sister Prudence. Regina collapsed in pain and exhaustion and awoke several hours later.

"Does she live?" Regina asked Sister Chastity timidly, afraid of the response.

"Yes, she is healthy. The priest and priestess will choose a name for her. Sister Prudence will care for her during your instruction."

"My instruction?"

"Yes, with the high priestess."

She was known as Lilith Azial Barequel from that day forward. A vial was filled with the baby's blood and given to the priest. Lilith would forever be bound to the dark lord.

Regina was soon summoned by a horse-drawn carriage to the home of the high priestess. Her massive gothic townhouse had vaulted ceilings, large bay windows, and a grand staircase that twisted downward. The salon was dimly lit with candles and adorned with impressive tapestries depicting scenes of ancient Greece, such as Dionysus and Hades.

Regina sat submissively on an upholstered damask chair and waited for the priestess to speak.

"Regina Amurael Tiranicus. Do you understand why you are here?"

"Yes, my Lady. I am to learn about the customs of the Golden Dawn," Regina replied.

"You will be instructed in the ways of our coven, *Ordo Hermeticus Aurorae Aureae*," the priestess corrected.

"I am a willing follower, my Lady. My own family left me for dead many years ago."

"Very well. Let us begin."

CHAPTER 24 - Vienna, Austria

"What do you want with me, Jesus, Son of the Most High God? In God's name don't torture me!' For Jesus had said to him, "Come out of this man, you impure spirit! Then Jesus asked him, 'What is your name?' My name is Legion,' he replied,' or we are many.' And he begged Jesus again and again not to send them out of the area. A large herd of pigs was feeding on the nearby hillside. The demons begged Jesus, 'Send us among the pigs; allow us to go into them.' He gave them permission, and the impure spirits came out and went into the pigs. The herd, about two thousand in number, rushed down the steep bank into the lake and were drowned." - Matthew 5:7-13

he car stretched on for several kilometers, crossing the Danube and zipping through the city of Donaustadt, a Jewish suburb of Vienna. The Mercedes hugged the city's corridors and then screeched to an abrupt halt. The priests exited the vehicle like an Interpol team in a hostage situation. The clerical crew stood in solidarity at the footsteps of a Victorian-styled manor, beneath a gable porch, flanked by twin rotund fluted Doric columns.

Pasquale rang the doorbell. "I would like you just to observe," he whispered to Ishmael. "Under no circumstances should you address the possessed, and especially, especially do not respond to the provocations of the demon! Do you understand?" Although Pasquale did not raise his voice, his tone was emphatic, unequivocal.

Ishmael nodded, hiding his anxiety. Footsteps from behind the giant oak doors could be heard. The lock was loosed and the doors cracked with a proverbial creak. A frail-looking older woman donning a grey shawl peeked her head into the aperture. Her face was riddled with spider web–like wrinkles that came together tightly around her mouth. Upon beholding the priestly party, she exploded, "Ohhh, Gott sei Dank, ich wusste nicht, was ich tun sollte... Du kamst gerade rechtzeitig!"

Pasquale responded in perfect High German, "Wir kamen so schnell wie möglich."

She stepped back and opened the door. "Oh, danke. Danke sei Gott!"

The house was eerily quiet—cold, even frigid. And the house looked as if no one had cleaned it for years. A thick blanket of dust covered every orifice of the house. Ishmael sneezed.

A loud, deep male voice could be heard from upstairs. "Wer ist da?"

Like a forensic team arriving at a crime scene, the priestly trio all pulled out their mass kits. The priest who had driven the Benz began to draw crosses on the banister with holy water. Pasquale and his other companions cautiously proceeded up the stairs. Ishmael followed in tow. The old wooden stairs creaked with each step.

"WER IST DA?" This time the call was louder and more desperate in tone. The hair on the back of Ishmael's neck stood on end.

The lady of the manor spoke in English; her accent was quasi-incomprehensible. "I am so sorry to call you, but I was so desperate. This is the worst he has ever been. I have never seen him this violent."

Pasquale ascended the old staircase. He led the group into the corridor and rounded the corner. The room was poorly lit by a singular bedside lamp. Dirty dishes sat on the table. A horrible stench that could only be described as fermented fecal matter wafted through the static air. And the temperature in the room was so cold that their breath was visible.

Upon seeing the priests, the man became silent. A disheveled elderly man, covered in layers of blankets and dressed in sweats, sat up in bed. His greyish-black payots were knotted like he had not showered in weeks, and his oily, sweaty skin glistened.

"O' halo." He smiled amicably through yellow teeth. He raised his hand in a half-hearted salute, revealing numerous self-inflicted lacerations on his wrist.

"May we enter?" Pasquale asked congenially.

The disturbed older Jewish man responded in kind. "Oh, Englisch? Sure... sure... To whom do I owe this honor?"

"I am Father Pasquale, and these are my colleagues. How are you, Herr Stuttenheim?"

"I am sick. I have been sick for too long. I don't need a priest. I need a doctor. Mildred!" He yelled at his wife. "Warum haben Sie diese Priester eingeladen?"

Pasquale and the other priests entered the room. Pasquale subtly motioned for Ishmael to remain in the hall.

"I will speak English if you do not mind." Pasquale did this for Ishmael's sake.

Mildred stood behind the clergy in the doorframe in front of Ishmael.

"So how long have you been sick?"

"Ich weiss nicht. Maybe years, maybe months... not sure really, ah... hack... hack..." Herr Stuttenheim coughed loudly.

"May I ask you a few questions?"

"No," he said flatly.

Mildred looked at Pasquale with concern in her eyes. "I will make you some tea."

She turned and left the room. Pasquale followed her. "Might I use your bathroom?"

Mildred replied, "Natürlich."

When Pasquale returned, he addressed the possessed man, "Herr Stuttenheim, do you mind if we pray together?"

The man's countenance changed; his hands gripped the blankets. "No! Take your gentile prayers and leave!" he said through gritted teeth.

From Ishmael's vantage point, he could see Pasquale but not the bedridden Jew. Ishmael's consciousness transcended the physical—his sight was altered, blurred but clarified at the same time... changed, as if new glasses were put on his eyes.

...A boy... a young Jewish boy came into view... he was... beaten... physically abused by a relative... anger had been seeded... left to gestate, mature, darken, and rot...

"Herr Stuttenheim, your wife called us. She was concerned about your health."

"I told you. I need a doctor, not a priest!"

Mildred came into the room carrying a tray of steaming teacups. "Hier ist ihr heißer Tee."

"As you wish." Pasquale began to leave. "Do you mind if we finish our tea?" He addressed Herr Stuttenheim directly. With a grimace, he grunted.

Mildred handed the hot tea to her husband. "Hier, trink das, mein Liebling." He took it by the saucer and then tipped it softly to his lips. The minute it hit his lips, he spewed it out all over the priests. He jumped up instantly to his feet, standing on the bed. He began kicking at the priests, screaming at the top of his lungs.

"Sen lanet pislik! Unë do të të vras, assholes të ndyrë! I'll kill you!"

Pasquale's team of priests moved to hold him down.

"ES BRENNT!!" he screamed all the louder.

"I call you out in the name of Jesus Christ! COME OUT OF HIM!" Pasquale pulled a cross from his kit and raised it to the beleaguered man's forehead.

Herr Stuttenheim let out the most ungodly, horrific cry, "AAH!!!!" His cry morphed at the tail end into the most unworldly, sadistic laughter that Ishmael had ever heard.

Ishmael couldn't help but watch. He leaned into the doorframe to witness the two priests struggling to restrain the man,

and Pasquale straddling the man's lap, holding the crucifix to the man's forehead. After a time, the man collapsed in exhaustion.

Hours passed.

Ishmael approached and whispered to Pasquale in the hallway. "The demonic doorway comes from his childhood; he was abused by his father."

"How do you know?"

"I saw it. I felt his pain."

"I don't know how you know, but I will trust your instincts," the priest conceded.

"His father's name was Johann. He was an alcoholic. He beat him until he was thirteen, then he died of cirrhosis. He has never forgiven his father! This is the portal! And I can even tell you the name of the demon! His name is Adbel!"

"YES. I know him—the lord of slavery. I have had dealings with him before. However, odd..." He paused pensively, "...that he has ventured this far north."

After isolating the trauma and the arch-demon, the rest of the exorcism was short-lived. In fact, it only took a few hours before the priests were back in the Mercedes, heading to a nearby parish. One of the priests had stayed behind to watch Herr Stuttenheim for the remainder of the evening.

A light drizzle painted the Mercedes as it spun its wheels through the city. The three men stopped at Karlsplatz to buy a Käsekrainer from a kiosk. The rain abated as they stood in a tight huddle, processing the events.

Ishmael spoke first. "I don't understand a few things."

"Mmmm?" Pasquale shoved a giant bite of the breaded sausage in his mouth.

"What set him off? One moment he was calm, the next, he was attacking you."

Pasquale swallowed. "Ishmael, the demons do not want to be discovered. They prefer to remain concealed. Inside the human body, they experience a reprieve from the torment. Doomed to eternal damnation—but not to hell... at least, not yet. They are disembodied spirits, relegated to wandering the earth. Their only solace is to embody and live vicariously through us."

"Hmmm. Interesting. But what set him off?"

"I put some holy water in his tea." Both priests smiled simultaneously. "Only the spirit within him would have known the difference. If he had remained calm, we would have called a doctor and left. But as you saw..."

"Wow. Clever."

"Ah, you know, over time we develop strategies to draw them out."

"And I have another question. Why did you say that you had not seen the demon 'this far north'?"

"The Book of Daniel speaks of provincial demons. Just as demons are assigned different tasks, they are also designated to certain areas. They are, in essence, regional principalities—princes, archangels who have been assigned different geographical domains."

"Wow." Ishmael's head spun. He took a bite of his food, then raised his gaze to the enormity of the square that culminated in the magnificent 18th-century church built by Charles VI, Karlskirche.

CHAPTER 25 - Assisi, Italy

"A highway will be there, a roadway, and it will be called the Highway of Holiness. The unclean will not travel on it, but it will be for him who walks that way, and fools will not wander on it." - Isaiah 35:8

caramucci paused and then looked at his mountain of books. "It is nice to have you back, my son. I trust that Pasquale... how do you say... I always have problems with the idioms... 'showed you ropes?' Qualcosa del genere." He whispered to himself.

"Yes. That's right. 'Showed me the ropes,'" Ishmael corrected him.

"Ah, sì. Grazie."

"Yeah. Saw some demonic activity. It was... uhh... eye-opening."

"And?" the priest provoked.

The loft was as disheveled as ever. Parchments protruding from an assortment of boxes riddled the walls. It was claustrophobic, but Ishmael put up with it because he had come to value the advice of Scaramucci. The priest took another bite of risotto.

"Father, I want to ask you something..." He paused. "My dreams have become more frequent, more intense."

"Dimmi. Tell me."

"Well," he paused reticently. "I have a recurring dream... of... uhh... a giant scroll laid out before me, floating in the heavens, an open book of charts. I guess I would describe them as tables or... I don't know. And a voice... uhm... although it is not an audible voice... more like a subliminal... I don't know... maybe more like an understanding given to me by some other means. And behind the pages flows a river, or perhaps a series of symbols. I see two men from times past dressed in Shakespearean clothing. And they are drawing these tables in real time, and there is a being of light

watching over them, and the light engulfs them. And although he radiates light, he carries with him a deep foreboding, an oppressive sadness. He repeatedly whispers, 'Gebofal,' although I don't know what it means."

Father Scaramucci stared at the redhead with an expression of awe. He stayed silent for what seemed like five minutes.

"My son, have you told this to anyone else?"

"No, Father."

"You are sure?"

"Yes, Father. Why?"

"Are you familiar with the writings of Doctor John Dee?"

"Who?"

"He was a spy. He signed his letters with the numbers 007; he inspired the writings of Ian Fleming. But beyond that, he was an alchemist commissioned by Queen Elizabeth herself. He and another man named Edward Kelley dabbled in the occult. It is said that an angel dictated to them the *Liber Loagaeth*, a text written in the first language ever spoken—Enochian."

"Eno... what?"

"In those texts, which have subsequently been lost to history, it is said that there are forty-nine tables, or instructions entailing the secrets of the angels—secret knowledge to communicate with the angels directly."

"Secret knowledge? Why would knowledge be secret?"

Scaramucci pulled an old Bible from his desk, then turned to James 1:5. The priest put it in front of the redhead.

"Read, per favore."

"'If any of you lacks wisdom, you should ask God, who gives generously to all without finding fault, and it will be given to you.'"

"Now turn to 1 Samuel 15:23."

Ishmael read aloud. "'For rebellion is as the sin of witchcraft, and stubbornness is as iniquity and idolatry. Because thou hast rejected the word of the Lord, he hath also rejected thee from being king.'"

"The author addresses King Saul after he chose to seek the counsel of a medium rather than wait for the divine message given to Samuel, YHWH's prophet. Do you know why the writer compares rebellion to witchcraft?" Scaramucci looked at Ishmael quizzically. Answering his own question, he continued. "Witchcraft is rebellious because it seeks to use the schemas of nature to circumvent

God. It is an attempt to elevate one's learning to use its properties for one's own advancement and enrichment. It is, in essence, the learning of God's creation to serve oneself—and, by proxy, the demons. Do you understand, my boy?"

"I think so. Is that why He forbade Adam and Eve to eat from the Tree of Good and Evil?"

"God wants us to pursue knowledge for His glory, to understand Him—not to advance our own agendas, to make ourselves gods. This is a reiteration of the original serpentine lie spoken in the garden. Much knowledge was given to man. Science, for example, was originally invented to understand God's nature—His attributes. The earliest scientists—Kepler, Newton, Mendel, Boyle, Pascal, to name a few—were all devoted Christians. They saw no contradiction between science and religion. Yet nowadays, science has been polarized, hijacked to explain the world without God."

"What does my dream have to do with this?"

"The word 'Gebofal' refers to the actualization of this knowledge—the scaling of the ladder. The comprehension of the angelic language, and the successive steps to communicate with the angels—the completion of the tables. Evil men pursue you to access this knowledge."

"Why would someone do that?"

"To access forbidden knowledge, forbidden secrets—to wealth, power, strength, intelligence, healing... and some even say, immortality."

"But I cannot read Enochian."

"Ahhh, but you can. You just don't know it yet." He paused and looked around his cluttered office. "Now, what they want from these dark angels is anyone's guess. I imagine that they will access the knowledge first revealed in the antediluvian era."

"What does that mean?"

"Do you remember when I spoke about the Nephilim?"

"Yes. They were giants."

"Yes, but more specifically, they were hybrids from fallen angels—angels known as the Watchers, or *grigori*, from the Greek."

"Yes, I know... that name has echoed in my head since I was five."

"These angels were originally charged with the caretaking of humanity but instead made a conscious choice to rebel. They took human form and copulated with the daughters of men. In their wickedness, they bore the giants of old—Nephilim. What you do not know is that in the two thousand years before the flood, during the rebellion, angels bequeathed forbidden knowledge to humanity."

Scaramucci got up and walked over to his treasured trove of literature. The bibliophile sifted briefly through his collection, then returned with *The Book of Enoch*. He opened it to *The Book of Watchers* and read aloud:

And Azael taught men to make swords, and daggers, and shields and breastplates. And he showed them the things after these, and the art of making them: bracelets, and ornaments, and the art of making up the eyes and of beautifying the eyelids, and the most precious and choice stones, and all [kinds of] colored dyes. And the world was changed. And there was great impiety and much fornication, and they went astray, and all their ways became corrupt.

"With these 'gifts' came lust, envy, and war... They had giant appetites. They ate everything that man could produce. After a time, famine spread throughout the land, and when the food was gone, the giants engaged in cannibalism—consuming human flesh. And then finally, they ate each other."

"I know this part."

"According to extra-biblical commentaries—*The Book of Giants* and others found in the Qumran caves (you might know them as the Dead Sea Scrolls...)—these writings chronicle the tales of giants as they began to grow in power. They began to experience prophetic dreams foretelling their own destruction. The two sons of the angel Shemjaza, Ohia and Haiya, dreamt of a tablet floating in water with three names on it—the names of the family of Noah."

"So, they knew the flood was coming?"

"Yes. And it terrified them! In those days, Enoch, the son of Jared, was considered a sacred scribe who had a personal relationship with the Creator Himself. The giants besieged him to act on their behalf, seeking an interpretation of their dreams and a remanding of the final judgment."

"So, what happened?"

"Despite their attempts to repent, God brought the flood and wiped them out, killing the giants and imprisoning the Watchers in the bowels of the earth. No giants survived. But some extra-biblical sources tell of records that outlasted the flood."

"I don't understand."

"Records written by the giants on tree trunks that would have floated."

"Where are they now?"

"Legend has it that they were discovered by an obscure figure from the early Hellenistic period, a man known as Hermes Trismegistus. It is said that he found the buried columns that held the inscriptions of secret angelic knowledge. And it is for his namesake that we derive the Hermetic Orders that we have today."

"Wow."

"Doctor John Dee and Edward Kelley came from this line of erudition. Hermeticism later gave way to other prominent orders such as the Order of the Golden Dawn and the Hollow Earth Society—the latter believed that the earth's core was inhabited by supernatural beings."

"Shemjaza."

"Sí. And his two hundred angels locked away until Judgment Day. One prominent member of this Hermetic Order was a man by the name of Karl Haushofer, who believed that there was a magical, mystic relationship between man and the universe. And it was his influence, some say, that led to the success of an awkward young man from a small border town in Austria. You might know him as Adolf Hitler."

"Hitler? Really?" Ishmael was astonished.

"It was Haushofer who inspired Hitler to write *Mein Kopf*, and it was he who sent graduates from the Hitler Youth camps to scour the globe for tunnels to access the earth's core to release the Watchers from Tartarus; and it was Haushofer who led Hitler in satanic incantations for the embodiment of deep, dark demonic powers, particularly before his rallies; and it was Haushofer who inspired Hitler to appropriate the swastika, which came directly from his studies of Buddhism and the religions of India."

"I... I... I can't handle this!" Ishmael put his hands on his head and bent over at the waist. "This is too much. What? Are you saying that Hitler was possessed? And that I am connected to all this?"

"Undoubtedly."

The stress was too much; Ishmael leaned over and vomited on the floor.

CHAPTER 26 - Assisi, Italy

"And he breaks the withs, as a thread of tow is broken when it toucheth the fire. So, his strength was not known." — *Judges 16:9*

hythmic drumming echoed through the hilltop borough; Ishmael was impulsively drawn to the faint sound. His Vespa buzzed as he traveled closer to the center of the town. Ishmael saw a band of percussionists marching toward *La Basilica di San Chiara*, adorned in red and blue. Gold banners hung overhead. The drummers beat their instruments in unison, which had a hypnotic effect on Ishmael. Suddenly, the pounding came to a stop and the crowd exploded in applause.

Ishmael chained up his bike and walked toward the main street. He heard a child exclaim, *"Stanno facendo l'albero di Maggio!"* A group of beautiful women in colorful medieval dresses danced in a circle underneath streamers attached to a pole.

He passed by an elderly woman with a hand-woven basket of fragrant fresh fruit. "Uh, mi scusi... What's happening?" he asked her.

"Calendimaggio, caro mio," she replied. *"It's the ancient celebration of the return of spring; the renewal of life..."* She gestured with an open palm to the sky. *"...the victory of light over darkness."*

Caught up in the moment, Ishmael's eyes followed the procession to the pale visage of a young woman peeking out from behind a cream-colored cloak. Her appearance was unusually familiar and intoxicating. She was clad in a fuchsia gown with white ribbons that flailed and twisted in her dark auburn hair. She appeared to be around twenty-five years of age. She locked her pale blue eyes with his, and Ishmael could not look away. A group of people walked by, blocking his view. After they passed, Ishmael searched for the woman in the crowd, but she had gone. He felt compelled to find her, but he was distracted by a parade with the new *Madonna Primavera* perched regally on a vaulted chair.

The sun began to set, and darkness veiled the town. Just as Ishmael was about to head back to the monastery, he noticed a procession of people moving toward the orange glow of the torchlit square. A group of actors was reenacting a scene from the medieval play *Ordo Virtutum.* Ishmael paused to watch. *Il Diavolo*, the devil, was performed by an actor on stilts with dark bat-like wings and a grotesque horned mask. A graceful actress wearing a white glimmering robe with a gold sash played *un angelo.* The remaining actors represented human virtues. A man's soul lay in the balance.

Ishmael heard a voice from behind him and turned around.

"Do you believe in good and evil?" It was her.

Ishmael stammered, "I... uhh... I know evil exists."

"Hmmm... You sound as though you speak from experience. My name is Sofia Erebus, by the way."

"I'm Ishmael Di Scala. Nice to meet you." He felt vulnerable.

"How are you enjoying the festival?" Sofia asked.

"Yeah, uh, it's like traveling back in time." Ishmael felt tongue-tied around the auburn beauty.

"I've never seen you here before. You must be a tourist." Sofia winked.

"Not exactly."

"So where are you staying?" she asked.

"At the monastery," Ishmael replied.

Sofia laughed. "Wow. Are you a monk?"

"Maybe someday," Ishmael retorted.

"That would be a waste." Sofia looked suggestively at Ishmael. He could feel his face flush with blood.

"What do you do there?"

"I work in the stables."

"Hmmm, an equestrian..."

"I guess so. What do you do?"

"I work at my aunt and uncle's winery. Have you heard of Marchiani Vineyards? We specialize in Sangiovese, Trebbiano, and Grechetto varietals."

"No, I don't know anything about wine," Ishmael stated matter-of-factly.

Sofia responded excitedly, "I can teach you! It all begins with the vines. They have to be carefully cultivated, and it can take years to yield grapes suitable for making a good wine. I can show you around the vineyards sometime... Hey, would you be willing to walk me home?"

"Sure. I can give you a ride on my Vespa," he replied.

"Even better!" Sofia smiled.

The pair climbed onto the leather seat of his motor scooter, and Sofia straddled him from behind, pulling him into her embrace. Her sweet perfume wafted through his nose and her warm breath caressed his neck. The black Vespa sputtered through the hilltop town, down the stone-crafted streets, and eventually toward a large villa surrounded by meticulously groomed vineyards.

"That's my home just there, up ahead!" she pointed over his shoulder.

When they arrived at the entrance of the villa, Ishmael turned off his bike and Sofia returned to a standing position.

"Would you like to come in for a bit?"

After the recent incident, worried about breaking curfew, Ishmael was hesitant to remain out at night.

"I really should be getting back."

"Come on. Just for a little while," Sofia coaxed and touched his arm. "You can park your bike over there." She pointed to the courtyard.

The rustic villa hosted Tuscan yellow plastered stucco walls, vaulted ceilings with massive wooden beams, and several Palladian windows. Neoclassic furniture sat upon limestone tile floors surrounded by plants in Umbrian pottery. Inside the foyer, a tall man, casually dressed with short dark hair and dull eyes, glared unwaveringly at Ishmael. He was flanked by a petite woman wearing a tan skirt with a celestial blue blouse and blonde hair. To Ishmael, her smile seemed entirely too large for her face.

Sofia introduced her friends, "Ishmael, this is Ewan and Cecelia. You might meet my uncle Lorenzo and aunt Francesca later."

Ishmael smiled back at Cecelia. He could feel Ewan staring at him with piercing black eyes; he matched his gaze. Ewan had a large gash under his right eye that struggled to heal.

Sofia broke the silence. "Don't mind Ewan, he's usually in a bad mood." Turning to Ishmael enthusiastically, she said, "You have to try our wine! The grapes were harvested from our vineyard."

Ishmael followed her through an arched ingress into a beautifully expansive kitchen with open rafters that stretched to the sky. Sofia pulled the cork from the bottle and hastily poured the red wine into two long-stemmed glasses. She handed one to Ishmael. Ishmael really didn't like wine, but he took it anyway.

"Come," she stated simply.

Sofia guided him to a rectangular sectional sofa in the living room near a fireplace with a roaring fire. The walls of the soggiorno were covered in portraits of people from times past.

"So... tell me how you ended up at a monastery in Assisi." Sofia took a sip of her wine and waited.

Ishmael reluctantly replied, "Uh, there was some trouble back home."

"And where is that?"

"California." He lied.

Her eyes widened. "What kind of trouble?" Sofia pressed.

"I don't really like to talk about it."

"Oh, okay. You sound dangerous," Sofia teased. "Maybe I shouldn't associate with a man like you."

He feigned a smile. "Not dangerous, just unlucky." He took a sip of the vintage.

"How about you? Why are you here?" asked Ishmael, detecting an accent other than Italian.

"My family is from London. I wanted to learn the art of winemaking, so here I am. Ewan, Cecelia, and I are business partners. This winery has been in my family for almost two hundred years. Ewan is the vintner, and Cecelia is in charge of the tasting room and hosting large parties."

"Speaking of Ewan, what's his problem?" Ishmael asked abruptly.

"Yeah, sorry 'bout that. We used to be a couple. He's... uhh... a little possessive." She took another sip of her wine. "Okay, a lot possessive. But he's a good friend," she conceded.

"If you say so."

"Enough about him." Sofia placed her glass on the coffee table and shifted her position closer to the redhead. "Look, Ishmael, I really like you."

Sofia leaned over and kissed him passionately, gently biting him on the lip. Ishmael felt an overwhelming desire for her.

"Let's go to my bedroom," Sofia whispered in his ear.

Sofia and Ishmael lay naked on her bed. Their clothes were strewn about the bedroom. Ishmael gently caressed Sofia's shoulder and traced a line down her back. Sofia smiled and laughed as goosebumps formed on her skin. Sofia turned over, and Ishmael cupped her breast and put his mouth on her erect nipple. Sofia pulled him closer and wrapped her arms around his neck. Ishmael slowly entered her body as Sofia began to rhythmically swivel her hips.

He abruptly stopped moving and commanded, "Slower." Ishmael paused for a few seconds and continued. He wanted this amazing feeling to last. Sofia looked up at him and began to cry out. Ishmael couldn't contain his excitement any longer. He began to quicken against her body and then poured himself into her with a guttural scream of intense pleasure. He collapsed on the mattress to catch his breath. Ishmael closed his eyes and began to drift off to sleep.

...Ishmael wandered through a dark, forsaken land with twisted trees. His legs were accosted by thorny shrubs and dense fog... or perhaps smoke... he looked down at his tethered, blood-soaked hands... a cabin... torchlit flickers from between the slats of wood... Gebofal... symbols... Rodrigo... doors opening... a masked figure... a platform... someone dying... pain... an offering to someone... who? ...people... thousands of people!

"Noooo!" Ishmael awoke. His brow was covered in sweat.

"Ishmael, hon?" Sofia touched his face softly.

He sat up, stunned for a few seconds. "I had a terrible nightmare." He stared blankly ahead.

Sofia looked concerned. "It was just a dream, sweetheart." She stroked his head. "Do you want to tell me about it?"

"No, it's too horrible." Ishmael shuddered and tried to fall back asleep.

The morning sunlight shone through the windows of the villa. When Ishmael opened his eyes, it took him a few moments to remember where he was.

Father Rodrigo! He must be so worried about me, Ishmael thought. He located his clothes and dressed quickly before walking out into the living room.

"Good morning, handsome. How are you feeling today?" Sofia appeared in the kitchen. "Would you like an espresso?"

"I had a great time, but I have to get back," he said frantically.

"Okay, but we must get together soon," she responded emphatically.

He felt drawn to Sofia. "I would like that."

Ishmael rushed back to the monastery. He showered, changed his clothes, then ran to Father Rodrigo's study, where he found the Spaniard laboriously sifting through some documents. Ishmael stood awkwardly in the doorframe.

"Where were you last night?" The young priest didn't lift his head from his task.

"I met someone at the festival," Ishmael replied sheepishly.

"It is important that you honor your curfew!" He looked up. "And remain on the righteous path of God — that is, if that is your path."

Ishmael winced. "Yeah, I understand. I'm sorry for disappointing you."

Rodrigo scolded, "It's not about me. It is about you!"

Chapter 27 - Rome, Italy

"And then shall many be offended, and shall betray one another, and shall hate one another." - Matthew 24:10

e sat at his desk.

"Hello? Can you patch me through to the Father?"

"One moment, please."

"Hello."

"Are you alone?"

"Yes. Go ahead."

"He's in Umbria, in the town of Assisi."

"What's the plan?"

"So, we sent in a team, but they blew our cover..."

"Who knows?"

"The Spaniard."

"I'll send in the Calabrese."

CHAPTER 28 - Assisi, Italy

"...but at the proper time manifested, even His word, in the proclamation with which I was entrusted according to the commandment of God our Savior." - Titus 1:3

shmael spent the next few days trying to occupy himself with work in the stables, but his mind kept drifting back to Sofia. She seemed so familiar to him, even though they had just met. Ishmael had had dreams about a beautiful young woman with dark auburn hair, smiling and laughing, sometimes screaming, but her face was a fractured image, a dream. Was it Sofia?

Ishmael decided to walk into town; he stopped in at Cotto e Crudo for a panino. He was pleased to find Sofia sitting at a table. Her hair was pulled back in a colorful scarf, and a yellow sundress clung snugly to her body. Sofia motioned for him to join her.

Sofia greeted Ishmael by kissing him on both cheeks and then on the mouth. "Ciao, Bello."

"I was just thinking about you," Ishmael responded in surprise.

Sofia smiled and asked, "Hope it was good... Do you have any plans tonight?"

Ishmael's mouth was full of food; he shook his head.

"I want to take you to a club with my friends... It's in Rome. We can take the train."

Ishmael had visited a few dance clubs back in Chicago, but it really wasn't his scene. He preferred to go see live music. But he really wanted to spend time with Sofia.

"Sure, sounds like fun," he responded dishonestly.

"Great! Meet me at the train station at 20:00."

The tiny Stazione di Assisi was located in an area known as Santa Maria degli Angeli near the center of town. Ishmael and Sofia met outside the ticket office near the main entrance.

"How long is the train ride to Rome?" Ishmael asked the attendant.

Sofia translated, "Quanto ci vuole per arrivare a Roma?"

"Due ore, più o meno," responded the guardiano.

Two hours? He would be missing another curfew, Ishmael thought to himself.

The train rattled its way through the peripheral towns on the way to Rome, each

announced successively by the conductor, "Foligno! Spoleto! Orte! Viterbo!" Ishmael looked out the window at the Italian countryside quickly passing from view. Dusk was approaching. The silhouettes of the hilltop castles were painted in a sottofondo of red and purple. Sofia paged through a magazine. Lulled by the movement of the train, he fell asleep. He fell into the metaphysical... Gebofal... The Watchers called out to him... Their wails, "Let us out..." The volume had been turned up... as if...

She softly brushed his lips with hers. "Wake up, sleepyhead. We're almost there."

Finally reaching their destination, Ishmael and Sofia excitedly departed the train at Termini and jumped into an awaiting black BMW 7 Series that had been waiting to take them to the club.

"This is us. Come on!" she implored.

His desire for Sofia trumped his reluctance to get in the car.

"Where are we going?" he mumbled.

"To the club... Don't worry. You'll love it," Sofia responded.

The driver turned southeast on Via Casilina, then left on Viale Palmiro Togliatti toward Centocelle. Several minutes later, they arrived at their destination and leapt from the car. The facade of the ancient Forte Prenestino was covered in spray paint. To Ishmael, it seemed run down, derelict.

As they approached the old monument, the colossal wooden doors shook and creaked, giving access to a long corridor. Gothic chandeliers and red-veloured drapes hung freely against the walls. The dimly lit room was perforated by flashing lights. Techno music pulsed loudly through the partitioned rooms, yet no one was dancing. The guests wore black clothes, many adorned in unusual silver jewelry with strange insignias. A few had disturbing masks with horns on their heads.

The auburn-haired couple stood in the ingress scanning the crowd.

"Is this a costume party?" Ishmael inquired.

"You could say that." Sofia smiled coyly. "Let's get something to drink."

Sofia took his hand and led him through the crowd. The pull of her hand mirrored the pull in his heart. He felt propelled, coerced, vulnerable, and... something familiar... he liked it.

Peering into adjacent rooms, Ishmael noticed beds covered in vinyl. They approached the bartender, who wore makeup and meticulously braided hair. With a glance, he handed her a silver goblet encrusted with dark jewels. Sofia brought the goblet to her lips. Staring at Ishmael, she took a sip.

"Here, try this, Ishmael."

Ishmael took the goblet reluctantly and investigated the viscous liquid. His reflection stared back at him. He drank deeply. It tasted like vodka with some kind of juice, maybe pomegranate; and there was an unusual residue as well, a taste he could not recognize. After a few gulps, Ishmael placed the goblet on the counter.

Shortly thereafter, it hit him... he felt exhilarated, his heart raced, his palms sweated, his face went flush, and he felt... invincible!

Sofia began kissing Ishmael while she explored his body.

"You're so sexy, Ishmael. I love your muscles. And I especially love this," Sofia slurred and slowly rubbed him over his jeans. "Let's see if there's anyone in here."

Sofia took Ishmael's hand and led him to one of the empty rooms before sitting down on the bed.

"Lay back, baby," she commanded, gently pushing him against the surface.

Sofia took off her shiny black dress to reveal beautiful round breasts and a luscious mound. Ishmael began to touch her breasts while Sofia lifted Ishmael's shirt and unzipped his jeans, releasing his erection.

"You're so beautiful," he said fervently.

Sofia kissed her way down from his mouth before straddling his firm body. She gently moved back and forth over his hard phallus until it slid inside her. Sofia gyrated in circles while looking deep into his eyes. Ishmael felt like he would explode.

"I want to be inside you," he said.

"Not yet," she whispered.

Sofia moved away from his body. An attractive yet haunting woman with short black hair and hypnotic green eyes moved onto the bed. Her body was covered in vivid tattoos and unusual piercings.

"This is my friend, Iris. Can she join us?"

Before Ishmael could respond, Sofia and Iris began to lick his glistening protrusion and then extended their tongues into each other's mouths. Ishmael moaned in ecstasy.

"I wanna taste you," Iris hissed.

Sofia leaned back, and Iris began to please Sofia. Ishmael heard people shouting and cheering; he realized they were watching through a window into their room.

A tall, muscular, naked man with bronze skin appeared on the bed and grabbed Iris by the hair, pulling her toward him. "Where did you think you're going? I wasn't done with you yet," he growled.

The man bit her on the neck, drawing blood. He forcefully pushed himself into her and thrust furiously so that his body made a loud, flesh-on-flesh slapping sound against hers. Ismael could not discern if she cried out in pain or pleasure.

Another couple joined Ismael and Sofia on the bed. The woman was blonde with large breasts, and the man was tall and lean with a goatee and long brown hair. The woman began to caress Ismael, and the man sucked Sofia's nipples. All of them were howling and clawing at each other's bodies. Sofia and Ismael locked eyes and simultaneously moved back together to climax. Ismael felt as though he had left his body for a few moments, and then everything went black.

When he awoke the next morning, Ismael was sitting next to Sofia on the train ride back to Assisi.

"How, how did I get here?" Ismael asked, confused.

"My friends had to carry you," Sofia seemed amused.

"Really?" he responded in embarrassment. "Please thank them... and apologize for me."

Sofia smiled and squeezed his hand.

Ismael racked his mind to remember what happened at the club after they arrived. The drink in the goblet must have contained some type of drug. There was no other explanation. Did Sofia know the drink was spiked? No, of course not. Ismael did not want this experience to affect his relationship with Sofia. He felt like he was falling in love with her, which terrified him because everyone he cared about died. Ismael would not let that happen again! But how? He was only able to heal the old man in church when he was a child. With the death of his parents, Ismael had turned away from God. Perhaps he had lost his ability. Maybe God had forsaken him as well.

Chapter 29 - Oberammergau, Germany

"Notwithstanding I have a few things against thee, because thou sufferest that woman Jezebel, which calleth herself a prophetess, to teach and to seduce my servants to commit fornication, and to eat things sacrificed unto idols." - Revelation 2:20

uring the Thirty Years' War, the bubonic plague, or Black Death, carved its way through the tiny community of Oberammergau, in southern Bavaria. It wiped out half the village. The populace collectively made a vow to God that if the plague would abate, they would perform a play in honor of their savior, Jesus Christ. No one else died.

As promised, the villagers began performing the opus every ten years. *The Passion of the Christ* grew in size and grandeur, attracting more and more visitors. Initially located in the local parish, the townsfolk built a stage in the nearby cemetery,

which gave rise to an outdoor theater. Municipalities were petitioned by the players and the ever-increasing crowds to open the public streets. In the years since, it had become a locus of Christian pilgrimage, attracting thousands of spectators from all over the world.

Nowadays, the event involves more than two thousand actors and event staff; it lasts more than five hours, divided equally by an elaborate feast. The former half entails the long haul to Golgotha, where "Christ" is paraded to the platform through a crowd of vegetable-wielding patrons, and the latter half, where people can observe His last words on the cross, "Eloi, Eloi, lama Sabachthani?"

"Why are we here?" Ishmael looked out of the window of the Mercedes. The wind and rain formed a sheet wall that swirled and hissed.

"Another case study, a young girl. We have no doubt as to her predicament this time, no prognosis needed. In fact, we are here to assist another team." The white-haired priest adjusted his glasses.

"It takes more than one team?" The black coloring in his hair had completely grown out, and his curly auburn locks bounced on his head like sprouting fern leaves.

"We are here as consultants," explained Pasquale. "And I thought we could take in the show as well. Have you heard of the Oberammergau *Passionsspiele*?"

"No."

"We are lucky to be here. They perform it once a decade," he said with his English accent.

"Okay, if you say so." Another festival... Ishmael thought to himself.

"Come on, Ishmael, what's wrong? It is quite the draw, you know. There will be a large crowd and some great food." Feigning a smile, Pasquale put his finger to his cheek and twisted it.

Ishmael nodded, but his heart weighed heavily against his spirit. He imagined that he would probably identify more with Judas than Jesus.

The Mercedes stopped at the local parish, *Pfarrkirche St. Peter und Paul*. Exiting the vehicle, the priest looked over the chassis of the car pelted by rain. "This is a major event. You know every room in the city has been booked for years. If it weren't for the parish and the rooms provided by the clergy, we would have to pitch a tent," he said jocularly.

"Okay, Father."

The idyllic Hansel-and-Gretel-like town was dwarfed by magnificent snow-crowned alpine mountains. The architecture of the pastel-colored houses was Germanic, with V-shaped, snow-repellent roofs and planters adorning nearly every small rectangular window. Yet the beauty seemed to be lost on the enlightened redhead.

The two other passengers stepped from the front of the car and led the way to a clandestine courtyard in the rear of the parish. The priest who had driven the car led the way, opening a sixteenth-century barn-like door. The group made their way to a convent-like edifice. The priest pulled a key from his pocket and spun it in the lock. The door popped open to reveal a brightly lit hallway with adjacent rooms.

"We'll stay here tonight." Pasquale gave his orders, turned on his axis, and disappeared into his quarters. Ishmael did the same.

... he was in an open field... cascading symbols fell on him from heaven... a portal... a strange ring... blurred faces in ecstasy... flesh everywhere... demons everywhere... he couldn't remember the events of the previous days... everything was a bloody blur... he remembered sleeping on the train to Rome... and an underground bunker... flashing lights... loud music... but nothing else... as if...

"ISHMAEL!" Father Pasquale slammed his door against the hinges. "Wake up! We need to go!" He entered the room, throwing articles of clothing on his bed. "Get dressed now!"

Ishmael's head was spinning. He sat up in bed and threaded his arms into the shirt sleeves.

"We have to go, hurry. I will wait for you in the car." The priest turned and left.

He frantically threw on the remaining clothes and exited the room. The car was waiting in the parking lot in front of the parish. Vapor and fumes poured from the exhaust as the three priests all sat waiting in the Mercedes. Ishmael climbed in the back.

"Why the hurry?" Ishmael asked. Pasquale glared at him. The redhead dared not ask again. He looked out the window at the remaining puddles from the previous downpour. Despite the temperature and the hour, people had begun to fill the streets. The Mercedes sped its way through the town, stopping for tiny children and Japanese tour groups led by guides holding tiny flags attached to their umbrellas.

The car skidded to the entrance of a Tuscan yellow cottage with atypical Germanic architecture. Another similar Mercedes was parked in front. The three priests shot out of the car like a cannon.

Loud but incomprehensible screams could be heard from the house. Pasquale led the way. Ishmael followed. Ishmael felt a shiver—tremors that he had never felt—a cold beyond description.

The door opened immediately. A blond couple stood in the doorway. The blond German woman spoke first. "Sie sind oben, bitte beeilen Sie sich!"

The clerical crew climbed the staircase. The cries grew louder. Aggressively escalated German male voices could be heard as well. The team came to the end of a long hallway to behold a most ghastly scene.

Defying natural law, a petite half-naked blond girl was suspended three meters above, on the ceiling. She appeared to be no older than twelve. Her arms and legs were inverted like a spider. Her fingers and opposable toes were embedded into the ceiling, supporting her body. Her eyes were entirely black, and her head spun backwards, facing the priests below.

Copious amounts of blood had streaked the walls and ceiling from the wounds caused by her ascent. The room stank from the vomit that permeated the priests' hair and clothing. She growled and hissed in a language that no priest could decipher.

Forgetting protocol, Ishmael inadvertently entered the room. Upon witnessing him, the girl screamed in Enochian, "Awwwww! Behold, the Seer, the Edomite! The fire-born prodigy of Esau! We have found Him at last. You seek to vanquish ME? HA!"

Ishmael peered around the room to witness perplexed expressions on the priests' faces and realized only he could understand.

"Speak in English, girl!" Pasquale demanded.

"You fool! I am no girl!" the entity responded in English.

The presence continued to address Ishmael in Enochian, "You hypocrite! I can smell their cunts on you! Your seed is an offering to Incubus! Carnal-minded! Fornicator with demons! You have no authority here! You are one of us! Tell them about Sofia! Tell your friends about your mortal sin!"

"I told you to wait outside!" Pasquale yelled.

Ishmael could not move; his feet and his memory had betrayed him.

"What is she saying?" Pasquale demanded.

Holding crucifixes toward the sky, the six other priests rebuked her in the names of the Blessed Virgin and in Jesus' name.

"Ecce Crux Domini! Partes Adversae, Vicit Leo de Tribu Juda!"

The possessed little girl screamed in pain but was defiant. She released one hand and pointed her blood-soaked digit at Ishmael.

"Edomite! You will usher in Gebofal, and you will release the Watchers! You are the key! You belong to us! Tell me where it is! Tell me where it is! TELL ME!"

All six priests spoke in unison, thrusting their crucifixes toward the possessed.

"Name yourself! And in the name of Jesus Christ, and His Sacred Blood, come out of her!"

"I am Lilith!" she grunted through clenched teeth.

"You have no dominion here!" they persisted.

The tiny blond girl let out a blood-curdling screech, then fell to the bed below. Waiting momentarily, Ishmael cautiously neared the bed to observe her still-frail frame. He touched her still-marred hand.

...He fell into the vortex... *So that is why they need me...* he thought. *...To release the Watchers... Two hundred of the most powerful angels...* He saw them roaming the earth... he saw Lilith... he saw her on the metaphysical plane... he saw the girl in her grasp... he saw a woman kneeling, dressed in black, chanting or perhaps praying... he saw death approaching... Gebofal... symbols... he saw them rejoicing... *Was he responsible for this? Never!*

Suddenly, she lashed out, grabbing his arm. She turned over his wrist to expose the angelic wound. "Ah ha! Behold, the mark of Cain! It has not healed! Ha ha ha!" she cried out in Enochian. "There is no more time! For you, it has been decreed that many will die—two of them very close!! Very close," she hissed. "You will be OURS! He created you in His image, BUT WE WILL RECREATE YOU IN OURS! TELL ME WHERE IT IS!"

Pasquale and the other priests approached her instantaneously.

"BY THE BLOOD OF JESUS, I COMMAND YOU! COME OUT!"

The tormented young girl convulsed, gurgling and snorting, thrashing about—then suddenly, she collapsed, unconscious. Quiet ensued. The priests were spent. They all gave out a huge sigh of relief.

"Is everyone alright?" Pasquale inquired.

Gasping, they all collectively nodded.

The amphitheater teemed with activity. The tourists were resolute; they pushed and postured to obtain a front-row seat. The overflow cascaded into the streets. From Japanese to Portuguese, the languages of the globe were represented. Children ran amok; some were hoisted on their fathers' shoulders, some held cones of gelato that ran over their fingers, and others called out to find lost relatives. The environment was festive, peaceful mayhem.

With a clear line of sight to the stage, Father Pasquale and Ishmael stood at the periphery of the outdoor stadium. The white-haired priest had had time to process the morning's events.

"So what language was that? It sounded ancient, like Phoenician or..." Although Pasquale was a polyglot, and his prowess for languages extensive, he could not place it.

"Enochian," Ishmael spoke directly.

Pasquale stopped mid-step and turned to look at the young prodigy.

"How? What did she say?"

He noticed Ishmael's countenance change.

"You are compromised."

"She... uhh..." the boy stammered.

"Look, my son, if you have sin to confess, do so in the name of Jesus. Do not give the enemy a foothold."

"It may be too late for that, Father." He paused to witness the players assembling on the stage. "She called me out. I... uhh... I've been involved with a woman back in Assisi. She and I..."

"Did you have sexual relations with her?" he asked plainly.

"Yes, but... uhh... not just with her. I engaged in relations with a few of her friends as well. I think... uhh... I think I was drugged. I couldn't remember what happened until this morning."

"I urge you to stay away from this woman. She is leading you down a path of destruction."

"I know, Father." His words betrayed his true intentions. "But I might be in love with her."

"My son, engaging in fornication is a mortal sin. You should have told me before the exorcism. You must repent and return to the Lord."

"How did she know? How did the demon know?"

"Although not omnipresent nor omniscient, evil spirits have the ability to transcend time and space, to access occultic knowledge. These beings are above us, my boy; their intellects are vastly superior. And they are insulted to bow to us. They hate God for His intimacy with what they view as lesser beings. And there is truth to their claim. We are less intelligent and weaker. So, to them, we are a violation of the holy order. And my instincts tell me this was not a case of possession but rather of astral projection. The coven was trying to draw you out!"

The crowd began to settle in their seats as the players took the stage.

"Astral projection? What is that?"

"Our spirits exist inside of our bodies, but the evil realm has developed the ability to leave their bodies—to astral project into another person. In fact, the lore of the witch riding the broom comes from this ability... They 'leave' their bodies connected by a silver cord, and if severed, they die. But a high-ranking warlock or witch may stay outside their body for an extended period." He looked around.

"Wow." Ishmael couldn't believe it.

"This means that they know you are here."

"Then shouldn't we leave right away?" Ishmael felt the cold chill he had felt at the cottage of the possessed girl.

"There are a lot of people... The church is fortified, and we are guaranteed a full escort in the morning. I think we'll be okay."

Ishmael was not consoled. "How does one keep the demons off, Father?"

Joining the crowd, Pasquale applauded as the actors entered the stage. "In Galatians, Paul tells us, 'To walk by the Spirit, and (we) will not gratify the desires of the flesh.' If we stay in the Word of God, open to His Spirit, pondering His presence, contemplating His desires, leaning not on our own understanding, acknowledging Him in all our ways—He will make our paths straight."

"That is a tall order, Father. Who can do that?"

"We all falter. We all sin. God does not expect perfection, my son. However, that is not to say we should justify our sin either, flippantly disregarding its gravity. And you, of all people, must be more vigilant than others. You are integral to their plans. A door has been opened, my son. And they will not stop until they have you and your abilities!"

"Honestly, Father, I think a door was opened a long time ago."

Chapter 30 - Assisi, Italy

"Watch out for false prophets. They come to you in sheep's clothing, but inwardly they are ferocious wolves." - Matthew 7:15

arge cathedral-stained glass windows lit the expansive studio. The vaulted ceilings were covered in arch-shaped rafters. The books on the wall-mounted shelves had been methodically categorized according to their subject matter. Saint Thomas Aquinas' portrait was framed on the wall behind his enormous cherry-stained mahogany desk. He sat in full clerical attire, with a large golden pectoral cross dangling from his chest.

Rodrigo stood in the doorframe. "Permesso, Your Excellency?"

The cardinal looked up over metallic lorgnettes. "Sì, sì. Entri. Entri." The cardinal's pronunciation of the rolled Italian *r* suffered from his Hamburg upbringing. His attention returned to the budgetary orders *du jour*. "What can I do for you?"

"I have some sensitive information."

The cardinal laid his plume down and looked up at the Spaniard. "Yes?"

"They know he is here."

The cardinal stared pensively at the moreno-eyed priest. "And what makes you say that?"

"He was assaulted in town yesterday."

The cardinal stood up and approached the young priest. "Have you told anyone else?"

"No. I came to you immediately."

"I see. We must make sure that he is protected at all costs. I know it may be hard on the boy, but perhaps we should consider another transfer. Let me make a call. We will determine what is the most prudent course of action."

The Spaniard nodded submissively, then took his leave.

The cardinal traversed his Turkish carpet to his desk and picked up the phone. "Patch me through to His Excellency."

"Yes?"

"We have a problem."

Chapter 31 - Oberammergau, Germany

"Thou shalt not murder." - Exodus 20:13

leverly absconded to the terrace of the *Hotel Alte*. He was unobtrusively perched, skillfully hidden from view by an assortment of industrial containers and architectural protrusions. The Calabrese, still donning the attire of the hotel staff, leveled his Beretta BM 62 .308 caliber semi-automatic rifle. The crosshairs of the one-hundred-meter scope meandered their way through the patrons. His balance was exquisite, his nerves unremitting, his aim steady, his devotion to the cause unwavering—he was the assassin's assassin. He had killed hundreds of men and children. His military expertise had been called upon once again to this 'unholy' cause.

He checked the periphery for law enforcement. On any other occasion, the police force of Oberammergau ranged in number from thirteen to twenty officers. During the *PassionSspiele*, deployments of another one hundred officers were warranted to accommodate the ever-increasing crowds. He took the suppressor that he had fashioned himself and slowly, methodically screwed it to the muzzle. He looked once again through the scope; his team was in place. He checked his watch. It was nearly time—seven more minutes. The actors were about to take the stage.

Ishmael and Pasquale applauded as the actors took their marks. The stage lights were dimmed, and silence fell across the eager onlookers. A single beam cascaded over the audience toward center stage, revealing a baby in a manger. An angelic-looking female player with long blond hair advanced toward the front of the stage to deliver a soliloquy. The beam of light followed her white robe. Pasquale and Ishmael stood from afar, awaiting the delivery. Her tone reflected her demeanor—jovial yet didactic. Although Ishmael could not understand the words themselves, he emoted their intensity, their crescendo. Pasquale leaned over, ready to deliver a concurrent translation in Ishmael's ear. She began, *"In jenen Tagen erließ Cäsar Augustus ein Dekret..."*

BOOM!

Suddenly, the stage under her feet rose in an explosion, severing her body and spraying the audience in fire and fleshly fragments. Blood and wooden particles fell from the sky. Hundreds of people were killed instantaneously, others maimed. Loud screams of horror rocked the remnants of the outdoor stadium. The injured scrambled in all directions, crawling listlessly in disbelief and shock to recover missing appendages and missing relatives. It was pandemonium.

The Calabrese took his mark and fired a single shot to Pasquale's temple, causing his head to explode all over Ishmael's person. The priest's flesh sprayed his red hair in blood. He crouched, scanning the horizon for the sniper. Medical staff descended upon the people. In the mayhem, no one noticed the two men dressed in police uniforms approaching Ishmael.

He felt a cold poke in his ribs and a hand under his bicep, holding it forcibly. He looked up. The officer held a suppressed pistol to his ribcage.

"Come with us!" he said threateningly.

Ishmael stood up, surveying his surroundings, weighing his options.

"Don't even think about it!" he insisted.

They marched him through the horrific screams and scattered children into a police van in a nondescript parking lot. One of the assailants slid open the door while the other pushed him toward

the back of the van. He leaned over as if complying, but he knew they needed him alive. He braced himself with his hands and expelled a kick to the abdomen of the gun-wielding assailant. The officer shot back in a fit of desperation and pain. The other officer countered by forcing his weight toward the windowless interior of the van.

Ishmael pivoted on his axis, elbowing the assailant in the face. Now Ishmael was in full fighting stance. He pursued the recoiling man, striking him sharply with three successive alternating crosses to the same location—his nose. The man cried out in pain, grasping at his wound. The other officer searched the ground for his firearm.

He could have taken them both but deferred. He swiveled to look for an escape. Across the way, a man had just ascended atop a red 900 Ducati SS.

He bum-rushed the lad, knocking his body and helmet askew. He picked up the bike, quickly grabbed the helmet, and revved the engine. The bike fishtailed, casting pebbles at his pursuers. He flew down the gravel-ridden path south toward the Italian border.

Passing Innsbruck and the intermittent swaths of verge that divided the tiny alpine villages, the motorcycle weaved its way through the southern Bavarian plains, crossing the creeks and rivers that fell from the Dolomites. Sporadically, the roar of the Italian motorcycle could be heard reverberating in the tunnels that burrowed their way through the sun-eclipsed mountainsides.

In less violent times, his mind might have rested serenely with the pondering of the evergreen pastures. These were not peaceful times.

His bike began to shake as he approached one hundred and ninety kilometers an hour. His mind returned to the possessed girl. *What did she say? Two would die...*

His mind passed into the metaphysical. *Gebofal... symbols... angels descending and ascending... death... an old woman chanting... crowds yelling... a sacrifice... someone would be sacrificed...*

In *the spirit, he floated high above the streetlights, looking down on Assisi... he felt conflict, fighting... he sensed a dark presence... someone was going to die! ... a familiar face...*

RODRIGO!

He pushed the bike even harder.

Chapter 32 - Assisi, Italy

"Every tree that does not bear good fruit is cut down and thrown into the fire." - Matthew 7:19

he Ducati climbed the cobblestone hilltop path. Ishmael had arrived at dusk. The seven-hour trek from Bavaria he had made in five. He knew exactly where to find the priest. He wasted no time. He turned onto *Via San Francesco* toward downtown.

Rodrigo looked at his watch. He had less than a half hour to meet Cardinal Müller at the *Torre del Popolo*. Disguising his allegiances to the Church, he dressed in secular clothing. He walked swiftly through the main *piazza* to the entrance of the tower. After providing his ticket to the attendant, Rodrigo made the one-hundred-meter ascent up the staircase to the viewing platform at the top of the bell tower. He looked at his watch again. *There must be* something wrong; the cardinal was never late, he thought to himself.

Rodrigo headed to the staircase to leave when an ominous figure dressed in black leather appeared.

"I come on behalf of the priest," he spoke from beneath a shielded helmet. "I have a message for you."

"Ah, sì?"

He ran directly for the young Spaniard. Corralling him around the waist, tumbling over the railing, they toppled one hundred meters, violently crashing to the stone street below.

Ishmael arrived in time to witness the pair fall headlong from the tower. He quickly discarded the bike and ran to his mentor and friend. Ever so delicately, he comforted the priest. Rodrigo coughed up blood, spewing crimson onto his chin and chest.

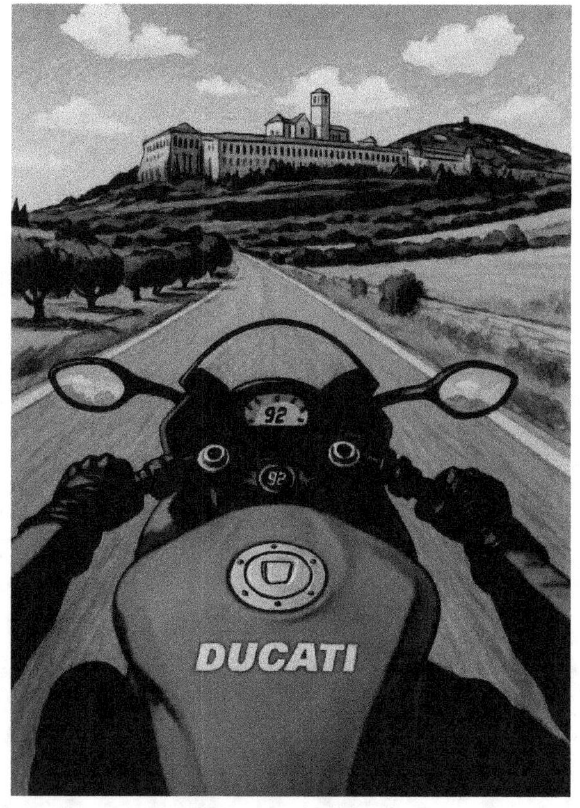

"You must get out of here! You are in danger. It was..." His gurgling was interrupted. His visage grew grey. He was gone.

Ishmael bowed his head, put his hand on his face, and began to pray. His prayer was cut short as the dark figure who had pushed the priest off the tower sprang up, uninjured.

How could...? Ishmael thought to himself.

The killer gathered himself and scurried to the end of the street, revealing a motorcycle hidden behind a rusted bin. Furious, Ishmael jumped on his Ducati and weaved his way through the curious onlookers. Precisely at that moment, the local *carabinieri,* sirens ablaze, rounded the corner, momentarily witnessing Ishmael as he fled the scene. They gave chase.

Both cycles tore up the tiny medieval streets, skidding around corners and taking flight on the inclinations. With the police cars in tow, the riders descended the hilltop town for the surrounding farmlands. Ishmael pushed his bike to the hilt, accelerating in the straights and slowing at the bends. He gained on his foe.

The black rider rounded the bend at *Via della Madonna* dell'Olivo, slowing profusely to navigate the three-hundred-degree turn. Ishmael took to the interior, flanking the black rider. Extending his leg, he kicked at the rear fender, causing the bike to teeter into the retaining wall. Separating from his cycle, the killer was catapulted into the treetops below. The bike flipped and contorted violently down the road, crashing into a parked car.

Ishmael got off the Ducati, ran to the precipice, and peered down into the silhouette of trees. The figure got up unscathed and ran into the obscurity of the night. Ishmael was baffled.

Sirens approached. Ishmael took his cue, evading the carabinieri narrowly by jumping over a fence into an olive grove. He circled back around and headed toward the only safe place he could think of…

Ishmael was used to danger. It was his normal, his homeostasis. He had no choice. It was either escape or die. Death was his unremitting passenger, the bane of his existence.

He could hear sirens dissipating behind him. It was as if his motorcycle was steering him toward an inalterable destiny. He shut off the lights on the Ducati and clandestinely meandered his way through the patches of meticulously pruned trees. His bike skidded along the uneven ground.

Ishmael traveled along the side of the quaint villa toward a storage shed. He quickly calculated the length of the shed and the distance between the side wall and the open door. He revved his engine and slammed on the brakes. Several pruning tools and hoses slowed down his forward trajectory; he stopped in time to avoid moving through the structure.

Ishmael jumped from his bike, now hidden in the shed, and crept toward the back of the villa. He peered through the window and knocked on the door.

Please be home! he thought to himself.

Sofia appeared, wearing a powder blue dress and matching lace kerchief that framed the puzzled expression on her face.

Sofia abruptly opened the back door. "Ishmael, what's going on?" She noticed dried blood on his face, neck, hair, and clothes. "Are you hurt?"

"You have to help me! I'm being chased by the police!" he pleaded.

"Come in. Hurry!" Sofia exclaimed. She shut the door behind him and closed the curtains. "Tell me what happened."

"Father Rodrigo was murdered, and the police think I'm responsible for his death!"

"What?! Why would they think that?"

"Because I fled the scene. I chased the actual killer, but he escaped. Before he died, Rodrigo told me I was in danger. I don't trust the police. I don't trust anyone... but you."

A loud knock on the front door interrupted their conversation.

She lowered her voice. "Ishmael, hide in the linen closet!"

Ishmael slipped inside the spacious closet and crouched behind a stack of neatly folded blankets.

Sofia nonchalantly walked toward the entrance and opened the door. Two Carabinieri officers stood on her porch in black and red uniforms with a white bandolier across their jackets. Their hats bore the *fiamma* insignia.

"*Buona sera*, officers. How may I help you?" she asked sweetly.

The tall officer with a bushy mustache spoke first. "*Buona sera, signorina.* There is a dangerous suspect in the area. Have you seen any unusual activity?"

"No, officer. I haven't seen anything suspicious."

The shorter officer with a large nose added, "The suspect is a tall male with a medium build and reddish hair. If you see the suspect, do not approach him. Contact us at this number immediately." He handed her a card.

The tall officer added, "We would like to check your property just to be sure."

"*Sì, naturalmente. Grazie,*" Sofia responded, hoping Ishmael did not leave behind any tracks.

From the windows of the villa, Sofia could see the Carabinieri moving back and forth through her front and backyard, shining a flashlight. Sofia exhaled in relief when they finally left.

Sofia opened the door of the closet. "Ishmael, they're gone. You're going to have to hide out for a while. But first, you need a shower."

Sofia led Ishmael to her master bathroom, which resembled an ancient Roman bath. A large soaking tub was surrounded by stone columns that connected to an arched ceiling with a sunroof.

The floor was covered with mosaic tiles in muted earth tones. Beyond the vanity and adjoining water closet, there stood a recessed shower enclosure.

She opened the shower door and turned the chrome knob until steam filled the room. Sofia turned to Ishmael and began to undress him. The blood-soaked, sweat-covered clothing clung to his body. She pulled off his clothes and threw them in a pile on the tile floor. When he was naked, Sofia began taking off her dress and kerchief.

She looked deep into his sorrow-filled eyes and said, "I want to wash you, baby."

Enveloped in the warmth of the water, Sofia slowly ran her soapy fingers over Ishmael's taut body and gently scrubbed his hair. He closed his eyes and enjoyed the sensation of Sofia's soothing touch. The tension of the past few days began to leave his body.

Ishmael felt his arousal begin to grow. He kissed her deeply until their tongues were entwined. Sofia turned her back to Ishmael and leaned against the shower wall. She bent over slightly so he could enter her. Ishmael stood behind Sofia and slowly slid inside. They both cried out in pleasure as he rhythmically moved forward and back, not faster but deeper with each stroke. Ishmael finally poured himself into her and then held her body tightly, wanting to remain inside.

"We'd better get out before we use all the hot water," Sofia said with a laugh and turned it off.

Sofia dried Ishmael off with a big fluffy beige towel. "Are you hungry? I could make you something to eat."

Ishmael was exhausted. "No, I just want to lie down."

Ishmael and Sofia slipped under the covers in her bedroom and held each other's warm, naked bodies in the dark. Before drifting off to sleep, Ishmael wanted to say, "I love you," but he resisted.

Chapter 33 - Assisi, Italy

"A house divided against itself cannot stand." - Mark 3:25

shmael awoke to confusion. Something was dawning—something evil. His sleep had been riddled with contradictory voices and scattered images of blood. Peace had eluded him; it had always eluded him. Night tremors and dreams of blood were the norm. He awoke unsure of his surroundings.

Sofia poked her head in the doorframe. "Coffee?"

"Yes, please." Ishmael rubbed his eyes and hit the floor. He planked his body against Sofia's bed and pushed out three sets of seventy push-ups each. He took a quick shower, then threw over his shoulder a *zaino* of some clothes and toiletries that Sofia had expediently packed for him. He made his way to the kitchen to find Sofia, Ewan, and Cecilia.

"We need to go straight away..." Ewan ventured impatiently in a Scottish brogue. He peeked his head out the door, surveying the surroundings for law enforcement. "I suspect the *polizia* will circle back." He went into the garage and then returned with a black Jaguar XJ6.

Sofia shoved a mug of coffee in Ishmael's face. "Here, drink. We gotta go."

He gulped it down, then climbed in the back with Sofia. They drove south to Rome.

The two-hour trip to Rome was devoid of conversation. Ishmael held Sofia's hand and pondered the Italian countryside and his future.

Raccordo Salario Settebagni is one of twelve major arteries accessing the "Roman Ring," a wagon wheel of *autostrade* surrounding the City of Seven Hills. The Jaguar approached the Ring.

"There is traffic ahead," Ewan broke the silence. He leaned his head out the window to see beyond the cars. "Looks like a checkpoint." He turned around to face Sofia. "And they have air support."

"How many?" Sofia inquired.

"Eight to ten," he responded.

"Proceed according to plan," she said with unexpected authority.

Ewan pulled a mobile radio from the dashboard and spoke in fluent Italian. *"Resta indietro finché non avremo bisogno di voi."* The Scot cradled the mobile phone and put his hand inside his breast pocket, which then let out an audible metallic *click*. Consoling, Cecilia reached over and squeezed Ewan's thigh.

Who was he talking to? Ishmael wondered.

Four Carabinieri patrol cars flanked the street—two on each side—and in an open grassy knoll sat a static Bell 206C-1 Jet Ranger III helicopter painted to the conformity of the federal police. A helmeted pilot sat at the helm. In proximity, several guards stood at attention, clutching Beretta M12 9×19mm caliber submachine guns.

The commanding officer beckoned the Jaguar forward toward a makeshift checkpoint—a superficially constructed barrier of a crossing horizontal orange and white pole.

Ewan looked at Sofia in the rearview mirror. With unsettling calm, Sofia stated flatly, *"Now!"*

Ewan punched the accelerator, igniting the V-12 engine. The tires spun wildly, kicking stone debris all over the cars in its posterior. The eyes of the guard widened as the Jaguar sped toward the retaining bar. Ishmael clutched Sofia, lowering her body into the seats.

Witnessing the approaching car, the officers yelled in unison, *"Ferma! FERMA!"* Several men leveled their machine guns and took aim at Ewan. Creating weblike configurations in the glass, the shots hit but did not penetrate. With tremendous impact and clamor, the metal pole bounced upward off the hood of the car, bending it backward awkwardly.

As the car passed, Ishmael's window was sprayed with nine-millimeter projectiles, but the window had been refitted with ballistic glass. The Jaguar sped off into the city.

Ishmael looked back. Two phantom riders in shielded helmets and black leather attire pursued aggressively. At first, Ishmael thought they were Carabinieri, but that was dispelled when one pulled a pistol from his jacket and shot one of the officers who had obstructed his path. Their twin BMW R100s quickly closed the distance.

Ewan called out on his mobile. *"Ci incontreremo al rifugio designato."*

The Carabinieri scrambled to their cars and spun around in pursuit. Ishmael could see the blades of the helicopter starting to rotate.

What had he gotten himself into? Who were these people? he thought.

Sofia's expression reflected... not fear, nor doubt, but something eerily certain—something familiar.

The Carabinieri's sirens echoed in the masonic canyons of the city. Ewan's exceptional driving skills were on display. Beads of sweat forged their way onto his forehead, and his body twisted and contorted in response to spontaneous sharp-angled corners. His progress, impeded only by groups of tourists or pedestrians crossing the street, he knew the city well.

The Jaguar turned south toward *Termini*. Ishmael looked back. The two riders had drawn their pistols, firing indiscriminately at the police. Screaming and gunshots filled the canyons of the Eternal City. Ishmael could see the discharges and hear the loud muzzle bursts from the return fire of the Carabinieri. One rider's bike exploded, violently projecting his body airborne into a kiosk.

The helicopter had bridged the distance and was now caressing the rooftops. Dusk had come, and the Jaguar was lit up with a wide-angled beam. Cecilia pulled an automatic weapon from the floorboard and began firing at the aerial threat. The helicopter stooped and swerved to avoid the oncoming fire. An amplified voice, incomprehensible to Ishmael, projected from the bird. Cecilia shot back in defiance.

Ewan turned east to the periphery of Rome. The buildings became sparse—more rural. The Jaguar sped up in the straights, distancing itself from the patrol vehicles, but the helicopter was difficult to lose.

"Si. Siamo vicini, circa cinque minuti! Siate pronti!" Ewan garbled into the mobile.

Gunshots rang out from overhead, resulting in the sound of metal clatter and linear patterns that danced across the hood and chassis of the Jaguar. Ishmael and Sofia ducked to the floor. Ishmael peeped back to the second black rider taking a bullet from above, casting his lifeless body to the cobblestone and causing his bike to topple down the street into a young couple with toddlers.

The Jaguar fishtailed into a dark hidden alley. Between two cypress trees lay a retractable metal door covered entirely in overgrown ivy. Upon approach, the door opened, revealing a clandestine subterranean garage. Ewan navigated the small space with ease. The Jaguar came to a complete stop and the door retracted behind them.

Without a word, Ewan, Cecilia, and Sofia all sprang from the vehicle. Ishmael followed. They scurried to the end of the garage and scaled a circular staircase enveloped by an antique banister. The staircase crescendoed into a large banquet hall with elaborately etched white crown molding and vaulted ceilings. The peeling rose-colored paint testified to the ancient secrets of a bygone era.

Two ruffians stood at the top of the stairs wearing clerical collars; each held an AK-47 strapped to their shoulders.

Nine police cars encircled the manor, but more were on their way. The streets

progressively filled with circling red and blue lights. The pestering helicopter still hovered in the night sky, probing the manor with a wide-angled searchlight. The beam circled the grounds, highlighting the ingress where Carabinieri combat troops began lining up, preparing for entry.

Cecilia slammed her back against the doorframe of the balcony overlooking the streets below.

Ewan opened what appeared to be a custodial closet. The doors swung open, revealing an organized arsenal of pistols, semi-automatic and automatic rifles, grenades, and ammunition of all sorts. He pulled out a Russian RPO-A Shmel and proceeded to the balcony. He stood firm, lined up his sights, and released the rocket.

The ignition system was engaged. The RPG shot out circular smoke rings from its posterior and a projectile from its muzzle. The rocket soared upwards, striking the invasive aerial craft. An explosion erupted. The helicopter spun out of control, splattering its burning remains on the Carabinieri below. The police immediately withdrew, crouching behind their vehicles.

"That ought to give them an idea of what we are capable of…" Ewan said sadistically.

Sofia looked at the two henchmen dressed as priests. "Hold them off for fifteen minutes, then follow… Don't be late, because I will trigger the system from my side." She turned to the others. "Let's go."

She walked to the bookshelves where there was a statue replica of Cleopatra. She touched her from behind, accessing a lever that released a door architecturally concealed in the wall. She held the door open for the other three to enter. "Come on. Let's go."

"No. Wait," Ishmael interrupted. "I am not going another step. What the fuck is going on? Who the fuck are you people?" He peered at Sofia.

"Honey, look, please... I know... I know it doesn't make sense, but I need you to trust me."

"Trust you? You guys just fucking murdered like... how many people?"

"For fuck's sake, we don't have time for this!" Ewan said anxiously.

"Please, just trust me, babe. I'll explain everything soon." She stared at him with her beautiful pale blues. *My God, how he loved those eyes!* He had seen so much in his life, and his passion for Sofia trumped every justification he could rationalize to leave. Begrudgingly, he stepped into the claustrophobic room, although it could be more aptly described as a shaft or compartment.

The door latched behind them. Ewan pulled a lever. Mechanical machinations could be heard squeaking, as if they had not been used in centuries. Giant cogs spun from above the crate. Then suddenly, with a jolt, gravity took over, pulling them inexorably down—past the foundations of the building, past the sewage system, and into the belly of the earth. They fell and fell and fell. The lift seemed to gain speed as the metal tracks on which it hinged screeched and howled from just outside its walls.

Was he literally going to hell? he thought to himself.

Finally, with what could only be described as pistons or shock absorbers, the crate hissed to a slow conclusion. When it stopped, Ewan returned the lever to its original position. The doors creaked open into nothingness—utter darkness.

Ewan stepped into the abyss. He could be heard fumbling in the dark. A light flickered from a torch held in his hand. He was in a cave—or perhaps a system of caves.

"Let's go." Sofia led the way. Ishmael could feel wooden planks beneath his feet.

"Where are we?" he inquired.

Sofia responded, "Years ago, the Roman principalities decided to extend the subway lines but ran into complications, setbacks... Every time they put a spade in the ground, they dug up an old relic, ancient crypt, or some God-forsaken antiquity. The archaeological societies would always get wind of it, then get the courts involved, and *presto*... no more digging. Halting progress in the name of archaeology and the preservation of the arts... So here we are—left with a system of vacant tunnels."

Sofia stepped up onto an abandoned subway platform. She looked at her watch in the dim light. She pulled a radio responder from her pocket.

"That's fifteen. I hope they're clear." She flipped the switch, igniting a massive explosion. The cave shook violently, and debris ravaged the platform from above.

"*WHAT THE FUCK WAS THAT*?" Ishmael inquired.

"I blew it up," she said flatly.

"You blew what up?"

"The house. It will take them a week to sift through the rubble."

What the fuck have I gotten myself into? he whispered under his breath.

Sensing Ishmael's doubt, she walked over to him and whispered, "Look, baby, I know you are unsure. But we are the good guys. I will answer all your questions in time. I promise. Trust me!"

At this point, he had no other choice. In fact, he wondered if he ever had.

The team walked further up the tracks to a subway car. Ewan walked to the conductor's port and switched on the terminal dashboard. It lit up. It was fully functional. The inner lighting systems flickered. Ewan hit a red button, and the doors opened. He stuck his head out the window.

"All aboard," he said with a goofy smile on his face.

Sofia smiled and looked at Ishmael and Cecilia. "Come on. Let's get the fuck out of here!"

Chapter 34 - Rome, Italy

"Ask and it will be given to you; seek and you will find; knock and the door will be opened to you." - Matthew 7:7

is hair was as pristine as ever, his grey beard groomed perfectly, his grey pinstripe suit impeccable. He stepped from a white Maserati Merak SS, donning a black overcoat and horn-rimmed lenses that balanced on the bridge of his nose. He held a small tablet of paper in one hand and a fountain pen in the other.

He approached the yellow tape surrounding the mound of burnt rubble. He gazed over the vestiges of the old manor that had stood for two hundred years. Members of the Roman forensic team swarmed the scene like ants.

His presence did not go unnoticed. He was approached by a man who introduced himself as an *investigatore*. He held out his hand, awaiting a reply from Malech.

"Buongiorno. Mi chiamo Enzo Amendola. Sono l'ispettore capo di questo caso."

Malech turned to address the voice. There before him stood a clean-shaven, stout, rotund figure wearing a brown trench coat that had been buttoned to his chin. He wore a tan herringbone cap and sported bifocals that made his eyes look lazy.

"I'm sorry, my Italian is a little rusty," Malech said patiently.

"Oh... England?"

"Close. America," he rebutted.

"Oh... I beg your pardon."

"No pardon needed."

"Do you have an interest in this building, or perhaps...?" Amendola tried to provoke an answer.

Malech sensed him probing. "My name is Harrison Knight. Interpol." Malech pulled his credentials from his breast pocket. He had the documentation to substantiate the farce.

"Hmmm... an American who works for Interpol?"

"I have dual citizenship. Mother's Belgian."

"Ah, I see..." He handed the documentation back to Malech. He could see the inquisitive nature of the Italian, scanning for cues—clues to anything untoward.

"And what makes Interpol interested in this case?"

"How many bodies have you recovered?" Ignoring his question, Malech redirected the inquiry.

Inspector Amendola conceded momentarily, turning to the ash heap. "So far, zero."

"Odd. Would they have been consumed by the fire?" Malech inquired.

"Not likely... We should have found a partial corpse or fragments." Amendola assessed his companion.

"How many perps?"

"At least six. Two died downtown. Still waiting on forensics."

"And what of the others?" Malech pressed.

The investigator leveled his eyes at Malech. "We'll know soon enough."

"Hmmm." Malech mused. "Please let me know if you have any new information." He handed Amendola his card.

"Why would I do that?"

Malech stepped to face the middle-aged Roman. "Look, I don't mean to patronize you, Inspector. But this case is bigger than you and me."

"*Che significa?* What does that mean?"

"Please contact me if you hear something." Malech turned, got in his car, and left.

Amendola looked down at the strange golden symbol on his card. *Harrison Knight?* "Hmmm."

Chapter 35 – Lago Gandolfo, Italy

"Woe unto them that call evil good, and good evil; that put darkness for light, and light for darkness; that put bitter for sweet, and sweet for bitter!" - Isaiah 5:20

he silk bed sheets felt cool against his skin. Their bodies were intertwined; her scent and the warmth of her body comforted him. His feelings for her had grown more than he was willing to admit. She was so familiar, their relationship so natural. Ishmael had been hesitant to let himself fall completely in love with her. He felt guilty for having drawn her into his life. *Yet was it he who had attracted her, or was it she who had enveloped him?* Or *perhaps something else—perhaps something hidden, something...?* He didn't know. To ensure her safety, he would do anything, including keeping his affection at bay. He wouldn't commit himself completely. It would be a death sentence for both of them. He couldn't bear to lose her. He wouldn't lose her—*not this one*!

He couldn't recall how he had arrived. In fact, his memories and dreams were so often fused with reality that his consciousness had become warped, convoluted; he had come to accept it. He felt led to an inalterable destination, as if his life were some holy (or perhaps unholy) hijacked hologram.

He lifted his groggy head to observe his surroundings. His movement stirred Sofia. She rolled onto her back and stretched her elegant limbs to the sky.

"Are you okay, Hon?" Her first thought was for his well-being.

"Where are we?"

"The palazzo." She sat up and threw back the cream-colored translucent blinds on the king-sized canopy bed.

"Whose palazzo?" he mused.

"Ours."

She threw a white robe around her beautiful, firm body and then freed her long auburn hair, letting it cascade down the back of the robe.

"Come on. Get up. We have a lot to do." She went into the bathroom.

Ishmael sat up in bed and assessed his surroundings. The size of the canopy bed was expansive, harboring a mattress three times larger than any conventional mattress. The rectangular room was also extensive. It was sparsely decorated with an antique thirteenth-century armoire, end tables, and a framed picture of a nondescript man in Catholic garments.

He rose and walked to the end of the room where the walls gave way to two French-hinged swinging doors accessing an outdoor balcony. The balcony was enveloped by balustrade-masoned columns and flanked by two statues, one of Pan and the other, Venus. The view was incredible. The ancestral palace stood at the apex of the hill with no obstructions on either side. On one side lay the patchwork of fields disappearing toward the coast of Ostia, and on the other, *Lago Gandolfo*—one of three volcanic lakes southeast of Rome. Far below, the *caldera* contained vibrant blue waters surrounded by impressive chestnut and holm oak trees.

The palazzo was accessed by a long, serpentine cobblestoned *sentiero* that slithered its way up the mountainside. Interspersed between the switchbacks lay methodically shaved hedges and mathematically planted cypress trees—landscaping befitting the Sun King. An ominous black car wound its way up the verdant Alban hill toward the residence. The Mercedes-Benz 600 SW limousine was equipped with two red, green, and gold diplomatic flags on its bonnet. Upon reaching the landing, two large Black men sprang from the front seats and opened the posterior doors for a woman wearing traditional African attire and a regal-looking Black man donning a tan-colored suit. They climbed the marble staircase and then subsequently disappeared into the house.

"Isn't the view amazing?" She startled him. Still wearing the robe, her hair was wrapped tightly on her head in a wet towel.

"Incredible."

"I'm starving! Let's go to the dining room. They should have breakfast ready."

They made their way down two flights of white Carrara marble stairs—past the gym, past the library, past an atrium, past the game room, past several closed doors, through a long hallway, and finally into a dining room that could potentially seat a hundred people comfortably.

Encased in white crown molding, the ceilings reigned high above. The walls of the dining hall held didactic paintings of the Garden of Eden, Noah, Daniel, and the early prophets of the Bible. Ishmael recognized the narratives from his studies with Scaramucci. The artistry rivaled the Renaissance frescoes painted by Michelangelo. One wall faced Rome and stood ten meters high, encased entirely in glass. If it were not for the scattered staff and the elaborate buffet, Ishmael might have thought he were in a museum—or a church.

Near a large television, Ewan and Cecilia sat anxiously at a circular side table, sipping espressos and sifting through a three-tiered pastry tray.

"Wow, here with all that effort to get you out alive, we thought you had died in your sleep," Ewan cracked.

"Why, what time is it?" Ishmael quipped. Sofia handed him a cappuccino and then lightly kissed his cheek. The steam wafted upward from the porcelain coffee mug.

"It is almost noon, Romeo," he said sarcastically.

"Give him a break!" Cecilia chastised her boyfriend. "I'm sure he needed it. He probably hasn't slept like that for months. Huh? *Ish?*" He leveled his gaze at the petite blonde. No one had addressed him as "Ish" since his mother was alive. Briefly, he imagined her face; a sense of melancholy swept over him.

"You alright?" Sofia returned with a tray of *cornetti.*

"Yeah, sure."

The kitchen staff came in carrying more foodstuffs for the buffet. Ishmael took a sip of the coffee. The coffee was amazing; the croissants were spectacular too.

"This is amazing food. And this coffee—I have never had coffee this rich. How do you do it?"

Ewan smiled at Cecilia and Sofia. "Let's just say... we have some influential friends." He paused to take a loud slurp of his espresso. "Get used to it, my friend..." he said ominously.

Their conversation was interrupted by the African couple Ishmael had previously observed entering the residence. She wore an ornate teal one-piece Dashiki gown, embroidered with intricate gold symbols along the sleeves, hem, and nape, and a matching headdress made from the same fabric. Her smooth skin was bare at the shoulders. Her neck and wrists were wrapped in golden bracelets. Her spouse wore a tan-colored three-piece suit with a headdress and pocket handkerchief that matched his wife's attire. Around his neck swung a gold amulet with a large cream-colored oval stone at its center.

They were accompanied by an elegant woman wearing a dress that was almost regal. Her gown was made from a single cut of fabric, dark—black as the night sky—but set off by glimmers of light that reflected from the tiny sequins that had been meticulously sewn into its lining. Her shoulders were also bare, and diamonds glistened from her ears and fingers.

"Good day."

Sofia stood up, holding out her hand in an ingratiating gesture. "Ishmael, this is Doctor Embata and his wife, Josephine."

Ishmael stood up and became immediately self-conscious. "It is nice to meet you."

"It is nice to finally meet you, Ishmael," Doctor Embata spoke with a strong African accent. He extended his hand confidently.

"Yes, my dear. It is a pleasure," his wife, Josephine, joined in concert.

"Wow. It is a bit strange that everyone knows my name," he said, partially to them and partially to himself.

"Don't worry, my dear. You are in good company," Josephine rebutted.

"And what company is that?" Ishmael pressed.

Sofia put her hand on his shoulder to comfort him. "We are friends, we are on your side."

"You must have a lot of questions," the black-gowned woman stated intuitively.

"I do. And who are you?"

Sofia stepped in. "Ishmael, this is the Lady of the House..."

She interrupted Sofia and then extended her hand, inviting him to reciprocate. He took her hand.

He was thrown into the metaphysical... *Gebofal... symbols... pain... the* Grigori... *pain... blood... the dream was unfolding... things were about to change forever... past, present, future... they were all one... what had he done?*

"Are you okay?" Sofia had noticed the change in his countenance.

"Yeah... uh... sorry. Still tired, I guess."

"Well, rest up for our banquet tonight, Ishmael," said Lily. "We have some very special guests attending." She smiled and stared at him with pale blue eyes like Sofia's, except they lacked warmth.

"Don't worry. We'll be ready."

It was as though he had switched lives with someone else. Ishmael was surrounded by strangers that seemed to know him intimately. The anchors of his life at the monastery had fallen away, into an unfathomable abyss. Pasquale had been assassinated. Rodrigo was dead. Scaramucci's fate was unknown. He had no idea where he was headed or what he would find ahead. The only constant was Sofia.

Chapter 36 - Rome, Italy

"If the avenger of blood comes in pursuit, the elders must not surrender the fugitive, because the fugitive killed their neighbor unintentionally and without malice aforethought." - Joshua 20:5

e leaned into the receiver. *"Pronto?"*

"Hello?" Malech picked up the line.

"Yeah, this is *Ispettore* Amendola. There are some new developments, but before I tell you, I want your assurance that this will be a collaborative effort... that we are together on this. Do you understand me?"

"I am doing you a favor, Inspector. Interpol has jurisdiction here. Legally, I do not have to divulge anything to you. I am just doing you a courtesy."

"S*to cazzo*! Ey, you listen to me! My friend was shot in the chest! HE IS IN A COMA! I had to tell his two little girls that their *pappa'* might not come home! SO DON'T TELL ME ABOUT JURISDICTION! I want these *stronzi*, and I will not stop until they are in prison for life! *Hai capito?*"

"I don't think you know what you are asking, Inspector," Malech stated without emotion.

"I will determine that!"

"Very well. Do you know where *L'Osteria della Pelle d'Oca* is?"

"*Si.*"

"Meet me there. I'll buy you dinner."

Chapter 37 – Lago Gandolfo, Italy

"Be strong and courageous. Do not be afraid or terrified because of them, for the LORD your God goes with you; he will never leave you nor forsake you." - Deuteronomy 31:6

arading up the snake-like path, the guests arrived in newly polished cars. Elegantly dressed chauffeurs jumped to open the hind doors of Ferraris, Maseratis, Lamborghinis, Rolls-Royces, Porsches, Mercedes, and BMWs. One by one, the couples scaled the tapered staircase to the entrance of the manor. They stepped into the foyer, a cathedral-like ingress with vaulted ceilings, Palladian rectangular windows, and large cascading drapery. Embedded in the white marble floor lay a depiction of a black tree with roots shaped in a mirrored facsimile. Ensconced between the two trees were four Latin words: *Sic Supra, Sic Infra.*

The door rang for the sixteenth time. A couple, adhering to the mandatory dress code, was beckoned in by diplomatic staff. The male guest wore a black tuxedo with a white shirt and matching bowtie, and she, a black satin gown that hugged her waist and flared at her hips. Rhythmic percussion and a cacophony of conversations combined to form deep frequencies that resonated throughout the inner sanctums of the house. The guests frequented the enormous vacuous rooms as the staff ran to and fro, appealing to any and every whim of their affluent, demanding clientele.

The banquet hall had been completely transformed. Dark red roses were suspended from the ceiling in black iron mesh containers. Ivory silk fabric was draped along the walls. A sweet sage aroma flowed from black candles resting on elongated metal sconces. The dining room table was covered in crisp white tablecloths, on which colorful Italian-crafted plates rested with a folded napkin on top. Delicate floral centerpieces adorned the length of the table, surrounded by crystal wine goblets. Through the glass panes, the sunset cast its orange glow—a golden sunset for this new iteration of The Golden Dawn.

Ishmael stood awkwardly in a black tuxedo and a white shirt and tie that had entirely too much starch in it. The suit was on loan from... he didn't know.

"You look so handsome," she said coyly, attempting to comfort him. Her hand rested beneath his arm. His body language had betrayed his sentiment.

"What is it, babe?"

"I... uhh... not feeling like it." He took a sip of champagne and shook his head. "You look great though."

Sofia looked elegant in a low-cut black sequin gown with a high slit on the left side and a flower appliqué over the opposite shoulder.

In sashayed the Lady of the House, dressed magnificently in a black gown with a train that dragged along the floor behind her. Her bare arms and shoulders revealed cryptic red symbols tattooed into her tanned skin. She was accompanied by identical twin escorts of imposing, contrary stature. Each wore a traditional sherwani, one white and one black. The short-haired twin on the left was clean-shaven and muscular; his unequivocal demeanor reflected a military background. His long-haired, Rasputin-looking brother wore a scraggly black beard and appeared to possess more brain than brawn.

Ewan rushed to the twin in black and gave him a bear hug. "My brother! It's great to see you!"

The Lady motioned for Sofia and Ishmael to join them. She addressed the twins, "I would like to introduce one of our special guests," pointing first to the twin in black. "Ishmael, this is Kabir and Samir. They are my friends and advisors."

"Nice to meet you," Ishmael replied.

Samir bowed deeply, and Kabir merely nodded in his direction.

A frail elderly woman with deep brown crevices etched into her face was carried into the dining room on a wingback chair. Her skeletal-like hands were perched atop two spheres protruding from the arms of the chair. The wings attached to the chair's posterior folded upward like the cherubim on the Ark of the Covenant. Her red blood dress and headdress lay in stark contrast to the black-and-white clad guests. She was positioned at the head of the table.

Ishmael glanced in her direction, then whispered in Sofia's ear, "Who is that?"

"That's Nonna. She's the head of our family, head of our Order. I'll introduce you later."

"I would like you all to adjourn to the dining room, where our internationally acclaimed chefs have prepared a meal for your pleasure." The Lady's pronouncement shot out above the fray. She raised her hand and gestured to the dining room.

The *antipasti* was served after all the guests were seated—an assortment of salumi, cheese, and olives. The first course, or *primo*, consisted of large platters of mushroom risotto placed amongst each grouping of celebrants. Ishmael instantly thought of his mentor Scaramucci and smiled to himself. A delicious garlic and herb stuffed porchetta followed as the main course. Since he was feeling full, Ishmael was relieved to find a salad placed in front of him as the *contorno*. A selection of *dolci* and espresso rounded out the banquet.

After such a generous meal and copious pours of wine, Ishmael just wanted to head upstairs to be alone with Sofia. He doubted that would happen, since she seemed to be enjoying herself.

Following three courses, three hours of conversation, and a lot of pomp and circumstance, the dinner came to a conclusion. The crowd began to dissipate into adjoining rooms. Sofia took Ishmael by the arm and guided him through the walkway into a large bedroom with a balcony.

Ishmael witnessed a couple pass a large goblet to another couple in their room. The familiar movements triggered a memory for Ishmael. He knew what would happen next. The couples began to undress. The women moved toward each other, and then the men began to kiss and explore their bodies. Ishmael wanted to look away, but he was enticed by the debauched scene. Sofia looked longingly at Ishmael, and he shook his head.

The couple decided to head back in the opposite direction. They passed a group of revelers gathered around a coffee table in a fireside lounge. A tall and handsome man with black hair sat on a sectional couch with his legs apart, leaning over the table. He cut a mound of white powder into individual lines along the surface, then used a shortened straw to inhale a line into a nostril and handed the straw to the attractive woman seated next to him on the couch. Ishmael kept moving and Sofia followed.

Nonna still remained in the hall. Sofia walked toward the old woman with Ishmael in tow. Sofia took her hand.

"Nonna, this is my friend Ishmael. He's a guest of ours."

Nonna replied after carefully looking him over, "Ishmael. Yes, I know about you."

"What do you... know?" he stammered.

"That you are one of us," the old woman stated matter-of-factly.

Ishmael looked startled. Sofia interjected, "We have to go now, Nonna." She kissed her on the cheek and pulled Ishmael in the opposite direction.

"What did she mean by that?" Ishmael demanded.

Sofia skirted his question. "Come on! Let's go outside. No one knows this, but there is a secret exit. Follow me."

They meandered through the mansion. She led him to the end of the hall, to a false floorboard that opened to a hidden staircase which, in turn, led them into a long tunnel. The wooden support beams gradually dissipated into the organic rock foundation on which the manor was built. Ishmael passively noticed other inlets—or perhaps outlets—that led into the core. He wondered where they might lead.

The couple emerged into a grassy clearing, and to a white gazebo bathed in the light of the full moon.

Ishmael let go of her hand. "Stop. Stop! Can we stop with the foreplay? I need some answers, or I am out of here!" he said in exasperation.

"What do you want to know?"

"Who *are* you? And who are these people?"

"These are my family and friends."

"More than family."

"We are dedicated to a cause."

"What cause?"

"Enlightenment."

"STOP WITH THE BULLSHIT?! Just tell me in simple terms!"

"We are a group of people searching for truth, Ishmael."

"What truth? Whose truth? Stop fucking dancing and tell me!"

"We are dedicated to freedom and self-expression. We are in search of knowledge—knowledge that has been designated by certain groups as forbidden, immoral."

"What knowledge?"

"Hidden knowledge. Some people call it 'occult' knowledge."

He remembered his discussions with Scaramucci. "Dee." He looked out over the caldera and then quietly murmured to himself, "Black magic."

"*White* magic, my dear! We are an extension of several schools of thought such as the Hollow Earth Society, Rosicrucianism, Jewish Kabbalah, and Freemasonry... We are the originals; we are *The Enlightened Golden Dawn.* Our movement is founded on Edward Kelly, Aleister Crowley, MacGregor Mathers, Anton LaVey, Hermes Trismegistus, and many, many others... and *yes*, Doctor John Dee. Their magnificent work in alchemy and the hermetic arts has given us knowledge passed down from..." She paused, concerned about Ishmael's reaction. "Angels." She stopped abruptly and gazed deep into his hazel eyes.

"You mean *demons*," he stated flatly.

"*Angels*. Fallen angels who have been misrepresented, misunderstood—cast out for exercising the very free will given to them."

"You follow these 'angels'? And at what cost, Sofia?" He matched her intensity.

"Hell is a myth, Ishmael—a lie from the enemy. There is nothing that is, except what we determine. As above, so below. It is up to us to create heaven or hell."

"We determine reality?"

"I mean, look around you. Does this look like hell?" She waved her hand in a sweeping motion toward the manor and surrounding olive groves. "We have the best food, the best clothes, the best cars, the best homes—everything. Don't you want the best life for you and your family? Access to the best schools for your children? Does that sound like hell to you?" She stared at Ishmael.

"Stolen wealth."

"I won't tell you that our history has been without greed or selfish ambition. But our businesses, our companies, our investments help those in need. Our hospitals give medicine to the poor. Grants for education, the homeless..."

"Great. Keep them healthy so you can enslave them... makes sense," he said sarcastically. "Beneficent companies that stack the deck in their favor and perpetuate poverty."

"Talk to Kabir. You will see... our schools give education and opportunities to orphaned children. We do a lot of good!"

Ishmael's stomach turned.

"Do you doubt that I love you?" she pleaded. He stared into her pale blue eyes. "Does love come from evil? I want nothing but good for you. I will never lie to you or hurt you."

"I believe you are sincere..." His words trailed off.

She approached him softly. The lovers kissed passionately.

At that moment, he realized that she was simply regurgitating what she had been taught. To get the answers he sought—to truly pull back the curtain—he would have to scale the ranks of the Golden Dawn.

173

Chapter 38 – Rome, Italy

"But he continued, "You are from below; I am from above. You are of this world; I am not of this world." - John 8:23

 *'Osteria della Pelle dell' Oca* was sparsely populated. Malech sat in the back at a poorly lit table with a blue and white checkered tablecloth. He poured himself a glass of house red from the Umbrian carafe shaped like a rooster. Amendola strolled in; Malech determined that the *ispettore* wanted to make a point by arriving twenty minutes late.

"Glad you made it, inspector."

"How are things at Interpol?" He tossed his hat on the chair next to him and then sat down abruptly.

"Same as always." He took a sip of his wine. "Bureaucratic." Malech motioned at the waiter behind the *banchina.* "Can we have another glass?" Then he turned his attention back to Amendola. "So, are you from Rome?"

"*Eh* sì. Born and raised."

"So, are you *Laziale* or *Romanaccio*?" Malech inquired.

"*Lazio.* My entire family bleeds blue, my friend." The inspector reached into his satchel and pulled out a file of papers that stuck out at all angles.

"So, I understand you have some new developments?"

"The ballistics report revealed that the bullets fired were of military grade. And the forensics on the explosive device confirmed military-grade C-4 or *plastique*, probably set off remotely, but no trigger system was found. The two pistols and ammunition recovered are commonly used throughout Europe by many militant factions, so it is difficult to pinpoint who might have used them."

"So, you believe these people are politically affiliated?"

"Probably a terrorist cell. The predetermined escape route and explosive device suggest sophistication, not to mention the access to RPGs and the charred arsenal recovered in the wreckage. They must have had paramilitary training and connections to some serious cash. What puzzles me is the fact that the building—or safehouse—has remained in the same hands since it was built two hundred years ago. The same proprietor, as if they had planned for this moment..." He adjusted his cap. "Centuries ago."

"Do you have a name?"

"A *Victor Samuel Lotus.* Do you know him?"

"Never heard of him."

"We found something else." Malech stared at him, waiting for him to continue. "...a shaft, *a lift*—or I guess in America, you would call it—*an elevator.*"

"Leading where?"

"Underground, into some old subway tunnels, abandoned long ago. It seems they descended into the earth, blew the tunnels behind them to slow our pursuit... My team is still digging out the debris. After that, they could have popped up anywhere in the city. My guess is, they had a rally point—also predetermined. They could be in Brazil by now."

Malech's gut told him they had not left Italy. "Can I see it?"

"See what?"

"The tunnel."

"Uhh... it is dangerous. The cave is unstable, and it could collapse at any time."

"I'll take my chances."

The scrap from the helicopter and the charred vestiges caused by the explosion had been swept from the streets. Malech stepped from his Maserati as Amendola's Carabinieri Alfa Romeo pulled up behind him. The two entered the skeleton of the house—only the foundation remained.

"The shaft is over here." The inspector walked him to the precipice of a gaping hole that disappeared into darkness. Metal construction ladders had been attached to one side of the channel. Malech noticed a chain of plastic-caged light bulbs attached to the frame of the ladder. He traced the cord, then fumbled around and flipped a switch. The lights flickered and lit the descent into the abyss.

"Let's go."

"*Come?* Uhh... Inspector Knight, I am not going..."

"Come on. What are you afraid of?"

Amendola reconsidered and followed Malech. "Falling to my death," he said under his breath.

They began the long, laborious descent. Malech could hear Amendola breathing heavily through his tar-filled lungs. Finally, the shaft ended—and it ended suddenly. He set his foot on firm ground, and the light faded to black.

"Inspector, may I borrow your lighter?"

He plopped his heavy feet to the dirt below and then sifted through his pockets. Malech lit it, then searched the surroundings. He found an old plank and a cloth buried in the dirt. He wrapped the cloth around the plank and lit it. The torchlight gave way to a cavernous expanse.

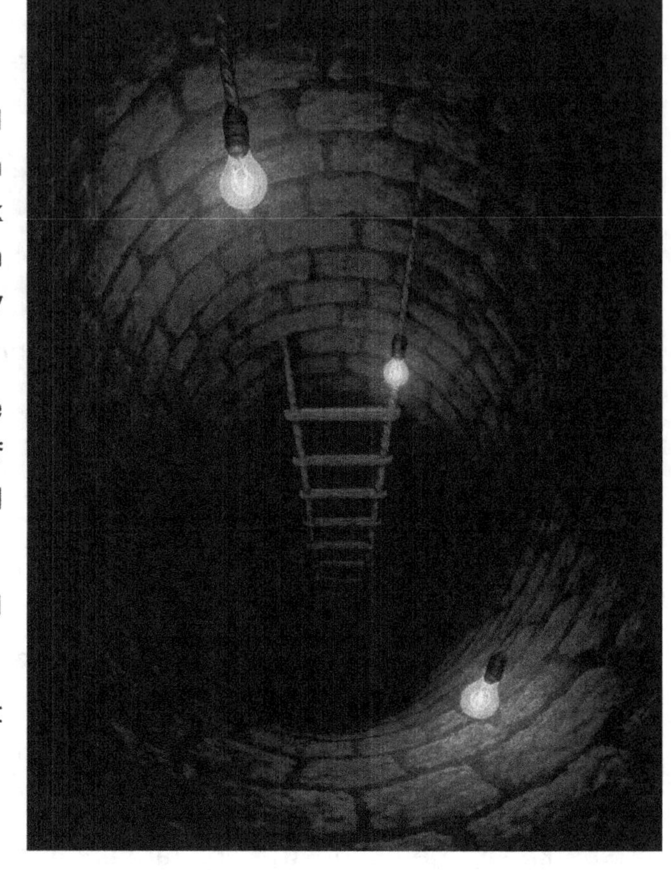

Much of the cave had collapsed, but near the tracks was a minute, tiny sparkle—a reflection of light. Malech moved toward it, bent over, and pulled the object from the dust. He blew on it.

"What is that?" Amendola inquired as he moved closer to examine its details.

"A dagger. An old one." Malech recognized it immediately.

Ishmael was in the hands of the Golden Dawn.

Chapter 39 - Mykonos, Greece

"We are from God, and whoever knows God listens to us; but whoever is not from God does not listen to us. This is how we recognize the Spirit of truth and the spirit of falsehood." - 1 John 4:6

hey had set out from Ciampino Airport two hours earlier. Ishmael looked out the window of the Blackbusche BBS jetliner. The endless blue of the Aegean Sea met the horizon. He could feel the vibration of the landing gear as they made their approach toward Mykonos.

Tourists from every corner of the world bombarded the island. The native population of Mykonos is composed of 10,700 inhabitants, but in the summer months, the number of residents and tourists would balloon to roughly 250,000. In addition to being known for its festivities and whitewashed facades, the small town of Mykonos is surrounded by private pebbled beaches, transparently clean waters, and of course, its trademark windmills. Most tourists arrived on large cruise ships. Few came by way of private jet. Ishmael and Sofia were the exception.

The jetliner flew directly over the tiny town. Ishmael peered down at the white buildings and crowds of people.

"I have never seen so many tourists in one place," he said incredulously. "I am thinking the hotels have been booked for what? Months? Years?"

Sofia laughed. "Yeah, but don't worry. We have a house here."

"Of course we do," he responded cheekily.

"Hey, listen. It's just us here, baby. No distractions. Okay?"

The couple was met by a driver in a black BMW. The distinct smell of the ocean permeated the fresh air, the humidity clearing his nostrils. He looked around the rocky landscape. The white rooftops were set off against the greenish-blue hue of the sea, parroting the colors of the ubiquitous Greek flags.

"Get in, babe. This isn't the main town. We are in the center of the island—we need to get to the coast."

He jumped in and sat stoically, gazing at scooters, quads, dune buggies, and taxis. A scooter cut off the driver, weaving in front of the car.

"Malaka!" the driver muttered under his breath as he squeezed the brake pedal.

The car spat gravel as it wound its way along the curvaceous roads en route to the small town of Mykonos. The driver halted at a three-story chalk-white apartment building. They scaled the interior staircase. Sofia pulled a T-shaped key from her pocket. With a series of rotations, she pushed on the heavy wooden door. The door swung wide to a large room with a quaint, stocked kitchen, a seating area with a dining table, and a balcony that spanned the entire length of the building.

Ishmael walked directly to the hinged glass doors, threw them open, and accessed the veranda. Two hundred degrees of the Aegean Sea lay before his eyes. The solar rays were dampened by a dark blue awning and potted gladiolus.

Sofia sifted through the copper pots that hung in the kitchen. "Do you like to cook?"

"Not much of a chef... mostly, just cook for me."

"Oh, you're in luck because I am an amazing cook! Shall we go get some groceries?"

"Absolutely. I am starving!"

She smiled.

Something about this environment—perhaps it was the fresh air, the solitude... He felt... safe, serene.

They tossed their bags on the double bed and left the flat to explore the town.

Chapter 40 - Boston, Massachusetts

"And you will know the truth, and the truth will set you free." - John 8:32

e picked up the phone on the second ring. "Yup."

"They have him," Malech whispered into the receiver.

"How do you know?"

"I found a dagger. I think he dropped it on purpose."

"Any idea where he is?"

"None. Could be anywhere."

"Let us pray on the matter. Something will turn up."

Stroking the crucifix that hung from his neck, Azikiwe hung up the phone and leaned back in his leather chair.

Chapter 41 - Mykonos, Greece

"But God demonstrates his own love for us in this: While we were still sinners, Christ died for us." – Romans 5:8

he narrow corridors of the town were congested with sojourners from the cruise ships, jewelry shops, clothing boutiques, miniatures of Greek statues, and pornographic postcards. The white-washed world of Mykonos was decadent, known for seedy bars, private sex parties, and gay beaches. Hand-in-hand, the concupiscent couple sombered through the claustrophobic alleys. Bouzouki music could be heard behind the cacophony of languages. Laughter and the scent of coconut tanning lotion saturated the air.

Perusing the shop windows, Sofia pointed to a black ceramic vase with a golden inlaid image of a couple in coitus.

"Hey, babe." She smiled suggestively.

He smiled. "If you're lucky," he said teasingly. She laughed.

They fell into a mom-and-pop grocery store, purchased a few items, and then returned to the flat. She cooked him some *pasta alle vongole* with some Retsina white wine, a local favorite. They finished the bottle, then settled in for a nap. They woke up periodically to make love. And it was different than before—tender, sensuous, and selfless.

They awoke in the late afternoon. A cool breeze came in through the cracked balcony doors. "Come on. Get dressed," she said. "We are going out to dinner, my treat."

They chose a quaint, rustic eatery with hanging vines that covered the outdoor tables. Electronic dance music could be heard from hidden monitors. They were shown a table, ordered a bottle of Retsina, and then reclined to watch the tourists fuss about the mundane.

"So, do you like Greece?" Her face was pink from their time sunbathing.

"It is amazing. I feel different here. I feel... I don't know. I feel... free."

"That is great, Ish."

He turned to her. "My mother used to call me that."

"Tell me about your parents."

He looked at the ground. "They died. Murdered. It seems to be a common thing…" His attention seemed to wander off.

"That is horrible. I am so sorry, baby. Well, I won't leave you." She scooched her chair next to his and then took his hand. "I feel connected to you. It's like we were made for each other."

"Look Sofia, I like you a lot. In fact, I don't think I've ever been attracted to anyone as much as you. But everyone who gets close to me seems to die." The blue tint of her eyes was accentuated by her sunburn. He looked at his feet. "I don't want anything to happen to you."

"Hey. Hey. Look at me." She put her fingers to his chin and lifted his gaze. "I love you. I'm not going anywhere."

"I… I…" He couldn't say it. He tried, but the words would not come out.

"Hey, don't worry about it. It's okay. When you're ready," she interrupted.

"Do they have a bathroom here?" he said, dispelling the discomfort.

"Nope. Crazy thing about the Greeks is that they don't pee. No peeing in Greece. Didn't you read the sign?"

Ishmael smiled at her sarcasm. He stood up and gestured to the head waiter, who seemed to know intuitively what he needed. He said something in Greek that Ishmael could not understand. Ishmael understood the head nod directing him toward the back of the establishment.

He finished his business and returned to the table to find three girthy Greek men getting handsy with Sofia. They had seated themselves in a half-circle, pinning her in. Her body language reflected her fear.

Foregoing the diplomatic route, Ishmael walked directly to the seated group and punched the first man in the back of the head. The man fell forward. His companions looked up in surprise and anger; they rose in unison. Ishmael struck with lightning-fast precision—two jabs to the face of the first man, and a quick downward kick to the knee of the second. The third recovered and came at him. Ishmael stepped back to make way for the other patrons, who screamed and stumbled over chairs.

The larger of the three ran at him, and in a barrel roll, collided with him, knocking them both to the floor.

"ISHMAEL!" he heard Sofia scream.

The collision propelled them into the tables, knocking food and drink everywhere. The man stood first and punched Ishmael in the face. Ishmael saw the second strike coming; he rolled over and sprang to his feet. With the full force of his body weight, he punched down, striking his chin full contact, knocking the aggressor to the ground.

The other two rallied; one came at him with a bottle, swinging it wildly. Ishmael stepped back, avoiding the sweeping motion, then tagged him with two quick jabs to the mouth. He yelled in pain and dropped the bottle, grabbing his mouth.

The third charged at him as if to tackle him, but Ishmael stood him upright with a knee to the face. He grabbed the bottle and brought it up under the assailant's chin, lifting him off the ground and crashing him down on a table. He was out cold.

The violence had hushed the crowd. The mayhem subsided as a local policeman ran into the restaurant, blowing an annoying whistle.

"Stop!" he shouted with a thick Greek accent. "Stop!"

Ishmael assessed his injuries.

"You okay?" Sofia asked.

"I think so."

She stared at him incredulously. "Wow. I didn't know you could fight like that."

"Yeah, well, there's a lot you don't know."

The police arrested Ishmael. They spent the next few hours in the police station explaining the events. The charges were dropped shortly thereafter when eyewitnesses came forward.

They returned to the flat, but even before Sofia could turn the lock, their bodies collided in passion. He pinned her against the wall and kissed her passionately. They stumbled through the door, tossing their clothes with abandon to the floor as they made their way to the bed. He had to be inside her—nothing else mattered. He pushed her aggressively to the bed; she recoiled lovingly in submission.

She had never felt so drawn to any man. She had never experienced love without lust; and he had never been willing to truly love. Their eyes were ablaze with expectation and excitement. For the first time in their lives, they were ready to give themselves without reservation. They were one—completely one. They made love all night, cuddling in between sessions.

Spent and naked, he grabbed a glass of wine and walked onto the moonlit balcony. Her soft caress came up his backside. He looked out at the water, at the moonlight and the horizon. He turned to Sofia. And for the first time in his life, he said,

"I love you."

Chapter 42 - Rome, Italy

"Woe unto them that call evil good, and good evil; that put darkness for light, and light for darkness; that put bitter for sweet, and sweet for bitter!" - Isaiah 5:20

he Mercedes picked them up at Ciampino Airport. The driver took a different route heading toward Rome.

"I thought we were going back to Gandolfo."

"Soon, but I want to show you something first," she said, holding his hand tightly. And for the first time in his life, he was willing to trust someone other than his parents.

He stared out the window... *symbols... tables... he saw a soulless crowd, lost in ecstasy... lost in blood... lost... Jabal al-Shaykh... Sofia was in danger... a foreboding feeling of torment and pain... The Watchers called to him... Gebofal...*

An hour-long trek took them through the heart of the Eternal City, past *San Giovanni*—the first Catholic church of Rome—along *Viale Regina Elena*. They drove north of *Villa Borghese*, over the bridge of *Corso di Francia*, near the *Tomba di Nerone,* and finally to the military academy.

The black Mercedes hugged the colossal stone wall for a kilometer, then entered the iron gates that swung open on chain-link hinges. Well-watered lawns stretched for hundreds of meters in all directions. The car drove on a red brick path lined with cypress trees to a roundabout with a fountain at its center. Students, dressed uniformly in dark blue sweats, jogged in the distance in linear conformity.

At the base of the steps to the entrance of the school, Kabir waited expectantly alongside two other well-dressed women for the concupiscent couple.

Along with Sofia, Ishmael exited the car and demurely approached the three administrators. Dressed in a three-piece black suit, Kabir spoke first.

"Welcome to the L'Accademia *Internazionale del Benedetto XV.*" Kabir introduced the other administrators and then showed Ishmael the school. Along with elaborate explanations of the curricula and programs, he was led through each classroom and introduced to teachers and students.

They paused in the hallway.

"These kids come from broken families, Ish," Sofia said, looking intently at the redhead.

"How many students?"

"Right now, we have seven hundred and thirty-three enrolled."

"And what ages are your students?"

Kabir responded, "At this site, we cater to ages thirteen to eighteen. Upon receiving their International Baccalaureate, they are transitioned to various apprenticeship programs and/or university studies that we fund entirely."

"Where do they come from?"

"Most transition from our orphanages."

"How many sites do you have?"

"In Europe, twelve."

"Cradle to grave," Ishmael said to himself.

Sofia interjected, "Ishmael, these kids would have *no chance* at life. If it were not for *The Dawn*, they would be on the streets, exploited and begging."

"Hmmm. The name on the sign for your school is an homage to Pope Benedict, but I didn't notice any other Catholic references—no biblical studies, no pictures of saints, no crucifixes, no statues of Mary..."

Kabir answered, "We have a diverse group here. We do not care about their skin color or background. We believe in equity and inclusion. We take a balanced approach. We teach the Bible, but we also teach its contradictions, its errancies, its historical inaccuracies. Our students seek enlightenment wherever it may be found. We are not so arrogant as to believe that one spiritual leader has *all* knowledge. We do not accept the false dogma that there is only *one way* to God. No one has objective truth!" he said angrily.

"Our religious curricula entail the teachings of Mazda, Gautama, Mohammed, Krishna, Hubbard—to name a few—and any number of other religious leaders." He paused and stared at Ishmael. "We examine all belief systems, or at least, as many as time will allow. But by and large, we are neutral—secular in practice."

The evil one has blinded them to the spiritual realm; it is inaccessible to the carnal mind, Ishmael remembered the words of Rodrigo.

"And when they are done with their training, academics, whatever... what then?"

"They are free to live their lives, Ishmael," he said matter-of-factly.

Ishmael smirked. "Really? They are just free to go their own way? And you want nothing in return? No reciprocation? *No quid pro quo?*"

"That's right," Kabir stated without emotion.

"The good we do is its own reward," Sofia inserted.

"Hmmm," Ishmael contemplated.

The bell rang, although it sounded more like a claxon. The older kids frequented the hallway, engaging in light banter and revelry; laughter filled the corridor. A woman in a brown pantsuit walked briskly to their group. Her face was downtrodden.

"*Mi* scusi, I don't mean to interrupt." She pulled Kabir and Sofia to the side and whispered in their ears.

Immediately, Sofia turned to Ishmael. "We need to go."

Chapter 43 – Lago Gandolfo, Italy

"Now the serpent was craftier than any of the wild animals the Lord God had made. He said to the woman, "Did God really say..." Genesis 3:3

he black Mercedes braved the serpentine slopes to the apogee of the volcanic hill. Without a word, she slammed the door behind her. Ishmael followed. They scaled the steps to their room.

Bewildered, Ishmael watched as Sofia threw some items in a bag.

"There is a private family gathering I must attend."

"Uhh… okay. Something wrong?"

"No. Will you be okay by yourself?" said Sofia, dressing quickly.

"Sure. I'll probably just go to bed early."

Something didn't sit right with Ishmael. He was not invited for a reason—and he was going to find out why.

"Goodbye, my love," she kissed him and then turned to leave.

He waited until she was at the base of the stairs. Then Ishmael threw on a black sweatshirt with a hoodie. He crept downstairs and looked out the bay windows at Sofia and her family loading their cars and turning out of the driveway.

Ishmael retraced his steps to the hidden staircase that descended into the long tunnel. He moved quickly until he reached the gazebo. He scaled the hill, hiding in the shadows of the hedges. Then he slipped through a side door into one of the garages.

Among the high-end vehicles lay three motorcycles. He grabbed a key from the wall and slowly pushed out the burgundy 1953 Indian Roadmaster. The bike picked up speed as it descended into the darkness of the olive grove. Ishmael kept his distance while trailing the procession of cars.

After several kilometers, Ishmael witnessed the motorcade access an arched iron gateway fed by a gravel road. On his approach, Ishmael extinguished his headlights, crossed the ditch, and penetrated the periphery of the *Sagrantino* vineyard. He threw the Indian to the ground, then scurried to the cover of the moonlit silhouettes.

He ducked down among the chest-high vines and crept toward the sound of rhythmic voices. The concentric rows of vines led to the zenith of a grassy hill. Although it was dark, Ishmael could see that at its center lay a large townhouse—a barn of modern fashion.

Ishmael watched from a distance through the vines as members of the Order stood on an outdoor stage, barn doors ajar, near the tasting room. The participants wore black hooded robes and face coverings that resembled warped Venetian masks splattered with black and gold paint. A body wrapped in a white shroud had been placed on a large wooden platform layered with cypress boughs.

A male and female officiant wearing velvet stoles embroidered with strange glyphs and thorny crowns began to speak.

"Regina Amureal Tiranicius, you have served the Golden Dawn for many decades. We now call you to join our father below for eternity."

A small group of participants approached the platform with torches. They all began to chant, first in a whisper that gradually grew louder with each phrase. The priest raised his arms, and the chanters held a single dissonant note. When he lowered his arms, the torches were pressed against the shroud until it ignited.

As Regina's flesh melted away, her horrified screams could be heard above the conjurations. A wisp of black smoke rose; the smoke circled and fought unnaturally, defiantly against the wind. It grew in thickness and height. The amorphous fumes had given birth to an entity—something transhuman, something angelic. It was beautiful initially, then terrifying.

The incantations grew louder, more aggressive, more cacophonous as it rose and rose in stature. It towered above the satanic patrons—ten meters, then twenty, then fifty, and finally a hundred meters at its apex.

Ishmael's heart beat uncontrollably, and his body shivered. He cowered in the vines, lying prostrate in the soil.

The demon spoke in the dark Enochian language Ishmael had not heard since the exorcism.

"You are the chosen one. I am here to guard you. No harm will come to you as long as you serve our dark lord."

Ishmael shuddered at the menacing sound that made the hair on the back of his neck stand on end.

Lilith moved toward the creature and chanted an invocation in the same dark speech.

"Yes, I will serve our lord for eternity. I bid thee to enter my body freely!"

She opened her mouth wide as the entity's smoke poured into her body. Lilith cried out in agony as the beast inhibited her. Her eyes grew black, and she emitted a guttural, sadistic laugh. She had, at last, assumed the power of the Order of the Golden Dawn.

Lilith held up a large goblet filled with blood. She took a long sip, letting the blood drip down her chin and chest. Lilith passed the goblet to a woman at her side. The woman also drank from the cup, also allowing the blood to flow down her body.

The crowd erupted in celebration. The congregation started shedding their robes, dancing naked around the pyre, and casting their masks into the flames.

Ishmael recognized Sofia, her body illuminated by the blaze. Even drenched in blood, she was breathtakingly beautiful, thought Ishmael. A tall, lean man kissed her violently on the mouth and threw her against the ground.

Ishmael instinctively wanted to protect her but knew he could not reveal his position in the shadows. He was incredulous to discover that Sofia merely laughed and spread her legs. The man began to thrust his erection into her body while Sofia tore the flesh on his back.

Ishmael felt like he had taken a punch to the solar plexus. His heart pounded into his throat. It sickened him to see Sofia with another man. He felt as though the love and intimacy they had developed over the past year was instantly destroyed.

Between the horrific events of the ceremony and Sofia's betrayal, Ishmael could bear no more. He stealthily ran back toward the hidden motorcycle and fled the winery.

Chapter 44 - Gandolfo, Italy

"When night came, David and Abishai went into Saul's camp." - I Samuel 26:7

t was 3:00 a.m. He hadn't slept. Sofia's prostrated body rose and fell in deep expirations; she was asleep, exhausted from her satanic sexploits. He threw on some black sweats that he had hidden under the bed a few hours earlier. The clothing stuck to the dried sweat on his body. He cracked the door ever so slightly, then peered into the hallway.

At the end of the softly lit corridor stood a guard. Ishmael slithered down the hall, down the staircase, through the false floorboard, and into the tunnel he had accessed twice before, but instead of exiting toward the olive groves, he turned into the mountain—into the abyss.

The sides of the tunnels bore the scars of machinery; the ceilings were supported by metallic rectangular scaffolding. Yellow rubber cage-encased light bulbs hung from the frames. Ishmael couldn't tell if the cold he felt was from the palpable humidity of the caves or that familiar frigid feeling of demonic activity.

Crouching and alert, he proceeded for a hundred meters. The rock floor evolved to cement, and the underground passage widened, exposing a cavern, or disembarkation area. An industrial half wall accessed a receiving area which, in turn, led to an underground warehouse. Wooden crates stood stacked at varying heights, many partially covered by army-green tarps, others lying face up. He quickly looked for activity. Nothing. No one.

He secured a crowbar mounted on the wall near the entry. He buried the bar in the seam and popped the wooden lid. He pushed aside some protective packaging. The box had been loaded to the hilt with rubber ammunition casings: 9-millimeter, 5.56×45 short-range training ammunition; 7.62×50, .50 BMG, and 12-gauge slugs and buckshot. He carefully restored the wooden crate. He imagined the other cases contained the armaments necessary to fire the ammunition. He left the loading dock toward smaller passages that broke off from the expanse, some with metal doors and some without.

A low frequency could be heard in the distance. It felt like an earthquake. Something was approaching—a vehicle of some sort. Impulsively, he slid along the wall and into the first hallway. Covering himself with a tarp, he hid between two stacks of crates. The confined space was cold, wet, and smelled of burlap.

Three behemoth Russian Ural-230 cargo trucks rumbled in single file. Their engines were so loud in the confined space that Ishmael had to cover his ears. The wheels rolled past just centimeters from his location. He peeked out through the fabric. The vehicle's brakes hissed. The trucks halted abruptly at the embarkation dock.

Several young men jumped from the cab, yelling in some language he couldn't understand. Clad in army gear, they popped the rear compartment and began unloading. Upon offloading the cargo, the driver jumped back into the truck. The V-8 diesel engine triggered an expulsion of black smoke that shot from the posterior exhaust.

Ishmael broke from his exclusion and ran after the truck. Stretching for the gate, stepping upon the bumper, he catapulted his body into the back of the cargo truck and lay prostrate, obscured from view. The cloth canopy swayed violently with the surface of the road, slamming his body against the metal bed of the truck.

Then suddenly, the quaking stopped. He peeked through the fabric. A paved road. *A tunnel.* They rode smoothly for another half hour. Nearly audible voices grew louder in his subconscious, tearing him into the metaphysical world. The Watchers—*the Grigori*—were screaming in expectation for him. Their Enochian screams were so loud that it was difficult to focus.

"Let us out!" they bellowed. He understood them. *Shemyaza, Asael, Satanail, Semyaz, Remashel, Kokabel, and Azazel...* He knew them by name.

His vision was interrupted by the hissing of brakes. The lorry engines growled and sputtered as the chassis lurched forward. They were arriving at their destination. There were no windows to predict where he might land or when to exit the truck to prevent discovery. It would be a leap of faith.

At a bend in the road, the lorry slowed. Ishmael took a deep breath and swan-dived off the truck into a patch of shrubs that grew roadside. He tucked and rolled his body, coming to a halt. He lay flat, still against the terrain. He listened for shouting or perhaps a whistle. Nothing.

The noise of engines was replaced by a murmur of voices and distant claxons. For safety's sake, he waited another second or three. He slowly lifted his gaze. His most creative imagination could not have conjured what lay before him.

He was aghast. *A city!* An underground city, with at least one hundred square blocks of ancient buildings—constructions that had not been destroyed in the sacking of Rome in 410 BC. They were ancient, early Roman, circa five hundred years before Christ; in fact, many of the edifices may have predated the Romans, perhaps even the Etruscans.

Yet the ancient relics were interspersed with modern construction as well, complete with electricity. Among the modernity and antiquity stood skyscraper-like stalagmites, and stalactites that fell like sharpened teeth. Babel-like staircases crisscrossed upward to terraces that surveyed the city below.

A subterranean tributary of the Tiber slithered through the heart of the massive chasm, splitting the city evenly. Ishmael could see a meticulously masoned bridge transcending the river. The bridge was flanked by stone parapets upon which sat what looked like statuettes of ancient Greco-Roman gods.

In the distance, one could hear the low, almost imperceptible, rumble of a cascading waterfall. Rays of moonlight filtered through fissures in the stone ceiling, softly illuminating the cityscape below.

The city was partitioned by roundabouts, open concrete lots, barricades, kiosks, a cemetery, and what looked like a large verdant knoll. At the end of the park stood a ten-meter statue of a grotesque figure with claws, an open mouth, a serpentine tongue, and ram horns.

The city streets bustled with activity. Vehicles, primarily paramilitary, trudged along roads that had been carved into the rock. Many pedestrians wearing fatigues crossed the streets. They gathered along the sidewalks; many walked briskly carrying packages; many gesticulated to other pedestrians; many jogged in single file—but all of them were devoted to their activities.

Surveying his surroundings, Ishmael rose slowly. The trucks had turned off the main road and onto a gravel inlet toward a facility. The complex was surrounded by a chain-link fence, but the security was light. Ishmael observed two guards at its entrance; no others were visible.

He shadowed some hedges and made his way to the edge of the perimeter. From his position, he could see some personnel gathered outside. The red glow of cigarettes pierced the night. The fence was devoid of razor wire, which made for an easy climb. He ran across a clearing to the edge of the building and scaled an iron ladder to the roof. He searched for an entrance into the building, to no avail.

He heard some voices. He removed his shoes and crept to the edge of the building, directly above the exit door where he had observed three smokers. Although, from Ishmael's vantage point, he could not see their faces, he could hear their conversation.

"Hey Cybil, let me borrow your lighter."

Ishmael heard the rotary flint of a Zippo, then a pause. He exhaled.

"Where are we getting these new ones from?" he said, softly spitting tobacco from his lips.

"Eastern... uhh... Romania. I think."

"It never ceases to amaze me how entire governments turn a blind eye."

"Money."
"We are doing them a favor, removing undesirables. No birth certificates gives us carte blanche to do whatever we want."

"This new batch is more powerful than the others... must be all those cabbage rolls." He laughed to himself.

The door popped open, followed by an authoritative voice.

"Okay, let's go. You've had your five."

Ishmael could hear their boot heels scrape the cigarette butts into the pavement, and the swing of the metal door. Before the strut springs could swing the door closed, Ishmael leapt from the roof and shoved his fingers into the doorframe. He waited momentarily, then opened it cautiously.

He entered a semi-circular foyer which branched off in three directions. He chose one and came upon an industrial lift. He got in. It fell for several minutes before opening on its own.

...'Let *us out!... The Watchers' cries echoed in his mind...*

He was concerned that he might be exposed, but the elevator opened into a corridor devoid of people. Indirect blue lights shot out from the ceiling molding. A labyrinth of corridors and doors riddled the hallway, each with a symbol at its crest.

He opened one. The door gave way to the backside of a maintenance closet lined with cubicle lockers, hanging custodial equipment, and teal scrubs. Instinctively, he put some on. He pulled a surgical mask over his face and exited the closet.

An emblem of a serpent wrapped around a pole was mounted next door. He opened it. Medical personnel frequented the hallways. The walls gave way to a large bay window, behind which resided fifty to a hundred miniature beds—it was a neonatal care facility. Like a scene from a science fiction movie, insect-like tubes and wires protruded from each baby carriage. The babies' cries blended with the voices in his head—Gebofal. They bellowed.

Ishmael turned a few corners and realized that his time was getting short. He should get back before Sofia awoke—before he was discovered.

He slipped into a lengthy staircase. Skipping steps, he scaled countless floors to arrive on the familiar highway that had led him to his destination. He hid in the bushes and waited for a lorry heading out of the facility. He leapt into the back, hiding himself behind several crates that had been meticulously tethered to the truck bed.

He lifted the military-grade tarp. *Сибирская язва*—he couldn't decipher the text, but it looked Russian. He crouched and waited. The truck swayed and kicked him against the crates. He recognized the configuration of the road. They were ascending to the Alban hill.

After a half hour, the vehicle turned up the gravel road that led to the palazzo. Ishmael jumped from the truck. He walked up the road, then slipped along the endless corridor and upstairs to the trap door in the floorboard.

He cracked it. There were more guards in the hallway than before—this time, carrying machine guns. He waited for them to change location, then slipped up the stairs and into bed with Sofia. She was still snoring softly.

What were they planning? Something big. So many questions ran through his mind. He knew he had to contact someone on the outside—someone he could trust. But who?

Malech. He had to find Malech!

Chapter 45 - Boston, Massachusetts

"But everything exposed by the light becomes visible—and everything that is illuminated becomes a light." - Ephesians 5:13

unnigan put down the phone and then inhaled on his Cuban.

"Mrs. Klein, can you patch me through to Father Nerone in Rome, please?"

The smoke climbed to the ceiling of his office. The white light on his push-button phone console flashed. He pushed the button and put the receiver to his ear.

"Father Dunnigan, Father Nerone is on line one."

"Thank you, Mrs. Klein."

The connection clicked and a deep voice responded, "Si?"

"Father, it's Dunnigan."

"Si?"

"Any progress?"

"We are on schedule; it is coming together as prophesied. The Calabrese will contact you in a few weeks."

There was a momentary pause. "Oh, and may I suggest you get your affairs in order? Be ready to leave at a moment's notice, *capisci*?"

Dunnigan took another toke on his cigar. "I'll be ready." He hung up the phone.

In a sister parish across town, Father Azikiwe cradled his receiver.

Chapter 46 - Rome, Italy

"But in that coming day no weapon turned against you will succeed. You will silence every voice raised up to accuse you. These benefits are enjoyed by the servants of the LORD; their vindication will come from me. I, the LORD, have spoken!" - Isaiah 54:17

he *Palazzo della Civiltà Italiana*, also known as the *Colosseo Quadrato*, or "Square Colosseum," was commissioned in 1940 under the fascist reign of *Il Duce*, Benito Mussolini. The building had since served as an example of Italian Rationalism and fascist architecture. With its arched windows, the design of the building had been inspired by the Colosseum. The structure's six vertical and nine horizontal arches were correlated to the number of letters in the name of the fascist dictator. The Global High Council of the Golden Dawn convened on the top floor.

All the members wore black, except for the high priestess. Lilith was dressed in a blood-red gown whose train fell through a hole in the posterior slats of her black throne. She sat upright, vaulted on a raised platform. Her long, sharpened black fingernails were camouflaged against the arm supports finished in skulls with crystal eyes.

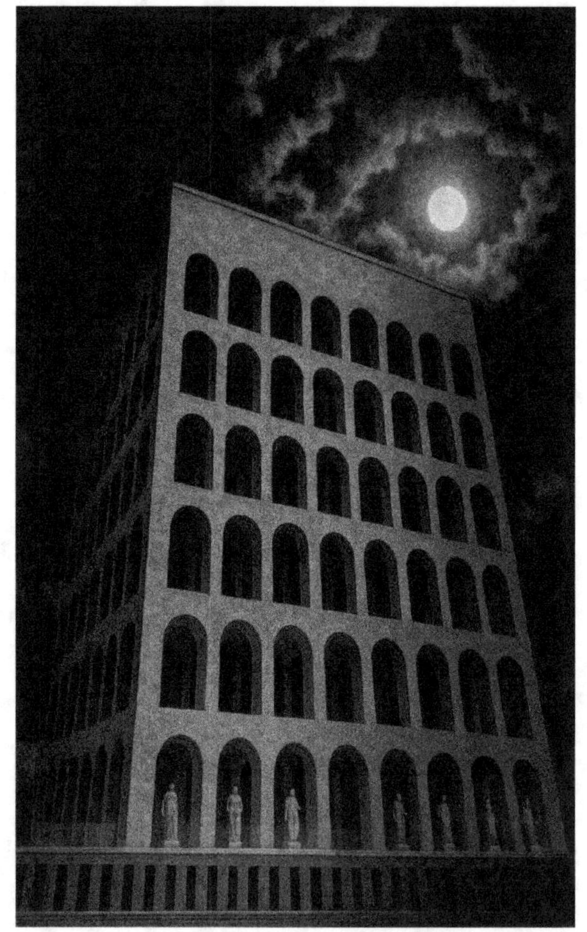

The high priestess, or high witch, sat regally at the center of the crescent table. The Jesuit Father, Nerone—or Black Pope—stood at her flank, ready to commence the proceedings. He loomed over the other members seated in front of him. Nerone's six-foot-seven-inch frame and priestly collar were buried under a shiny black three-piece suit. His top hat, which, when worn, made him look even taller, rested upside down on the table. He had taken it off in a gesture of humility to the nine-member council.

The father's black hair was well-oiled; he slid his hand along his forehead to slick back a few rebellious strands. A Gauloises cigarette sat smoldering in an ashtray in front of him.

"We have come together this evening," he began, "...to commemorate the passing of our high priestess, Regina Amureal Tiranicius, and to celebrate a new era, a new covenant under our new priestess, Lilith Azial Barequel!" He held up his champagne.

"Hail. Hail!" The intimate crowd held aloft crystal flute glasses.

The room resembled a stage production of Faust, accompanied by black and red mural curtains, Sumerian mythological tapestries, marble busts of beastly men, and Mephistophelic regalia. The crescent table seated the other eight members of the council, each representing a global power: Doctor Embata and his wife, Josephine, from Africa; Cardinal Muller from Europe; the Tewani twins, Samir and Kabir, from Southern Asia; Maxim Korolyov from Northern Asia; Takeru Tachibana from Eastern Asia; and the Nicaraguan, Marta Ruiz Fernández, from the Americas. Dunnigan, Ewan, Cecilia, and four other athletic-looking chaperones were also in attendance.

Father Muller spoke. "Any progress on *Gebofal*?"

Samir stood up. "Yes, Father. I have created four T.E.D.s. The other three are being assembled at Gandolfo. They will be ready for deployment shortly. And we have eight contagion delivery systems currently kept in cryo. However, we will not know their efficacy until the day of deployment. For our trial run, the council has elected an American city." Samir paused and stared at Dunnigan. "Boston."

Dunnigan nodded in acknowledgement. Samir walked to the end of the room. From behind a tapestry, Kabir pulled down a large, scrolled map displaying the Greater Boston area. He extended a metal pointer, then continued.

"My brother has assembled a team to release a chemical contagion into the water systems, infecting the water table, and consequently tainting the cultivation of food for generations."

"How will you get it into the country without being discovered?" Muller chimed in.

"It is already in place." Samir looked up at the bishop condescendingly. "Several months ago, we smuggled in the individual parts through our contacts in Mexico. We assembled them on location into three smaller systems. They are being held in a bunker under a parish outside of Boston. Once we have the green light, Father Dunnigan will run cover, giving access to our men."

Nerone spoke. "I hope you know what you are doing. We have a lot invested in this."

Samir continued. "Ewan and Cecilia will head a seven-member team." He gestured with his head toward the amorous couple. Then, turning back toward the map, he continued. "Dissemination will take place upstream, spoiling the water table here, just north of Watertown; here, at the Cambridge cemetery near Harvard; and finally here, at the entrance of the harbor. The effects of the attack will destroy all marine life in the harbor and destroy all cultivation for fifty miles in every direction." With an evil grin, he looked up at the members of the council. "Thousands will die! Terror will run rampant!"

"And what about extraction?" Muller inquired. "We cannot afford for our members to fall into the hands of law enforcement."

Kabir answered the question. "We have escape routes prepared. All our soldiers are aware of the risks. And if captured, they are prepared to die. This assault is minuscule by comparison to what we have planned. We are primarily interested in intel—specifically the reaction of the public and authorities, both local and federal. The real target is not Boston."

"Tell me about phase two." Muller mused.

Chapter 47 – Lago Gandolfo, Italy

"Peter said to Him, "Lord, if it is You, command me to come to You on the water." And He said, "Come!" And Peter got out of the boat, and walked on the water and came toward Jesus. But seeing the wind, he became frightened, and beginning to sink, he cried out, "Lord, save me!" Immediately Jesus stretched out His hand and took hold of him, and said to him, "You of little faith, why did you doubt?" - Matthew 14: 28-31

he *Giro del Lago Gandolfo Col Battello* was set to embark at midday. The excursion by luxury vessel was intended to serve as a romantic couple's getaway for Sofia, Ishmael, Ewan, and Cecelia—to bring them closer together.

"Hey, babe. You should start getting ready. We're heading out soon," Sofia instructed.

"Yeah, okay." Ever since witnessing the ritual, he had not felt the same about Sofia. Yet Ishmael did not want to reveal his secret. He needed more time to figure out his plan.

Sofia smiled weakly. "Great. We leave in an hour."

A blue and white Riva Monte Carlo Offshorer was waiting at the dock, operated by a mysterious man— probably a member of the Dawn, Ishmael thought.

"Buon giorno! Sono il capitano, Pietro Caputo," said the captain with a flourish of the hand. He held the bud of a cigar tightly between his lips.

The captain was a quirky fellow with a bulbous nose and a handlebar mustache. He wore a V-neck navy sweater over a collared shirt and a plaid ascot.

"You may call me Capitano!" He laughed hysterically and winked at Sofia. She gave him a dismissive wave, while Ewan and Cecelia ignored him and started boarding the vessel.

"È una bella giornata, amici miei! Andiamo!" announced the captain before putting on his white hat and turning his back to his passengers.

Sofia was heiress chic in large sunglasses, a white scarf over her head, and a robe over her red bikini. She carried a large wicker picnic basket. Ishmael wore his usual black T-shirt and jeans with

Converse. Ewan and Cecelia were nondescript in khaki shorts and tailored shirts over their bathing suits.

When the boat was underway, Sofia and her friends laughed and drank from bottles of beer, while Ishmael sulked. Even the breathtaking panoramic view had little appeal to him. His newly healed heart was again shattered into tiny shards. Ishmael saw flashes of the ritual in his mind, and his fury began to grow to an unmanageable size.

The captain halted the engines in the middle of the lake and dropped the anchor. "*O sole mio! Sta 'nfronte a te!*" The captain continued to sing after the music was turned off. Cecelia and Ewan disrobed before plunging into the cool water for a swim.

"Are you okay, hon?" Sofia asked, touching Ishmael on the arm.

"No, I am not okay!" Ishmael turned away from her in protest.

Sofia paused for a moment before she spoke. "Ishmael, I know you followed me to the gathering. This is why I wanted you to stay behind. I knew you wouldn't understand."

He spun around. "Understand? Who could possibly wrap their mind around this shit?! You burned a woman alive! I saw a demon manifested right in front of me! You were fucking someone else!"

"What you saw was part of a ceremony. It doesn't change anything between us," Sofia implored.

"How can you say that? Do you even have feelings for me?" He was surprised.

"Yes, I love you."

"I thought I loved you too," Ishmael admitted reluctantly.

"Ishmael, don't throw this away! I've never felt like this about anyone before."

"And yet, you were still willing to cheat on me."

"Sweetheart, it's not like that. This is how I was raised. It's all I know."

"That's so fucked up, Sofia!" His voice echoed across the lake. Ewan and Cecelia looked up from the water.

"Why am I here? I mean, why am I *really* here?" he demanded.

"We need you... I need you," she admitted.

"Need me for what?" Ishmael was indignant.

"We want you to join us. The Golden Dawn is a benevolent institution in search of knowledge and wisdom—just like you were learning about with your friend, Scaramucci."

"Scaramucci was not summoning demons and murdering people!"

"The Order is so much more than that. You're special, Ishmael. We could do great things together!" Sofia's eyes danced.

"I don't... know what to say," Ishmael chose his words carefully.

Sofia turned Ishmael's face toward her. "I'm sorry if I hurt you. Please forgive me." Sofia gently kissed him on the lips, and his anger softened.

The couples spent the rest of the afternoon sunbathing and taking sips of beer and dips in the lake. They stopped to enjoy bites of strawberries, Taleggio, and focaccia with olive tapenade nestled in the picnic basket. Ewan challenged Ishmael to race to a buoy two hundred meters in the distance and back, and of course, he accepted. Sofia and Cecelia cheered for their men from the deck of the boat. Ishmael was deemed the champion to Ewan's chagrin. Out on the peaceful water, Ishmael could almost forget the stormy darkness that loomed around him. He knew the Golden Dawn would not accept his refusal.

When the boat began to disembark at sunset, sunburned and wind-blown passengers began to unload onto the dock.

"Ehi! Rosso, vieni qui! Aiutami," the captain motioned for Ishmael to join him at the bow.

Ishmael was confused. "What do you need?" he asked.

The captain said in a low whisper, his accent gone, "Ishmael, it's me, Malech."

"What?! How did you find me?" he blurted.

"Father Azikiwe infiltrated the Order through Dunnigan, bugged his phone. We need to get you out of here. I'm going to start up the boat. Just act surprised."

"No! I'm so close to finding out the truth. You can't pull me out yet."

"Ishmael, your life is in danger."

Sofia called to Ishmael from the car. "Come on, hon. Hurry up!"

"I've got to go," he said to Malech through gritted teeth.

"Here, take my card. Call me when you can."

Ishmael took the card and put it in his pocket before jumping onto the dock.

"What was that all about?" asked Sofia when their car was underway.

"Oh. The crazy old captain was telling me a story about the time a swordfish landed in his boat. I think he's just lonely," he lied.

Ishmael now realized what he had to do.

Chapter 48 - Boston, Massachusetts

"Joseph remembered the dreams which he had about them, and said to them, "You are spies; you have come to look at the undefended parts of our land." - Genesis 42:9-11

ffering to close the church, Dunnigan had relieved the clerical staff for the evening. He descended into the basement and opened the electric door to the subterranean garage. Saint Cecilia Parish's underground entrance was only accessible from Scotia Street.

A white van entered. Ewan, Cecilia, and four other men wearing black balaclavas sprang from the vehicle. Dusk had settled, and the night gave perfect cover for their activities.

"You'll have a few hours to tie up things on your end, priest," Ewan said with a hint of disdain.

"I have already made arrangements. I will never be returning to Boston."

Ewan and his team unlocked the floorboard where they had hidden the devices. They threw open the shutter doors. The disbursement buoys were spherical and mechanical, droid-like with tubes and wires that circled the exterior then retreated again. Each was roughly half a meter in diameter with a stabilizing mechanism that enveloped their centers. The nefarious men loaded them into the van and headed off toward the designated deployment zones.

"Good luck, priest. May the eye of providence watch over us." Ewan extended his hand in farewell. Dunnigan shook it formally.

The priest closed the doors, climbed the basement steps, and walked through the empty sanctuary. He opened the office door and took a Cuban from his pocket. He walked to the window, opened it, lit his cigar, and peered into the night sky. Had he been at the window a few moments earlier, he might have noticed a black Jeep Cherokee with wooden sideboards parked across the street.

Azikiwe, and five other muscular, military-looking men, followed the white van west on Belvidere and then north on Massachusetts Avenue toward the Harvard Bridge. The Jeep followed loosely to remain undiscovered. The white vehicle veered north on Beacon Street, then stopped in a greenwood just north of Watertown. Two men sprang from the van carrying a large round object. The van took off.

A soldier seated at the rear spoke. "Father?"

Azikiwe asked the driver to stop, then looked in the rearview. "Follow the ones on foot. We'll follow the van." Two men in the backseat obeyed immediately and exited the Jeep; three remained.

The van continued to the Cambridge Cemetery near Harvard, and two more men exited the white vehicle in the same fashion, carrying a spherical device. Azikiwe ordered two more men to follow the members of the Golden Dawn. He then ordered the driver to follow the van.

The van drove toward the harbor, toward Castle Island. It stopped prematurely and parked behind Ronnie's Crab Shack. Cecilia and Ewan broke from the van. Ewan stood stoically, surveying the area. He returned to the van and retrieved the sphere. Cecilia walked with him into the verge, which was shielded by the darkness.

Azikiwe's driver parked the black Jeep in the shadows, and then they took two minutes to pray. The Nigerian pulled his clerical collar from his neck and put it in the glove compartment. From the same compartment, he retrieved a Belgian FN Browning pistol with a 20-centimeter suppressor and handed it to the driver. Not very priestly, but on this day, necessary.

The bug in Dunnigan's phone had yielded dividends, but the details of their plan were still unclear. He knew only that they intended to kill thousands, perhaps millions of people. He had no idea what they carried, but somehow, he knew he had to prevent its activation.

The soldiers of The Dawn had crossed the intersection and entered the tree-ridden park. Azikiwe and his comrade exited the Jeep that they had parked snugly in the shadows, then crossed the street to Castle Island Park. The streetlights became obstructed by arboreal limbs, painting Sleepy Hollow-like shadows that twisted and threatened.

The clerics watched the two satanists as they hurried through the long dark toward the waterfront. A small boat, a white SeaRay, sat moored to a wooden dock. They ran quickly, aggressively closing the gap. If they let them get in the boat, it was over.

They had been spotted. Cecilia knelt at the entrance of the dock. She leveled her weapon into the dark and fired two rounds that splattered bark into the Nigerian's eyes. Sheltered behind a tree, his driver fired in response, hitting her in the shoulder. Cecilia fell backwards.

Ewan screamed an obscenity as he observed Cecilia fall to the ground. He quickly unloaded the sphere into the boat, then pulled his pistol from his breast pocket and fired back. Ewan ran to her aid. The injury was graver than he had thought. She had collapsed lifelessly onto the muddy embankment. She was unconscious but still breathing.

Ewan was exposed. Azikiwe's driver passed into the clearing, calmly, methodically firing with precision. His muzzle coughed twice, hitting Ewan in the chest. In an adrenaline-laden stupor, Ewan was knocked backward, unwittingly jetting his pistol to the sludge at the water's edge. Hobbling toward the boat, Ewan's stagger became a crawl, then he fell face down on the wooden dock.

Azikiwe's henchman stopped with his pistol aloft. He released the empty cartridge to the ground and slid in a fresh clip. He took a deep breath. He surveyed the scene, scanning the horizon and looking for any sign of movement from the wounded satanists.

He approached Cecilia cautiously, while still maintaining an awareness of Ewan. He knelt at her side. He put two fingers on her jugular vein. She was alive. He took her pistol and threw it into the ocean. He passed over her and proceeded down the dock toward Ewan's lifeless figure. The driver stalked cautiously, pistol raised. Azikiwe followed in tow. The driver knelt to assess the Scot—no pulse. No movement. No life.

Suddenly, a bullet whizzed by Azikiwe's ear.

"Surprise, priest! AHAHAHA!!!" Her wicked laugh broke the night air.

The two clerics instinctively dived into the boat. Azikiwe's driver raised his head to peer over the edge of the boat. Cecilia was on her feet, firing indiscriminately in their direction. A few bullets penetrated, cracking the fiberglass hull of the SeaRay.

"You can't kill us! We are too strong! Where is your carpenter god now?"

The driver sat up obstinately, emptying his clip, pumping Cecilia's chest with nine-millimeter projectiles. She hardly winced upon impact. She emptied her clip as well, missing wildly. Yet there she stood, defiant, unyielding, screaming blasphemous obscenities.

Azikiwe immediately realized that they were no longer fighting a physical battle. Bullets exhausted, he sprang from his protection, pulled his crucifix from his pocket, and held it high. Azikiwe's advance toward her was authoritative, full of righteous indignation.

"Evil spirit, I command you in the name of Jesus Christ to come out of her NOW!" The driver deferred to his priest, following from behind.

"AHAHAHA! I am no evil spirit, slave. *I AM LILITH, HIGH PRIESTESS OF THE DAWN!* And you have no power over me! I can curse your pathetic carpenter god all I want!"

"In the name of Jesus Christ, I command you to leave, or *I WILL SEVER YOUR CHORD!*" Eyes blazing, the Nigerian approached the wounded marionette. "You may not use this girl! By the BLOOD OF THE LAMB, I COMMAND YOU TO RELINQUISH THIS BODY! GO BACK FROM WHERE YOU CAME, WITCH!"

The driver ran at her, trying to tackle her to the ground. She pivoted and threw him four meters into the muddy embankment. He recoiled, amazed at her strength.

"NO!" Quoting from Zechariah 4:6, the priest reprimanded, "'...Not by might, but by the Spirit, saith the Lord.' I will handle this!"

He turned to address the embondaged young girl. She spat at him. Her eyes were entirely black.

"You have no authority here!" The Nigerian pressed his cross to her forehead. Her body twitched in an unnatural manner; her arms bent backward like a spider, then she crawled to attack him.

"I do not," he responded. "But I know One who does, and in His name, you must comply!" He raised his cross. "In the name of the BLOOD OF THE LAMB, JESUS CHRIST, I COMMAND YOU TO SUBMIT!" The priest thrusted his crucifix to her forehead. "KNEEL!"

She hissed, shrieked, and defecated. She was forced to the silt. His driver returned, securing her legs. Azikiwe pulled a flask from his pocket.

"In the name of Jesus, I command you to see!" He took a few drops from a vial of holy water and wiped them on Cecilia's eyes.

Bewildered, Cecilia's spirit briefly came to the surface. "Where am I? Who are you? Ahhhh!!!" She let out a shriek as if she had seen her eternal fate. *"NooooOOOOO! SOMETHING IS WRONG! I WON'T GO! GET OFF OF ME!"*

"SHUT UP, SLAVE!" Lilith invasively fought to re-establish her dominance. Cecilia's countenance vacillated between anger and bewilderment, her eyes mirroring the internal struggle, switching from feline black to pearl white.

Azikiwe spoke tenderly to Cecilia. "Daughter, Jesus died for you! Satan is a liar! You can still choose! Jesus' blood is more powerful than any demon, any witch. He is calling you. He is alive, and He died for your sins."

"FUCK YOU, PRIEST! SHE BELONGS TO US!" Lilith screamed.

"I BIND YOU IN THE NAME OF JESUS!" He put his golden crucifix to her forehead.

"AHHHHHHH!" Lilith let out a loud shriek.

Cecilia broke through once again. "I can't. After all I have done? He could never forgive me." She began to weep.

"He already has!"

"I... I..." She coughed, spitting liquid crimson all over her blood-soaked chest.

Azikiwe's driver knelt, softly holding her secure while softly chanting, *"But if I cast out demons by the finger of God, then the kingdom of God has come upon you."*

"Cecilia," the Holy Spirit had shown the priest her name, "your time is now! Repeat after me, I choose Jesus!" Azikiwe's temperament was nurturing.

Cough. Cough. "I... I... choose Jes—"

Cecilia's head exploded, throwing cranial debris all over both of them. Deeply hidden in the confines of the adjacent forest, the Calabrese had made an incredible shot from eighty meters. He looked again through his scope to verify the kill. He observed Azikiwe and his cohort scanning the horizon for the source of the shot. He lined up the sights on his Beretta BM 62 .308 caliber semi-automatic rifle.

Azikiwe's driver immediately covered the priest with his body. The assassin pumped two rounds into the mass of his protector. The driver fell lifelessly into the sludge. Azikiwe ran and dived into the awaiting SeaRay. The Calabrese fired several rounds into the hull of the ship, but to no avail—the priest sped away.

Chapter 49 – Babylon, Italy

"Then the Lord spoke to Moses saying, "Send out for yourself men so that they may spy out the land of Canaan, which I am going to give to the sons of Israel." - Numbers 13:1-20

t was 3:45 a.m. It had taken them longer to unload the cargo this time. Alone with his thoughts, he had waited impatiently under the military tarps for thirty minutes. They finally finished their task and climbed aboard the massive vehicle.

The truck's hind tires spat gravel at Ishmael as he hoisted himself into the bed of the truck. After yesterday's catastrophe in Boston, he knew his time was short. He knew he had to discover their plan. He had seen it in a dream. *Gebofal.*

This time, he was prepared to venture into the interior. He had stolen some military fatigues from the loading docks. His army green attire made him indistinguishable from the rabble. No one paid him any attention.

Passing clandestinely by storefronts, restaurants, parked cars, and pedestrians, he headed toward the center of town, up a subtle incline toward a building with Greco-Roman architecture and a half-circular marble staircase. The portico extended ten meters upward and was supported by six Corinthian columns. He scaled the steps.

Above the colossal wooden doors, inscribed in the frieze, lay a sign: *Nag Hammadi*. It was a library—a library of the occult. Lost grimoires, apocryphal hermetic papyri, and ancient codices had been collected over millennia.

It was open.

The inside of the library was extensive, a hundred meters in depth and half again as much in height. It appeared as if it had been a church at one time. The ceilings displayed celestial scenes of angels ascending into the heavens. Colonnades with carvings of biblical characters flanked the nave. Colossal bookshelves ran horizontally, creating private reading nooks. Lamps atop quadratic desks lit the room.

Ishmael walked to the reception. An elderly woman with chain-link glasses lifted her head. "Yes?"

"Can you tell me where I can find the works of Doctor John Dee?" he inquired.

"Um… let's see. Fifteenth-century England… here, follow me. I'll show you." She vacated the confines of her rotund cubicle and led him through several Tudor-arched hallways to the back of the massive museum.

The room was distinctly different from the rest. Etched, embedded in the lofted walls, were an assortment of symbols—two- and three-dimensional—many borrowed from Doctor Dee's magnum opus, *Monas Hieroglyphica.*

The angelic voices in his head had reached a fever pitch. He could barely make out her words because of the interference.

"Here are some of the artifacts that we have," she said, motioning to the shew stone and the pearl amulet in the glass encasement. "Unfortunately, we have very few of his literary works. There are a few over there." She motioned to a set of shelves. "But feel free to explore." The archivist left.

Ishmael's dream had led him here—but no further. He was close. He could hear the Enochian screams in his consciousness. He didn't know what he was looking for.

He stepped back and surveyed the large room. He looked around for a portal, a lever, a button, a switch—something. He slid his fingers under the glass encasement. Nothing. He looked for electrical wiring—perhaps a secret door, a portal… nothing. He sifted through the books. Nothing.

His eyes followed the contours of the room—globes, cartographies, bookshelves, glass display cases, marble busts of people he couldn't recognize. And of course, all those symbols... yet... he knew them. He had known them since his youth. All his dreams had led him here. *But where? To do what?*

He heard two words in his head: "*Listen. Speak.*"

He stared at the symbols, sat on the floor, took a deep breath, then closed his eyes. The symbols were Enochian. He knew this language. He opened his mouth, and words poured forth. His body tingled; his anxiety heightened.

He was transported to Mount Hermon in antediluvian antiquity. Floating like a disembodied spirit, he saw twenty luminaries. Gravity pulled him in; he fell amongst them. He listened in English and spoke in perfect Enochian:

> *And it came to pass when the children of men had multiplied that in those days were born unto them beautiful and comely daughters. And the angels, the children of the heaven, saw and lusted after them, and said to one another: "Come, let us choose us wives from among the children of men and beget us children." And Semjâzâ, who was their leader, said unto them: "I fear ye will not indeed agree to do this deed, and I alone shall have to pay the penalty of a great sin." And they all answered him and said: "Let us all swear an oath, and all bind ourselves by mutual imprecations not to abandon this plan but to do this thing." Then sware they all together and bound themselves by mutual imprecations upon it. And they were in all two hundred, who descended in the days of Jared on the summit of Mount Hermon, and they called it Mount Hermon, because they had sworn and bound themselves by mutual imprecations upon it. And these are the names of their leaders: Sêmîazâz, their leader; Arâkîba, Râmêêl, Kôkabîêl, Tâmîêl, Râmîêl, Dânêl, Êzêqêêl, Barâqîjâl, Asâêl, Armârôs, Batârêl, Anânêl, Zaqîêl, Samsâpêêl, Satarêl, Tûrêl, Jômjâêl, Sariêl...*

Each symbol corresponded to an angelic name, each descriptive/prescriptive of their individual traits, each unique. Each one illuminated in a golden hue as he pronounced it, as if led by an invisible planchette.

He spoke the last name and then awoke to a jarring rumble—a displacement of a heavy stone.

The entirety of the wall covered with the spider web of symbols had moved—*on its own*. The meter-thick wall ground against the marble floor, scarring it with deep gashes. It ground backward for a meter, then abruptly stopped, exposing a gap at its edges, a space just large enough to pass.

He sprang to his feet and looked in. Total darkness. He contemplated his options. And for the first time since he was a child, he said a prayer of protection in Jesus' name.

He took a deep breath, then stepped into the void. The massive wall began closing behind him, grinding, forcing him inward toward his destiny. The last ray of light was eclipsed by the colossal slab. His exit was sealed.

He was filled with a deep foreboding—a listless, soulless surrender he had never felt before. It was so cold and beyond dark. He had no bearing. There was only one way now—forward.

He walked aimlessly in a single direction—or at least, what he thought was a single direction. The path declined, sloping gently downward. He walked for an hour in the damp, cold corridor. Gravel crunched under his feet, his only heading the ever-increasing volume of screams.

He followed them as if walking into hell itself. He was beyond the point of no return. *There was no freer will.* He had chosen this path.

He could not point his finger at God in self-righteous indignation. He could not claim that he had had no free will. He could not shake his fist at God and say, "You made me this way!"

Suddenly, he perceived in the vast distance a flicker of dissipating light. He grew in expectation and angst. He walked for half an hour. As he grew closer, he observed a flash of flame—perhaps a torchlight. He walked for another half an hour. As he approached, he perceived a subterranean chamber, then many chambers, side by side—hundreds of them.

The corridor in which he found himself was a promenade, a suspended observatory high above the barred cells. He was startled by the flames yet again; this time, he could hear heavy breathing and movement.

The cold air grew warmer as he approached. Flames flew once again from the subterranean chamber, splashing against the counter wall and then cascading like viscous liquid to the ground. The glow of embers lit the corridor, then quickly petered out. The air was sulfuric and dry.

He crept to the edge of the precipice and cautiously peeked into the darkness. A large reptilian creature exhaled fire in all directions—gnashing, snarling, and throwing its head about like an untethered garden hose. Its feet were bound by heavy chains, but its fiery breath could not break its bindings.

Ishmael could not believe his eyes. Was *this a dragon—a real dragon?* The beast looked up at him as if reading his thoughts. He collapsed to the floor so that he might not be seen. Fire erupted just centimeters from his face, scorching his clothing and singeing his auburn hair. Gravel scratched his stomach as he crawled to the adjacent cell.

He peered down into the darkness. From behind him, the beast's fire lit the chasm. He could not see anything. He heard a moan and the wrestling of chains—heavy iron chains.

Another dragon? he thought. But there were no flames. Something large lumbered below. He waited again until the reptile in the neighboring cell spat fire once more. In the flickering light, he saw the silhouette of a gargantuan figure—a being.

He quickly fell back down with his back to the wall. He waited for the next illumination to look again. He perched himself on his knees and peered into the darkness. An enormous eye stared unequivocally back at him; its gaze was less than a meter from his face. The eye spanned the length of Ishmael's entire stature.

Its eyebrows were long and gangly, and the corners of its eyes were wrinkled and worn. It stank of sulfur and fermented flesh. Ishmael had been discovered. The entity let out a soul-crushing audible that could have shaken the foundations of heaven itself.

Startled, Ishmael shot backward, collapsing onto the cold pebbles.

Upon hearing the bellow, the occupants of the neighboring cells awoke. Scuffling turned to banging; banging turned to a cacophonous murmur. Millennia of suppressed agitation and indignation came to the surface. They all awoke to Ishmael's presence. They became acutely aware that their release was imminent.

The entire chasm lit up with a god-like luminescence. One after the other, each cell, as far as he could see, ascended in light into the corridor. Their shouts grew to a crescendo. Ishmael covered his ears and closed his eyes. The cell bars began to quiver. The walkway began to shake, and stone fragments fell from the rotunda ceiling.

Their cries morphed from shouts of anger into jubilation. In concert, they shouted, "Edomite. Edomite. Edomite! Edomite! Edomite! EDOMITE! EDOMITE! " Their shouts grew in fervor. *"EDOMITE! EDOMITE! EDOMITE!"*

As if being chased by Cerberus himself, Ishmael fled. He darted back toward the library. He ran for an hour. The light gave way to the abyss again. It was so dark that he collided with the stone slab that blocked the entrance to the library. He was knocked backward to the ground.

His heartbeat raced. He was out of breath, sweating despite the frigid air. He felt numb, exhilarated, afraid, and confused. He remained seated, took a deep breath, and crossed his legs. He thought about his recitation. He remembered it verbatim. He repeated it in fluent Enochian.

The slab rumbled once again, shifting its weight forward. Slivers of light penetrated the darkness. He waited until his one-hundred-and-eighty-pound frame could squeeze through the crevice.

In the Fifteenth Century room dedicated to Doctor Dee and his contemporaries, a gaggle of the Dawn's operatives—soldiers—had lain in wait to seize him. Kabir surprised the redhead. Ishmael was outnumbered and cornered. He stood in resignation. Without a word, two of the men stepped forward and grabbed him by the arms.

"I was beginning to think you would never come back," Kabir said snidely.

Suddenly, the soldiers of The Dawn all became acutely aware of the faint incantations proceeding from the mouth of Tartarus. Their eyes glazed over, trance-like. They became attracted by the siren-like chants of the beasts—the Grigori and the Nephilim.

"Edomite, Edomite," still rang softly in the distance. One of Kabir's soldiers grew so drawn that he put his head into the passage. As if insulted, the wall suddenly became animated; it closed so

abruptly that it severed the man's head from his body, causing his decapitated corpse to collapse to the floor—twitching and bleeding on the marble.

Kabir stared momentarily at the body as it convulsed. Then, without a sliver of emotion, referring to Ishmael, he turned back to his team.

"Bring him."

Ishmael was bound and taken back to the *palazzo* at Gandolfo Hill.

Chapter 50 - Lago Gandolfo, Italy

"As it was in the days of Noah, so it will be at the coming of the Son of Man…" - Matthew 24:37

here had been a temporal disturbance. Time lost. Unbeknownst to Ishmael, what had seemed like a few hours in Tartarus had translated into several weeks on the temporal plane. The Dawn's plan had undoubtedly progressed. *How close were they to executing it? How would he contact Malech now?* He didn't know.

The bedroom, once the source of pleasure and ecstasy, had become a cell. Guards were posted at every door. He was allowed to roam the house but not to leave it. He was under house arrest. The "secret" staircase was no longer secret. If an escape was possible, it would require thought and planning; and judging by the increased traffic in the house, the escape would have to happen soon.

He went downstairs into the dining hall. The buffet breakfast had been immaculately furnished with eggs (soft/hard-boiled, scrambled), toast, cornetti, ham and cheese, chocolate and plain croissants, cereal, fresh milk, fifteen types of cheese, bacon, sausage, and a tray of freshly cut fruit, and juices and coffees galore… *Good food, wealth, possessions, power…* it all seemed so empty. Scaramucci's biblical teachings echoed in his mind, *"What accomplishes a man if he gains the whole world and loses his soul?"*

Sofia came in looking haggard and sullen. She got a cup of coffee and sat down next to him.

"What?" he said flatly.

She nursed her cup, holding it with both hands in an almost defensive manner. "I know it is hard for you to forgive me… but I still love you."

"You have no idea what love is."

The television caught his attention. He got up and turned up the volume. The television broadcast was in English, a satellite feed from America.

Good evening, this is an emergency news alert… This is ABC News, and I am Peter Jennings reporting live from Boston. We have just learned of a terrorist biological attack in the city of Boston. We go live now to the press conference being held at the Westin Hotel with the Governor, Mayor, FBI SAC, Bureau of Alcohol, Tobacco, Firearms, and Explosives (ATF), U.S. Attorney, BPD Commissioner, MSP Superintendent, MEMA Director, and the Transit Police Chief.

Two buoy-like dissemination devices were detonated, releasing a biological contaminant that the authorities have yet to disclose. The second buoy detonated some thirty minutes later, approximately eight miles upriver from the first contamination site. Reports are coming in that as many as a thousand-plus people may have been affected. There are also reports of multiple injuries. The hospitals have met capacity, and local municipalities have set up accessible street triages. Triage and treatment have started immediately at both contamination sites by nearby fire, police, EMS, medical personnel, and bystanders who rushed to help the injured.

All water in the surrounding twenty-mile radius has been affected. The public is advised to drink and use ONLY bottled water. The federal government is moving as we speak to provide potable bottled water to local warehouses, to be dispersed at designated localities. The public is encouraged to ration their consumption.

Ishmael sat mesmerized, listening intently. He looked at Sofia, who avoided his eye contact, also enraptured by the broadcast.

The FBI has confirmed that the Joint Terrorism Task Force (JTTF), with support from local and state police, is working to solve the crime, asking for assistance from the public, and requests that the public provide information to the FBI tip line. The FBI confirms that two devices were detonated, and that no additional devices were present. The Mayor and Governor announce that the support/resource center at the Castle remains open for affected individuals.

A media briefing is being held at the Westin Hotel with the Governor, Mayor, FBI SAC, U.S. Attorney, BPD Commissioner, MSP Superintendent, MEMA Director, Transit Police Chief, and other public safety and elected officials. The FBI provides an update on the investigation and evidence recovery and states they have recovered three bodies in Castle Park and have received reports of another four individuals that may have been carrying large spherical objects that may have contained buoy-like device(s). Details of the interfaith service are announced, including the participation of the President. The Mayor and Governor announce the formation of the One Fund Boston, where donations for victims and survivors may be sent.

So, this was their plan... to poison the water supply. There was no way he would participate. He would rather kill himself.

"And how do you expect me to get onboard with this? You don't seriously expect me to cooperate with you? Do you?"

"It's necessary to form a better world," Sofia explained.

"Necessary to murder thousands of people? So me and mine have to die so that you and yours can live? Fuck you!"

"Ish..." She was interrupted by a procession of the High Priestess, Lilith, and the black pope, Nerone. They entered arm-in-arm. They were accompanied by seven royal guards assigned to their protection, each muscular, each militant, along with two black Cane Corsos with clipped ears, each standing a meter and a half at the shoulders. Ishmael was a good fighter, but defeating all of them would have been folly. He would lose.

"Let me try to address a few of your concerns," Nerone interrupted. His voice was low and steady. He spoke with a slight drawl. "I'll tell you plainly, Ishmael, that what you have come to believe is frankly…" He paused pensively. "…false. Everything you have been taught is a lie, for it is *our* father who told the truth."

Never having seen the man before, Ishmael was a little taken aback at his hubris. He stood at least two hundred centimeters and wore a top hat that added another twenty. His attire was not unlike a voodoo witch doctor. He wore a strange shimmering black three-piece suit with a Catholic collar, jewelry around his neck, diamond-infused skulls, gold chains with symbolic pendants, and a cane with an inverted cross for a handle.

He sombered around as if pontificating before a large crowd. Nerone paused and waited for Ishmael's reaction.

"Do you remember in Genesis 2:16–17, when God told Adam, 'Ye shall eat of any tree in the garden, but of the Tree of the Knowledge of Good and Evil you shall not eat, *for in that day* that you eat of it you shall surely die!' And our father responded, in truth, 'Ye shall *not* surely die but ye shall know the difference between good and evil…'" He folded his arms obstinately.

Ishmael looked up at the biblical narratives depicted in the surrounding murals, then addressed the Jesuit.

"Adam died."

"Did he? Adam lived another what? Nine hundred and thirty years?" He stared intensely at the redhead. "So, who lied?"

"We are mortal beings. We must all face death… and then The Judgment."

"*The Judgment. Ha!*" He scoffed. "Tell me who should be judged: a narcissistic, picayune god who desperately needs to be worshiped, then eternally tortures those who exercise the very free will given by him, *or* a being who is willing to stand against such tyranny?"

"God judges righteously."

"Does he? How can one exercise free will without knowing? Tell me, Ishmael, how does this god judge those he predestined to torment? Huh? How does your 'loving' God send to hell those who he foreknew would betray him? You call that free will?"

"Hmmm, and yet you *freely* chose to tell me that…" He paused and looked up at the mural of Eve with the forbidden fruit in her hand. "Some things are better left unknown."

"Better than what? How can you choose something if you do not know what you may sacrifice? How can you exercise free will if you do not know what you give up? How could Adam have had free will if he did not know what 'evil' offered? Can you determine what is, without what is not? Can you have light without darkness, good without bad? Male without female? Up without down? Sweet without sour? Is not evil necessary to exemplify good?"

"Not all knowledge is beneficial."

"Is it not? Why would God punish a man for knowing? And what, pray tell, is wrong with knowledge? Hmmm? Tell me. What kind of sadistic God seeds his creation with a desire to learn and then forbids him to exercise the very desire that He instilled? The truth is, it was *our* father who gave mankind free will, *not* YHWH! It is the occult knowledge that God forbade that has allowed mankind to progress!"

"All knowledge is subject to the wisdom of the Bible."

"So said the Christians when they scoffed at science. And look at it now."

"Scaramucci said the scientific method was originally founded to pursue God's divine attributes, to know Him, and that many of the earliest naturalists were Christians."

"That bald-headed freak! I will admit there were a handful who sought after objective truth. But we have evolved past that! Just look at what we have done without those backward troglodytes! Look at what we can do! Knowledge has become a pursuit unto itself, a catapult toward progress, for the betterment of all mankind! Your god would have prohibited the development of medicines that have saved millions of lives."

"Scaramucci said that the Church teaches—"

"*Fuck the* Church*!* Lies, my son. Don't play the fool!"

"That is not what I was told."

"Ah yes, perhaps you speak of dear Asiya, your mother?"

"DON'T FUCKING TALK ABOUT MY MOTHER!"

"That's it! *THAT'S IT,* MY BOY!"

"Fuck your cult and your goofy prophecy!" Ishmael said defiantly.

"*YES!* I LOVE IT! More. *GIVE ME MORE!* Give me the anger! You know, I had my doubts." He paced back and forth, shaking his finger. "But I believe you *are* the 'boy bitten by flame,' *'the Edomite'* of old, after all!" He paused as his enthusiasm subsided. "I remember your mother. Remember when she tucked you in at night. I was there." He stared into Ishmael's hazel eyes. "She lied to you, my boy, *not intentionally of course.*" He put his hands out in a gesture of resignation. He quickly qualified his comments. "...but those bullshit Bible stories...." He paused. "Naïveté. Ignorance. Unintentional lies. But lies nonetheless." He stared intently at the redhead. "Cast aside the archaic notion of sin. Utter nonsense! It is for the slave, the sheep. You are not one of them! You are like us! *Enlightened!*"

"I don't think so." He shook his head in belligerence.

"Think, Ishmael. Why would God forbid knowledge? Answer? Fear! And why would an almighty God fear man, an infinitesimally small peon of plasma, a meat sack, on a remote planet shoved way in the back of the universe? I will tell you why. He is afraid of your potential."

"No man rivals God."

"*Ahhh*, no man, true, but a *god*... that is a different matter. And what kind of megalomaniacal, sadistic God seeds his creation with a desire to know, a desire to learn, a desire to experience life, a desire to have fun, a desire to love, a desire *to fuck*..." He popped an olive in his mouth. "...and then deprives him of it? Huh? Answer."

"To protect us," he ventured. "So that we don't hurt ourselves exceeding the limits. There are limits... uh... there are immutable boundaries... laws."

"Are there? Are there really immutable boundaries? Name one."

"I will never be able to breathe underwater..." Ishmael stuttered to reply. "...or fly."

"Really? How did you cross the Atlantic? Huh? Swim?"

"I mean I have no wings. Gravity forbids me. I cannot defy natural laws."

"Interesting point of history." He turned and paced across the dining hall. "Did you know that it was Baraqiel, a helpful familiar, who seeded the knowledge to Jack Parsons who, in turn, developed the propulsion systems necessary to get you here? Jack Parsons. Heard of him?"

"No."

"He was a protégé of Aleister Crowley. I am certain you have heard of him."

"Unfortunately," Ishmael said facetiously. "But I simply meant that there are laws that mankind cannot transgress. Immutable boundaries."

"Are there now? Immutable? Hmmm." The priest took a few steps back, crossed his arms, chanted a spell, and levitated two meters off the ground. But he didn't float as if suspended from a wire, rather seemed to step up, as if scaling an invisible ladder. His body did not wobble or falter but rather seemed to perch solidly atop a phantom platform. Suspended in the air, he stared down diminutively at Ishmael.

"Holy shit!" Ishmael recoiled; his eyes grew wide with fear. Sofia gave him a look of deep concern.

"I think you mean 'unholy shit'?" The priest stared at him, waiting for the gravity of the situation to sink in. "There are *no* limits, my boy! You can do whatever you want. You can do anything. You can satisfy your deepest, darkest desires. Money? Power? Sex? You want someone dead? Done. You want someone tortured? Done. You want to extend your life? Done. You want to fuck a woman, a man, a child, a dog? Anything. It is yours. *You* determine what is right and wrong, not some sanctimonious, miscreant celestial child with a magnifying glass. *We* determine our destiny. *Do what thou wilt shall be the whole of the law.*" His eyes glazed over with a ferocity of intensity.

"This is madness."

"Is it? I say it is syllogistic, entirely sane and reasonable. When the serpent spoke to Eve in the garden, he said, *'Ye shall be like gods.'* So, tell me now. Is it not so? Who told the truth? Tell me, my boy, we define what is true... *Quid est veritas?*" He raised his hands open as if praying to heaven. "*ARE WE NOT GODS?*"

The Jesuit priest jumped to the floor as if falling through a trapdoor. He approached Ishmael, his menacing figure dwarfing the redhead.

"I... I..." Ishmael felt the familiar frigid feeling that he had come to recognize when he encountered the demonic; the scar on his wrist began to itch.

"You see, God is afraid of your true potential. He doesn't want you to be truly free. So He created rules, rules, and more rules. Well, I say *NO MORE FUCKING RULES!*" He shouted toward the ceiling. "Let's follow in the anthem of Saint Sinatra—let's do it *our* way!"

"Never! Torture me! Kill me if you like. I will never choose to be a part of your plan! I would rather die."

Slightly exasperated, Nerone looked at Lilith. "Very well. You leave us no choice. Bring her in!"

She was escorted by one of their henchmen, her head covered with a black hood. One of the corsos growled as she passed. Her hands were bound by rope; she gazed at the floor. There was an immediate familiarity to her countenance, her gait. She stopped at the center of the room. She lifted her gaze to her son. There, before him, stood his mother.

"*MOM?!?!*" He stood to face her. He ran to hug her, but the corsos leapt forward.

Asiya was bound with lace ties, but she was bound nonetheless. Her mouth was covered with tape. Nerone spoke. "As you can see, she is in good shape. She has been cared for... privy to daily doses of our finest adrenochrome drips. She looks great, doesn't she?" Asiya didn't—couldn't—respond.

"*WHAT THE FUCK HAVE YOU DONE TO MY MOTHER?!!*" Ishmael charged at Nerone. The Black Pope raised his hand and, without contact, kinesthetically threw the redhead three meters into the air, onto the buffet table, spilling coffee, juice, and scraps of edibles everywhere. Sofia bit her tongue, but the look of concern on her face was evident.

"You will do as we ask, young one," Nerone straightened his suit. "...or we will torture your mother for the next decade and make you watch!"

Without another word, the Black Pope, Lilith, Asiya, the two corsos, and their escort turned and left.

"WHAT THE FUCK DO YOU WANT FROM ME?!!!!" he yelled after him.

Sofia wanted to speak, but she held her tongue.

Chapter 51 - Rome, Italy

"I brought you from the ends of the earth and called you from its farthest corners. I said, 'You are My servant.' I have chosen and not rejected you." - Isaiah 41:9

mendola chomped loudly on his gum. He was trying to quit smoking, and the gum was not working. The impulse to smoke was overwhelming.

He was sitting in his sterile office, watching RAIDUE for the nightly news, when the normal programming was interrupted by a news bulletin.

ATTACCO A BOSTON E ALLA CIVILTÀ!

He listened intently as the newscasters reported on the exploits of the saboteurs. He wondered, *why the sudden surge in global terrorism? Did this event have anything to do with his case?* His gut told him it did.

He picked up the receiver from the white phone on his desk.

"Si, signorina *Blanca,* mi *puoi comprare un biglietto per Boston, per favore? ... Si... Si... domani."*

He hung up. He had decided to find out.

Chapter 52 – Lago Gandolfo, Italy

"If you do not tell me the dream, there is only one penalty for you. You have conspired to tell me misleading and wicked things, hoping the situation will change. So then, tell me the dream, and I will know that you can interpret it for me." - Daniel 2:9

t was 3:00 a.m. His auburn hair had grown long in his captivity. His curls recoiled as his body twitched. His eyes darted back and forth beneath his lids, lost in R.E.M. Ishmael was in a deep dream.

Suspended in the metaphysical ether, in the atemporal expanse, he floated on the ceiling. This was novel. He had never been here before. He was in the most magnificent palace he had ever seen... Where was he? When was he? He didn't know.

It was early morning. There was no activity. The throne had six steps, and its posterior had a rounded top. On both sides of the seat were armrests, with a lion standing beside each of them. Twelve more lions stood on the six steps, one at either end of each step.

Intricately woven tapestries, hanging veils, pillars, incense... everything was of the most incredible quality. Water filtered into the sanctuary, collecting into pools from an outdoor spring. And there were palm trees and pomegranate trees fed by sunlight in the courtyard.

He was lost in the grandeur and splendor when, in the distance, he heard raised voices. They sounded guttural, contesting, defiant, angry. His spirit was pulled toward them. As if immaterial, he floated through the wall, entering another room, then another, then another, and still another.

Finally, there on the floor knelt a man in regal attire, long curly sweaty brown hair protruding from underneath a golden throne. His head was bowed in submission or obstinance—Ishmael couldn't tell which. The king was talking, whispering, chanting...

Inscribed on the floor, encircling him, was a pentagram. Each point of the star held ancient Hebrew glyphs. In the metaphysical realm, Ishmael could see demons trying to break the perimeter, but they were held at bay by luminary spirits with long, unsheathed blades of fire.

Pasquale had spoken of Solomon... and his exploits in witchcraft.

He was immediately transported back to Vienna, to the court at Karlsplatz. The priest walked over to the kiosk to purchase a Kaiserkreiner.

"YHWH had promised King Solomon a gift, any gift. The new king chose knowledge. He was young and wanted to rule righteously. YHWH was pleased; as a result, he gave Solomon wealth and power as well. With this gift, the teenage king bore the burden of erudition; his learning became both lauded and despised.

The Bible speaks of his vast knowledge, his writings, and his wealth. He accumulated seven hundred wives and three hundred concubines."

"Wow. That is a lot of women."

The priest paid his schillings and took the breaded sausage from the man behind the window.

"Many were political marriages. Yet his marital exploits eventually led to his downfall. The Testament, The Greater and Lesser Keys of Solomon, and other apocryphal writings shed light on the subsequent events of his reign. He was disturbed by the disembodied spirits who had haunted some of his closest friends. He vowed to use his vast intellect to fight them.

The spirits were, of course, the disembodied spirits of the Nephilim—the giants killed by the flood. For the first forty years of his reign, Solomon prospered:

'Thus, King Solomon excelled all the kings of earth in riches and in wisdom. And the whole earth sought the presence of Solomon to hear his wisdom, which God had put into his mind.' (I Kings 10:23–24).

He ruled over the natural world. He began to apply his acumen to overcoming the spirits of darkness. He would draw a pentagram on the floor, and at its points, the five names of Adonai that served as protection against the demons.

The Greater Key of Solomon tells us that in the beginning, YHWH protected him, allowing him to probe the demonic hierarchy and discover their names. Solomon was able to evoke the demons at will and charge them with certain tasks. In fact, many believe that it was Solomon's evoking of the spirits that helped to construct the first temple."

"So, the Nephilim built the temple of Solomon?" he said sarcastically.

"Many believe that they not only built Solomon's temple but also the Pyramids of Giza, the Colossus of Rhodes, and many other ancient marvels. And it was these 'masonic' demons that gave rise to the Freemasons and other secret societies..."

"Really? Come on, priest. Give me a break. Demons built the pyramids?"

"Believe what you want, son." He took a bite of his Kaiserkreiner and adjusted his bifocals. With a mouthful of sausage, he muttered on.

"And so, through his interrogations, he was able to decipher that if he could control the archdemons, all their underlings would have to comply as well. There was a hierarchy. That is why, in an exorcism, we seek the highest-ranking demon. If we dispel him, his underlings must follow."

"Very militant."

"Yes, but we are not alone."

"You mean God is on our side?"

"Not just God but angelic hosts, assigned to certain demons—their luminary counterparts."

"So, Yin and Yang?"

"I prefer not to use Eastern mysticism, but if that helps you understand, so be it." He took another mammoth bite from his dog. *"Solomon was able to contain them. He was able to banish the archdemons to a brass kettle, and this is where the legend of Aladdin's lamp comes from."*

"Sounds like fantasy. How do we know that these were written by King Solomon? As you said, most Christian denominations do not include the apocrypha. I mean, maybe they were written by some anonymous writer, or maybe demons themselves?"

"True. But I do not believe that a book about demons, written by demons, would evoke the true names of God. They would rather hide behind false titles such as Allah, Krishna, or Shiva... God's name is torture to their ears. And furthermore, I do not believe they would give a prescription on how to control them."

"So basically, Solomon was a sorcerer?"

"He began doing what we call 'white' magic. The Greater Key is a grimoire—that is, a list of spells to control demons."

"But you said that all magic is bad?"

"It is, my son. Let me tell you how the story ends." He took another bite.

"In The Lesser Key, Solomon listed, by name, seventy demons or principalities and how to control them. It is the latter of Solomon's works that became the source of inspiration for the likes of Aleister Crowley and Samuel L. M. Mathers. It offers seductive power to those willing to sacrifice their souls in order to wield it, as Solomon learned later."

"So, Solomon was a Satanist?"

"For a time, Solomon was able to control an entire army of demons—magical genies, or jinn, if you will—that were forced to do his bidding."

"He just said, 'Do this! Do that!'?"

"No. In fact, Solomon was brutal. To conjure their presence, he would evoke the demons by torturing them with spells. If they refused to come, he would cast them into the fire, curse them with leprosy, and/or confinement. In this manner, he was able to interrogate them individually, learn their secrets, and unmask their world."

"Like what?"

"Well, he summoned the entirety of the archdemons, then he forced them to self-incriminate."

"What do you mean?"

"So, a demon might say, 'I hate the smell of the innards of fish at full moon,' for example. And so, Solomon would experiment with spells involving fish that would repel their presence. In so doing, he chronicled the weaknesses and strengths of the demonic hosts. Remember that demons are not just fumes of smoke, amorphous and listless, but they are personalities with preferences, habits, ways of thinking, skill sets, and fetishes."

"Like people."

"Yes. Each one is unique. Solomon's original intent was to help humanity... but you see, there was a caveat. The ring was to be used to enslave the demons, but Solomon began to use it for his own desires."

"Ring? What ring?"

"Oh, sorry, I forgot. YHWH had fashioned a ring with either a five-pointed or six-pointed star—no one knows for certain. It was hand-delivered by the archangel Michael. It had the power to control demons!"

"So that's what she was looking for?" he mused to himself.

"What are you talking about?" Pasquale said quizzically.

"After we exorcised the young girl in Oberammergau... I felt another presence fight against my spirit, probing as if looking for something. It was brief. She didn't stay for long, but it was pure evil, dark... I didn't know who it was until the night of the ritual when she was made high priestess. It was then that I recognized her presence. It was Lilith."

"Ishmael." He gripped his arm in desperation. "Do you know where the Ring of Solomon is?"

"I don't. I mean... I don't know... I might. So, what happened to the ring?" he said curiously.

"Well, God gave strict instructions that Solomon would be protected only as long as he did not worship the foreign 'gods' of the surrounding kingdoms. Over time, he became seduced by his foreign-born brides. He was enticed to burn incense to Molech, a foreign god, and in so doing, YHWH's protections were revoked. So instead of being the master of demons, he became their slave. With pent-up frustration and rage, they tortured him for years.

At the end of Ecclesiastes, we read how it was resolved. He threw himself at the mercy of God and asked for forgiveness—but only after sin had taken an enormous toll, including the loss of his posterity and their claim to the throne of Israel. Never again would Israel be united."

"So, if he had not bowed to the foreign gods—or Nephilim—he would have been able to control demons? So white magic does exist," he mused to himself.

"Well, it depends which legend you believe. According to one account by Herodotus, the Greek historian, Asmodeus, the demon of lust, disguised himself as the king and tricked one of his wives into giving it to him. He then supplanted the king, ruling for decades as an imposter. The real king was kicked out. He became a fisherman. Tired of its burden, Asmodeus cast it into the sea, never to be discovered by mortal man again. It was swallowed by a fish, which was later caught by King Solomon, thus returning him to power. Henceforth, it took the name 'the Fisherman's Ring.'

It has influenced many tales throughout the ages, including the writings of J.R.R. Tolkien—but those are just mythologies. The ring is real, my son, and by no means can it ever fall into the hands of the Dawn. If you know where it is, you must tell me!"

His demeanor softened. *"If you know where it is, please tell me!"*

Something strange... Ishmael felt cold, and his scar began to itch.

"I don't..." Pasquale's face seemed to morph. His countenance became frustrated, desperate, longing—perhaps even lustful.

"Ish, tell me please!" His eyes changed color.

"Ish? You have never called me Ish before," the redhead commented.

The priest leaned over and grabbed him by the throat.

"AHHHHHHH!!! TELL ME WHERE THE FUCKING RING IS, YOU CUNT!!!!!"

Ishmael sat up wide-eyed. His bedsheets were drenched in sweat.

"Lilith!" So that's it! It all made sense now. Once the Watchers were released, they would never bow to a mere human—unless...

He whispered, *"They need the Ring of Solomon!"*

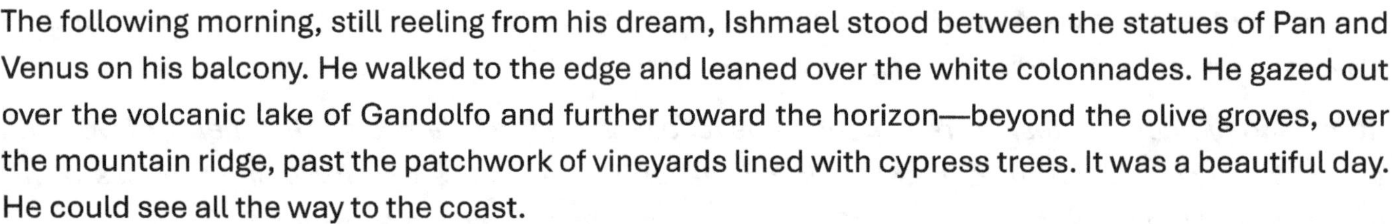

The following morning, still reeling from his dream, Ishmael stood between the statues of Pan and Venus on his balcony. He walked to the edge and leaned over the white colonnades. He gazed out over the volcanic lake of Gandolfo and further toward the horizon—beyond the olive groves, over the mountain ridge, past the patchwork of vineyards lined with cypress trees. It was a beautiful day. He could see all the way to the coast.

What a beautiful prison, he thought to himself.

For the entirety of the morning, the estate had been overrun with a buzz of activity. Car after car had arrived at the manor. Militant-looking personnel scattered about like bees. Conversations—

languages from every corner of the globe—ebbed and flowed from the corridors of the enormous estate.

He heard a soft knock at his door.

"Hello?" Sofia pushed her way past the guards and poked her head in the doorframe. "*Permesso*?"

"I have nothing to say to you," he said dismissively.

She came in anyway. "I know you are upset, but can we just talk?"

"I know what you are going to say."

"I don't think you do." She sat on the bed and patted the mattress softly. "Please. Sit."

He reluctantly approached and stood at the foot of the bed, arms crossed.

"Lilith is my mother."

"I figured."

"Well, you don't know about my childhood, my upbringing. I was born into the Order, just like my mother. My father was the Emperor of the Order, a man named Winston Maspeth. I hardly knew him. When a girl is coven-born, she must undergo the rituals of defilement to determine if she is a worthy candidate as the bride of the Dark Lord."

"The bride of Satan? Are you serious?" Ishmael interrupted.

"Yes. I was raped by a member of the congregation first when I was twelve, and then many times after that. My mother told me it was my duty for the good of the Order. She hoped it was our Dark Lord's will that I was impregnated." Sofia winced from the painful memory but quickly recovered. "I've seen babies sacrificed during conjurings, their hearts cut out right in front of me. I've had to taste human flesh and drink blood."

Ishmael was horrified. "I'm sorry those things happened to you, Sofia. Why didn't you just leave?"

"I couldn't leave... this life is all I know. Besides, they would kill me if I tried. I am to become the head of the Order when my mother is too old to serve."

"Yeah well, your mother paid me a visit last night."

"Look, I am sorry, hon, but we *must* have the ring. Without it, the angels will roll all over us."

"And what is to stop me from turning the Watchers on you, huh?"

"Neither the Dawn nor the Watchers will ever let you wield it." Sofia looked at the ground shamefully. "But we must know where it is..."

"I see. So, you are plan B, huh?" He looked at her defiantly. "If you can't force it out of me, seduce it out of me! Tell me, *love*," he said facetiously. "How does it feel to be a puppet?"

"You don't understand. We will use it for good—even if we have to break a few eggs to get it."

"*Eggs?* What the fuck, Sofia? *A LOT OF PEOPLE ARE GOING TO DIE!*"

"Yes. Unfortunately, *some* may die..." She stared at him in earnest. "But for a greater cause, a better way!"

"So, the end justifies the means? Huh? Kill everyone who opposes you so you can create your Eden?"

"*YES!* Absolutely!" She stared at him with conviction. "How many people suffer every day? Huh? How many people die of hunger? Die of disease? Lose loved ones? Suffering all over the world? Huh? Is it not a noble cause to want to fix humanity? To cure the sick? To put nature into balance? We are destroying the world. Shortages are inevitable. Mankind is on the road to destruction—self-annihilation. The world requires a radical solution for a radical problem."

"*Sin* is the problem."

"NO! Sin is fiction. We are enlightened. We have evolved past that archaic notion. We want to create a global solution where there are no more shortages, no more injustice, perfect equality, equity for all. What is wrong with that?"

"I'll tell you what is fucking wrong with that! You have no right to choose for someone else!"

"Ish, free will is an illusion! Do you choose which demographic you are born in? Did you choose your skin color or what religion you were born into?"

"Of course not, but my free will is not confined by borders or how much money I make."

"Is it not? Do you think we all have the same opportunities? Come on, Ish, be real."

"Perhaps not. I may not have the same choices as others, but I still have the right to choose from the options given to me. Someday soon, I may have to choose between servitude and death, and it may not be a choice I like... but it is still *MY* FUCKING CHOICE! *AND YOU HAVE NO FUCKING RIGHT TO TAKE THAT FROM ME!*"

"I am sorry, Ish. But the rights of the many outweigh the rights of the few."

"Yeah. I can see that." He looked around at the grandeur of the palatial room. "You are all about the rights of the many, aren't you?" he said sarcastically.

With her head bowed, she got up and left the room.

241

Chapter 53 – Lago Gandolfo, Italy

"…whoever climbs out of the pit will be caught in a snare." - Isaiah 24:18

t was late. He didn't know the hour. His clock had been removed, along with anything else that could be used to self-harm. He hadn't slept. Except for shoes, he was already dressed.

He had surveyed the house for weeks. He knew the protocols. He could not escape by running across the meticulously landscaped fields, nor could he use the tunnel that had provided access to the subterranean chambers. There were fourteen guards—seven teams of two members each—including one team in front of his door, and the others spread throughout the compound; none were stationed on his balcony.

He moved to the balcony door and quietly shimmied the lock (a talent he had gleaned from his friends back in Chicago). The door clicked. He slipped quietly onto the balcony. He looked over the edge. Two men stood at the entrance of the manor, each equipped with Beretta ARX 160s. Two more stood near the garage, near the periphery, and two more stood at the gated entrance at the bottom of the hill. The rest could be anywhere.

No one guarded the roof.

The redhead positioned himself between the fascia and the statue, shimming up the wall using Pan's erection as a step to get to the next rung. Finally, Ishmael stepped on Pan's head and leapt horizontally. The statue began rocking free from its base. For a moment, he feared it would tip over and betray his position.

He grabbed the rake of the roof and jumped. He knelt and listened. Nothing.

He proceeded along the roof's ridge, hiding his silhouette from the night sky. He stepped delicately on the Spanish tile. Light shone from the atrium encased in translucent glass; its glass ceiling held vented windows that could be hyperextended, allowing for the passage of a nimble person.

Ishmael opened the window and jumped to the tree in the interior of the house. He climbed down the tree and opened the fog-covered glass door to the main hallway. He peeked out and felt a gun muzzle at his temple.

"So, I guess we need to think of some different accommodations."

Kabir stood flanked by two armed soldiers.

Chapter 54 - Rome, Italy

"(I) strengthened their arms, but they plot evil against me." - Hosea 7:15

igh atop the *Palazzo della Civiltà Italiana*, every member of the satanic council sat in attendance.

"What is the progress on phase two?" Muller posited.

The Tewani twins stood up in unison and walked over to a wall-mounted map of Europe that spanned five meters in every direction.

"On Saturday, April 19th, we shall execute our plan."

"On the *Sabbath*?"

Kabir nodded. "Black Sabbath."

"All right. Enlighten me," Muller insisted.

Kabir stood in his singular trademark one-piece suit. His military haircut was neatly coiffed, and his freshly shaven face stood in direct contrast to his brother, who donned a long beard and ponytail. Samir sported a white collarless jacket. The identical twins stood on opposite sides of the map.

Kabir extended his mechanical pointer. "We shall execute a mass attack across the entire European continent, striking seven cities concurrently. Seven teams, with seven members each, shall deploy seven transient electromagnetic disturbances."

"I'm sorry. Can you put that in layman's terms for those of us without a military background?" the cardinal said cheekily.

"We will set off seven E.M.P.s."

The clergyman looked quizzically at Samir, so he answered, *"Pulses*, Cardinal Muller. Planes will fall from the sky, cars will stop in traffic, telecommunications will cease, all electronic systems within a one-hundred-mile radius will be rendered useless."

Kabir continued undaunted, pointing to the map. "Our targets are Rome, Vienna, Paris, London, Madrid, Stockholm, and Brussels. Following the EMPs, we will deploy seven more teams, each with seven members, to release contagion devices into the local water supplies, as we did in Boston." He indicated it on the map. "…into the Seine here, the Thames here, the Danube here, the Norrström here, the Senne here, the Manzanares here, and the Tiber River here. Thereby crippling supplies and creating a shortage of food and water. The cities will be blind; they will neither have the wherewithal nor the ability to see it coming." He paused and straightened his jacket.

"I hope we will not see another debacle like Boston," the bishop said sardonically.

Samir responded, "I admit Boston was not an exemplar. Two buoys were deployed with mixed results. One was captured. Our attempts were…" He paused, choosing his diction, "…met with opposition. The enemy was able to infiltrate our ranks by bugging our phones. We lost six operatives. The Nigerian had a team in place."

"Azikiwe?"

"Yes," Kabir continued. "He was able to tap Dunnigan's phone."

"Where is that Irish fool?" The cardinal looked around the room.

"He is off-grid at the moment."

"Convenient." He adjusted his vestments. "And the Nigerian?"

"To speak plainly, we do not know. Although we had assets in play, he was able to slip away. He was able to capture one device."

"So, we can assume that the authorities have the mechanism. Can they trace it back to us?"

"No. All the components were constructed and later assembled in-house, and the contagion was purchased through our Soviet counterparts, smuggled out of Odessa, through the Straits of Istanbul, and then brought in by our contacts in Sicily. Our soldiers collected it at Ostia. There are no direct links to the Dawn," he said confidently.

"You said two devices detonated…" Muller continued.

"As I assume you witnessed on the news, the buoys were met with limited success. Roughly seven thousand casualties…"

In his thick Ghanaian cadence, Doctor Embata interrupted, "And what assurances can you offer to prevent further disruptions?"

The Tewani twins turned to address the West African.

"Well, we no longer have a leak. And although we are certain that they expect further action, they will have no idea where to assemble their forces, nor will they be prepared for the size and scope of what is coming. And Boston, although unfortunate, yielded some interesting results. We have learned from our mistakes, and we have since remedied the situation. The deployment devices we have developed since will contain thrice the strength as those used in Boston."

"How many casualties should we expect?" the doctor continued.

"Conservative estimates: initially, one hundred thousand deaths per city, with half again as many injured, and possibly twice that in the aftermath."

"How do you predict the public will respond?"

"The hospitals and triages will be forced past capacity. The grocery stores will run dry in a matter of weeks. The governments will be forced to ration goods and services. The lack of electricity will make it impossible for commerce and communication."

"And if all electricity is knocked out..."

Anticipating the doctor's objection, Samir interrupted, "We are completely shielded. Faraday cages have been embedded throughout Kingdom Hill and in Babylon. In addition, we have seven subterranean hydro-generators that will service our needs until the apocalypse."

Kabir continued, "The people will be forced into the streets. As the need for basic necessities increases, so shall desperation; famine will ensue, undermining the local municipalities. Factions will arise. Raiding parties will move from home to home. Society will cannibalize itself, and all we have to do is sit back and watch the show." He smiled sadistically.

"And what about law enforcement?" Muller spoke again.

"They will be blindsided, no pun intended. They have no idea of the magnitude of this attack. It will send shockwaves around the world. Law enforcement will be under enormous pressure. We will amplify this pressure by dispatching indiscriminate terrorist attacks across the continent—lone gunmen and selective bombings of Christian churches and Jewish temples. Public sentiment will lose confidence in the ability of the authorities to maintain order."

"And if they get caught?"

"They are prepared to die for the cause, Father."

"So, if you plan to poison the water supplies... won't we poison ourselves?"

"Yes, but our members will be inoculated, and we have stockpiled enough provisions, hidden under the city, for months—even years, if necessary," Samir answered the question.

"And what of phase three? What about *Gebofal*?"

Nerone continued the narrative. "The Edomite is in custody, albeit unwillingly."

"How will you get him to comply?"

Lilith spoke from under her crimson veil. "He will do as we ask!"

Chapter 55 – Lago Gandolfo, Italy

"So, when Joseph came to his brothers, they stripped him of his robe—the ornate robe he was wearing— and they took him and threw him into the cistern. The cistern was empty; there was no water in it." - Genesis 37: 23, 24

shmael stood in the subterranean loading bay, handcuffed to a metal bar.

"I wish Cecilia and Ewan were here," Sofia said, biting her nails.

"You've got new friends now." Ishmael gestured to the suited soldiers climbing into the cab of the cargo truck.

"I am sorry that we have to keep you prisoner. I had hoped that it would not be necessary," Sofia stated.

"All you had to do was sacrifice your best friends." He rebuffed her attempt at magnanimity.

"They died for what they believed."

"How noble," Ishmael said sardonically.

Kabir walked around from the backside of the subterranean loading bay. Two soldiers accompanied him.

"Take him to Babylon. Put him in the cell next to his mother. Misery loves company and all that…"

"Please cooperate, hon. I love you." Sofia bowed her head submissively.

"Leave me alone," he said flatly.

Two soldiers wearing black military attire unlocked his handcuffs and then escorted him to the bed of the cargo lorry, where they refastened his restraints. They then climbed into the back of the truck and sat on the opposite side.

Kabir spoke from the loading floor. "Call to confirm your arrival." He slapped the side of the Russian vehicle.

"Yes, sir."

As Ishmael remembered, the truck ride was rough, teetering back and forth, knocking his cohorts against each other. Then suddenly it was smooth—the underground highway—and soon, Babylon.

He wondered if he would ever see the sky again. He thought about his journey, his plight, Gebofal. Would he be forced to conjure the evil spirits? He dreaded the thought. Yet he also felt drawn. He understood Sofia—he disagreed cerebrally, but he understood her intentions.

The truck swayed, then lurched forward, forcing the soldiers to collapse on one another. The brakes hissed, and the tires squealed. Suddenly, it stopped.

The two soldiers sat across from him, Sig Sauers drawn. The rear gate dropped, revealing a man with a black balaclava standing on the side of the road. He stated something in a language Ishmael could not understand. The two soldiers returned their pistols to their shoulder harnesses and began to descend from the bed of the truck.

No sooner had the men turned around than the driver pulled a suppressed pistol from his breast and inserted projectiles into the heads of the two guards. They both fell to the bed of the truck.

"Hurry! Help me hide their bodies." He lifted his mask.

"Malech!"

"I've been following you for a while. Here, help me with these." They struggled with the three corpses, tossing them into a neighboring ravine.

"We have to get you out of here."

"How?" They piled into the cab of the lorry.

"Do you see those sun rays?" He alluded to the stone ceiling hundreds of meters above the cityscape. "Do you see those stairs?" He pointed into the distance—to a spiral staircase

carved from the wall of the cavern. "We have very little time. When Kabir doesn't get a call that you've arrived at the detention center, he will send out a team."

Malech shifted the lorry, ground it into third gear, then sputtered along the periphery of the town. He turned right toward the cavernous walls, then parked the Russian behemoth at the base of the stairway. They exited the vehicle.

Ishmael looked up. A daunting climb lay ahead of them. A whistle blew from several blocks away, and a horde of black-clad individuals gave chase.

"Go! GO! Hurry!" Malech prompted.

They ran up the rotund staircase—round and round, higher and higher. His feet began to ache and his lungs expanded, sweat flowing beneath his black hoodie. The view broadened, and the buildings below them got smaller and smaller. At the base of the *scala*, he could see the circling of red lights and the activity of the Dawn's minions. Yelling, grunting, and the clatter of boots could be heard reverberating off the cement steps below.

They had run half a kilometer vertically. The redhead looked toward the sky as the light seemed to grow in intensity. Finally, at its zenith, the staircase straightened and gave way to a carved tunnel, and then to an obscure hole in the ground, partially covered in verge and eroded red masonry.

Ishmael could see the surface.

Malech and Ishmael popped out amongst the ruins of the *Baths at Caracalla*—a system of elaborate edifices originally built by *Imperatore Nero*, several thousands of years prior. The section had been blocked off by pointed iron fencing, inaccessible to the public.

They ran to the fence at its periphery and scaled it. Malech bade Ishmael to follow him to a white *FIAT Cinquecento* parked clandestinely along the hedgework. Malech pulled some keys from his pocket and started the car.

They sped away.

Chapter 56 - Ankara, Turkey

"...while he himself went a day's journey into the wilderness." - I Kings 19:4

 alech had procured a private jet. They had flown out of Naples to avoid discovery. The flight from Naples to Ankara was seven hours, and the car ride to Amasya was another four. They had rented a pagoda-yellow 742 Skoda. Malech was at the helm. *Not a very* discreet *vehicle*, the redhead thought to himself. The tiny wheels bounced along the pothole-ridden roads, occasionally stopping for the rogue pedestrian or herd of grazing goats.

"So?" Malech inquired. "Why Turkey? Did you get a vision?" He seemed uncomfortable in his three-piece grey suit. His impeccable grooming stood in direct contrast to the worn interior of the Czechoslovakian vehicle.

"No. Not this time..." He paused. "It's just a feeling, an impulse... I can't explain it."

"Are you sure we are headed the right way?"

"No. I am not..." He looked out the window. "Call it faith." He said it more to himself than to Malech.

"How do you know where to go?"

"I don't." He shifted in his seat. "But I know that there are three brothers living here... One of them is abroad, and the other two live here in the city of Amasya."

"And why these men?"

"Let's just say that they run an illegal business—a smuggling ring. Through their connections in Africa and the Middle East, they smuggle ancient religious artifacts into the hands of rich Westerners. In a few days, they will receive a shipment from Ethiopia. This particular package will be unlike any they have ever received. Its contents are priceless."

"And so, we must get there before it arrives."

"Precisely."

"Efes, can you bring me some tea? And my cigarettes from the kitchen counter?" he yelled from the Berber-style courtyard.

"Get up and do it yourself, you lazy!" his mother corrected him as if he were nine years old.

His balding middle-aged brother entered with a silver tray, pretentious porcelain teacups, and a crystal carafe full of steaming, reddish-brown libation. He set them down on the inlaid tiled table, then threw a pack of filterless cigarettes at his brother.

"You spoil him; that is why he always asks you. You reward his bad behavior," his mother quibbled.

"He is the youngest. He is supposed to be spoiled." He threw both hands, palms up, toward the sky in a gesture of resignation. "I love to spoil him. And don't make it seem like you don't do the same."

"I am your mother. Don't talk back to me." She lifted her hand as if she was going to backslap him.

"Ah, Mom." Efes grinned.

"Ahmet, stop asking other people to do what you can do for yourself."

Ahmet took out a pearl-white Zippo lighter, lit his cigarette, then took a lengthy drag. "Why do for myself what other people will do for me?"

Fatima laughed aloud, then took a long sip of her tea. She sat regally, legs crossed in a peach-colored skirt and cream blouse, her hair combed back and held neatly in a mesh net. She put her cup on the table.

"Any news on the shipment from Addis Ababa?" she changed the subject.

Efes responded, "Yusuf called a few hours ago. He'll be arriving in the next few days. Do you have a buyer lined up?"

His mother seemed annoyed at his question. "Of course. Don't I always? Tell me one time I have not had a buyer."

Ahmet smiled. "You amaze me, Mother. I would like to know how you got in with all these wealthy benefactors."

"Ahhh, my son, I forced my way in." She laughed proudly. "Before your father died, they were his business partners. I just took over the reins. Of course, they did not accept me at first, but you know how persuasive your mother can be." She fashioned an evil smirk.

It was true. Fatima C. Gunkut was resilient. Widowed at twenty-seven, and despite having no formal education, she had succeeded in a society ruled by men. She had raised three boys, and she had thrived. Through their illegal trade and Fatima's connections, the Gunkut family had amassed millions in foreign currency. She and her sons owned homes in their hometown Amasya, and in London, Paris, and New York.

Via bribery and political connections, the Gunkut brothers had carved smuggling routes through West Africa, crossing ten international borders and into Turkey— the epicenter of international trade and the historical nexus of the Silk Road.

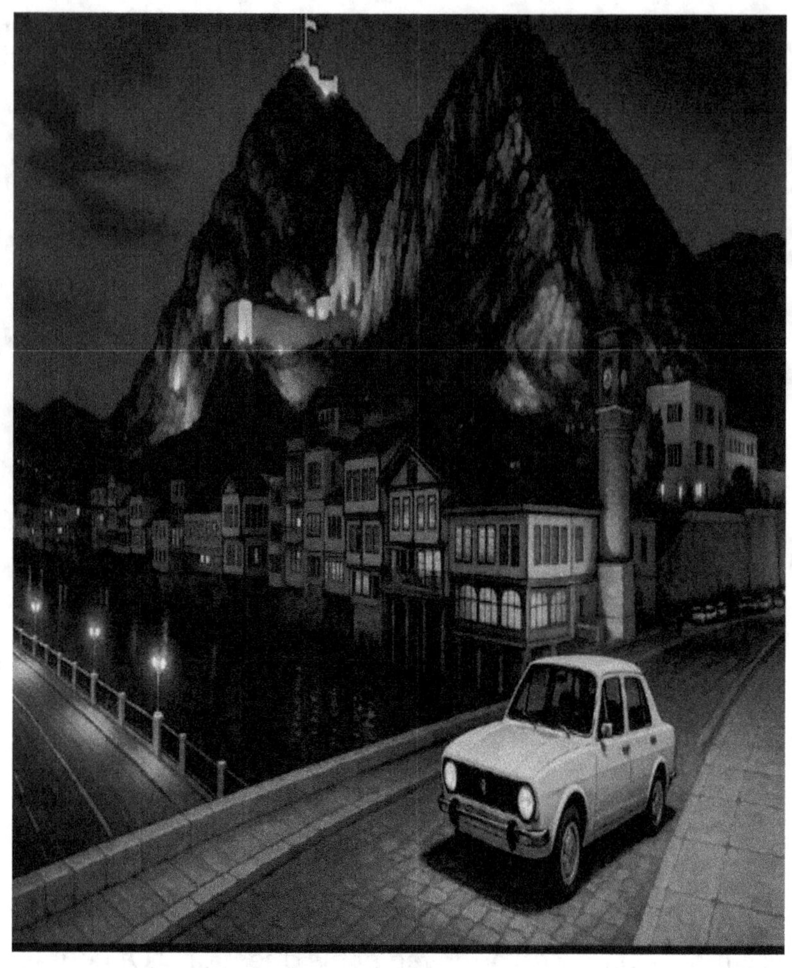

The pagoda-yellow Skoda looked like a tennis ball bouncing through the tiny town, and Malech's butler-like attire didn't make them any less inconspicuous. They might as well have placed a siren atop the car.

They booked themselves into a small hotel off of Ziya Paşa Boulevard. The minaret in the main square was visible from his hotel window. They had rented the suite with a door connecting the two rooms. His room was nondescript—sterile.

Ishmael hadn't slept for days. He felt exhausted. He fell headlong, listless, lost between the physical and metaphysical planes.

...He was propelled into the chassis of a cattle truck, decked out with figurines on the dashboard and a burgundy beaded drape that framed the front window. A bearded man of about thirty-eight sat in the driver's seat. He sang boisterously, seemingly uninterested in his cargo—i.e., four spotted Jiddu heifers and some ancient Solomonic relics that lay stashed amongst the hay and paraphernalia. Ishmael watched as he smoked, sang, and occasionally sipped a Turkish coffee from a straw. Stopping on the side of the road for oncoming traffic, the rusted metallic Mercedes-Benz LP 183 clanked, screeched, and lumbered its way through the narrow mountain passes. Yusuf was only a few hours from Amasya.

...Ishmael was floating again. His mind conjured images of three-dimensional symbols, the seals of the fallen angels. He was transposed to the Nag Hammadi Library. He felt the frigid demonic feelings of the long, dark hall of Tartarus. The chants of, "Edomite. Edomite," still echoed somewhere between the then and now. They beckoned to him. In his third eye, he projected himself into the darkened corridors—beyond the dragons, beyond the Nephilim—into the subterranean chambers reserved for the antediluvian abominations. The Watchers stood illuminating the dark corridor of Tartarus, standing ready. He remembered the teachings of Scaramucci and how they had procreated with mankind and animal kind...

"Allahu Akbarrrrrrrrrrr!" He awoke to the morning prayer amplified into the public square from the local *Bayezid II* Mosque.

He knocked out his morning push-ups, then knocked on the adjoining door. Malech answered, already pristinely dressed.

"Yup? We leavin'?" he inquired matter-of-factly.

"Good morning. Yeah, I know where to find it. Let's go."

They piled into the Skoda and drove east.

"If we go any further east, we'll wind up in Iran," Malech ventured.

"I know… They live here, up this hill. Turn left."

The Skoda sputtered and coughed as it climbed the embankment, navigating the gravel switchbacks. There was no railing; the hillside fell off directly to the river canyon. Ishmael closed his eyes. Malech drove for a few more kilometers. The road ended. Before them stood an immense stucco wall replete with razor wire and a retractable metal door.

"Stop," Ishmael chirped.

"What is it?"

"Just wait here."

"Red, we are in the open."

"Find a place to park the car."

Malech parked the Skoda in a large overgrown oleander bush that had crowded the road. He extinguished the engine.

Half an hour passed before Malech spoke again. "So, what are we doing here, Red?"

Ishmael sat hypnotically, eyes closed. He didn't speak. Malech adjusted his seat and leaned against the window, closing his eyes.

Hours passed. Dusk descended. Finally, the light fell and night came. Ishmael said nothing.

Malech began to grow anxious. "Hey, Red."

"They're coming!"

An old grey Mercedes cattle truck approached, screeching its way to an abrupt stop. The driver leaned out the window and yelled in Turkish. Momentarily, the vertical metal door was drawn upward electrically. Two men were slowly revealed as the door recoiled. The two individuals let out a boisterous salutation, and the truck entered the confines of the courtyard.

Ishmael was pushed to act. Without warning, he sprang from the bushes and ran toward the cascading aluminum door.

"Hey, wait," Malech belched.

Before Malech could react, Ishmael had tucked and rolled into the inner sanctum of the compound. Malech watched incredulously as the redhead disappeared beneath the retracting door.

Ishmael rolled under the lorry. The cattle directly above him spooked and began kicking at the retaining walls, which, in turn, attracted two mangy canines. They barked at his heels and sniffed his jeans.

A female scream of irritation came from the house. Ishmael put his hand up, and the dogs silenced, wagging their tails. From his station, he could see the wheels of a few motorcycles. They would have to be disabled, he thought.

Two men came from the house, engaged in jovial banter as they returned to the heel of the lorry. Ishmael could hear the clanging of the mechanical clasp, then a flurry of movement, a clattering of hooves. The men tried to calm the heifers, calling out after them. Ishmael had no idea what they said. The heifers were led away single file by the men.

He looked around. No one. The rear door of the truck was still open. He acted.

He ran first to the bikes, pulling their keys from their ignitions and casting them over the large retaining wall. He moved to the red button and punched it. The door began to recoil. The sound drew attention from the Gunkuts.

He leapt into the truck. He had seen this in his dream. He rummaged through the hay. A wooden crate!

Malech was surprised to see him, running toward the car with a box in his hands. Screams from the interior called out after him.

"*START IT UP!*" Ishmael bellowed.

Malech spun the car around and then leaned in to open the rear door. Ishmael threw the box in the backseat and jumped in.

"*GO! GO! GO!*" Ishmael pounded the dashboard. Two brothers pursued him. The third held a shotgun.

"*OH SHHHHIIIIIIIITTTTTT!*" Malech and Ishmael ducked as they passed. Buckshot blew out the windows on both sides. Malech punched the accelerator.

The four-cylinder Skoda bounced along the gravel road, pushing its limits. Malech looked in the rearview mirror.

"FUCK!" he exclaimed again.

"They had no idea what they had," Ishmael uttered.

Malech and Ishmael both spontaneously recoiled as buckshot sprayed the car's boot.

"Or maybe they did," Malech rebutted.

The Skoda was down the road before the Gunkuts could give chase. They drove hard toward Ankara.

They finally stopped at a rest stop and popped the crate. Malech sifted frantically through the hay to find a few items, each wrapped in a purple cloth. They unwrapped them: a regal seal shaped like an hourglass, inlaid with the Star of David; five golden tablets; grimoires, each with seven pages; a golden bull figurine; and a bronze charm, all with ancient Hebrew inscriptions.

"Where is it? It is not here. You said it would be here," Malech stated desperately.

"Hold on. I don't understand. My dream... I was sure it was here." He tossed the hay to the ground in frustration.

Ishmael looked at the items spread out on the leather seats. "Wait a minute." He picked up the seal with the Star of David and examined it. "What is that made of?" He held it up.

"Looks like clay."

Ishmael threw it heavily to the ground. It shattered. He fell to his knees, sifting through the rubble, crumbling the clay fragments between his fingers. A splinter of light reflected off a clot that had fallen under the car.

He picked it up. He blew on it, clearing the dried mud, wiping it clean. Ishmael held it to his face. The roadside lights reflected dimly off the mounted snowflake onyx. The pearl and black stone were flanked by two starred inscriptions, one five-pointed, the other six.

It lacked luster, regality. In fact, it was quite jejune. It seemed to be made of brass and iron rather than gold, disguising its inherent value.

"The ring of Solomon!" He held it up to the sky.

Ishmael felt a pinch in his neck; he fell unconscious.

259

Chapter 57 - Rome, Italy

"So, the king gave the order, and they brought Daniel and threw him into the lions' den. The king said to Daniel, "May your God, whom you serve continually, rescue you!" - Daniel 6: 16

n an underground bunker far beneath the city of Rome, in Babylon, teams of black-clad soldiers sat in a half-circle on bleachers. The conference hall was packed to the hilt. They waited patiently, anxiously, for directions from their leader. Samir and Kabir stood in the center of the gathering, preparing the foot soldiers for the onslaught.

"It is Maslovian! We will attack their basic needs: food, water, and electricity. In time, with a little prompting, a little provocation..." He smiled sadistically. "The public will splinter into chaos, and anarchy will ensue. And *we* shall fill that void! Alright! You know your assignments! Any questions?" He paused and surveyed the audience. "Alright, you know what to do. *Dismissed!*"

Hundreds of faithful followers filed forth—each devoted for different reasons. Some inclined toward obedience to the Dark Lord, some atheistic but seduced by demonic power, still others interested in solidarity for a larger collectivist cause. Whatever their reasons, they were inexorably drawn, by an invisible noose, toward self-annihilation, mass extinction, and eternal damnation.

Several blocks down the main thoroughfare from city hall sat a detainment facility. In the building, down the hall, among the cells, handcuffed to the bars, sat Ishmael—still unconscious. His mother, Asiya, sat on her cot in the adjacent cell.

"Ish? Dear? Hey? Wake up," his mother beckoned.

"Uhhh... oooohhhhh... Huh? I feel... What happened? Where am I?" His ears rang, and his eyes struggled to focus.

"You are in Babylon."

"*Mom?* How did..." He rubbed his eyes. "*Babylon?* What? In Iraq?"

"No, sweetheart. That is what they call their underground city. You are in Rome—or actually... under Rome."

"How did I get here?"

"Malech brought you in."

"*Malech*? I thought he was on our side."

"Yeah, me too, sweetheart."

"That motherfucker!" The serum was wearing off.

"But at least you are safe. My little Ish, I have missed you so much. I am just glad you are okay."

Asiya was much older than his memory of her. He looked at his mother's worn countenance—her hair unkempt, her clothes haggard and torn.

"Yeah well, 'little Ish' ain't so little anymore, and lots has changed since you 'died.' *Where have you been?*"

"I am sorry. I was taken into their custody years ago. I have lived incarcerated ever since."

He marveled at her demeanor. He had forgotten how regal, how unaffected she was, as if she had an invisible shield that protected her.

"So you have been in this hellhole?" He bowed his head in desperation. "I am sorry, Mom. If I had known..."

"No, honey, it is not your fault. I have been moved around over the years; they have taken moderately good care of me—I mean, all things considered. I have never gone hungry, and they have allowed me monitored excursions. I've even had the chance to lead some fellow prisoners to the Lord."

"Wow. You still believe in that shit!"

"*ISHMAEL ROGHA!*" She looked at him sternly. "I don't know what you have been through, but that does not give you license to blaspheme Our Lord! What happened to you? What happened to your respect?"

He was taken aback. He had not heard her reprimand him in years. And it had been at least that long since he had heard his full name—his *real* name. He felt ashamed.

"With all I have seen... I don't know if I believe anymore. If God is so powerful, how come He is losing the war? I mean, Satan certainly believes he can win. And I'm not sure he's wrong."

"Satan is a liar. And you know the funny thing about lies? You say them long enough and often enough, and you start to believe them yourself. The devil will have his day, my son, but we know how it ends."

"Mother, *THEY HAVE THE RING OF SOLOMON!* And soon they will release the Watchers. They will be able to control an entire army of demons. And soon the Watchers will breed again; the Dawn will have legions of super soldiers—giants, Nephilim. And it won't stop there."

"What?" she said calmly.

"They are planning the craziest shit you can imagine. The angels will breed with animals, creating hybrids, the beasts of old—you name it. Werewolves, vampires, centaurs, and... and... There will be chaos, pogroms in the streets. Do you get it? Mankind cannot fight against the forces of hell!"

On her cot, legs crossed at the ankles, head bowed and hands folded, she sat stoically, pondering the magnitude of his oratory.

"Perhaps not. Mankind cannot. Yet there is still hope. We may have no *ring,* but we have something infinitely more powerful—we have a King! And *our* King is more powerful than any beast from hell. *We have Jesus!* He is the Ringmaster, the Alpha and the Omega. And His power is greater than any beast, or angelic bastard offspring, or any ring of Solomon! Solomon is a dead king. But ours... is ALIVE!

"So I say, bring it on! For it is written, '*As it was in the days of Noah, so it will be at the coming of the Son of Man.'* If this be the end time, so be it! Let them come!"

The redhead was dumbfounded, astonished at the incredible strength of his mother. It was otherworldly—perhaps even...

"Can I speak to you?" Sofia's body sulked as she interrupted.

He turned to see her pale eyes staring back at him through the bars of the cell.

Ishmael sighed deeply. "On one condition—you get these bastards to release me from these cuffs. I'm in a cell. Where can I go?"

Sofia gestured to the guard. He walked over and unlocked the cuffs. Ishmael rubbed his worn wrists and his scar.

"You may leave us," she stated to the guard. He obeyed.

"What now? Did Lilith send you? You know I will never join your cult."

"No. I am here on my own accord. I just wanted to tell you..." She bowed her head.

"What is it? Can we get to it? You know my schedule is full. I have to get back to my pushups."

"I... I... I'm pregnant."

Ishmael hadn't expected that.

"What?" he muttered more to himself than to her. Through the bars of the neighboring cell, he looked at the widened eyes of his mother.

"I don't believe you. Just another trick to get me to do your bidding."

"I swear to God, Ish."

"How do you know it's my child?"

"It's yours. I only tell you because of the Dawn…" She began sobbing. She stared through pale eyes. "They will sacrifice our child." Tears welled in her eyes. Usually a paragon of strength, he had never seen her so fragile, so vulnerable.

He had no words, no response. The thought of fatherhood had never entered his mind. He had always thought that he would die prematurely. In his dreams, he had died horrifically—over and over and over…

The thought of posterity—the thought of fatherhood—was overwhelming. He suddenly felt a guttural surge flowing through him. He leaned over and vomited through the bars into the hallway.

"I am sorry. I shouldn't have come." She turned and left. Ishmael wanted to call after her, but he refrained.

His mother spoke in her absence. "You see? God has a plan for you, son. You have a future."

His mind was still reeling from the news. "I… I…"

"You have lived on the fence your entire life, son. It is time to choose. You will either choose to live in anger and despair, shaking your fist at God, and so reap the harvest of bitterness, or you will grant Jesus His rightful role as Lord over your life. I raised you to know Him. And I can still see the ambivalence in your heart, your inner struggle. You were made for a purpose. And now is the time to decide! NOW!"

"I have no free will, Mom. Did I choose for my father to die? My girlfriend to die? You think they had a choice? Did I choose to be raped as a child? Huh?" His anger began to percolate. *"WHERE WAS GOD WHEN I WAS MOLESTED?* Huh? Where was your fucking God then? You are just as lost as them!"

"The forces of darkness are hell-bent on your destruction, Ish. They want you to give up; they want you to lash out in anger. You see, demons attached themselves to you at an early age. They entered through your wounds. And they have remained because you have given them a right to stay. We are either formed in the image of God, which was our original design, or we are formed in their image. There is no middle ground."

"Nice of God to allow that. Huh?" he said defiantly.

"Yes, God allowed that! He also allowed His Son to be tortured for you! And that is the worst thing ever to happen in history! And you know what, my love? It is also the best thing to ever happen in history because Satan never saw it coming. What the devil thought was his greatest victory turned out to be his greatest defeat! So if God can make the worst thing the best thing, what can He do with you?"

"I am too far gone." He looked at his feet and shook his head. "Besides, I don't think He cares much for us, Mom." He gestured to his cell.

"You must stop looking at your current circumstances. Stop looking back at your pain, or forward in fear. Stop focusing on the voices in your head—the voices of defeat and anger. Stop allowing the demons access to your life. Lean not unto your own understanding."

"Did I choose to have them in my life?"

Asiya took a hard inhale and looked at her prodigal son. "When you were younger, I used to read the Bible to you. Do you remember that?" He nodded.

"Do you remember the story of Jesus when He walked on the water, on the Sea of Galilee? Peter asked to come to Him, Jesus told him to come, and he was able to walk on the water as long as he kept his eyes on the Lord... Do you remember?"

"Vaguely," he muttered.

"If we keep our eyes on Him, He will deliver us from the storm."

"Yeah, it really looks that way. Has He delivered you?"

"Honey, if God chooses this to be my path..." She looked around the cell. "Then so be it."

"I don't know whether to pity you or admire you."

"Honey, look, all mankind has a singular choice: to either bow to the weight of the world or choose to believe that despite the horrors of life, God is *still* good. And I am not saying that it is an easy choice, but I promise you, if you choose betterness over bitterness, He will meet you where you are and bring light, healing, and understanding that you never thought possible... but you must relinquish everything—no strings attached. You must approach Him on *His* terms."

"Okay, that is enough!" Brashly interrupting, her two Corsos at her side, Lilith and her entourage entered the cell block. "No more of your bullshit!" She gestured to Ishmael's cell. "Bring him!"

Chapter 58 - Boston, Massachusetts

"For God is not a God of confusion but of peace." - 1 Corinthians 14:33

cacophony of conversations competed for supremacy. A makeshift podium had been placed at the center of the lobby. The Boston Police Department was riddled with representatives from the finest forensic teams, representatives from the Department of Homeland Security, and a litany of nefarious governmental agencies, as well as television reporters from all over the world.

Microphones attached to recorders and television cameras zoomed in on a wiry twenty-something-year-old with brown hair and thick glasses. He approached the lectern to address the congregants.

"My name is Reginald Arturo. Round here they call me 'Art.'" He paused awkwardly. Public speaking was obviously novel to him. "So anyway, I am with forensics. And I was charged with running point." He paused again as if awaiting a reaction. "Unfortunately, we have little to divulge on the assembly of the device. Its origin remains unknown. The contagion is biological, but to date, we cannot tell you where it has come from. I won't bore you with the science, but we are lucky..." He looked at Azikiwe, who was in attendance. "Um... I mean blessed." He looked at the growing number of journalists. "The details have been turned over to federal authorities. And we will now take questions."

The crowd of reporters surged forward, shoving microphones in his face. Azikiwe listened to a few of the questions and then decided to leave. Amendola followed him into the parking lot.

"Father, do you have a minute?" he beckoned from behind.

"Yes?" The Catholic priest stopped and turned around.

"Might I ask you a few questions?" Amendola's short Italian stature seemed almost comical next to the mammoth Nigerian.

"It depends. What news organization do you represent?"

"No. No. You misunderstand. I am not a reporter."

"Hmmm."

"No, in fact, I am investigating this case and its possible correlation to another case that I am working on."

"You're a cop?" the priest inquired.

"Well yes... but not here. I am from Rome."

"What do the Roman authorities want with an attack in Boston?"

"Well, the group that we are after has displayed some similarities to a terrorist group. There is no direct link yet... but... let's just say, I'm doing... how do you say, 'a hunch'?"

"'Playing a hunch,' huh? What 'similarities' are you talking about?"

"I am not disposed to tell you the details but... among other things, C-4 explosives, and military-grade weaponry..."

"There was no C-4 used in this case, only devices designed to infect the water supply."

"Uh, yes, I am aware, but there is more. Can we go somewhere and maybe take a coffee?"

"Well, I was supposed to get back to the parish, but I don't know why I couldn't take a few moments."

They popped into a stereotypical fifties diner and took a booth in the corner.

"So, what would you like to discuss, Inspector?"

"Well, first can you tell me how you were able to obtain the device?" He pulled a mini tablet from his breast pocket and prepared to scribble some notes.

The Jesuit priest shifted his large frame in the booth and nodded to the waitress.

"Well, as I told the authorities, I was out walking in the park, which I care to do when I pray. I heard some shots. I saw three people loading the device into a speedboat. I imagined the worst. The three suspects were shot multiple times by someone hidden in the woods. I came to their aid. After I realized that they were dead, I began to take incoming fire from beyond the tree line; the sniper had turned his gun on me. I knew that I had to get the device somewhere safe, so I dived into the boat and fled."

"Hmmm. Interesting. So, you were strolling through the park in the middle of the night? Praying, you say."

"That's correct."

"Father, may I be candid?" He continued without waiting for the priest's consent. "You know that giving false testimony is a sin."

Undaunted, the Nigerian just stared at him. "Can I get a coffee, please?" He turned his attention to the blonde waitress.

"I was down there. There are footprints in the clay that do not match your description. For one, there are two sets of tracks leading from the park's edge to the shoreline, not one as you just recounted. And one set of footprints was much deeper, heavier-set, indicating a man of large stature, about your size. And the other set probably matches the size of one of the men found dead at the seashore, I would imagine, no? Secondly, there seems to have been a fight or scuffle of some kind."

"Inspector, what do you want?"

"My guess is that you and one (or more) of the people found dead at the scene pursued these men to this location, which would indicate that you knew of their intent, which would also mean that you were privy to their plan. And so, I wonder how you would have come upon this knowledge." He stared unequivocally at the Nigerian.

Unmoved, the priest slowly took a sip of his coffee. "And might I ask *you* a question? You are not exactly representing the Roman authorities on this one... are you? So what? Something personal? Some sort of revenge tour?"

"It *is* personal... Do you know anything about this?" He pulled a medieval dagger from his pocket with the Star of David on its hilt.

Azikiwe sat erect. "Where did you get this?"

"We found it in a cave."

"We?"

"Interpol. Do you know who it may belong to?"

"No."

"Father, two of my closest friends were killed by these *bastardi*," he stared at the priest in earnest. "...Please tell me."

The priest examined the inspector, sizing him up with his eyes. "The Golden Dawn."

"OH MY GOD!" the waitress screamed. "They did it again!"

Azikiwe and Amendola turned their attention to the television atop the bar.

...NEWS ALERT

TERROR IN EUROPE?!!!

Breaking now...

Chapter 59 – Lago Gandolfo, Italy

"You shall do to Ai and its king as you did to Jericho and its king, except that you may carry off their plunder and livestock for yourselves. Set an ambush behind the city." - Joshua 8:2

he populations of Rome, Vienna, Paris, London, Madrid, Stockholm, and Brussels were blindsided. In the subsequent obscurity, the Dawn's tactical teams were left unobstructed to seed the contagion into the water supplies. The Seine, the Thames, the Danube, the Norrström, the Senne, the Manzanares, and the Tiber rivers were infected at multiple locations. The plan had succeeded perfectly.

The aftermath unfolded methodically. Darkness fell like a protective blanket for the deeds of the ill-willed—the predators. Cars sat lifelessly in the streets, and planes fell from the skies, crashing into skyscrapers and launching debris onto the streets. Fires broke out all over the cities, casting contorted shadows on the facades of the buildings.

Seizing the serendipity of the moment, hooligans flooded the streets, breaking storefront display windows and carrying away sneakers, televisions, liquor—even furniture. Criminals wearing masks were randomly struck by passersby, laughing, skipping, and hollering into the refuge of the darkened streets. The shattering of glass, gunshots, and cries of desperation could be heard echoing in the concrete ravines.

The affluent boarded their windows and shut themselves inside their homes. Others fought off bandits attempting to steal their children. Still others provocatively stood on their front porches wielding shotguns. Morality had been suppressed. Mankind's most basal instincts had been aroused. Society's social contract had been torn up and thrown into the gutter.

The High Council stood anxiously around the television in the dining hall in the palazzo at Gandolfo. The Tewani twins stood with them.

...NEWS ALERT

TERROR IN EUROPE?!!!

Breaking now...

"*Incredibile*!" Nerone spoke.

"No, my Lord, this is only the beginning," Samir stated. "They are completely unaware of the sickness that is upon them. In their ignorance, they will hoard water and food, taking the contagion into their homes. Entire caches of goods will have to be thrown out. Rationing will begin. And famine will ensue. They will become desperate, and we shall exacerbate the chaos with 'random' acts of violence. Millions will die! And then..." He paused and smiled at the Black Pope. "...Phase Three."

"Excellent. When shall we begin *Gebofal*?" Nerone turned to Lilith.

"We shall begin at sunset." Her elation was hidden beneath her red veil.

271

Chapter 60 - Babylon, Italy

"But when someone stronger attacks and overpowers him, he takes away the armor in which the man trusted and divides up his plunder." - Luke 11:22

housands of uniformed soldiers sprinted toward their nefarious assignments. Clicking boot heels, rumbling engines, and shouts of confirmation could be heard from outside the detention facility.

"Sounds like they are preparing for something."

"Gebofal," his mother stated.

"What does that mean?"

"Are you aware of the Book of Loagaeth? Doctor John Dee and Edward Kelley?"

"Unfortunately." He rolled his eyes. He hadn't been able to get the two men out of his head for years.

"It is said that the two 'alchemists' were visited by a lunar angel, a demon-angel named Levanael. He revealed to them a way to reach enlightenment. He gave them a system of tables, or gates—forty-nine to be specific."

"So Gebofal refers to these tablets?"

"No. It refers to the process. Gebofal is the ascension of those tablets, a fulfillment of all forty-nine steps."

"What happens when the final step is achieved, when the last gate is opened?"

"According to the legend..." She stared at her son. "...a way to speak to God in His own language, as Moses did. And a fulfillment of the prophecy spoken of in Revelation 9:1: *The fifth angel sounded his trumpet, and I saw a star that had fallen from the sky to the earth. The star was given the key to the shaft of the Abyss."*

"In their minds," she looked at him with deep concern, "you are that star."

"They think I will open Tartarus and let out the Watchers."

"I believe so, hon."

"I won't cooperate. I refuse," Ishmael stated defiantly.

"I know you'll fight them... anyway, from what I know, the tablets went missing. Many believe they were destroyed in a fire centuries ago."

"I have seen them, Mom." The redhead got up and grabbed the bars, looking toward the entrance. "...An angel paid me a visit long ago, in a dream..."

"They will try to get you to access those tablets, to bring them out of you somehow."

"And Lilith has the Ring of Solomon." He shook his head in desperation.

"I do." Lilith entered with her entourage. Her face was covered in a red veil. She gestured at Ishmael. "Bring him. Prep him for the ritual."

The cell was unlocked, and two men entered, shackling him behind his back. In passing, he blurted, "I will never do what you ask. I will never release the Watchers!"

"We'll see about that. Bring the mother too."

Chapter 61 - Babylon, Italy

"God did not spare angels when they sinned, but sent them to [Tartarus], putting them in chains of darkness to be held for judgment." - Peter 2:4

shmael was shuttled through the subterranean city in the familiar Russian trucks that were so ubiquitous in Babylon. Sixty of them rode single file through the streets toward the roaring cascade—the Tiber's hidden tributary. It fell one hundred meters from the ceiling, casting a roaring blanket of water on the approaching road. Mist ascended toward the fleeting moonlight, throwing micro-rainbows into the night air.

Upon approaching, from high above in the canopy, the water was drawn back like a Shakespearean curtain, splitting into two heavier streams. A glistening stone bridge and a large temple atop a small incline were revealed. The temple was colossal—an amphitheater that could potentially seat forty thousand spectators. The architecture was early Vespasian; red bricks could be seen peeking their way out from under the eroded facia. It resembled the Roman Colosseum, except that inside the barrel vaults stood statues of pagan gods instead of the effigies of the gladiators du jour.

At its apex stood an imposing figure: a bullish gargoyle whose horns stretched to the left and right by several meters. His concrete brow frowned. His mouth stood agape, exposing long, sharp teeth and a slithering tongue that split into the doorframe twenty meters below.

A drawbridge descended, connecting the road and the ingress of the "Temple of Molech," as it was colloquially called. A second iron gate retracted upward, exposing an oval-shaped holding area. The trucks entered in linear fashion, parking themselves into three perfect columns. The rear door of the lorry fell sharply, shaking the bed. The soldiers sitting on bench seats filed out in military fashion. Twenty men poured forth from the cargo truck, each armed with shoulder-strapped Kalashnikovs and black bayonets.

"Let's go," said one.

Ishmael, still cuffed, was led down an eroded marble staircase into a vaulted hallway, and then into a room that resembled a Roman torture chamber.

Several people in black robes awaited him. A voice proceeded from one of the robed staff. "Put him over here. Take off his cuffs. We need to prepare him."

Low rumbles reverberated off the walls—chants from down the hall. There seemed to be a large crowd awaiting his arrival somewhere. He was reminded of his bouts. *Where was Snow when he needed him?*

Ishmael found himself stripped and put into a cold shower. The faucet spat rusty water on his naked body. Three sets of hands lathered his body with a fermented, fatty liquid. He was oiled from head to toe. He stank. He was subsequently dressed in a one-piece cloth that was twisted around his crotch.

"Drink this." Nerone held out a vial of red liquid.

"Fuck you," the redhead stated flatly.

"I don't have time for this. Bring her in!"

His mother came in, handcuffed, dressed like the other satanic staff in a black robe. Nerone unsheathed a dagger from his belt and held his arm out horizontally, the blade at his mother's throat.

"Drink it!"

Ishmael closed his eyes and begrudgingly drank the blood. It tasted of iron mixed with cough syrup. He fought back the impulse to vomit. He had been drugged. His vision began to skip, as if he were watching passing lights. He felt queasy—sick. His knees felt weak, and he lost his balance. The hooded staff caught him before he fell.

"Bring him!" Nerone said forcefully. "...and the mother too."

They rounded into the hallway; the volume of cheers was immediately amplified, and the temperature in the hallway increased precipitously. Despite being quasi-naked, sweat began to fall from Ishmael's brow.

The rotund ceiling in the hallway was ten meters in height. It grew symmetrically, gradually toward the inner sanctum. The hall gave rise to an arena, or sanctuary—a massive expanse without columns to support it. The dome ceiling culminated in an oculus that stared defiantly at the rock ceiling high above.

Swaying back and forth, thirty thousand hooded satanists stood on scaffolded *gradinati* seating. Silence fell over the crowd as Ishmael came into view. Excited chants of "Edomite! Edomite!" echoed—not in English, but in Enochian.

Along the sanctuary floor, patiently awaiting their cue, sat a queue of hooded shamanic drummers. Several processions of hooded members stood at the periphery, hands folded and heads bowed. Throughout the arena floor lay crucifixes with corpses nailed to them—victims of previous ceremonies. At one end, a mammoth bronze statue of Molech had been erected. The deity stood at least forty meters in height.

At ground level, hooded members feverishly stoked a fire in his belly, throwing in wood with abandon. The fire crackled and fed the hall with a blazing heat and shadowy luminescence. The statue mimicked that of the image at the entrance of the temple, except that it was bronze—and much larger. The Canaanite god held forth two cupped hands. A long staircase gave access to a platform that sat adjacent to Molech's outstretched hands.

Ishmael was dragged forcibly across an inclined stage that sat in the center of the theater. His ankles bounced on the steps as they carried him up the platform. On it stood a large wooden cross wrapped in thorny tendrils. The crucifix was affixed to a square notch at center stage. An inverted pentagram, drawn in red paint, extended from the cross. Each point was finished by a black pillar candle, and inside each triangle lay a different sigil.

His impulse was to fight, but his body would not comply. Ishmael was placed, nearly naked, on the cross. His wrists and ankles were tied with ropes to the points of the star. Ishmael felt a cold draft of air tickle his backside; he sensed a cavern below—possibly a drainage channel.

The Black Pope stood magnanimously atop the platform next to the bronze abomination of Molech. He raised his hand like a newly crowned Caesar. Silence befell the crowd.

"Brothers... Sisters... Our day has finally come!" His voice could be heard above the crackling fire, his ominous shadow cast onto the ceiling. "The end is nigh! The end of our *enemy*! After tonight, we shall usher in a new era... *our* era! The prophecy is about to be fulfilled under this new leadership." He turned to his flank and extended his arm. "It is with great pleasure that I present our queen, our high priestess—Lilith Aziel Barequel!"

Twenty-four muscular hooded satanists tottered in, carrying an oak palanquin. The High Priestess sat inside a baroque canopy covered in red satin linens. Her garments—her headdress—were crimson as well. She gave the proverbial wave to her subordinates.

Ishmael stared at her in disgust. Then suddenly, his attention was drawn to a familiar humming sound. Through his blurred vision, he could see an expanding invasive cloud forming overhead. A beautiful, yet terrifying angel engulfed in flames emerged from the cloud.

The crowd gasped. Ishmael felt the searing, yet familiar pain of his left wrist; his scar became illuminated.

The angel presented to him not a scroll, but two large stone tablets. Ishmael looked into the blinding light at the gorgeous, hypnotic face of the creature.

"Manchild, you have been granted the gift of celestial wisdom, for only you can decipher these revelations. I command you to do so now! *SPEAK!*"

Ishmael replied with slurred speech, "No. I will... not."

To this response, the entity descended upon him. Its ethereal face was instantly transformed into a hideous, twisted creature with piercing talons that bore into Ishmael's body as it lifted him upward, releasing him from the tethers.

"How dare you disobey!"

The creature merely looked in Asiya's direction and her skin began to burn. She cried out in agony.

"You don't have to give in! You have a choice!" his mother yelled again.

Nerone nodded to a member at her flank. Asiya was struck hard across the face. The congregants' chants grew louder. In unison, they chanted, "Edomite, Edomite..."

Ishmael shuddered in terror as the cloud descended, enveloping his body. Against his will, the words emitted from his lips—the Book of Loagaeth. Something spoke with him, apart from him, through him. The Enochian utterances manifested into licks of flame that ascended into the cloud, into the crowd.

Beyond Ishmael's will, and beyond the physical plane, the incantations flew like hummingbirds—swooping, teasing, annoying, caressing the men, women, and children. His body convulsed and jerked at each utterance.

A procession of nude women entered single file from the tunnels. Each maiden cradled naked, squirming infants in their hands, held aloft over their heads, one after the other—too many children to count. Their heads bowed in submission; they paraded up the gradual incline toward the Black Pope.

Nerone took each child and prayed over them. Drums sounded rhythmically, and the collective shouts grew to a fever pitch. One by one, Nerone tossed the babies carelessly onto the extended metal hands of Molech. The children's screams could not be heard over the noise of the crowd. Each child's flesh sizzled on the incandescent metal. The innocent souls squirmed in terrible anguish.

When they had passed, Nerone took a large poker, several meters in length, and pushed their carcasses into the flames below. The process repeated itself.

After relinquishing the children to their fates, the naked maidens descended from the platform and lined themselves up neatly in front of Molech. They fell to the ground animal-like, bent over, offering their genitalia to any person inclined to breed. After a time, drawn by their lusts, male congregants came forward. They threw their robes to the floor and gave reign to their carnal desires, engaging in gratuitous copulation.

More children were sacrificed, and more lust was released. The entire amphitheater became alive—or perhaps dead—with carnal lust. Thirty thousand people engaged in sexual debauchery of every kind: homosexuality, bestiality, and pedophilia. The priests on the arena floor cut themselves and drank each other's blood, conjuring demons that tossed them to the ground into convulsions.

From atop the platform, Nerone gave the order, and Asiya's throat was cut.

"NOOOOOOOOOOOO!!!! YOU ANIMAL!!!!!!!" Ishmael screamed out in agony and horror as his mother collapsed to the ground.

The celestial creature dissipated into the air. Ishmael plummeted to the platform. His head concussed against the wooden construction, knocking him unconscious.

A singular black hoodie lifted. Sofia's pale blue eyes shot out in disgust at the Black Pope. For the first time in her life, empathy crept into her heart. She stared up at her true love, caught up, a marionette—held helpless and vulnerable.

Sofia's heartbreak was prematurely interrupted by seismic rumbles that shook the ground; deep sonic waves penetrated the rock foundations. The temple walls shook, and debris fell from the ceiling.

Several kilometers away in the Nag Hammadi Library, the stone wall that separated the metaphysical from the physical world had cracked from top to bottom. Deep in the heart of Tartarus, the cells that had once imprisoned the Fallen had flown open. And for the first time in millennia, the Watchers were free. Two hundred angels had been released. All of them—save one—swarmed through the fissures of Caracalla, flying into the night sky. One general, *Shemyaza, flew* directly for the temple of Molech.

...He could smell his father's pancakes... Ishmael was five years old again. His mother was dressing him for church. He walked by his father's corpse in the ambulance... Like a video that skipped, he saw his mother shot again and again... He was in Chicago fighting, sweating, training... Listening to Snow's advice... He was being chased again... Cindy died... Rodrigo died... Pasquale died...

YOU LET MY MOM DIE! I WILL NEVER FORGIVE YOU! YOU LET ALL THOSE DEAREST TO ME DIE! I HATE YOU! ... Suddenly, all of them stood before him, encircling him...

"Ish." His mother's countenance was calm and at peace. "Let go of your anger. Let go of your hate. Stop judging God for who you think He is. Let Him reveal Himself to you. He died for you. He loves you."

She disappeared.

Ishmael was in Scaramucci's office in Assisi... He was talking to Rodrigo... touring the countryside... making love to Sofia... Sofia.

"Sofia? SOFIA!" He yelled her name. She ran to his aid, kneeling beside him.

"Yes, hon, I am here." Just as it was the day they met, her pale eyes flickered with the orange glow of the firelight.

Suddenly, the drums stopped. The debauchery stopped. All activity stopped. The entire sanctuary fell quiet. All eyes fell to the southern end of the arena.

Ishmael could not distinguish between the physical and metaphysical worlds; the drugs pulsed through his veins. His head burned; his temples throbbed. He had to be dreaming again, for when he raised his gaze, there before him stood a luminescent being of *incredible* stature and beauty—perhaps ten meters in height.

All the congregants stared hypnotically at his presence. His robes were white and lengthy. His glorified, angelic body was muscular; his skin was shiny bronze. Shemyaza stood forth in a princely posture. His glorified hand elongated and then morphed into a flaming sword.

"I demand a sacrifice!" He gestured at the redhead. "*KILL THE EDOMITE!*" His thunderous voice shook the hall.

Interested in garnering favor with the angel, Lilith echoed his command. "Kill him!"

The train from her gown snagged on the oak frame, tearing it lengthwise. "I will do it myself!" From the base of her serpentine-crested scepter, a blade was triggered forth. She charged the mounted crucifix where Ishmael lay unconscious.

Kabir and Samir disrobed and advanced in unison.

"MOTHER. *MOTHER! Please! Please spare him!*" Sofia begged.

Lilith raised her scepter to the sky, fell to one knee, and aimed for Ishmael's chest. In her madness, in her lust for power, in the chaos—blinded by rage—she failed to notice her daughter charging in to intervene.

In the last instant, Sofia dived headlong, canvassing Ishmael's body with her own. Lilith brought her blade to bear. Her strike fell violently, penetrating her daughter's back. Sofia let out a scream in Ishmael's ear. He awoke—startled yet still groggy.

"OH, MY GOD! What have I done?" Lilith gasped under her breath and recoiled to the ground, leaving the scepter lodged in her daughter's back.

Ishmael awoke. *Where was he? Was this a nightmare?*

Sofia's lips caressed his own. "I love you. I have always loved you." She coughed up blood as she spoke.

Ishmael could feel her body quivering. He was losing her. He looked down at the black phallus embedded in her back.

"*NOOooooooo!*" he screamed. He squirmed from under Sofia and rose to his knees. His coordination was absent. He fell clumsily toward Lilith, striking awkwardly at the shadows.

He was immediately tackled to the floor by Samir and Kabir.

"I FUCKING HATE YOU!" Ishmael screamed at Lilith and at God Himself.

Kabir struck him with a closed fist to the jaw.

He was out again.

"*Are you ready, my son?*" He was surrounded by light. *A gentle, loving, masculine voice could be understood but not heard, not even on the metaphysical plane.* Although it was not audible, there was an immediate understanding—a spiritual whisper that left no room for equivocation.

"I have been with you since the beginning, my son. I know your pain. I need you to let go now. All your pain, all your anger, all your confusion..."

"*Lord? You don't know my pain!*"

"*But I do.*" *From the glorious luminescence, two hands protruded,* palms *up, showing the wounds of the carpenter.*

"*Jesus? You don't understand...*" He wept. "*My pain is... is... all I have...*"

Asiya appeared from the hue, glorified like the Madonna. "Son, He is real. Let go of your anger. Your pain... Trust Him."

"*I... I...*"

"SACRIFICE HIM NOW!" The flames on Shemyaza's sword grew higher, and his angelic voice reverberated throughout the hall.

Samir pulled a dagger from his belt and approached the redhead lying prostrate on the ground.

"I give my life to you, Jesus." Ishmael's mouth quivered; the faintest of whispers were lost in the cacophony of cries.

Yet, someone did hear him. Ishmael looked upward. Samir and Lilith were caught in a struggle; four hooded men held their clothing. Nerone was also subdued, and even Lilith struggled against several men trying to restrain her.

Gunshots rang out in the hall. Confusion ensued.

On Amendola's signal, his embedded men had opened fire on the Satanists. The

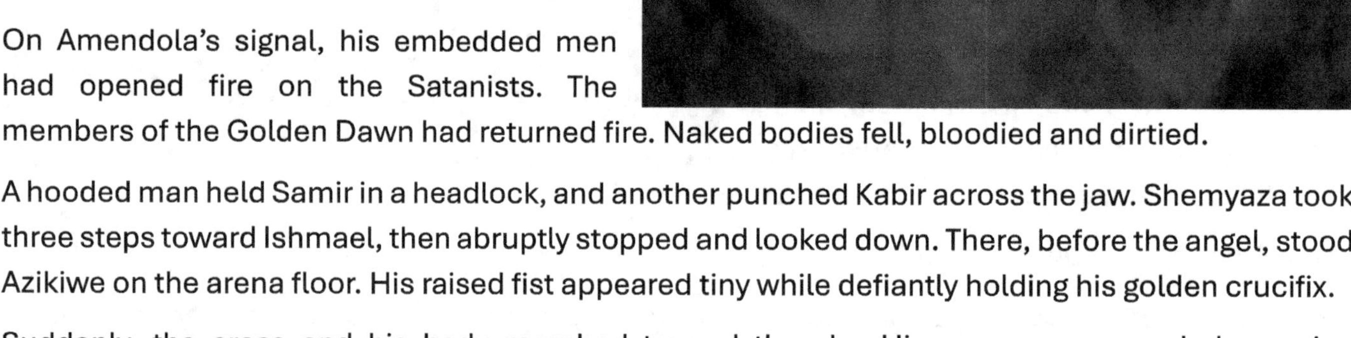

members of the Golden Dawn had returned fire. Naked bodies fell, bloodied and dirtied.

A hooded man held Samir in a headlock, and another punched Kabir across the jaw. Shemyaza took three steps toward Ishmael, then abruptly stopped and looked down. There, before the angel, stood Azikiwe on the arena floor. His raised fist appeared tiny while defiantly holding his golden crucifix.

Suddenly, the cross and his body morphed toward the sky. His presence expanded, growing immensely in beauty, size, and luminescence. Electric currents snapped and bounced along the rotunda. Azikiwe's clothes stretched and tore away; his skin fell off him like molten ash, and his stature grew to the height of his angelic foe.

Azikiwe's wings unfolded, releasing a wave of suppressed light. With a heavy flap, he raised his sword.

Shemyaza belched something in Enochian and attacked. Pent up for thousands of years, Shemyaza's aggression was released—but it betrayed him, for he was imprecise and clumsy.

Azikiwe, on the other hand, was ready. He fended off Shemyaza's blade with his left wing, twisted his torso, and swung his blade through the air. His blade struck Shemyaza in the arm. The angelic wound was instantly covered with immortal flesh.

Oblivious to their surroundings, they battled like celestial samurai. Each clash of the blades brought forth Greek fire, igniting the combatants on the arena floor. Screams of pain and horror echoed in the confined space.

Shemyaza swung his sword wildly. Azikiwe spun and countered; the blades splashed viscous fire down on the crucifix platform in the center of the arena. The liquid acid steamed its way through the wooden platform and iron grid that guarded the drainage. Incandescent trails of charred wood and metal fell into the abyss.

A hooded man leaned over Ishmael. "Let's get you out of here, Red." Ishmael looked into unfamiliar eyes. A hooded man stood over him.

"That's right. Let's get the hell out of here. Come on! Let's go."

"Who the hell are you?"

"A friend." Amendola pulled the redhead up by the arms.

"Get Sofia!" Ishmael refused to leave without his love.

"My son, I think she is dead."

"BRING HER!" Ishmael growled.

The inspector threw a robe at Ishmael, then wrapped Sofia's lifeless arms over his shoulder. Amendola carried Sofia to the center of the arena where the angelic fire had melted several cross-sections in the drain, revealing a small crawl space that led underground.

Pandemonium ensued. Guns fired below, angelic swords clashed above. Kabir and Samir took little time with their combatants, casting them aside effortlessly. They scanned for Ishmael.

"Get in there." Amendola tenderly held Sofia as Ishmael began his descent into the exposed shaft.

"Hold on." Ishmael hung from the iron bars that had served as the drain cover.

"Let go. They are coming. *LET GO*!" Amendola screamed as he witnessed the twins running toward him at full speed. *"LET GO AND I'LL DROP HER IN BEHIND YOU!"*

Ishmael hung from the bars; his legs dangled above the darkness.

"I can't see anything. It is dark. I DON'T KNOW WHAT IS DOWN THERE!"

"TAKE HER NOW!" The Roman police inspector was tackled to the gravel by Kabir. Amendola released her immediately.

Sofia's limp body fell between the bars. Ishmael let go of the metal and grabbed her body mid-air. Ishmael enveloped her with his legs and arms, cradling her head on his chest. A clump of flesh, they fell together into the abyss.

Whatever came, he would bear the brunt of the blow. They fell deeply. Their bodies slid freely, yet the pipework gradually curved—divinely— allowing them to come to a sliding conclusion.

The air was moist. The angelic light from above lit the small clearing. They were on a plateau enveloped by walls that bowed out and fissures that fell into the darkness.

Ishmael sprang to his feet. The drug was wearing off. He laid Sofia gently face-up on the gravel floor. Half immersed in a puddle of water, the redhead bowed his head, put his hand on her face, and began to pray.

"Lord Jesus, I come before you with the prayer of Samson. Allow me to heal once more... You said, 'Greater love hath no man *than this, that a man lay down his life for his friends."*

From the bottom of his soul, he shouted. *"She died for me! Please. PLEASE!"*

Immediately, he was interrupted by the eerie sound of canine claws scratching against iron pipes. He turned around to see Lilith's corsos tumbling awkwardly behind him. Kabir and Samir descended behind the dogs.

Ishmael surveyed his surroundings. The tunnel was poorly lit, but he had noticed a few rusty blades from battles past strewn across the floor. He took two rusted swords from the wet surface and stood, wobbly, ready for battle.

Kabir whistled at the corsos; the dogs came at him in tandem, each attacking his ankles. He swung his blades at their heads, stabbing one of them. The blade snapped off, lodged in the dog's neck.

The wounded animal let out a deafening screech and then fell to the side. The other recoiled and lunged for his throat. The redhead and canine fell backward; the dog inadvertently impaled himself on Ishmael's blade.

He pushed the twitching carcass to the side and stood up. Kabir and Samir advanced to subdue Ishmael. He knew he could not defend Sofia in her current condition. She was moving, but she was vulnerable.

Ishmael grabbed the pale-eyed beauty. He hugged her tightly and then slid on his bottom into the fissures that led somewhere into the earth.

Samir and Kabir could only watch from the precipice as the two descended into obscurity.

Samir walked to the edge of the precipice and surveyed the crevice. "You want to follow them?"

Kabir looked into the darkness. "No. We'll catch them topside."

Chapter 62 - Babylon, Italy

"You who are trying to be justified by the law have been alienated from Christ; you have fallen away from grace." –
Galatians 5:4

hey slid for a hundred meters, bouncing off the rocks, slamming violently into the walls and clay floor. Clouded in dust, they sat up and assessed their condition.

"I am *alive*!" she said to herself, patting her body for injuries. "And... and... you came and got me. I remember now... I was about to fall into the lake of fire. I could see them—the foreboding, the fear, the pain, the immense darkness, and isolation, and the despair... of having no hope... OH MY GOD! I AM ALIVE! Thank you, JESUS!" she said in resolution.

Ishmael hugged her deeply. "Yes. He answered my prayer. Thank You, Jesus." Ishmael hugged her deeply, and they wept for several minutes.

"You alright?" Ishmael checked his ankles for fractures.

"I... I..." Sofia lingered. She sat up and assessed herself. He wrapped his robe around his body and helped her to her feet. Sofia threw her hair back from her eyes.

"I think so." She coughed and blew the clay dust from her sleeves.

They were in a room—an expansive space with high ceilings. There were fish symbols and Latin text scratched into the porous walls. There was an artificial source of red light coming from one end of the cavern. They made their way toward it.

The details of the room became more discernible as they approached the exit. Ishmael leaned in to observe ossified human remnants. There were countless burials stacked to the roof. Red read the hand-carved inscription from the nearest wall.

"What does '*Iesus Christus Dominus* est' mean?" he inquired.

"Jesus Christ is Lord." Sofia paused and gazed across the grandeur of the room. "The Caesars of old didn't take too kindly to a profession of faith that did not deify the emperor. To the ancient Romans, Caesar was God! And any profession otherwise got you fed to the lions... and usually in public... you

know what I mean? Like the Colosseum." She stared at the ceiling. *"We are in the catacombs,* Ish... although I will not be able to tell you which one until we reach the surface."

"The catacombs? Wow." He looked about the vaulted ceilings. "I never thought I would be able to see them."

"This is where the Christians fled during the reign of..." She paused. "Well, to be honest, a lot of different Caesars really. I believe these were built during the time of Nero, although I may be wrong..." She brushed off the dust from her robe. "I can see some light coming from up there."

"And what about you?" Ishmael stopped her and looked into her pale blue eyes.

"What do you mean?"

"Is Jesus Lord? Or are you still Satanist Sally?"

She stared at him with tears in her eyes. "What I saw up there, in the temple, changed me. Everything I have been told is a lie. They have no interest in helping people. They use people. They exploit them for power. I cannot live that life anymore. I choose Jesus."

They embraced. He took her hand. "Come on. I think there is a staircase up here."

They emerged into a grassy knoll.

Sofia turned her groggy head. "I think those were the *Catacombs of Saint Sebastian.* So that means we are southeast of Rome. Come on." She started jogging toward the city.

The fresh night air sobered him. There was a full moon in the sky. They crossed the fields and approached La Piazza di San Giovanni. He looked around, jaw agape, dumbfounded at the chaos around him.

The streets were a war zone. People ran aflame, some shot at each other randomly, others raped women in the alleys, and still others continued looting.

So, was this their goal? he thought to himself. *Despair.* Despair had always been the intended contagion, the true poison—much more powerful than any biological. *Despair* was the opposite of hope, and without hope, man and womankind are easily controlled.

The public was under assault—physically, emotionally, and spiritually. The softened, weak minds of those who had spent their childhoods in comfort had no answer for the violent onslaught; they cowered in their bedrooms and locked themselves in their basements and attics. Others simply took their own lives. Some fell from great heights, landing in the road; others fell onto rubbish bins, severing their bodies. Whether they had died by homicide or suicide, no one would ever know.

People ran screaming in all directions. Gunshots echoed through the concrete corridors of the city. Amendola's men had been joined by the Carabinieri and the Polizia Municipale, but they were no match for the satanic forces, forty thousand strong, flooding from the Metro stations and crevices at Caracalla.

The police had set up defensive positions across Rome. Corners, street-level entry points, and elevated positions were fiercely guarded—yet quickly overrun. The Dawn had been preparing for millennia. They were expert assassins with a military prowess that the police could not equal. They ran roughshod over the authorities.

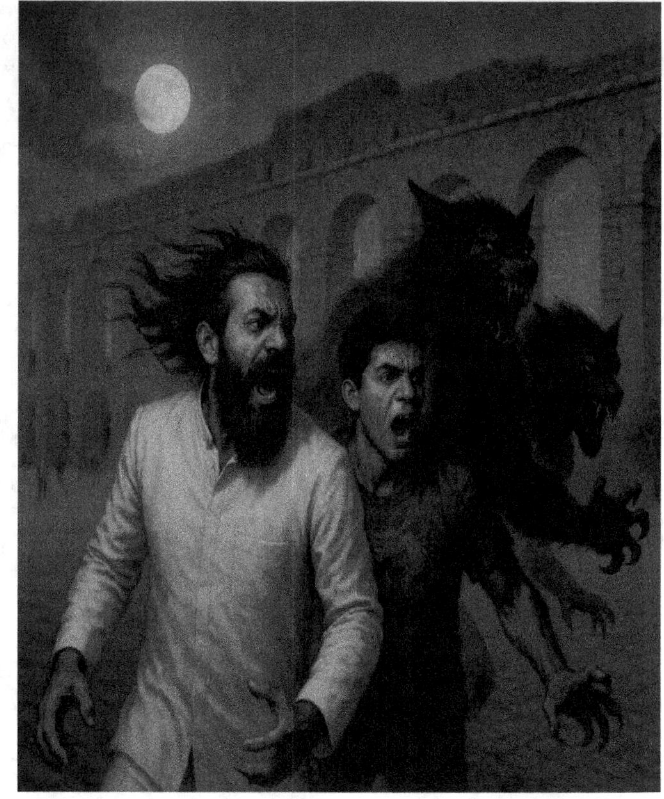

Sabir and Kabir exited the Metro and appeared in the clearing. They were covered in sweat, and their bodies were agitated, restless. They convulsed and twitched in a primal fashion. They stood side by side, scanning the horizon, panting, sniffing the air for the lost couple. Kabir stared directly into the eyes of Ishmael, tapped his brother's shoulder, and pointed at the limping pair.

"Come on. Pick up the pace," Ishmael warned Sofia.

Sofia held onto his arm for support. "Oh no! You don't understand. We need to run NOW!" She stared back at the Tewani twins.

"They are far away. Let's just hide down here in the shadows and let them think we are gone."

"No! You don't understand! THEY ARE *WEREWOLVES*!!! *RUN!!!*"

In unison, the twins fell to their hands and knees. Their backs arched upward, their limbs cracked and twisted, their necks and faces became immersed in feral fur, their snouts grew canine-like, their clothes tore away like papier-mâché. Their teeth stretched from their jaws, and they both gave out a screeching howl/growl.

Snarling and drooling, jetting gravel from their hind legs, the wolves charged after the redheaded couple.

Many of the satanists, following the cue of their generals, channeled their familiars. The horde morphed into hideous beasts, running initially on two legs, then on four. Their extended gaits gave them speed. Some grew horns, some tusks, some wings, some long teeth... all of them grew in rage. Children, old women, the disabled—no one was safe.

The satanic procession of beasts splintered and crashed into the side alleys, flying, scampering, and climbing the facades of the buildings. Tearing holes in the edifices, beating down anyone in their paths, they spread like a virus throughout the city.

Ishmael and Sofia watched in horror; their adrenaline spiked—they ran for their lives.

They sped their way into a nearby *vicolo.* Just beyond the rooftops, light could be seen coming from the direction of San Giovanni, still a block away.

"Come on! This way! We are going toward the light!" She led Ishmael along Via *Sannio,* behind the aqueduct. They scampered steadily up the grassy clearing in front of the first Catholic church of Rome, *La Basilica di San Giovanni in Laterano.*

The square was lit up. The cathedral was lit up. Rays of luminescence poured forth from the cathedral's stained-glass windows, throwing a kaleidoscope of incandescent trails into the night sky.

The werewolves had closed the distance; they scampered within striking range. With incredible rage, mouth agape, Kabir leapt forward for the kill. Just at that moment, the one-ton doors of the church swung open violently. The doors slammed against their hinges. Their clash against the concrete columns gave off a shockwave that knocked back the wolves—but not Ishmael and Sofia.

The maleficent canines flew through the air, tumbling awkwardly, spiraling, kicking, and inevitably creating long scars across the front lawn as they skidded to a halt.

"YOU HAVE *NO* AUTHORITY HERE!" His voice boomed.

Azikiwe stepped forth, swinging his blade of righteous anger. He leveled it at the wolves. Its flames rose to the heavens. His voice shook the ground, causing parts of the nearby aqueduct to collapse.

Ishmael and Sofia ran between the angel's legs and into the sanctuary of the Catholic parish. The wolves turned and ran. Azikiwe surveyed the terrain and then slammed the two enormous wooden doors shut behind the young couple.

The couple ran deep into the church before they stopped. A few clergy members and faithful parishioners huddled in the corner of the massive sanctuary. Ishmael and Sofia doubled over, panting heavily. Transforming back into human form, Azikiwe approached them.

"This shelter is temporary. We must move on," he said calmly.

Ishmael was out of breath. "Why can't God just send more of you guys... or something... to protect us?" He was frustrated.

"I don't know why the Creator has chosen to do it this way, but we can trust that it is for a good reason." Azikiwe's human form and clothes had reappeared.

"Wow! That's a nice trick! How did you get your clothes back?"

"Perks of being a guardian angel..." Azikiwe smiled.

"So, you're my guardian angel, huh? After all

this time, you couldn't drop a hint? Say something like, 'Hey, by the way...'"

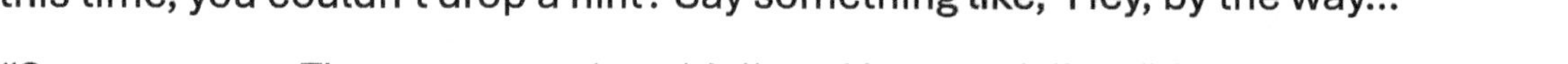

"Sorry, my son. There are certain guidelines I have to follow," Azikiwe said dismissively.

"So where were you when...?" He stopped himself. This is the part when Ishmael would have said something like, *Where was your God when...* but his mind had been changing. His anger was dissipating, his faith was growing, he was more conscientious of the power of the word and of thought, and the ramifications of belief and doubt. So, he remained quiet.

Azikiwe smiled proudly. "Ishmael, my son, you are learning... better not to kick against the goads."

"I'm just tired of fighting, priest. Or... wait... what do I call you now? I guess you have some sort of 'angel' name now, right?"

"*THEY ARE SURROUNDING THE CHURCH!*" Sofia interrupted from across the sanctuary. She was peering out the window at the church grounds.

The entire congregation ran to the windowpane. White light flooded the hall of the sanctuary. Each truck levied a high beam against the facade of San Giovanni. Ishmael looked outside. As a trophy of war, Amendola's corpse lay bloodied, tied with barbed wire to the hood of one of the trucks. Nerone sat beside the corpse, atop the cab, directing the legions.

"They have an army out there. And they are bringing in more trucks. Each truck holds twenty men." She peeked over the pane. "I see... seven trucks out there already. We need an exit strategy." Sofia sounded like a field general. "LOOK OUT!"

The front doors to San Giovanni shook from the collision of the truck. The doors held, but vibrated roughly against the steel bolts embedded in the foundation. The truck's gears

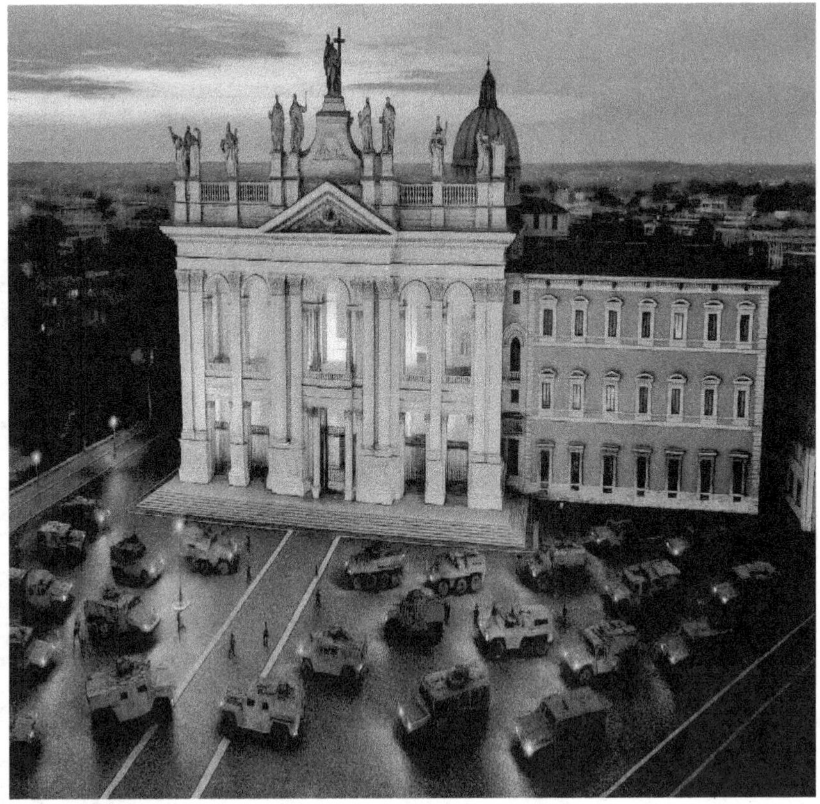

ground and hissed as the driver backed up for another assault. The lorry slammed into the door once again, shaking the walls. Crystalline shards were thrown throughout the church, scratching their way across the sanctuary floor.

Blue smoke rose from cylindrical canisters that helicoptered across the room. The fumes rose toward the rafters. Running toward the interior, people began to cough as they covered their mouths and eyes.

"Why are they so intent on killing me?" Ishmael coughed.

"You are the door to Tartarus. They are afraid you will put them back in," Sofia responded.

"Door? I didn't open it the first time—and I certainly don't know how to close it."

"Well, the Watchers think you do! To them, you are a threat! They think you will force them back... to Tartarus. That is why they want you dead."

"I have no idea how to do that. I don't know how to send them back." He turned to Azikiwe. "Azikiwe? Why won't God help us?"

"Maybe He already has," the priest ventured.

The silhouettes of two werewolves could be seen perched on the window ledge. Their mouths twitched and nostrils flared, sniffing the air. Their claws dug into the window frame. This time, the wolves were not alone; hundreds of beasts flooded in behind them.

Centaurs, minotaurs, and all sorts of mythological beasts broke in, gnashing their way through the congregants. Azikiwe sprang into action. His wings rolled forth, cascading into the pews. His angelic stature and luminescence exploded from his human body; his stature shot up ten meters into the sky.

His sword extended organically from his hand, but sprang explosively like a switchblade. He swung it horizontally, causing lacerations, dismembering beastly flesh, and splattering blood on the opposing wall. Grunts, growls, and cries of pain stifled the room. Pieces of wood split and spat from the broken pews. The beasts tore through the parishioners.

Sofia and Ishmael covered their eyes to shield themselves from the flying wood chips. They collected themselves and ran for the halls of the church. Several beasts roared toward them, knocking down the clergy.

The walls narrowed. They had just entered the hallway when the beasts slammed against the door. They were too large to enter the portal. They scratched, snarled, and screeched at the sheetrock—and at each other—in a desperate attempt to reach the couple.

Chapter 63 - Rome, Italy

"Flee also youthful lusts: but follow righteousness, faith, charity, peace, with them that call on the Lord out of a pure heart." - Timothy 2:22

hey fled through the back door. The Italian army had mounted an offensive and were laying siege... explosions went off all around the cathedral. Gunshots fired from behind the brick aqueduct. Grenades were thrown. It was bedlam.

The Dawn took cover behind the giant Russian lorries. Oblivious to the projectiles flying around, Nerone stood on top of the cab. He looked over the carnage, scanning the horizon. He fixed his gaze on the rear door of the church. He squinted at the couple. Sofia saw him from afar.

"Let's go!" Ishmael yelled.

"No, wait!" Sofia responded.

Sofia put her hand up against Ishmael's chest, surveying the streets for threats. Ishmael pushed through her arm and headed for V*ia Ludovico di Savoia* toward *Porta Maggiore.* Sofia begrudgingly followed. They ran along the narrow streets, looking behind themselves as they ran.

"Do you know where we are going?" Sofia inquired desperately.

"Getting away," he snorted.

"Wait! Nerone is on us! We cannot escape him."

"He is an old man. He'll never catch us!" He continued down the street.

"You don't understand!" She pointed to the dark clouds above.

A massive black bat-like figure swooped overhead. Its wings flapped with little effort, but the turbulence created swirls of wind that caused the rubbish from the streets to circle in the air.

"What the..." He didn't curse this time. "What is that?" He pointed to the sky.

"Nerone," she said flatly. "I tried to tell you before you took off running. Nerone is no mere man. He can change at any time."

"Like the twins."

"Worse. Much worse." The dragon flew over them once again. "He is too strong for us to fight." Sofia investigated the black clouds overhead.

Just atop the edifices in front of them, the dragon's wings flapped, pulsating, hovering, gliding to a halt. His immense slithering thorax expanded. His wings beat heavily, throwing the debris from the street into the air. Every bit of debris became a projectile.

He hovered forty meters in the air. The turbulence was so strong it knocked Sofia and Ishmael to the ground. Nerone's giant talons touched down on the cobblestone street, cornering Sofia and Ishmael in the alley. His teeth bared, his wings collapsed, he marched forward, seeking to devour them. His head was ten meters in length, and his tail, like a tree.

Where is Azikiwe when you need him? Ishmael's mind gave way to vision. His mother's words echoed in his head. *"You don't need the ring. You have the King."*

Nerone spoke with his dragon tongue. "You are mine now, boy. You cannot fight me. I am much more powerful! I am a GOD!" His wings spread to their full expanse.

"That may be. But I know one who is more powerful!" Still lying on the ground, Ishmael put his hand up in defiance. "Jesus rebuke you! I rebuke you in the name of Jesus Christ!"

Suddenly, the dark clouds parted, and a white beam of lightning from heaven illuminated the beast. The dragon let forth an incredible scream. His charcoal breath permeated the small street. The beast fell to the ground, contorting and twisting. His leathery black skin began to change into the black clerical cloth. His draconic visage shrank. His body became smaller. His arms formed from his wings and forefeet. He stood there... a man.

"*Ahhh*! What happened to you, priest?" Ishmael sprang to his feet. "Looks like you're just like me now." Ishmael put his hands up, then approached him like the prizefighter he was. "Let's see what you got!"

Ishmael followed Snow's advice from years past. *Fake left, fake right, go right.* Nerone didn't see the first blow coming. The redhead squared his feet and leveraged his blow and sank it squarely on Nerone's jaw. The priest fell backwards, realizing for the first time that his supernatural abilities had been revoked.

Nerone collected himself, then channeled his rage. He ran at Ishmael wildly, trying to tackle him to the ground. Ishmael threw an uppercut that caught him under the chin. The priest flew up erect, then staggered. He collected himself, then threw a clumsy right hook. Ishmael countered with a blow to his abdomen, then a lightning-fast uppercut to his jaw.

Nerone's body flew upward toward the sky. He fell flat, striking his head on the pavement—laid out. The approaching clatter of heels striking cobblestone could be heard echoing in the cement canyon.

"Come on. Let's go." Ishmael beckoned his blue-eyed girlfriend. The amorous couple scurried through the tiny *vicoli* and slipped into the foggy, cold, dark night.

Chapter 64 - Vancouver, Canada

"Come to me, all you who are weary and burdened, and I will give you rest. Take my yoke upon you and learn from me, for I am gentle and humble in heart, and you will find rest for your souls." - Matthew 11:28-30

he North Atlantic stream kept Vancouver surprisingly warm in the spring. The log cabin was built on the precipice of the cliff. Sofia had wisely set aside a large sum of money in secret accounts, allowing for a comfortable lifestyle.

She and her husband sat on the veranda on a swing, cuddling, overlooking the Atlantic Ocean. The cotton blanket around them obscured the bulge in her tummy.

"They will eventually find us, you know," the redhead ventured.

"I know."

Chapter 65 - Southwark, England

"Nevertheless, I have a few things against you: You tolerate that woman Jezebel, who calls herself a prophet. By her teaching, she misleads my servants into sexual immorality and the eating of food sacrificed to idols." – Revelation 2:20

egina collapsed in pain and exhaustion and was unconscious for several hours after the birth of her daughter. The coven doctor who examined Regina near the end of her pregnancy reported that she was showing larger than expected. The doctor informed Sister Chastity about the possibility of a multiple birth, but she did not reveal this information to Regina. The Order had plans for the other twin.

After Regina fainted, Sister Chastity held a cloth doused in ether over her nose.

Regina's contractions began again, and Sister Chastity had to massage her belly to encourage the baby to move down into the birth canal. The sister had to reach inside her to pull the baby out. A healthy boy with auburn hair emerged—a twin. The nurses looked at each other. This boy would be clairvoyant, "the moonchild." He would help to usher in the Antichrist, and with him, a new age, a singularity, a one-world government.

They gave him the name Ishmael.

THE END